Calabrian Tales

Calabrian Tales

by
Peter Chiarella

REGENT PRESS
OAKLAND, CA

Library of Congress Cataloging-in-Publication Data

Chiarella, Peter, 1932-
    Calabrian tales / by Peter Chiarella.
        p. cm.
    ISBN 978-1-58790-030-0
        1. Calabria (Italy)--Fiction. 2. Mistresses--Fiction.
        I. Title.

PS3603.H537 C35 2002
813'.6--dc21   2002073863

Fourth Printing

REGENT PRESS
2747 Regent Street
Berkeley, CA 94705
www.regentpress.net

Dedication

To my parents, Ralph and Catherine, whose constant encouragement and inspiration throughout my life has fed my motivation to write this book.

Acknowledgements

There were many contributors to this book, but I wish to acknowledge two people whose special hard work and encouragement inspired me to carry out the project to completion. First and foremost my brother, Anthony, whose constant counsel and remembrances of the stories we first heard as children, helped fashion the very core of the book. His wife, Marie, was my other partner in the crafting of this book. Her experience as a writer and mentor served me well and her tireless efforts at editing my manuscripts were invaluable.

Needless to say, my thanks go to Frances Marie, my partner in life, who has brought joy to the past half century of my life, and who has patiently cajoled and endured along the way.

Contents

Prologue

To truly understand and enjoy this book, one must reflect on a small bit of history dating back to ancient times. Bruttium, as Calabria was known by the ancients, was first settled by the Greeks many centuries before the birth of Christ. It was part of Magna Graecia in the fifth and sixth centuries BC, and was at its apex of prosperity in those times. The Romans conquered the region in the third century BC and began a protracted period of domination by a series of conquerors. The locals were treated as possessions to be used for the enrichment of the foreign lords. Even the Risorgimento, Italy's war of unification, could not break the yoke of outside interference with the destiny of the Calabrian people. The region was virtually ignored by King Victor Emanuel and his advisors. They considered it a wild and backward addendum to an otherwise cultured nation. The kingdom's resources were directed to the North and to a series of unsuccessful wars. Calabrian aspirations were dashed so often by intruders that a fatalistic character was embedded in their psyche over the centuries.

If adverse politics were not enough, the climate of the region was additionally stultifying. It is underscored by the legendary Sirocco wind, blowing in from across the Mediterranean Sea for much of the time, bringing searing temperatures and humid air filled with the mysterious maladies of the African continent. Cholera, malaria, dysentery and a multitude of lesser-known diseases were commonplace. Not only was the Calabrian sentenced to a thankless life of drudgery, but his work was performed under dangerous and adverse conditions.

Is it any wonder that the people of Calabria became known for their skepticism and stubbornness? It has been said that change is the tool of optimism and belief is the result of beneficence. Neither of these conditions was known in Calabria. The result was that nineteenth century Calabria was unable to make the transition to the modern world. Growth and progress were measured by how well the family survived. Hence, the functioning of daily life was governed by old and outdated methods. There was little opportunity for education, even as late as the mid twentieth century. The young learned from the old, not from reading books or listening to the learned. Mostly, the *literati* were transplants from other parts of Italy. So, too, were the gentry who had been handsomely rewarded with huge tracts of land for their acts of loyalty to the king, or had inherited their *fiefdom* from a forebear. The land was virtually out of reach for the ordinary Calabrian. He was thus made to be the laborer for an aristocratic landlord. To be sure, there were those who rose from the ranks of the ordinary to become landholders. But these were extremely rare and there was usually a tale of avarice to accompany the elevation of a man's status to that of landlord.

Calabrian Tales covers the period immediately following the Risorgimento through the culmination of The Great War, or roughly 1860 to 1920. The stories told about these Calabrians are based on truth stranger than fiction. They are a collection of events about the people who inherited the calamitous social order of the southernmost province of the Italian boot. Their story is worth telling because it is a capsule of an extinct period, told in the perspective of the people who lived it. Their story has been carried, orally, through successive generations to the present, in astonishing detail. Their progeny has made it a part of the landscape of America. This was a period in Italian history following the unification of the many foreign-dominated Italian states into a new Kingdom of Italy. It was a time of great pride in a new nation, coupled with intense poverty and struggle. The tales documented here resurrect real people and their lives, loves, joys and heartaches from a time that is forever gone.

Chapter 1

Marianna

In the white heat of the Calabrian sun, a teen-age peasant girl labors in the field. It is hard work to which she has become accustomed. She straightens her aching back and lifts the hem of her dress to wipe the sweat of her brow. Her bare legs glisten. They are strong and sensual, rising to shapely buttocks and broad hips that press against threadbare fabric. Her breasts are firm and as round as prize oranges. An artisan of cameos would not choose her for his model; the nose is too substantial, the lips too sure and full. The eyes, though, the sparkling eyes as brown as dark chocolate, would need a Michelangelo to do them justice, to capture their fire. Impatiently she grasps the unruly fall of raven hair and twists it into a great, moist knot before she bends again to resume her work. As yet, she is unaware that, this day, an event will occur that will alter her life forever.

It is 1885, a generation beyond the historic Risorgimento, and little has changed in Italy's southern region of Calabria. The hopes and ideals of the Calabrian men who marched off to join Garibaldi in the fight to unify Italy seem to have been forgotten by the new government. The women and children work in the fields alongside the men, in a life of stolen youth and hardship. It is as though Calabria has traded its Spanish Bourbon yoke for the shackles of a government dominated by northern Italian statesmen. Class distinction remains. The land is owned by a few rich landlords who permit local farmers to work for a share of the crop, often resulting in poverty and deprivation for the sharecropper and his family.

The Soluri family is perhaps less poor than others, since Guiseppe receives a stipend from the new government for having been disabled in the war. His injuries ostensibly prevent him from working, but his daughters labor in the orchards of Count Leone Capurro, the richest land baron of the region.

"Marianna! Marianna! Vieni subito!" Stella Soluri calls to her daughter from the edge of the orchard. The girl must leave her work abruptly. She is only mildly surprised by the summons from her overbearing mother. She slings the hoe onto her shoulder and moves at her own moderate pace through the warm, rich earth that she has just manured, relishing the feel of the soft dirt between her toes.

"What is it, ma? What do you want?" She senses the tense promise in her mother's voice and it confuses her. What possible reason could there be for hastening her pace? Nothing ever changes in this netherworld of repression. Or does it?

"I want you to come home with me right now. You must get washed and dressed."

"What's going on?"

Stella explains, as they near the house, "My dear, I have made arrangements for you to live and work in the home of Count Leone. You need to dress and get over there at once."

"Oh? And what will I do there? All I know is farm work."

"Don't worry. You'll be taught all that you need to know. You're going to be a chambermaid for Leone. You'll get to eat lots of good food with the rest of the workers and sleep in a bed with a mattress; and you'll no longer need to work in the burning sun with only a bottle of water to keep you from drying up."

"Why me? There must be many others who would wish to be Leone's chambermaid."

Stella looks directly into Marianna's face. There is a moment of silent exchange, her eyes breaking away and then looking down before she speaks. "I will be honest with you, Marianna. You are being given the opportunity to put your beauty to good use. Leone is taken with you. You may decide, after a time of living and working at his villa, to get closer to him. If you succeed, it will benefit us all."

Marianna is startled. She has seen this side of her mother before, but never so brazen, never so crass. *Damn her*, she thinks. *She selfishly schemes to hand me over to Leone like a sack of grain, to be used as a handmaid and perhaps even a concubine. She tells me about my beauty and how I can now repay her for giving me life by offering myself to Leone.*

"And what of Lorenzo?" she blurts. "He has already declared his intentions and were we a bit older, you would have to take us seriously." Lorenzo, a farm laborer from Gagliano, is but nineteen years old, a year senior to Marianna. Tall and handsome, he has won her affection.

Over the months of increasing familiarity with one another, he has also taken her virginity, a prize not lightly given in these times and in this place.

"Forget him, Marianna. He will never amount to anything. Leone can make a life of luxury for you such as you have never imagined. One day you will be known as Donna Marianna." At age forty and the mother of two girls, Stella still has a young, pretty face and shapely torso. And, despite the male-dominated society in which they live, her husband has deferred to her entirely in their relationship. Marianna's destiny is hers to mold, with no permission sought from Giuseppe.

Their home in the ancient town of Gagliano is a ragged, two-story masonry building wedged between two others of the same square design. The rear room of the first floor contains a large wooden tub used for bathing. The two women are alone as they pour out the heated water that Stella has prepared for Marianna's bath. Stella takes great care in preparing her daughter for her trip to the Capurro villa. The bath fills the room with the aroma of citrus. There is olive oil balm for Marianna's lips and strawberry rouge for her cheeks. The curve of Marianna's hips and the ascent of her torso from her slim waist to her full, round breasts authenticate the desire that Leone feels for her. Her raven colored hair that has been left to grow long and her darting brown eyes are a precise complement to her glowing young skin. As she helps Marianna to slip into her dress, Stella is proud of this creature that she has spawned, flesh of the flesh. Little wonder, Stella thinks, that Lorenzo's passion is aroused. Leone will be pleased.

"How is it that Leone desires *me*?" Marianna asks.

"Some weeks ago, as we carried water to his home, Leone rode into his courtyard and saw you working there.

His stare was long and his passion noticeable. I later spoke with him, and he admitted to me that he had noticed you at other times as well, working in his vineyard. He tried to get your attention once, but you did not notice."

"Yes, I did notice, mother, but I defied him."

"Why, for God's sake?"

"Because he is a foul old man who owns everything and makes us all work for nothing!"

"Marianna, you are wrong. You will see that when you meet him. He is not foul at all and his wealth was not stolen from others. It is rumored that he is a friend of the king and fought the Bourbons at the side of Garibaldi. And, they say his reward for the Italian victory placed him in the position he is in today. He must follow the system that prevails in our region."

Marianna looks at Stella. She is silent, but she thinks, *I know I will detest him. And to think that my own mother has put me in this position.*

It is time for the two women to leave for Leone's villa, and as they step into the street outside their door, they notice several of their neighbors peering at them curiously. Gagliano, a village of 400 people, is not conducive to privacy. The neighbors have detected a change in the rhythm of the morning, and the Soluri women have confirmed their suspicions as Marianna makes her appearance in full dress in the middle of an ordinary day. The hens among the women have come out to seek their grist and the hawkish men enjoy their catch of news to accompany their grappa. Anita Cecchini, the mother of Marianna's closest friend, thinks, *What is going on? This little tramp and her mother are up to something. What can it be? And where are they going?* She does not speak, but her pinched face betrays her thoughts. Marianna and Stella are aware of her inquisitive look, but ignore her.

"Bon giorno, signora e signorina." They turn to see that they are being greeted by a nun of the village, the white of her collar gleaming in the sun. "Bon giorno," Stella responds, and hurriedly walks up the street to avoid further contact.

The journey to Leone's villa is seven miles long. All along the way, Stella and Marianna are aware of eyes upon them. They seem to be the topic of the day. Giuseppe Soluri has made himself conspicuously absent since his wife has been on her mission to advance the Soluri family by her sordid means. Oftentimes, when Stella presses her superior will, Giuseppe will roam the streets of Gagliano, smoking his rope cigar and murmuring about *my Stella* and how she is having *another of her fits*. He will then wait for her to calm down before returning home in his usual complicity with precious Stella's wishes. Now he must bear the bruise of embarrassment with his cronies as they fight the urge to inquire as to where his daughter may be going, looking her very best. They sip their coffee knowingly and the short, rotund Guiseppe draws on his cigar and wishes for a more abiding world.

The mid-morning air is clean and pure, sweet with the scent of lemons and oranges. The valley that is formed by the descent of the terrain westerly from Gagliano yields abundant produce that springs forth despite the sparse soils and steep incline. It is a tribute to the hard work and ingenuity of the farmers of Gagliano. Though neither Marianna nor Lorenzo have been outside of this little world, she thinks of how they have contrasted it to farming in the New World.

Lorenzo says that the soil in Argentina and America is rich for many feet into the ground and there is so much land that the least of farmers owns forty acres. There is water everywhere for irrigating crops and every harvest is large and brings high prices. Lorenzo and I will go to this world as man and wife. We will earn our fortune there and send for our families in Calabria. Lorenzo insists on going to America and I tease him about wanting to settle in Argentina.

She thinks of how Lorenzo will react when he hears of her new association with Leone. Perhaps he already knows.

The buildings along the road are mostly private dwellings. Many still stand from the middle ages. They were built sturdily to prevent destruction by hordes of invaders from the north and east that sacked the hundreds of towns along their way. The surviving structures have been patched and restored many times over the centuries. Lacking architecture, they are constructed of poured masonry and brick, with as few portals as possible. Only a doorway and perhaps one window are fitted to the front of an otherwise bland and uninviting structure. Two-story buildings contain more openings, allowing for two windows in symmetry above the height of man on horse. The town is hardly two miles from end to end and less than one wide. It is built on the instep of the descending Apennines. The descent continues past the village for another six miles before the turf ascends to create a valley. As one enters Gagliano from the north, stone wall three feet high girds the terrain on the left, protecting the main road from eroding soil. The wall is constructed of *petra viva*, the living stone that has been placed in position whole so as to last forever. Some of the oldest homes are constructed of the same stone.

As they near Catanzaro, the principal city of the province, a road appears to the left. They turn and head for a gate perhaps a half-mile away. A guard appears amid tranquil green trees and a handsome iron portal. A shotgun hangs from one shoulder and he seems ready to swing into motion despite his easy recognition of the women.

"I cannot help but wonder why all the protection is needed," Marianna says.

"And at such expense," says Stella. "I have heard that the men of Gagliano have often expressed their loathing of Leone and speak of joining forces to break through his defenses and pressure him to reform the system. As if it were *Leone's* system to do with as he pleases!"

The guard moves in mock salute as they pass into the luxuriant ground of the Capurro villa. He is aware they were summoned. There is a large berm ahead, from which they sight the main house. It is not unfamiliar to either of the women. Marianna has worked here before and Stella has come here to meet with the Count to cultivate his interest in her daughter. Now Marianna views the villa in a different light. She is not here because Leone needs water for his guests' morning comfort, nor is she here to assist with pruning. When pretense is put aside, Marianna is here for Leone's personal pleasure. To be sure, she will have a choice of whether to stay or depart, but who in these times would choose the latter. Here she will be sheltered from the harsh peasant life, with its constant work and meager rewards. No longer will she need to look forward to the inevitable dinner of *pasta faggiole* at the end of her workday. And perhaps she will sleep on a real mattress and have all of the covers she needs to keep warm on cold winter nights. Someone else will be assigned to bring in the firewood and set the fireplaces ablaze. All that she will need to do is clean and mend and keep order in the Count's chamber.

Marianna's thoughts are diverted as she looks out upon

a marvellous view. Here in the humble countryside of Calabria is a garden of flowers and fruit trees heralding their presence by their aroma and color and placing a sensuous touch on the scene. A series of paths leads to several small one-story buildings used either for storage or for housing Leone's guests. In the midst of the compound is a large swimming pool built in the Roman style, complete with gods and emperors. The main structure, the Capurro residence, is of a painted, rough textured, concrete that forms walls eighteen inches thick. All windows are shuttered behind iron grates matched to the design of the entry gate. The rooftop is of curved red tile and pitched to form an angle that is more associated with the Bourbon Spaniards than with the native Italianate design. The entry doors are fifteen feet high and nine wide and are intricately carved to resemble the Baptistry doors in the Duomo square in Florence. A wall nine feet high and eighteen inches thick contains the entire four-acre compound.

Stella escorts Marianna to a side door and calls quietly for someone to grant entry. A buxom, matronly woman arrives at the door. As Stella takes her leave, she looks lovingly into Marianna's eyes and smiles reassurance. She places her hand to her lips and throws a kiss of encouragement. She now seems less matriarchal, perhaps even revealing another, softer side. Marianna notices her gleaming hazel eyes and flowing brown hair. If Marianna's presence is alluring, then Stella is surely the origin of her beauty. At age 44, she is slim and tall. Her long neck distinguishes her as having descended from Etruscan stock, and her stride tells of a self confident and determined woman.

"You are here to work as a chambermaid, yes?" Marianna nods. The woman servant continues, "Understand that I am usually free to make these appointments, but this case is special. The Count will ultimately decide if you stay. My name is Concetta and I am in charge of the house staff. Come with me."

As Marianna follows, she feels a surge of uncertainty and foreboding. Her body shivers as though she is cold, and she is only vaguely aware of the opulent interior of Leone's home and of the presence of another guard. They climb to the third floor of the house and enter the servants' quarters.

"You will share this room with Angela. She cooks for us all. Your bed is the one on the left." Marianna quickly notices that there is a fine, thick mattress and there are several layers of bed clothing. Her mood changes and she calms.

"You will begin by readying the Count's bed this evening. He will leave clothing out for laundering and mending. They should be brought to me. In the morning, while you are working, Aldo will go to your home and fetch your belongings."

Chapter 2

Angelo

The snows seldom fall on the Southern Apennines of the Calabrian peninsula. Even in the worst of winters, the southerly breezes coming off the African continent reduce the crystals of airborne vapor into droplets of rain. Snow is a special occasion. The villagers here say *ogni settani,* every seven years, there is a snowfall. And they prepare for it. Large underground spaces are readied to receive the snow, storing it to use as the main ingredient for a local *gelati* in warmer weather. Snowfall is greeted with enthusiasm and thanksgiving, a sort of manna from heaven. But this jubilation is not shared by all.

It is the winter of 1898. The breezes have stilled long enough for the hills to be veiled in white lace, documenting the movements of all creatures that inhabit the area.

"There. I knew I saw his tracks. This time we'll get him. His wife couldn't convince him to give himself up, but now that we can track him, we no longer need to invite him to surrender." The young Carabiniere officer turns to the two mounted troopers at his rear and belts out a hearty laugh. They are here to apprehend Angelo Chiarella, a fugitive who keeps the law at bay by covering his tracks and survives by plundering the inhabitants of the remote mountaintop villages. But now the snow has come and has at last created a handy way for the soldiers to track him. The horses trudge up the stony mountain where twisted Balkan pines cling to rock beneath the snow. The patches of dense forest that surround them are a combination of pine, oak, beech and alder. Not since Roman times, when the forests were felled to obtain their pitch, has the tree cover been so full. There is evidence everywhere of wolves and bears. The temperature hovers at the point of freezing and the dense humidity and constant wind combine to form a piercing cold. Only a desperate and resourceful man could survive this harsh environment.

Angelo is awakened with a start. He hears the sound of a horse snorting in the distance and the faint voices of men. The snow covering the ground has remained smooth and he has thus been unable to accomplish his usual disappearance. His tracks show clearly in the snow, and his encampment in a formation of rocks encircled by a thicket of trees, is suddenly vulnerable.

Oh, Lord, what will I do? I'll never surrender to those bastardi. I'd rather die than return to Asinara. I'll fight them to the death.

Angelo is enraged by the prospect of capture and return to prison on the remote island of Asinara off the northern coast of Sardinia. Imprisoned there for nine years, the thought of ever returning has kept alive Angelo's will to survive the hardships of his mountain refuge. Only the occasional visits by Gesuzza, his wife of eighteen years, is a respite from this hell. She brings him the foods that only she could prepare and the creature comforts that only she can provide. There is vegetable bean soup made with fennel and thin pasta with red meat sauce. And, always, her homemade red wine that rivals the best in Gagliano.

But Gesuzza's visits are infrequent and dangerous. The rugged life in the hills makes it impossible for her to remain for more than a day or two at a time. On an earlier visit, a bear approached their camp seeking the food he smelled from afar. Angelo was prepared for him and fought him off with a spear he had managed to find on one of his forays into the nearby village of Cropani. Gesuzza required a month to recover her courage to return. When she did, it was to tell Angelo that she had become pregnant with his child. Despondent that there would soon be another mouth to feed, Angelo had raged at Gesuzza, desperately proclaiming, "Now you can *mongia cazzo*," a filthy expression that somehow calmed his fury. As she left weeping, he called after her. "Gesuzza, you bring that baby to the wheel as soon as it is born. Let the nuns raise it." She sobbed all the way home, knowing that she needed to heed her husband's command to place the yet unborn baby in the hands of the clergy as soon as she delivered.

The soldiers approach to within a few yards of the camp. The lieutenant calls out, "Angelo Chiarella. Come out with your hands high. You are under arrest for physical attack upon two officers of the law on September the 24th, 1896. You have also committed acts of violence and theft against certain residents of Cropani and Sersale. You are to return with us to Catanzaro, where you will be tried for your crimes."

"Go away! I will not surrender as long as I have a breath in my body."

"Angelo, come peaceably and we will assure you of a fair trial."

"Ha! That's a laugh. *Fangul!* You'll have to come get me if you dare."

The officer dismounts and motions for the other two troopers to do so as well. They confer for a few moments before the young lieutenant approaches the entrance to Angelo's fortification. He is armed only with the truncheon issued to the military assigned to police duty. It is tucked into its holder on the back of his service belt.

"Get away! Don't come any further," Angelo scowls. Anger and fright redden his face. "I warn you. Don't come any further!" With height in excess of six feet, the muscular, blonde, blue-eyed man of forty-four years towers over most of the men of Calabria. The lieutenant is no exception, but Angelo's huge size and frightening demeanor will not intimidate him.

"For the last time, Angelo, give yourself up. I will assure you of a fair trial."

"A fair trial? What is that? My trial ten years ago was a mockery! The Bourbons treated us better. Italian justice be damned!"

"Then, I have no other choice." The lieutenant advances on Angelo, reaching back to free his truncheon from its holster. The men collide before the trooper can clear the weapon and Angelo forces his arm back and a loud snap proclaims the agony of a broken limb. The lieutenant falls to the ground groaning as his two comrades race to his assistance and resume the fight. Angelo disables one trooper by pushing him headlong into a dirt pile behind him. He throws his arms around the second man in a vise-like bear hug and begins to squeeze the breath out of him. The man responds by bringing his leg up sharply into Angelo's groin. As he doubles, Angelo sees the first trooper rising from his unflattering position, ready to join the scrap. Angelo is desperate. He must do something to take another of the threesome out of the fight. He is still holding the trooper around the chest. He rams the man's face with his head and then takes the man's ear in his mouth and bites down. Blood begins streaming down the man's face and he cries out in unmerciful pain. He is out of the fray.

But all of the fighting is for naught. As Angelo turns toward the last of the soldiers, a truncheon meets him squarely and heavily on the head. He falls to the ground in a single motion, dead or unconscious. The trooper takes no chances. He places shackles on Angelo's wrists and ankles. Later, with the help of the others, he hoists Angelo's limp body over one of the horses and begins the trip to Catanzaro.

Where am I? What's happened? What is that God-awful pain in my head? And why am I hog-tied to this horse?

"Ah, he's alive. He'll soon wish he were dead." The soldier notices that his prisoner has come around and is now awake. His muttering brings Angelo back to his senses and he is again overcome with the anguish of knowing that he is inevitably headed back to prison. This time he is guilty of several crimes, including having mauled his captors. They hunch over their mounts nursing their wounds, and silently vow revenge for their intense pain. Angelo becomes lost in thought.

How did this come to pass? What went wrong and where did it all begin?

I started life as the youngest of three sons born to a goat herder in the village of Gimigliano, high above the farmlands of Catanzaro province. There were fewer than four hundred residents of the town and less than fifty buildings. Mostly, they were framed huts made from mud and straw and logs cut from the thick pine forests that surround the town. The streets were bare earth that the frequent rain turned to mud. Cheese making was the main occupation, and this meant that there were goats in every yard. Their pungent smell filled the air and their clamor was heard everywhere.

Contact with the rest of the world was infrequent. It was usually with a cheese buyer from one of the towns below the mountains, who had come to bargain for the wares of the locals. There was also the occasional trip down the mountain with my brothers. We mostly went to Gagliano and raised hell in a local tavern. The Gaglianese were frightened by our size and boisterous manner and wished that we would pick some other town to vent our frustrations. I remember thinking to myself that I would one day escape the clutches of my family and settle down in Gagliano.

My father was a mountain man. Some say that he was part animal and that he had mystical power over other creatures. He could tame wolves and direct their course by an animal sound that emanated from his throat. He was able to keep them from attacking certain villages in the dead of winter when the hunt for food was most difficult. Or, he could send them coursing in packs through an errant town seeking any bit of food they could find in refuse piles and, often, in homes whose doors had not been secured. Occasionally, a small child would be missing and believed carried off by a wolf to become the next meal for the pack.

Father rarely slept at home or ever thought of his family. He was out on the land somewhere, hunting or trapping and defending his goats from predators. His bed was the last pine grove he happened to stumble onto and the stars were his evening's entertainment. *He would occasionally return home with his catch and we would feast for a time. He was a very large man from whom I inherited my size. He was also very stern and demanding, another trait I acquired.*

My mother was a slight woman who passed her fair complexion, blonde hair and blue eyes on to her sons. She, too, was a strong-willed person. She worked from the moment of sun-up until she laid her head down to sleep for the night. When she was not working the rock-filled landscape for its grudging yield of vegetables and fruit, she was the head cheese-maker of the family. In between, she cooked, cleaned and washed for us all. She obeyed my father's every command and never complained. Unfortunately for all of us, she was stricken with the fever and died when I was only eight years old.

Later on, father married Nina, my stepmother. She had substantial knowledge of cheesemaking and took over from where my deceased mother had left off. But she had very little patience with all of us and cared not a whit about our well being. When father was away on his frequent trips, she was particularly cruel, requiring us all to fetch and clean and do additional chores before we were permitted to eat. Even then, our meals were slight and poorly prepared.

Father eventually was killed by a pack of wolves that attacked him while he was sleeping under the stars. The wolves ripped his body to shreds as though they were tired of his mastery. Some said they were taking revenge for all the animals he had trapped and killed. My brother Constantino, the eldest, took command of the family after that.

My two older brothers - Constantino and Raffaele - have despised our rugged upbringing, and often took their frustrations out on me. Constantino would beat me for the slightest of reasons. Once, when I spilled a cask of goat curd awaiting my mother's attention, he beat me so badly that I bore the welts for weeks. And Raffaele, likewise, was not reluctant to use his fists to make his point. As I got old enough to defend myself, they became more brotherly. In fact, they insisted that I participate in their forays into the more established villages. Mostly, they were drunk-fests in which we ended up overnight in strange beds with even stranger women. More than once, a cuckolded lover would come looking for Constantino, weapon in hand, and just as often, one look at the three of us sent the irate man fleeing to his sanctuary. We were, all three, very tall and muscular and our ruddy complexions were unlike that of most Calabrians. We were likely to be wearing the old garb, a sort of medieval look that other Calabrians had abandoned. We wore a large, loose blouse tied at the waist by crude hemp twine over fitted pants that were inserted into boots that barely reached our ankles. The hat to accompany this dress was pointed and drooped over the ears and forehead. This look somehow created the impression that we were strangely backward, which, of course, we were.

Raffaele has since found a life in the city of Cosenza. There, he settled down with his lover, Maria, and has recently married her and is the father of two girls. Maria had previously been married to a rugged individual who went about his life as though he were still a bachelor. Even the lovely daughter they had to-gether could not get Salvatore to remain at home. No one knew where he would go, but more than once Maria suspected him of betraying her with another woman. One evening, as Maria and Angela were cleaning up after dinner, Salvatore burst unex-pectedly into the house and retreated to the bedroom, where he locked himself in. He had once again been on a mysterious soi-ree, but had returned early. Moments later, a loud knock on their door brought the teen-aged Angela to the door. As she opened the portal, she was met with a death-dealing blow to the head with an axe. She fell dead on the threshold of her home, her head split open. The killer was gone into the night and was never found; but rumor persists to this day that the murderer was the husband of Salvatore's secret lover. The agony of the tragedy so affected Salvatore that he eventually killed himself with his own shotgun. Maria showed her contempt for her dead husband by taking up with Raffaele in the unheard of time period of less than one year.

Raffaele's cheese-making skills, taught him by our mother, have made him a most respected citizen of Cosenza. It is rumored that the city's long established cheese purveyor (who purchases his cheese from producers) was very upset over having to compete with Raffaele and tried to intimidate him by sending his two sons to ask Raffaele to "go back to Gimigliano" and take his cheese with him. This approach was what Raffaele expected. After listening to their chatter and threats for a few minutes, Raffaele simply said "no." One of the brothers then made the mistake of turning over a table containing several cheese wheels. It was the last straw. Raffaele swung into action, using a huge wooden ladle carved from hardened oak. The first brother received a swipe across the face and a back swing to the throat. He dropped to the floor gasping for air and bleeding from the cheek. As Raffaele turned toward the second brother, he hesitated. The second man was stopped in his tracks by the fearsome sight of this large man beating on his brother. Raffaele then gave the man instruction to take his brother home and to tell his father to never try using force on him again, and –oh yes- 'don't mention any of this to the police.' Thereafter, Raffaele prospered and was never again approached by his competitor.

Constantino remains in Gimigliano, the inheritor of our parents' cheese business. His wife of eighteen years, Millicenta, came from Cropani and has borne him a son and two daughters. She has taken up the role that our mother and stepmother had, that of head cheese-maker and homemaker. Her life is a little easier than our mothers' was because she has daughters to com-

miserate with. I am told that Constantino behaves much as our father did. He is rarely seen by anyone, but an occasional rifle shot is heard off in the distance and it is assumed that he is either killing prey or defending himself from the ever-present wolves and bears. He and Raffaele squabbled for a time over his possession of our dead parents' property, but when Constantino offered to take in Raffaele and his family, it ended the discussion for all time.

"He looks pretty bad." The trooper breaks in on Angelo's thoughts, referring to the beaten man, who is swollen with pain and whose eyes are shut tight from the blow received to his forehead.

"Too bad!" The lieutenant responds sharply. "He should have surrendered when he had the chance. And look at what he's done to us. My arm is broken and Luigi's ear is gone. He'll pay for this, I tell you."

The long trip down the mountain to Catanzaro is tedious on horseback. Though the winter weather is cool, all four men perspire under their wool clothing as the midday sun emerges like a gleaming oracle in the sky above them. The soldiers swig from their wine bottles and chew at their cheese and bread. They ignore Angelo, who seems far away in thought.

I can remember the day I first set eyes on her. My brothers and I had arrived in Gagliano as the summer sun was setting on the evening strollers. There in the Town Square were the old men promenading arm in arm, some smoking their rope cigars and some waving their arms in conversation. There were the elderly ladies, many clothed in black, walking and talking with their friends, occasionally covering their mouths with their hands as if some forbidden secret was being passed on which only they were privileged to know. And then there were the young couples, who walked without touching and within earshot of the ever-

present squad of lady chaperones.

And there she was. My gaze fixed on her from the moment she appeared. They say that opposites attract. Well, she was everything I was not. She was olive complexioned, with raven-colored hair and dark brown eyes that danced as she talked. Her face was so perfectly formed that she resembled the Greek sculpture atop the fountain in the town square. She was as petite as a fawn and her movements displayed a well shaped torso. She seemed exhilarated as she strolled alongside a young man who looked as though he could have been her brother, talking excitedly and ignoring the older women trailing them. I felt an immediate dislike of the man and had the urge to confront him and seize her attention. Somehow, I was frozen and couldn't act out my impulse. This had never before happened to me, and I knew that I was experiencing something momentous.

"Who is that girl?" I asked one of the ladies following the couple.

"She is Gesuzza Soluri, and she is betrothed to the young man she is walking with."

"And what is his name?"

"Andrea Andalusa."

"And how do I find the home of Gesuzza Soluri?" I was feeling bold. Such a request could cause quite a stir. Besides, this lady might have even been related to the boy.

"Ask her mother. She is right there. Her name is Stella." The woman pointed to one of the chaperones.

I would never have imagined before that day that I would ever meekly approach anyone, much less the mother of a woman who had caught my eye. Now I walked up to Stella and timidly proclaimed my attraction to her daughter, fully expecting the wrath of a complacent matron.

"Signora Soluri, I must speak with you privately."

"Yes, I have seen that look before. What is it that you want?

Speak up."

"I want to ask for permission to court your daughter." I couldn't believe that the words came from my mouth, but suddenly I was pleading for the hand of this lovely stranger who was already committed to another. *'"I am a man of substance. My goat herd numbers into the hundreds, and I am a skilled cheese-maker."* I had exaggerated my wealth, but I felt justified in that desperate moment.

"Come to my home at eight this evening. It is on the edge of town and not easily missed. The name Soluri is on the door. What is your name?"

"Angelo. Angelo Chiarella."

That evening as I walked into the Soluri home, I encountered immediate disdain from Gesuzza's father, Giuseppe. He was aware of me and my brothers and our reputation for frequenting the saloons and brothels of Gagliano and creating disturbances wherever we went. Moreover, what was I doing asking to court his daughter? She was already set in betrothal to Andrea, a respectable boy from Gagliano. Things like this just weren't done.

But Stella was of a different mind. My apparent wealth intrigued her and she seemed open to negotiation. I decided to play along and to pretend that I was a man of substantial means. In fact, I had built a goatherd from three goats to more than a hundred. And I had understudied my mother and become somewhat of a cheese maker myself. I even had a fair number of shops and households that were buying my cheese.

"Are you aware that my daughter is promised to another man?" Stella had begun her negotiation. *""He is the son of the boot merchant of Gagliano."*

"Ha!" I confidently declared, *""the son of a poor merchant. And how many more sons does this boot merchant have? Surely a lovely young maiden like Gesuzza deserves better."*

"And what do you have to offer? Are you so rich that you can provide her with more than any other?" At that moment Stella betrayed her inner thoughts by seeming to open up the possibility that my fortune could win her approval. Giuseppe glared at me disapprovingly, but dared not speak.

"Signora Soluri, I come with love in my heart and a promise to elevate your daughter and her family beyond their present state. Should our courtship take root, I will ask for Gesuzza's hand in marriage. I will bring my herd to Gagliano and purchase a home for Gesuzza and me in which to live and raise our family. I ask for nothing from you other than your daughter's hand in marriage."

At that moment Gesuzza walked into the room and I was frozen. She wore a simple white dress that tucked in at the waist and reached down past her calves. Her lips were full and red as cherries. Her face was smooth, and the swarthy color of her skin gave contrast to the milky white that surrounded the piercing brown of her eyes. Her thick, full crop of black hair was tied to the back of her head with a white ribbon and it appeared as though she had just stepped out of a painting.

I had already said everything I could to win her. The rest was up to them. My desire for her must have been apparent as Stella introduced us. As I shook her hand, I felt an exquisite passion surge through my body and I vowed to reform my existence if only God would see fit to let me live the rest of my life with this woman. I left the Soluri home a few moments later, my destiny in Stella's hands.

The following day, as I prepared to return to Gimigliano, a pretty young girl approached me. "My name is Marianna Soluri. My mother sent me to ask you to come to our house. She must speak with you."

I was elated. Surely I had won Gesuzza's hand. Why else would Stella bother to send her little girl to summon me? I charged over to the Soluri house.

Stella looked solemn. "Angelo, I will be frank with you. Your promising future and your manliness is befitting of Gesuzza, but she insists on continuing her courtship with Andrea." The words rang out in my head. I could not believe it. "Damn him!" I scowled. ""I'm going to kill him."

"Calm down, Angelo. You must not have such thoughts. Go to Andrea and calmly explain your situation to him. He will not stand in Gesuzza's way if he knows that she will benefit. In the meantime, I will try to soften Gesuzza's stand." Surely Stella must have known that I was not capable of having a rational talk with my competitor for Gesuzza's hand. She must have anticipated what would happen.

Within the hour I had found Andrea and confronted him. He was in his father's boot shop fitting shoes to a young man's feet. The front of the shop was completely open to the street, a width of twenty-five feet, and piles of merchandise were displayed on wooden racks jutting out partially in the pathway. Andrea's customer could see that I had important business with him, and left. We were alone in the shop when I gave him the news.

"I have seen you walking with Gesuzza Soluri and I have come to tell you that I will be courting her with the intention of marrying her. You may no longer see her."

His face became drawn as though he had become another person. "What right have you to come here and frighten away my customer and tell me what I can or can't do? Gesuzza and I are betrothed and intend to be married. Be gone and don't come back again." He gripped a long metal tool as he talked. He trembled so that his body shook.

He must have noticed, in my face, the rage that was building. He raised the metal object above his head in a motion that was meant to put me in retreat. At that moment I lost control and lunged forward, all the while remembering Stella's demand that I control myself. I seized the steel bar from Andrea's hand and swung it wide and far. The racks of leather came crashing to the floor, as did the dozens of pairs of boots and shoes. The noise was deafening and soon Andrea's father emerged from the living quarters behind the shop to see what was going on.

"Jesus! What in hell is going on?" He could not believe his eyes as he witnessed my rage and the havoc I had visited upon his shop. "I'm ruined!"

Andrea was by now in a state of shock and stared up at me, but dared not speak. I towered over him, and my crazed eyes must have been fearsome. I took his shirt collar in my hand and squeezed it tight. "The next time we meet, I will kill you with my bare hands." I was afraid that I had run afoul of Stella, but I could not control myself. In the next moment, father and son were shouting at one another.

"Andrea, fight back! Defend your honor!"

"That's easy for you to say, father! This brute will kill me if I resist!"

"You coward!"

In a fit of rage, Andrea wrested himself free of my grip and fled. I am told that he left Italy and sailed for South America. I was never to see him again.

Word reached Gesuzza about the violent confrontation between Andrea and Angelo and the subsequent departure of Andrea. But she had not heard from her beloved Andrea. The news came to her from a friend who saw him climb onto the cart that made the daily journey to Cosenza, the first stopping point on the way to the seaport of Naples. He had all of his possessions with him. She wondered why Andrea had chosen to leave without first informing her of the incident and his reasons for leaving. If he loved her, wouldn't he have wanted to take her with him? They might have arranged for Father Zinzi to marry them and then gone off together as man and wife. After all, their bans had been announced and there was no reason to wait. It did not occur to her that Andrea was soundly embarrassed about his refusal to fight Angelo and could not face her. She concluded that Andrea could not have loved her in the true sense if he could leave her behind.

She thought next of Angelo. What had possessed him to act so deliberately and violently to gain her hand in marriage? She had heard romantic stories about how men have been affected by the passion for a woman they truly desire, but did not think that it would ever happen to her. She thought of herself as plain and with little appeal. Why, then, would she completely dismiss his advances as boorish and infantile? There were those who would have been his for the asking. He was tall and handsome, a blonde with blue eyes and ruddy complexion. And, he was a man of means. Perhaps he was not as affluent as he would have them believe, but he did have goats and sheep and could make cheese and could farm as well. Most of all, he showed his passion for her in the most explicit way: he fought for her.

Having caused the sudden disappearance of Andrea, I waited a fortnight before calling on the Soluri household. Even then I timed my visit so that Gesuzza would be away, working in the fields. I needed to talk to Stella alone.

"And how is Gesuzza these days?" My tone was tenuous.

"Angelo, it was not my intent that you would use violent means to discourage Andrea. However, it appears that our ruse has worked. Gesuzza is questioning the sincerity of Andrea's intentions if he was so easily dissuaded. Give me another week with her and then come calling again. I believe she will be receptive to you by then."

I was elated! Andrea was gone and Gesuzza doubted him. The possibility of courting Gesuzza at last looked real. All man-

ner of thought danced through my mind. I could not afford a mistake if I were to end up with Gesuzza as my own. I thought of how I needed to be near her if I were to court her properly and how I needed to give Stella some sign that there was substance to my claim of abundance. She must never know that my claims were exaggerated.

I went home to Gimigliano to tend to my business and serve out the sentence placed on me by my co-conspirator, Stella. In that week I sold all of my possessions except two sturdy goats, a large pig and my dog, Ciao. I said farewell to my family and gave assurances that I would be no farther from Gimigliano than the little hamlet of Gagliano. Then, with the sale proceeds snugly in my pocket, I moved to Gagliano and purchased a small house in utter disrepair on a small plot on the western edge of town. The house was constructed of dried masonry, had a front room with a large fireplace and a back room with just enough space to fit a bed, a trunk and a cabinet. Each room had one window, and the front room had a doorway leading to and from the outside. The stench of animal dung that rose from the dirt floor made it unlikely that anyone had lived there in a while. The dull, gray walls were covered with black flies of the type that were said to transmit malaria. The windows were small and dirty, with a veneer of slime left by the spiders that had had their fill of flies and other creatures that found themselves trapped in their sticky webs.

The yard was also in terrible condition. A wood fence encircled mud and small piles of manure. It was sufficiently battered that it needed to be torn out and replaced. But the yard had enough space to adequately hold a small flock of sheep, which I planned to purchase. And, there was room for all of my other animals as well. I leapt joyfully into the task of cleaning and repairing the house in which Gesuzza and I were to begin our life together and the yard that would contain my new animals.

Stella seemed not to notice that my new home was not quite

up to her expectations, perhaps thinking that I had kept my wealth in reserve for future requirements. She was delighted at having finally won over Gesuzza for me. It was weeks since Gesuzza had heard about Andrea and it was all but certain that he was gone for good. Her pride injured and her mother repeatedly urging her to act, she suddenly looked to me as a worthy suitor. We began courting in earnest and soon received the endorsement of Giuseppe and Stella, should we decide to marry. When the news surfaced that the marriage was to take place, it seemed that the whole town rejoiced. Women referred to my blond ruddiness as mezzo giorno and to Gesuzza's dark swarthiness as mezza notte. The romantic notion of the joining of two lovers of opposite coloring seemed to give the women of Gagliano grist for their daily chatter.

A huge crowd attended the wedding. It seemed that every man, woman and child in Gagliano was there. Father Zinzi performed the wedding in conjunction with a mass, sending his altar boys to the rear of the altar to obtain more communion hosts in order to satisfy the record demand. The procession from The Church of the Holy Rosary to the town square gave final notice to anyone not already aware, that a wedding reception was about to take place. Thankfully, food was provided, prepared and served by many of Stella's friends. The music blared for most of the day and into the night. The Tarantella seemed to be the most frequent melody, giving most of the crowd a chance to dance merrily into the night. A few of the men needed assistance finding their way home after consuming too much wine. The a busta bag filled rapidly with good wishes and small cash gifts from many of the Soluri's closest friends. My family journeyed down from the mountaintop, giving ample opportunity for all the townspeople of Gagliano to meet my father, the strange mountain man whose lore they had whispered about over the years, and whose presence was deemed to be the reason for such an abundant crowd. There were those who eyed my brothers with suspicion and hatred, remembering some shameful act that they were alleged to have performed at some time in the past. *All in all, the wedding was well received by most and I was at last joined for life to this lovely woman who only a few months ago was set to marry another.*

It was not long before a son was born to us. Pietro arrived shortly before our first anniversary. It was evident from the start that he would resemble me. He was blonde, blue-eyed and very tall. But his demeanor was like his mother. He was kind and gentle and he bonded with Gesuzza in a special way. Mother and son had a sense of each other that was uncanny. Pietro almost never cried as an infant. Gesuzza, inexperienced though she was, sensed when it was time to feed Pietro and changed his soiled diaper almost before the boy realized it was necessary. And Pietro never complained when he knew his mother was tired or sleeping after an exhausting day. He would wait patiently in his crib for his mother to awaken, and of course she would then run to his aid. I can even recall their finishing sentences for one another, almost from the time that Pietro was able to speak. It was as though they could read each other's mind. There were times when I envied them for the love they felt towards each other. I loved them both more than I ever imagined I could love other human beings. I would occasionally awaken at night and watch Gesuzza sleeping. My whole body felt a surge of warmth and pride. She was mine. How lucky I was that Stella had favored me over Andrea.

Six years passed before our second child was born. It was another boy, whom we named Giuseppe after his maternal grandfather. Though he had my blue eyes, Giuseppe had his mother's coloring and size. He would grow to where he barely reached his older brother's shoulder in height. His features were those of the Soluri family. Unlike his brother, however, Giuseppe had my temperament. He flew off the handle easily and was always scrap-

ping with the other town rascals. He had little rapport with his mother, though she gave him the same loving upbringing that she gave to Pietro. Gesuzza prayed daily that he would calm and mature as he grew into manhood.

The exaggeration of my wealth was soon forgotten and my new life, though not overly comfortable, allowed my family to have the essentials of life as long as we were all willing to work. My yard contained a small flock of sheep, a few goats and a pig. I made a small amount of cheese for sale, produced some wool for the buyer from Milan and shared the crop from a small farm that I worked for Count Leone, the largest land baron of the province. Even Stella seemed to have accepted me for who I really was.

The boys lived in the main room of the house, where they shared a straw bed. It was roomy enough until harvest time arrived. Then, they shared it with cousins and others who helped us to gather the crops. There were seven in all. Nine boys in the same bed on hot autumn nights was stifling, even for a few weeks. There was no schooling for the boys and there was no escape for any of us from the hopeless peasant existence, but we were a family and that was all that mattered.

And then it happened. It was the most extraordinary event of my life, yet it seemed like nothing at all. Gesuzza and I were asleep in our bed in the middle of the night when we heard a knock at our door. The boys were in a deep sleep in their perch on the floor in front of the fireplace and were undisturbed. The black of night was lit by a half moon, casting shadows everywhere and creating an eerie feeling. I thought I heard the animals stir, an unusual sound for the middle of the night. I opened the door.

The caller was Roberto Borrelli, a neighbor and friend from my bachelor days. Although a well-meaning person, Roberto had a way of intruding on his friends, often to their regret. He once had produced a bad smelling cheese from the milk of a dy-

ing goat. It had the lingering smell of death. All of his friends warned him against selling or eating the cheese, but Roberto convinced the local grocer to purchase it at half price. As a precaution, the grocer fed it first to his own family. The result was that his wife and one child became desperately ill and were brought to Catanzaro to have their stomachs pumped out at the new medical clinic. Then there was the time when his goats tore down a section of fence enclosing his herd. The animals roamed freely for a time until Roberto got several of his friends to help round them up. Later in the day it was determined that some of the herded goats belonged to Count Leone. All of the men involved in the roundup were under suspicion of theft and it appeared that they would be arrested awaiting trial. Thankfully, Roberto was able to convince the Count's purser that the caper was an honest mistake and the charges were dropped. Roberto eventually became so unpopular that everyone shunned him. Only his closest friends would acknowledge him and even they were suspicious of him. Now he was at my door in the middle of the night.

"What is it, Roberto? Don't you know you're disturbing us?"

"I need your help, Angelo."

"I figured that. What do you want?"

"I have this goat who is new to my herd and is being hacked at by the herd leader for heaven knows why. I would deal with it myself, but I need to go quickly to Gimigliano. My mother is deathly ill and is not expected to live. May I leave the animal with you?"

"No, Roberto, you may not. The last time your friends tried to help you they almost ended up in jail. Do you think I'm crazy?"

"Angelo, please, you're my last hope. You know my mother. She's dying. If I don't get to her side immediately, she'll be gone and I will have missed her last words to me." Roberto began to sob pitifully.

At that moment Gesuzza spoke. "Angelo, you can't turn Roberto away. He is your friend and he needs your help. Imagine yourself in his shoes."

Angrily, I shouted at Roberto, "Very well, you can put the goat in with mine, but you get back here quickly and take him home with you. Now, let's all get some sleep."

"May the Lord bless you." Roberto was truly grateful and expressed his thanks as he made his way to the yard where the goat was already in with my animals. Gesuzza and I were finally able to get back to our rest.

For the next two days, I tended Roberto's goat along with my own. There was no problem at all with its acceptance by my herd. It was a nanny and its teats were full with milk, requiring milking twice daily. Its coat was longer than those of my goats, and it seemed to gleam in the light as the goat moved about. The goat's milk was creamy and formed a light curd with the least effort on my part. I thought that I must ask Roberto where he had obtained this wonderful animal.

On the morning of the third day, three Carabinieri soldiers from the local garrison arrived at my door.

"Hey, Angelo, we need to check over your animals."

"What the hell for?"

"It seems that the Count is missing some livestock and his purser is really pissed."

"Why bother me? I'm an honest man. I've nothing to hide, but why am I suspected?"

"We don't give the orders, we just follow them. Now let us in to check over your animals."

To my astonishment, the goat left by Roberto bore a mark indicating that it was owned by Count Leone. The officers placed me under arrest. Gesuzza came into the yard in tears, pleading my innocence.

"You are making a mistake. This goat belongs to Roberto

Borrelli. He asked my husband to care for it while he visits his dying mother."

"Signora, we are very sorry, but we must place your husband under arrest. If what you say is true, he will be released."

At this point, Gesuzza was sobbing and begging for my release. I looked at her reassuringly. "Don't worry, Gesuzza, I will be freed as soon as Roberto returns." She seemed to calm, but became upset again as they placed manacles on my wrists and led me away. The disturbance attracted a crowd of neighbors, all of whom witnessed my arrest. There was a moment of pride as some of the onlookers called out to the police and vouched for my honesty. I had gained the respect of the townspeople for my hard work and dedication to my family. My past as a maverick had at last been forgiven. It was too bad that the acknowledgement had come at this time of misunderstanding with the authorities. Now it was up to Roberto to return to Gagliano and clear my name.

The jail was not very far from our home, a distance of not more than a couple of miles. But it was a different world entirely. From the moment I entered the building I could sense hostility to all that entered who were not in the uniform of the Carabiniere. We were assumed to be guilty and treated accordingly. I caught a glimpse of a barracks off to one side of the building that looked like it might house a small troop. It was being swept by an elderly woman and looked clean and orderly. The other side of the building contained the prison cells, which were behind a large wooden door that was reinforced with steel bars. Only bars separated the prison cells, and the outside wall of the building was made of stone. The condition of the prison was unlike the barracks. It was dirty and had a lingering odor of sweat and urine. I was placed in a cell with two unfortunate souls awaiting trial and, since the cell was made to accommodate only two persons, I was given a straw mattress and told to

*sleep on the floor. It was then that I noticed the presence of sev-
eral long, brown cockroaches. One of the other prisoners warned
me not to complain or the guards would not let my wife bring
food in to me. He also warned me about keeping food around in
the cell, since there were rats that would appear in the middle of
the night to claim their share of whatever was available. I gave
thanks to God that I would be here only long enough for Roberto
to return and straighten everything out. It troubled me that I had
not even asked him how long it would be before he expected to
return.*

Chapter 3

Capurro Villa

For the first few days that Marianna tends to Leone, she sees nothing of him. His bed is slept in and his soiled clothing is left for cleaning, but nowhere is Leone to be seen. On the fourth day, Concetta summons Marianna.

"Leone is entertaining a lady at dinner on the patio tonight and Antonio is down with the fever. You will be needed to serve and clear the dishes."

"Yes, of course." Marianna is at last to get a glimpse of the Count up close and in a social setting. She is elated. But why would Leone be entertaining a woman? It is rumored that he has been a sexual recluse since the death of Countess Beatrice two years ago, and that he has vowed never to marry again. Ah, but perhaps the dinner is to serve a purpose unfamiliar to a peasant girl. "I am Marianna and I will be serving you this evening, Count."

Marianna smiles at a curious Count Leone and then at the lady sitting across from him, a shapely and well-preserved woman who Marianna guesses is fifty years old. She appears lovely in her evening dress of light blue silk studded with sparkling stones that Marianna has never before seen.

Marianna tries not to be obvious in her first close-up look at Leone. Stella was right. He is not a foul old man at all. When he stands to pour his favorite wine for his guest, Marianna can see that he is tall, slim and muscular. His hair is a mix of brown and gray and his eyes are hazel. He is olive complexioned and his tan is mild, unlike that of the men who labor under the punishing Calabrian sun. His hair is full and long and brushed back, belying his true age of sixty. He wears a silk shirt tailored to his torso, the sleeves ending in a slight cuff and secured by tiny lion-faced spikes. His trousers are linen and creased to perfection. They are cuffed and sit neatly upon highly polished brown shoes. Draped across a nearby chair is a suit coat, the obvious mate to his trousers. There is an odd pride in Marianna's thoughts, since she herself has cleaned and pressed the clothes Leone is wearing, and even polished the shoes. As she serves the dinner and removes the empty plates, she strains to eavesdrop on the conversation.

"Madam, you are especially lovely tonight. I have so anticipated these moments that we are sharing, that I have asked my cook to prepare her specialities and I have brought my favorite Brunello to the table."

"Leone, I haven't noticed the food or the wine. I have been watching you all evening and can't help but wonder."

"If I have created mystery, you may ask me any question at all and I promise a forthright response."

His encouragement emboldens Gina to ask quite bluntly, "Why, after two years, do you keep Beatrice's body in a coffin in a room in your house? Why do you not bury her and end all of the pain that her death brings you?"

"My marriage to Beatrice of some thirty years was extremely blissful. To now place her in the ground would be to deny the happiness we shared and perhaps even risk the chance that we could end up in different crypts. Thankfully, the embalmer I retain has excellent powers of restoration and preservation, and is able to hold back the forces of nature from causing Beatrice's body to decay." His face is pained as he continues with his confession. "As most people know, I was publicly ex-communicated from the Church along with all of the principal supporters of our king, Victor Emmanuel, and our liberator, Guiseppe Garibaldi. They, too, were ex-communicated for acting upon their enormous love for Italy in defiance of the Pope and what once was his temporal power over much of Italy. I have taken over the support of The Church of the Holy Rosary in Gagliano in order to gain the favor of the pastor, Father Saverio Zinzi, so that when I die, he will see that I am entombed in the St. Rosalia Church cemetery together with Beatrice, despite my status as an excommunicant. That is my plan, plain and simple."

"Not so simple, Leone." Gina is at once appalled and annoyed with Leone's explanations. Obviously, her interests are not quite as mysterious as Marianna had imagined. The girl has received quite an earful of conversation for one night. As the dinner ends, the couple walks off into the garden and is not seen again.

Her normal routine having been interrupted, Marianna now remembers that she must get to Leone's chamber to prepare his bed. It is late and she is concerned that he may already be in bed. As she approaches Leone's door, she carefully and quietly turns the doorknob and finds herself in the room unnoticed. As she looks around, she observes clothes strewn about. The beautiful gem-studded blue dress is among them. There on the bed she sees Leone with Gina on top of him in an ardent sexual embrace. Their murmuring and groans are easily loud enough to have drowned out any sound that Marianna has made, and Marianna surprises herself as she takes pleasure in having found herself the unwitting voyeur of this liaison. Leone is prone and reaches up to cup his hands over Gina's breasts. Gina's sensuous body is copulating furiously, her inky hair falling into Leone's face. She calls out his name and then swoons as she orgasms. Leone suddenly turns and mounts Gina. Marianna is able to see his pubic hair and erect penis for a fleeting moment. He copulates forcefully and Gina continues to groan and call Leone's name as he climaxes and falls into her arms. All is silent as Marianna makes a hushed exit.

As Marianna returns to her room, her thoughts are of Lorenzo and his lovemaking. Observing Leone's rapture has excited her and brought to mind moments of passion she herself has experienced. She and Lorenzo have never had a setting such as Leone's large and very private room with massive, canopied four-poster bed and satin sheets; but their passion was just as strong and their love for one another was confirmed by their lovemaking time and again. Now she thinks of Leone, this man who has confessed his passion for her to her mother and has brought her to his villa to be part of his life while he entertains the lovely Gina. Does he really need her? Isn't Gina enough? One thing is for sure. Her former perceptions of Leone are forever dashed.

━┅•❂•┅━

As the weeks pass, Marianna performs her role as chambermaid well. There is even faint praise from Concetta, who has found Marianna to be a willing worker and easy to direct. Though Marianna has felt homesick and has thought frequently of her family, she has longed for the strong embrace of Lorenzo and the feel of his manly body against hers. The new surroundings have mitigated her yearnings, but her concern for the whereabouts of Lorenzo overcome her complacency. She decides to find out. As she exits her room, Concetta approaches. Marianna feels comfortable enough at this point to engage her superior in a conversation on a personal level.

"Concetta, may I ask a question?"

"Yes, of course. What is it?"

"Lorenzo Fusco. Before I came here, we were close, nearly betrothed. Will I be permitted to contact him, perhaps even see him?"

The older woman falls silent. Even at her young age, Marianna is able to sense a sudden reticence to share the truth of what Concetta knows.

"Is there something you know about Lorenzo?"

"Some things are better not talked about."

"Oh, please, Concetta, you must let me know what has happened. Please!"

"I thought you were told. I am truly sorry that I must be the one to tell you."

"*Tell me?* Concetta! Please! What has happened?" Marianna's eyes fill and her breathing is forced and heavy.

"Two weeks ago, Lorenzo came to the villa looking

for you. He was turned away, but later he petitioned to speak with Leone. Leone was away and would probably not have agreed to such a meeting anyhow, but Aldo met with Lorenzo. He was apparently authorized by Leone to deal with the situation."

"Yes, yes?" Marianna shows her anxiety and impatience with the pace of the conversation.

"Oh, Marianna, I detest having to tell you this, but Lorenzo left for America two days ago. He was given a sum of money sufficient to guarantee his success there."

Suddenly, the world seems to have closed in around Marianna. The blood drains from her face and she begins to lose consciousness. She falls into Concetta's arms and both women drop to the floor.

"Aiute! Aiute!" Concetta calls frantically for help. Marianna is brought quietly to her bed and the door to her room closed. Leone must never know of this incident.

▸┄◂▸─◦─◂▸┄◂

There has been ample time for Marianna's physical recovery, but the emotional shock of Lorenzo's departure for America has not worn off. Marianna has been able to resume her normal duties, but her emotions are exhausted and she makes a conscious effort to avoid thinking of Gagliano and her home and family. Just as she thinks she has succeeded at isolating herself, she sights Anita Cecchini walking up the road to the house and recalls the day that Anita's face told of suspicion as she observed Stella escorting Marianna to her new domicile. Now it is Marianna's turn to suspect and wonder what Anita is up to.

Mariana turns to Concetta, "What is that woman doing here?"

"She has somehow gotten Leone to meet with her, but only heaven knows why."

"She is my best friend's mother," Marianna says, "but I have never liked her or trusted her. Who knows what she is up to with Leone."

Nighttime arrives and, following the evening meal, Marianna makes her way to Leone's room. She must turn down the bed and see to his clothing. It will take her but a moment, considering that she has spent the better part of the afternoon in the room, diligently cleaning. As she enters, she recalls the scene with Gina and Leone that she observed only a few days before. Her thoughts turn unavoidably to Lorenzo, and she falls into a window seat and with head in hands, begins to weep.

"Good evening." Marianna looks up to see Leone's face. Her eyes and face are streaming tears. She murmurs a response, embarrassed that Leone is seeing her in this state. After a moment of quiet, he speaks. "Marianna, I have not had the opportunity before now to tell you how pleased I have been with your work and the fact that you are here. Have you been happy here?"

"Yes, I have."

He moves closer to her. "Then why do you weep? Has someone offended you?"

"Oh, no, no. Everyone here has been very kind."

"Then why do you cry?" Leone asks a second time.

Hardly able to raise her head, Marianna tells Leone, "The man I had hoped to wed has left suddenly for America, and I will probably never see him again. In fact, I *hope* I never see him again!" Tears stream down her face as she tries to control her sobs.

Leone moves closer and takes her hand in his, placing the other hand on her cheek. "My dear, I am sorry that you are so saddened, but often the passage of time turns sadness to joy."

"Oh, Sir, at this moment that possibility is difficult to imagine."

"I can assure you that it's true." Leone is seated alongside her and gently pulls her toward him. He places a kiss on her mouth. Her sudden feeling of passion for him and complete lack of reserve astonish her. Recalling the tryst that she had witnessed between Leone and Gina, she looks deeply into his eyes.

"Oh, Leone", she mutters as he envelops her in his arms. They kiss on the window seat for several minutes, further arousing their desire and establishing their resolve to move across the room to the bed. Once there, they make quick work of undressing and are naked in one another's arms. Marianna is able to detect a notable difference in Leone's passion for her compared to Gina. Perhaps he is driven by the aromatic balm that Marianna has obediently worn every day since Stella instructed her. Certainly middle aged Gina is no match for Marianna's sleek, fresh body, and Leone seems well aware of it. Though gentle, his hands and mouth feverishly find every bend and curve of her torso. As their passion increases in intensity, Marianna thinks she hears Leone mutter the name Beatrice. Then, he is on top of her and has found entry to her willing body. He copulates wildly as Marianna's long legs hold him firm to her. She inhales the lingering aroma of his citrus face lotion. In his final moment of ecstasy, he cries out, "Marianna, Marianna!" To her utter amazement, she, too, reaches climax and calls Leone's name over and over. And, to think that she had dreaded this moment as her *awful fate*. Then, she revels in the thought that her relationship with Leone has been so passionately consummated.

Marianna falls back in a moment of respite, engulfed in a sea of satin and finery such as she has never known. She is overwhelmed by the contrast to her lovemaking with Lorenzo in the tall grass and of her life in general. Then she turns back to Leone and is fulfilled by his passion, his charm and his elegance. Despite his advanced age, he is able to respond to his wish to have Marianna a second time. They make love again, as they will over and over for years to come.

It has been weeks since Silvia Cecchini presented herself to Leone, in accord with the wishes of her mother, Anita. Alas, not a word from Leone. Signora Cecchini is confident still, but nervous that too much time has passed and that Leone has not come bargaining for Silvia's favors. Anita decides to take matters into her own hands, dispatching a note to Leone.

"Signoro Leone, may we meet to discuss my daughter's future position in your household?" Leone responds promptly, indicating that he will visit her tomorrow at eleven O'clock in the morning. Anita Cecchini is ecstatic. At last she has lured the lion from his den, and trapped him into admitting that he needs her daughter to light up his life and save him from an otherwise drab existence. She will dress up her front room as best she can. There she will invite him to sit, sip coffee and offer her the fortune to which she is rightly entitled, in exchange for the privilege of bedding her Silvia. If Stella could do it, why not she?

Leone arrives promptly. Surely, this is a sign of his intention to ask for Silvia's inclusion in his life. He is dressed in his usual finery, but looking a little peaked and tired. Anita cannot help admiring Leone's handsome face, thinking that perhaps under different circumstances, she herself might have appealed to him. She takes pity and decides that she will exact only a fair price for her merchandise. After all, how much will it take to comfort her for giving up her beautiful daughter to this lonely man?

Anita thinks, *Ah, Providence, at last thou hast seen fit to come to my door. No longer will I need to scrape by, depriving myself of the barest pleasures of life and fearing misfortune in my old age. Who does this Soluri woman think she is? What nerve to believe that her Marianna can compete with my Silvia. Surely, she will be crushed when the word reaches her that Leone has chosen Silvia.*

Leone enters and sits in a large oak chair that dominates the room. Anita serves coffee and cruller. He appears to be a monarch on his throne; issuing a decree that will affect the lives of every person in the humble village. Such power! Anita is duly impressed. How does she open conversation with this sovereign? What words does she use to break the silence? A feeling of exuberance fills her body and she blurts out, "Signor, shall I summon Silvia?"

"No, that will not be necessary," Leone responds, "we will be but a moment, and this matter is best discussed between us."

Anita is nervous, but remains outwardly calm. "Signor", she says at last, "I am not very experienced at this type of thing, but can you tell me what sort of financial arrangement you had in mind?"

Calmly, Leone puts down his coffee cup and looks up to Anita, "…financial arrangement? Madam, I am here to tell you that, after much careful thought, I have chosen Marianna Soluri for the position in my household. I would have spared you this moment except that you sought me out and requested my presence. I am truly sorry if you were misled by my actions."

Anita is stunned. She is unable to speak. Her mouth is open and finally she blurts out "Marianna? That whore! How could you possibly choose her over my beautiful Silvia? Sir, you have no taste!"

She has overstepped her position with the most offensive of insults. *Oh, lord, what is going to happen now, how could everything have gone so wrong?*

Leone's face is crimson, as though it has been soundly slapped. He pulls himself up to his full height and flings the embroidered napkin she had given him to her feet. "Madame", he says, "Marianna's *behind* is many times more exquisite than your daughter's face." With that, he turns and leaves. Anita is never to have the pleasure of his company again.

⊱━━━⊰

It is a dreary, rainy morning as Leone's carriage pulls up to the Soluri home and Aldo disembarks. He knocks gently at the door and calls for Stella.

"What is it?" Stella answers the door.

"Marianna asked me to summon you to the Capurro villa."

"Is she all right?" Stella is concerned. Though she has been kept abreast of Marianna's well being, she has not actually seen her for two months.

"Never better," Aldo responds, "Can we go now?"

"Give me a moment."

The carriage, with an iron lantern on each side, is a black box that looks as though it will easily fit two persons in the enclosed cab. The interior is dark tufted velvet, well worn from many years and scores of journeys, but still rich and soft to the touch. Aldo is dressed as any man of the village might be: open shirt, trousers with suspenders and a peaked cap. It is only because of the rain that he wears a light coat. He holds a whip in one hand and the reins in the other. The horse is a striking and sleek sorrel mare with flowing mane and tail. The short ride to the villa seems interminable.

Concetta is there to greet Stella and escort her up to Marianna's shared room. She then courteously leaves them alone.

"Marianna. Thank heavens you're all right. I was afraid that some terrible thing had happened. Why am I here? Is something wrong?"

"Mother, I'm pregnant with Leone's child."

Chapter 4

Miscarriage of Justice

Mario Martinez had come a long way in life. From humble beginnings as an orphan in Naples, he had risen to the post of Justice of the Criminal Court. Still in his formative years in the Orphanage of the Holy Ghost in Naples, he had been taught to read and write before coming of age and leaving the orphanage. Out on his own, he had offered his services as a scribe to the scores of women whose husbands, fathers or brothers had immigrated to the Americas in search of a better life than the new Italian Kingdom had to offer. Since there were many such women, none of whom could read or write, Mario had as much business as he could handle and was able to charge a handsome fee for his services. After a while, he found that he could earn enough money in just a few hours a day to permit him to further his education. Eventually, he earned a law degree at the University of Naples and established a law practice in which he defended the accused in criminal court. His successes in the courts were impressive and he was soon asked to accept an appointment as judge. He was assigned to the province of Catanzaro, where his cool, impartial justice earned him respect in the community. As with most self-made intellectuals of the time, Mario married late in life, taking a young Calabrian woman as his wife. They settled in a fine house in her hometown of Gagliano. The marriage produced a daughter who quickly became the focus of Mario's life. As Tina grew up to become an attractive woman, he became extremely protective of her virtue to the point of repulsing her suitors.

Tina soon found herself isolated from the young eligible men of the town. In the midst of her misery, she chanced upon Angelo's brother Constantino, who was in Gagliano on some hedonistic sortie. Out on the town square on an errand, Tina stood out in her colorful blue sheath dress and white sandals, her well-shaped torso forming a sensual sight. Constantino spotted her and could not contain himself.

"And who might you be...the queen of England?"

"I beg your pardon, signore, but do I know you?"

"No, but you should."

"And why is that?"

"Because I am more fun than anyone you know."

The conversation continued until Constantino felt comfortable about asking Tina to join him for the evening. Since this was the first man who had the courage to approach her in spite of her father's stern dominance, she accepted his invitation, casting aside the purchases she had made and leaving the square with him, arm in arm. Clearly this strange-looking giant, who now eyed her with considerable lust, mystified her. After a few glasses of wine, Constantino convinced Tina to accompany him to a local brothel, where she was exposed to a more squalid side of life than she had ever known. Her young and innocent face contrasted with the hardened residents of that vile place. In the main room of the establishment, five women awaited their prey, dressed scantily and seated provocatively in easy chairs fashioned of wood and finished in leather. The clothing they wore was garishly colored and they wore many golden bracelets and large earrings. They looked up as Constantino made his entrance. Tina's innocence and youthful good looks seemed to eclipse them. The mature, buxomy madam, Maria, who had undoubtedly seen much service in this oldest of professions, called out to Constantino.

"Hey, what gives? Aren't my beauties good enough for you any more?"

"Never mind. We'll talk about that another time. Where can we go to be alone?"

Ushered to a room on the second floor of the building, Constantino and Tina walked past rooms where moans of ecstasy gave vocal testimony to the activities therein. The couple entered a room with a large bed that was unmade and had obviously been slept in or otherwise used during the earlier hours of the day. It did not seem to matter to either of them. They immediately came together intensely and passionately, tearing at one another's clothes. When they were completely naked, Tina said softly to Constantino, "Please be gentle. I have never been with a man before."

Constantino could not believe what he had heard. How

was it possible for a complete novice to have allowed herself to be lured to a place such as this? He turned to Tina and held her head in his hands, scattering the pins that held her rich brown hair. His mouth was on hers in the next moment as they responded to the burning lust that they both felt. As they fell onto the bed, their bodies fused and they felt the culmination of their passion in a hot explosion like that of a volcano erupting. She was oblivious to the pain from the separation of vaginal tissue and the consequent bleeding. She knew only that she wanted more from Constantino. They lay panting in their euphoria for a time and then repeated the act, this time more deliberate and controlled.

Awakening from a deep sleep, Tina nudged Constantino. "I need to get home right away. It's the middle of the night. My father will be frantic."

"Where do you live?"

"I live with my parents here in Gagliano. My father is Don Mario Martinez."

"Where have I heard that name before?"

"He is judge of the Criminal Court."

Constantino held his head in mock pain. "Oh, my God. Why didn't you tell me that when we first met? He'll kill me for what I've done."

"It's what *we've* done, Constantino. You've done nothing that I didn't agree to, and I am old enough to make my own decisions. Don't worry, I'll see that he doesn't blame you." As they hurriedly dressed and passed through the main hall of the brothel on their way out, Maria was there and tuned in to their conversation.

"You must know that your father has put terror into the hearts of all of the young men of Gagliano when it comes to your virtue," Constantino said. " There is no explanation that he will accept. I'm a dead man."

"Constantino, what's wrong?" asked Maria.

"Oh, Maria, this time I've really done it. This lady is Don Mario's daughter."

"You must get her home right away. Then return here and I will solve your problem for you."

Wide-eyed, Constantino silently made his exit with Tina in tow, and walked her quickly to her home. There was a lamp burning in the window on the second floor. The noise of their walking up the front walk brought Don Mario to the door.

"Where the hell have you been? Do you know what hour it is? And who is that with you?"

Tina spoke strongly and loudly. "Father, this man has escorted me through the evening and has brought me home. He has acted with my permission. There is nothing more to discuss."

"Like hell! You were seen entering Maria's whorehouse with him. I am going to take him apart with my own hands. Come over here you son of a bitch." As Mario lunged at Constantino, he was prevented from doing any harm by Constantino's huge arms and frame. Constantino signalled good night to Tina and left.

Intrigued by Maria's mysterious invitation and desperate for a solution to his hopeless dilemma, he returned to the brothel. Maria was waiting for him.

"I've just come from Don Mario's home. He would have killed me on the spot if I didn't restrain him. Maria, I'm a dead man."

"No, you're not. I will give you information that will keep Don Mario away from you for as long as you live."

"Tell me, Maria, what is it?"

"Constantino, you and your brothers have been

wretched mishaps in Gagliano. You have partied at the expense of others and have upset many of the men in town. But you have always treated me well and been more than generous with my girls. You have never looked upon any of us with scorn, and have even defended us. Hence, I have always considered you to be my good friend. For that reason, I will share information with you that will save you from harm. Don Mario is not as innocent as he would have everyone believe. He has been a valued client here for many years. For the last two years, he sees one woman only, whom he has met in my house and demands be kept away from other men. He comes unannounced in the middle of the night so that he is not noticed by anyone and so that he can test the woman's loyalty to him. They are closer than man and wife and her identity is kept secret."

"How can I use this information to save myself from Don Mario's wrath?"

"You do not have to do anything. I will let him know that if any harm comes to you, I will reveal his relationship with the woman. It will work, believe me."

"Bless you, Maria, may you live *per centi anni*."

⊷

The guard entered the cellblock that I had been held in for the past week. I was relieved to hear him call my name. "Angelo Chiarella, you are to be tried today in the Criminal Court in Catanzaro. Gather your belongings and come with me."

On her visit to the jail the day before, Gesuzza had told me the news that Roberto had returned from Gimigliano and was immediately seized by the Carabinieri. His mother was indeed gravely ill and had died the day following Roberto's arrival. After a three-day wake, she was buried in the cemetery of the little

Church of the Nativity in Gimigliano, after which Roberto made his grief-filled trek back to Gagliano. The Carabinieri were waiting for him.

"Roberto Borrelli, you are under arrest for the theft of a goat belonging to Count Leone."

"What do you mean? I have done no such thing."

"The goat in question was found in the possession of Angelo Chiarella, and he has told us that you brought the animal to him for safekeeping while you were away. Is this true?"

"I did leave a goat with Angelo, but it was from my herd, not the Count's."

"Then you must testify against Angelo in court."

"Oh my God, have you accused him of stealing the goat?"

"Yes, he is in our custody awaiting your return to Gagliano. He has told us that your testimony will free him from responsibility for the theft of the goat."

"It is true that I left the goat with him. He is an innocent man."

"Then you admit that you stole the goat?"

When Roberto failed to answer, he was taken to a holding cell at the court in Catanzaro so that we could neither see nor speak to one another before the trial. Then, because I had been held for a week, the case was given priority and placed on the Court agenda for the next day. The judge was Mario Martinez.

From the moment I entered the courtroom I felt the terrible stare of the judge on me, as though he knew me and was aware of my past misdeeds. Since those actions were not in any way connected with the charges against me, I was certain that the trial would be short and that I would be cleared very quickly. I was right about the length of the trial. It was short.

The prosecutor questioned Roberto mercilessly and eventually got him to admit that he had stolen the goat. Roberto made it clear that I was unaware that the animal was stolen, but the *prosecutor refused to accept that part of the testimony, inferring that Roberto was simply covering up my guilt. Since neither of us could afford to hire a defense lawyer, there was no one to object to the unjust proceeding. The judge seemed satisfied that he had heard enough to convict Roberto, and since provincial law gave him the sole power to decide, he brought his gavel down with a loud crack.*

"Guilty as charged. Roberto Borrelli, you are hereby sentenced to nine years at hard labor. Your sentence will begin immediately and you will be moved to the penitentiary at Asinara without delay."

Roberto's family, a wife, two daughters and a son, was noticeably absent from the courtroom, an indication of how they felt the decision would go. Roberto's looseness about the law was bound to catch up with him sooner or later and chances were that this was the time. They were right. Now, their plight was to survive during Roberto's long absence and they were already making arrangements to take over his contract to work a farm belonging to Count Leone.

Against my wishes, Gesuzza had come to Catanzaro to witness my trial. Thankfully, she had decided to leave my sons behind in Gagliano. I could see from the corner of my eye the apprehension she felt towards the proceedings. Roberto had been lead away to his fate and it was now my turn before the bar of justice.

The prosecutor began. "Angelo Chiarella, you are of the family from Gimigliano?"

I did not like the subtle referral to my past. "Yes, I am. But I have lived honorably in Gagliano for the past nine years. I am married and have two sons, and I farm a property belonging to Count Leone Capurro."

"How did you come upon his goat, the one that was found in your animal pen?"

"It was brought to me in the middle of the night by Roberto

Borrelli. He asked that I care for it while he was attending his mother's funeral in Gimigliano."

Judge Martinez' face became hard and he scowled, "So! You admit that you assisted Borrelli in performing this crime."

"Absolutely not, your honor! I was not aware that the beast was stolen. Roberto has already told you that."

The prosecutor broke in. "Yes, you mean that your paisano Roberto testified to that lie so that you would go free. Your honor, this man is an accessory to the crime."

The judge peered at me from his perch high above the rest of us. He looked at me rather strangely, almost as though he knew me and hated me for what I had done. But what had I done? Aided my neighbor? Could he not see that?

In the next moment, his gavel crashed to its cradle on his bench with a loud crack. I could not believe he was saying the words that I heard. Was I dreaming? Could this be true?

"Angelo Antonio Chiarella, you are found guilty as accessory to the crime committed by Roberto Borrelli. You are hereby sentenced to serve nine years in the penitentiary in Asinara at hard labor. Your sentence will be carried out immediately."

I stood frozen as the guards came to take me away, but I could hear Gesuzza in the rear of the courtroom, screaming. "No! No! He's innocent. Jesus, don't let this happen. He's innocent."

As I looked back, I could see her slump to the floor. It was the last sight I would have of her for the next nine years.

Chapter 5

Voyage to Asinara

Two days after their conviction in the Criminal Court in Catanzaro, Roberto Borrelli and Angelo Chiarella were to be moved to Reggio di Calabria, along with 43 other prisoners from Catanzaro province. Reggio would be the last that they would see of their beloved Calabria, with its beautiful mountains, its streams and all the other familiar sights that made it home. Now that coastal city was to be the seaport from which they would be taken to Sardinia. Before leaving Catanzaro, they were placed in chains to assure their complete obedience to twelve Carabinieri assigned to escort them to Asinara. A single blacksmith pounded his hammer, riveting wrist manacles and ankle rings around their limbs. A chain between the manacles allowed them to spread their arms only three feet apart. The ankle rings were linked so that their stride could not exceed two feet, forcing their walk into a shuffle. The right ankle ring was made just large enough to allow a space through which a chain could be fed to keep all of the prisoners tethered in two long columns. *As we made our way to the horse-drawn carts that took us to Reggio, the Carabinieri made it plain that they were in command and that the trip to Asinara would be oppressive. They used every opportunity to assert their authority. Chained as we were, walking a straight line was almost impossible. Yet, with every stumble or waiver we were dealt bruises and bloodied faces from rifle butts and truncheons. Roberto was one of the unfortunate victims of this brutality. As he tripped over his tangled foot and fell to the ground, a soldier was upon him and beat him until blood poured from his nose and he begged for mercy. I felt rage and anger towards all that was happening at that moment and all that had happened to place me in this position, but I was totally helpless and could do nothing but accept my fate. In spite of Roberto's pitiful state, I wanted to slit his throat for the misery I knew was ahead of me because of his stupidity in implicating me in his blunder.*

Throughout their journey on foot through Catanzaro and in carts to Reggio, townspeople gathered along the way to stare at the miserable prisoners heading to some horrible place, a few of them for the rest of their lives. There were some hecklers and some sympathizers. A few family members of the prisoners were present. Angelo looked for Gesuzza, but she was not there. He wondered about her well being and longed for her as never before. For sure, there would be no visits by Gesuzza to this faraway place that Angelo had never before heard of. There would be no more of Gesuzza's cooking and homemade wine. Most of all, there would be no Gesuzza to hold and make love to.

As he peered at the onlookers, he could not help but notice the diverse profiles, shades of skin, eye and hair color and even the shapes of noses and lips. It was obvious that this place called Calabria had been a huge joining of people of various cultures. For centuries the tip of the great Italian peninsula had been a haven for the persecuted and a target for invaders. The Greeks and Romans were part founder, part conqueror. Jews fleeing the Arab onslaught had come seeking a place where they could live in peace with the inhabitants. The Saracens, Turks, French and Spaniards all had their turn at invasion and conquest. All left their mark on the faces of the people of this region, and those who remained suffered subsequent invasions.

"All right, you men, pick up your belongings and single file onto the ship." The guard poked at the prisoners who had fallen asleep awaiting the arrival of the sailing vessel that was to take them from Reggio around to the westerly coast of Sardinia and up to the island of Asinara.

The Brigantine sailing vessel was an old crate, barely sixty-five feet long and thirty wide. It had two masts and four sails. Two of the sails hung at right angles to the length of the ship and two were slung fore and aft. Its dilapidated condition told of long service as a warship in past encounters. In these times, when much of the world was turning to modern steam powered ships, this relic of the high seas would take two weeks to sail a mere 600 miles. The return trip would be even longer because of the predominance of the southerly wind. Nevertheless, it would be adequate to ferry these men to their unwelcome destiny. Their haste to end the journey would be driven only by the miserable conditions on the ship and by the continued cruelty of the guards.

The prisoners would be kept on deck at all times, some

of them being required to assist with hoisting and lowering sails and scrubbing the deck clean of salt left by the occasional sweep of the sea across the deck. Others would be responsible for collecting the pails used by the prisoners as latrines and heaving their contents windward into the sea. Meals consisted of hardtack and water.

My mind kept racing all of the time. I was frantic. I was separated from my family. I had lost my freedom. I was chained like a dog and treated even worse. Escape was impossible. Nine years of this! My thoughts turned desperately to suicide. I looked for an instrument that I could use to end my life, but could find nothing. I slung the chain between my wrists around my neck and pulled tight. As I felt myself losing consciousness, I could see a guard headed towards me and as he pulled the chain from around my neck, I blacked out.

━┅━◆━०━◆━┅━

Guido and Luigi Rossi were twin brothers from the city of Cosenza. Identical in looks and actions, they had chosen a life of crime after their mother was severely beaten and abandoned by their father when they were of adolescent age. No explanation was ever given by either of their parents, and they never saw their father again. The brothers worked as a team, stealing outright at first and then turning to burglary after being arrested and let off with a warning for openly taking a wheel of cheese from the local grocery store. Their mother had never been better supported, but they all lived in fear of the inevitable brush with the law. After one caper in which they were found locked in a warehouse overnight, the twins decided to flee to Argentina only moments before they would be arrested and tried. Their escapade there lasted only weeks, and, after running afoul of the Buenos Aires police, they returned to Italy to resume their life of crime. This time, however, they settled in Catanzaro since their hometown of Cosenza was off limits.

If burglary and theft were not enough, Guido and Luigi added violent crime to their repertoire. Early one morning as a young maiden was out sweeping the street in front of her family's clothing store, the two men abducted her and brought her to an abandoned loft at the edge of the city. Originally intending to hold her for ransom, the boys could not resist her good looks and alluring figure. Instead, they stripped her naked and took turns raping her. After several hours, they left her behind as they made their escape to the hills. In short order, they were arrested, convicted and sentenced to a prison term of twenty years at hard labor. They were among the chained prisoners awaiting transfer from Reggio to Sardinia.

The Rossi twins added to the misery of our voyage to Sardinia. At first, they seemed to accept their fate, eating the miserable food and sleeping on the hard deck without a murmur. On the third day, however, as the ship tossed in the swells of the sea and many of the men became sick, the deck was slick with vomit. Only an occasional spray of spume aided the stench as the ship clashed with the sea. The crew and the guards had sought refuge in the bowels of the vessel, leaving the prisoners to themselves. As the men slid on deck, chained together as they were, they bumped one another. Eventually fights broke out between the prisoners. When Guido suddenly lost his footing and fell onto another prisoner-a fellow named Enrico- the man shoved Guido ferociously in a moment of exasperation. To his utter surprise and dismay, he was assaulted by both brothers in as vicious a display as I had seen up to that point. While Guido slashed at Enrico's face with a knife he had hidden away, Luigi produced a hammer, with which he broke both the man's kneecaps in a matter of moments. It was a repulsive sight.

"Aiute! Aiute!" The guards raced onto the deck to witness the Rossi's attack on Enrico. Enraged by the need to leave the relative safety of the ship's hull, the guards drew their clubs and began beating on the Rossi twins. Their fury was interrupted.

"Wait!" It was Ernesto, the in-charge officer of the Carabinieri. "A crime such as this requires a proper punishment. Secure the two to the mast for now while we wait for the sea to calm."

Enrico had passed out from the pain of his wounds and it was feared that he might never walk again without immediate attention. It seemed that he had also lost an eye. He was brought below and we did not see him again. Some said that the guards could not stand his screams of pain and that he was thrown overboard in the dead of night, to drown while we were all sleeping. Others said that he was deemed to have suffered enough and was sent back to his family in Calabria.

The day following the incident, the sea calmed. Guido and Luigi had spent the entire time lashed to the main mast with their arms tied back, each occupying one side of the upright pole. They were given water and were fed their small ration of bread by the other prisoners, but they were in terrible pain and discomfort. Both men had dried blood on their faces from the beating they had taken from the guards in the first moments following their attack on Enrico. Their bonds had cut into their arms, and their wrists and ankles showed the bloody result of having been dragged to the mast the day before.

"So, Guido, you like the use of a knife, do you? And you, Luigi, hammers appeal to you, do they?" It was Ernesto, stripped to the waist and holding a garrote, the favorite tool used for executions.

As vicious as their crime was, the Rossi's had not commit-

ted a crime justifying execution, unless Enrico were dead. Even then, it would seem that the Rossis were entitled to a trial. All forty-five captives were motionless as they awaited Ernesto's next move.

"Prisoners!" he called out. "You will now see what happens to those convicted criminals who persist in committing hideous crimes, even as they are in the custody of the law. Remember this as you begin your period of atonement." He walked up to the terrified Guido and stared him straight in the face.

"Beg for forgiveness, you son of a whore!"

Guido was so frightened that he could hardly speak. He mustered up all his strength and shouted, "God, forgive me!"

Just then, Ernesto slipped the garrotte around Guido's neck and pulled it together in a motion that cut off all air to Guido's throat. The gurgling sound of imminent death riveted the prisoners all the more. As Guido lost consciousness, Ernesto opened the garrotte at the last moment and removed it from his victim's throat. Guido came around and immediately heaved slime from his vacant belly. He lost control of his bladder and bowels, adding to the putrid mess that was already there from the previous day. Twice more, Ernesto brought Guido to the point of death and then allowed him to live. Guido's body began to shake and heave as though it had been occupied by a devil. Some of the prisoners began begging Ernesto to let up and take Guido down from the mast.

"So! You do not like to be the victim, eh?" Looking in our direction, Ernesto was tormenting us all for what the Rossi's had done. He left Guido, but would soon have us begging for Luigi's life as well.

Ernesto strode over to Luigi. "You lousy bastard, beg. You are about to die!"

Luigi must have decided that he would be sent to meet his maker. He made not a murmur as the garrotte slipped around *his neck. Ernesto was ever so careful not to produce the fatal tug.*

"Who will help you now? Are you ready to die?"

Luigi continued his resolute silence, although the gurgling sound came from his throat and he lost consciousness each time the garrotte was applied almost to the fatal point. But Ernesto would not let up until he received a plea for life from Luigi.

"Beg, you bastard!" Still, Luigi was motionless. Fearing that he had indeed gone too far and taken Luigi's life in the presence of fifty witnesses, Ernesto allowed the prisoners' cries for mercy to be heard.

"You are lucky that your fellow prisoners are too squeamish to allow me to continue. Perhaps you will some day give me another chance to end your life."

When he was finished, the two men were released and put back in chains on the deck. There would be no further fighting among the men. The other prisoners nursed the Rossi's for the remainder of the trip to Asinara.

━━◦◦◦━━

It had not been easy for Gesuzza to explain the whereabouts of his father to Pietro. The eight-year-old knew only that his stalwart provider was gone and that somehow his family had to survive. There was talk in Gagliano about how his father had committed a crime and had been sent to a prison in a far away land, but Gesuzza assured him that his father was not a criminal and that some horrible mistake had been made that resulted in his imprisonment.

"How will we live, mother? Who will farm the property and care for the goats and sheep? And who will make the cheese?"

"It will be up to us, Pietro. Your brother is still very

young, but you and I can carry on with the farm and the animals. You'll see. We're strong and we can do it. When your father returns, he'll be proud of you and what you have been able to accomplish in his absence."

"My friends say that my father is a criminal and that he has been sent away to repent for his sins. They say that he is in another part of the world and that he will never return. They tease me about not having a father at all and the taller boys sometimes want to fight with me."

"Don't worry, Pietro, we know better than they. Your father is coming back. You'll see. And besides, we're too busy to be bothered with those silly boys. Let them tend to their own work."

But deep in her heart, Gesuzza knew that the nine years without Angelo to provide and care for his family would be a hell on earth. Were it not for Stella and Giuseppe, her parents, she would have lacked the fortitude to go on. Stella reluctantly took on the frequent chore of looking after grandson Giuseppe while Gesuzza and Pietro labored at growing a crop of olives and wine grapes, caring for a flock of sheep and producing cheese from the milk they drew from their goats. They gave the landlord, Count Leone, his share of the crops, after which they were free to sell or use the remainder. It was a meager existence of constant work.

Gesuzza thought often of her sister, Marianna, who for the last four years had been the chambermaid and mistress to the widowed Count Leone, and lived in splendor in his villa near Catanzaro. Stella had done well for her younger daughter in encouraging the liaison with Leone. Or had she? It still remained a question as to where Marianna's wayward life would lead her. As Gesuzza looked now at her young sons, she wondered what her life would have been like had she conducted it differently, avoiding all the pain that had descended on her. Had she married the gentle Andrea, there would have been no possibility of this calamity in her life. Then, she looked at her boys again. They were her reward. She would do whatever was required to survive the nine years without Angelo.

Chapter 6

Andrea

The Buenos Aires of 1880 was already a beautiful European-style city. Having recently been named the Capital of Argentina, it was in fact the largest city of Latin America. Surviving three hundred years as a colony, it had won its independence from Spain and was set on a course of unprecedented development. Immigrants from all over Italy came to find their fortune in this land of opportunity. One of them was Andrea Andalusa.

Andrea had fled his father's reproach as much as he had feared Angelo's wrath in the struggle for Gesuzza's hand in marriage. His choice for refuge was Argentina, where he would learn the language in a few weeks and would be welcomed by a thriving community of Calabrians who had preceded him to this beautiful and fresh land. As luck would have it, he arrived in Buenos Aires at an opportune time. The city was in great need of shoe and boot makers, its gentry having made their fortune and having become an exclusive coterie of fops. Shoes became an obsession in this nation devoid of old-world craftsmanship. It was therefore elementary for Andrea to find work at a stylish bootery in Buenos Aires' fashionable *centro* district, where fancy shoes were made from local leathers to the foot measurements of the richest Argentineans.

"Sir, may I introduce you to Mr. Andalusa, one of our most skilled craftsman. He is Italian, of course, and has made shoes and boots for the King of Spain." The customer was duly impressed with this extraordinary credential being falsely attributed to Andrea. It mattered not, however. The sale was made and the fortunate customer was able to tell his friends that he uses the same boot maker as the Spanish King.

Andrea worked hard and learned all that was possible in this sheltered atmosphere. Because of his years of experience at making shoes in Gagliano, he was familiar with different types of leather, shoe and boot lasts, and, most importantly, the techniques used in making shoes for meager pocketbooks as well as for the rich. Now he had exposure to the source of the world's best hides. He observed the equipment that cured, tanned and pressed the rough skins into smooth and supple leather. Before long, he had a more complete understanding of the production of shoes and boots than any man in Buenos Aires. And, when the leather buyers arrived from Milan, they looked for someone whom they could trust and who spoke the language they understood, albeit a strange Southern dialect.

"Andrea, will this grade of leather make the finest quality boots?"

"Yes, but it is too heavy. Try the lighter gauge. It has almost the same strength and is half the weight. It will produce a more graceful boot."

Word of Andrea's product insight and flair for fashion spread to all of the boot makers in Italy. One by one, they came to him for his advice on the purchase of leather, shoes and other leather objects made in Argentina. From product counsellor, Andrea moved to purveyor and wholesaler. Soon he was brokering large shipments of goods to Italian producers from sources all over Argentina. Having functioned in his adopted country for a decade, he was now becoming rich.

When he was not at his work, Andrea lived a reclusive life. At home, an elderly servant woman from his hometown of Gagliano would cook him familiar dinners from foods imported to Argentina from Italy. His home was meticulously cleaned and kept for him. But, despite constant suggestions that he meet some of the most eligible ladies in Buenos Aires, he kept to himself.

"Andrea, it is not good for a man of your age and ambition to live alone. There are many lovely women here who find you a very attractive man. Why don't you give them a chance?" His housekeeper was stepping out of her bounds to urge her employer to seek happiness to complement his success.

While Andrea never allowed his inner feelings to be known, this time he responded. "There is only one woman who could ever interest me, and she is married to another man. There can never be another."

"Who is she, Andrea? What is her name?"

"Gesuzza Soluri...Chiarella"

"Are you talking about Stella Soluri's daughter?"

"Yes, that's the woman." Andrea's eyes seemed to

liquefy.

"Oh, that poor creature."

"What do you mean? Tell me what you know."

"Her husband was convicted of stealing a goat and sent to prison in Sardinia."

"Are you sure? How do you know that?" Andrea seemed to come alive with enthusiasm.

"There is a woman named Rosa, who arrived only a few weeks ago from Gagliano. She has been giving all of us the news from home."

"What did she say about Gesuzza?"

"Only that her husband stole a goat from Leone's herd and was caught and sent away for nine years to Sardinia. Poor Gesuzza is struggling to support her two little sons. She works a farm and cares for the animals and even makes cheese and wine to earn a few more lire to buy food and clothing for her boys. Her little boy Giuseppe burned his hand badly in a fire and two fingers are left withered. The older boy is a good worker, but he is not yet nine years old. Stella does all she can to ease Gesuzza's burden, but she is not a young woman and can only do so much."

Andrea's eyes lit up and he breathed in a deep breath. In the next moment, he was busy arranging for assistance in managing his affairs for the next several weeks. This would allow him to be away for an extended period. It was time for him to visit Gagliano.

⊢•◦•⊣

There was pretense in Andrea's trip to Calabria in that his supposed purpose was to visit his family there. His father had years earlier rebuked him because he was unwilling to fight Angelo for the hand of his betrothed. Now he was back and would flaunt his amazing success of the last ten years to his father. At least his mother would be proud of him for sure, and his true purpose for returning to Gagliano had nothing to do with either of them.

"Andrea, why do you not stay here with us?" His mother implores. "What does that pensione have that our home lacks?"

"Don't be offended, mother, I merely want independence to move about freely and not wish to account to anyone for my whereabouts." Andrea had provided for the privacy that he would need to covertly meet with Gesuzza. Though his purpose was not yet entirely clear even to him, he knew that he must see Gesuzza to reassess his feelings for her.

Andrea's father approached him with a piteous look. "Andrea, can you ever forgive me? I don't know what I was thinking when I encouraged you to fight Angelo. I know now that I was terribly wrong. I have missed you these ten years, and I want you to know how proud I am of your accomplishments in Argentina."

"Thank you, father, I forgive you. As you can see, it has all worked out for the best." But Andrea held back the prized offer to take them back to Buenos Aires with him, as so many of his contemporaries had done with their families.

"Andrea, are you aware of what has become of Gesuzza Soluri?"

"Yes, father I am. What do you make of it?"

"As you know, her husband, Angelo, is the most despicable man I have ever known, having caused a breech between us these many years. But, in fairness, I believe that a grave injustice was done to him. You know that buffoon, Roberto Borrelli, who was constantly causing problems for everyone. It appears that he somehow got his hands on one of Leone's prize goats and got Angelo to hold it for him so that he could visit his mother on her deathbed. The goat was discovered in Angelo's possession and the both of them were sent to prison for theft."

"Angelo won't get any sympathy from me."

"Nor from me. But it is very strange that judge Martinez, the fairest of all, has created this gross injustice."

"Angelo had it coming for what he did to me."

The following morning, Andrea dispatched a messenger to find Gesuzza and tell her that he was back and intended to see her, and that it would delight him if they could talk alone for a time. He wished to visit her in her home that evening at eight o'clock.

Gesuzza had been aware of the news that Andrea was back from his self-imposed exile to Latin America. She expected that he would want to see her, despite the taboo placed upon persons of the opposite sex meeting privately. In her case, a visit by a former suitor would be considered indecent, what with her husband imprisoned six hundred miles away. But the circumstances of the sudden break in her betrothal to Andrea preyed on Gesuzza and she eventually decided to receive him in her home in private. To do this, she needed to let Stella know of the meeting, so that Stella could take the children to her home for the evening.

"You of course know that Andrea has made his fortune in Argentina." Stella was in her usual form, despite the onslaught of arthritis and memory loss in her old age.

"Of what interest is that to me?"

"Haven't you learned anything from your misfortune? This world will continue to deal blow after blow to those who ignore opportunity. Andrea is rich. He is here to see you because he has not gotten over his passion for you. You are still a lovely, alluring young woman. Listen to what he has to say. Don't be hasty. Consider whatever he offers."

"And what makes you think he will make an offer? I am, after all, a married woman with two children."

"Gesuzza, don't be ridiculous. He didn't come all this way for nothing."

Andrea was like a young boy attending his first dance. He tried on every item of clothing in his possession and pondered which cologne he would use. He rehearsed his opening line over and over. *Gesuzza! It's you! You are still lovely after all these years. ...Or should I say, you are as lovely as ever...and leave out all the years.*

As he approached her house, he was so nervous that he feared he would drop the flowers he had brought with him. He had chosen to dress less opulently than he originally thought he would, wearing only the plain shirt and loosely fitted trousers that he normally wore in his leisure hours at home. A plain waistcoat completed the ensemble. At age thirty-two, he still had handsome facial features and a swarthy complexion. To be sure, he was still uncertain of his purpose in calling upon Gesuzza. He knew simply that he must see her.

"Anyone home?" Andrea had noticed the door ajar and called in to whoever might be at home.

"Come in, Andrea." It was unmistakably Gesuzza's voice, but it sounded more mature and deliberate than before. It was, after all, ten years since Andrea heard her voice. He could feel himself hesitate and then quickly enter.

There she stood, dressed very plainly in a long gray dress and looking darkly tanned. As she stood erect and looked at him, her bright eyes shining, he understood why his feelings for her had survived all this time and absence. Her features had not changed; her sweet affability still a part of her.

"Come in," she said simply, "will you have some coffee?"

"Yes, thank you."

He watched her go to the fireplace, take a pot from over the hearth and pour out the thick, black liquid into a cup. She poured another for herself. As she moved about, his eyes were fixed on her. She was indeed the adorable woman he recalled. Her small, thin body was older, but not much different. To be sure, the strain of her present life showed on her pretty face and her hands revealed the long, hard hours of labor in the fields. But the Gesuzza he had fallen deeply in love with many years ago was unchanged. How could he possibly have let her go? She had been worth fighting for. He might somehow have survived the fight with Angelo.

"I hear that you are a big success in Buenos Aires."

"Yes, I suppose that's true."

"Don't you want to talk about it?"

"How are you, Gesuzza? I have worried about you." Andrea chooses to get to the point.

"Why is that?"

"Because I Love you and heard that you were in trouble."

"That's a strange sentiment coming from you. The moment you were pressured, you ran off and were not heard from again. Was that the act of a loving person?"

"Do you know that Angelo threatened my life and sought to fight me? He is twice my size and I would not have stood a chance. What's more, my father felt dishonored by my refusal to fight Angelo and called me a coward. I felt that I had to leave his house and strike out on my own. I was very young, then, and stupidly left without trying to see you first. Can you forgive me, Gesuzza?"

"Why is my forgiving you important? Yes, I had heard

that Angelo challenged you. I was worried and confused. But, when time passed and I heard that you left Italy without so much as a word to me, I concluded that our love was not real. Angelo would have done anything to win my affection. He made it obvious to me and to everyone that he loved me and wanted me for his wife."

Andrea walked up to Gesuzza and put his arm around her. He pulled her in closely to him. She resisted by pulling back to separate their bodies, but did not leave his embrace entirely.

"Gesuzza, I love you! You must become part of my life."

"Don't be ridiculous, Andrea. A man such as you doesn't need me. There are plenty of women who would be more than happy to marry you. I am a married woman with two children."

"I cannot love any one else, Gesuzza. I have tried and it simply is not possible. My love for you has not ended and never will."

"But I am married and have a family."

"I know that, Gesuzza, but that's all right with me. Come with me to Argentina. I have money now and can provide a life for us beyond your wildest dreams."

"And what will I do with my children?" Andrea sensed a spark of hope.

"Take them with us. They will no longer have to work away their childhood.

They will go to school and have all the advantages of life."

"And what of Angelo?"

"Forget him, Gesuzza, he is a criminal now."

"He is an innocent man."

"Yes, perhaps, but he will always be under suspicion by the Carabinieri. He has been exposed to the criminal element in prison and will be hounded by the authorities as a suspect even after serving his sentence."

Gesuzza considered Andrea's words. Were she to accept his proposal, she would cease to experience the pain she had been suffering to this point. Her new life would be endowed with material advantage she had never before known. Perhaps even the boys would be better off with Andrea as their father. Her mind raced on, thinking of her place on earth and how this one gesture would deny all that she stood for. She would have to turn her back on her God. She would lose her self-respect. She pulled away from Andrea and walked to the other side of the room.

"You are blinded by your feelings for me, Andrea. What do you think Angelo would do when he returns to find his family gone? If he was willing to fight for my hand in marriage, how do you think he would act when he hears that his family has left him for you and a life apart from him?"

"I can handle him, Gesuzza, trust me."

"Even so, should I live a life of dishonor and force my children to do likewise?"

At this point, Andrea knew that he had lost her and pleaded, "Please, Gesuzza, you love me. You know you do. We can be happy."

"I'm sorry, Andrea, but my answer is 'no.' It has been very difficult for me without my husband to support me. My life will continue to be difficult for years to come, but when Angelo returns he will find me and the children here to welcome him back."

Never in all the time that Andrea had known Gesuzza had he felt more love for her than at that moment. But his love was mixed with resentment for not having won her over. He was speechless as they looked at each other for the last time. As he exited, he murmured, "Good luck, Gesuzza."

Chapter 7

Aldo

Aldo Caristi belongs to Leone more than any man alive. At age 46, he has been married and widowed, has worked in America to gain his stake, returned to Calabria to establish himself as a landowner, and lost everything in a moment of overwhelming mortal fear. Now he tends the gardens that surround the Capurro villa and caters to Leone as driver of his carriage and as his messenger.

Leaving Calabria as a mere teenager to earn his fortune in America, a common practice among his peers, Aldo made his way to western Pennsylvania. There he was hired on as a coal miner and sent deep into the dark shafts and tunnels of the mines to harvest the black anthracite used to heat American homes and fire up the factories that were operating all over America. Lowered into the ground in a wooden cradle with a dozen of his comrades, Aldo would choke as the coal dust emerged from the huge cavity in the ground to fill his lungs. Arriving at his post in the mine, he felt the continuous presence of imminent danger as he chipped away at the walls that encircled him. It reminded him of the team of miners that was fatally trapped by a cave-in only a few days after he had arrived at the mine.

Though his wages were meager, Aldo found that he could live very cheaply by rooming with scores of other Italians who also worked the mines, and by reducing his lifestyle below even that of the Calabrians back home. Mostly, he ate a soupy gumbo fashioned from scraps of food discarded by the local butchers and greengrocers, a decided decline from the *faggiole* of the Calabrian peasant. Others slept in his bed when he himself was not the occupant. But, by his reckoning, he would have enough money saved for passage back to Italy and to enable his becoming a landowner in Calabria, within two years.

"This is my opportunity to break the hold that the Calabrian landowners have on me and my family. I know it is difficult and dangerous work, but in the end it will have been worth it. I will dream of the property I will own in Calabria and the time will fly by."

At the time, his existence seemed like an interminable purgatory, but finally he accomplished his aim. Returning to Calabria with enough capital to acquire a forty-acre farm in the countryside between Gagliano and Catanzaro, Aldo married Giuseppina, his childhood friend. They were both from very poor families and so the bargaining for dowry was of little consequence. They moved into a stone hut that had been standing on their property since ancient times. It had the stale odor of dampness and the droppings of field rodents that had occupied it as its sole tenants for two centuries. Its dirt floor was stained with urine and fecal matter, and its small arched windows allowed only enough air to enter its one room to allow Aldo and Giuseppina to overcome the suffocating stench while they cleaned the place thoroughly.

"Oh, Aldo, this place is a toilet! Open the door and windows so we can breathe."

On one side of the room was a fireplace used for heating, cooking and incinerating; and the other side accommodated a bed the couple was given as a wedding gift from Giuseppina's parents. The center contained a table and two chairs fashioned from discarded wood and lumber that Aldo had found in the field behind the house. The building's redemption was to be found in its thick stone walls and heavy beamed ceiling, which protected its inhabitants from the intense summer heat. Soon, the aromas that filled the dwelling were Giuseppina's cooking, the smoke rising from the chimney, and the flowers in the garden just outside the front door. The animal pen and the latrine were now both far enough from the house that none of the foul smells ever reached them.

Ah, how the ancients lived, thought Aldo, shaking his head in loathing and vowing to improve on the dwelling, as providence would allow.

The land lay on a slope and was rocky. It had been farmed for centuries before foreign invaders overran the region and either killed or enslaved its inhabitants. Now it would be returned to a productive state. Together, the happy couple planted the cash crops that would fill their pockets with currency. Onions, garlic, fennel, fava beans, basil and other vegetables were always in demand by those who did not have access to sufficient land to plant their own vegetables, and the Caristi's would be there to supply them. They installed grapevines, fruit trees and an olive grove, all of which would be furnishing their bounty in just a few years. In short order, Giuseppina was with child, and the couple looked forward to a full life together.

"I am so happy, Giuseppina. I dreamed of this all the while I was working in America. I can hardly remember what it was like in the filthy coal mines and now here I am in Calabria with all that I have ever wanted."

In August of 1860, Aldo received a call to arms by Count Leone Capurro, the man who was to lead a force from Catanzaro province to Reggio di Calabria. There, on the shore off the Straits of Messina, they would join Giuseppe Garibaldi, the great liberator of the Italian people, in the fight against the Bourbon king who ruled their country. As a young Italian, Aldo felt the rage of his countrymen against the foreign rulers with their dominance of wealth and societal function. But, on the other hand, he had struggled to achieve his position in life and had revelled in it for so little a time. Besides, if he went off to war, how would Giuseppina get along without him?

"Giuseppina, I hope you will not think I am a coward for refusing to go with the rest of the men to Reggio, but I feel that I must remain here to protect you and the child you will soon bear."

"I understand, Aldo. It is only right that you remain here with me."

In the end, he was given no choice. All able-bodied men were obliged to serve the Risorgimento, despite even the opposition of Holy Mother Church. He kissed his now beloved Giuseppina goodbye and left with the others for the province of Reggio. There, 6,000 men from Catanzaro were billeted and would form the nucleus of the army that would follow Garibaldi into battle. Aldo missed Giuseppina terribly and his constant thoughts were of her and of the life they had built together. Now he would face death at the hands of the Bourbons, who, after all, had a force of greatly superior number and a garrison that was impregnable. Only the genius of Garibaldi could save him.

"They say he is a miracle worker. We need one now more than ever." Aldo commiserated with his comrades.

On the 21st of August in 1860, the Calabrian troop was met with fierce fighting by a Bourbon force, and after much blood was spilled on the beach below Reggio, the foreign regulars withdrew to the garrison on a cliff overlooking the Straits. It was a victory for the Calabrians. Leone was at the lead, excited, as Garibaldi turned to exclaim that the enemy's numbers had been exaggerated and that the fierce Calabrian retort was the demonstration that he needed to believe in their determination to oust the Bourbons. Aldo was terrified as he saw the bodies of his comrades torn suddenly from their earthly existence, a look of pain, terror and disbelief on their young faces, many still in their teen years. As Garibaldi gave the command to charge in pursuit of the Bourbons, Aldo began to weaken. Suddenly, the huge doors of the garrison opened and a mounted unit, lances in hand, surprised their enemy as they rode past the Bourbon regulars and charged the Calabrians. It was more than Aldo could bear. He felt his days on earth were over and saw his entire early life pass before him in moments. As he gathered his composure, he found himself in full retreat. The Calabrians around him shouted slurs of cowardice and some even threw objects at him as he ran past them to the rear. Aldo had deserted in the face of the enemy.

As the cheers of victory over the garrison at Reggio

arose and as Garibaldi praised the Calabrians for their first encounter as a military unit, Aldo sat in the rear beach area and wept in shame.

"Oh, my God, what have I done? I will be labelled a coward forever and I've brought shame on my family."

Later, a military guard apprehended him and placed him under arrest to await execution as a deserter. His despair increased as he thought of Giuseppina and her swollen body full of his unborn child. He thought fleetingly of taking his own life and then dismissed the idea. His last act would be in harmony with his Faith and there was at least some chance that he would eventually receive a place in heaven.

The following morning as his execution was being administered, there was a sudden, unexplained change and Aldo was taken down from the gallows and set free. He was permitted to return to his home, branded a coward, and ordered to surrender ownership of his land to the new government. He later learned that, as the only deserter from the Calabrian troop, he was thus granted clemency by Leone. Though his death sentence had been commuted, his land would be taken away. Now, Aldo had to tell Giuseppina of his cowardice and of the resulting loss of their land. His two-year sacrifice in the American mines had been for naught. They would no longer be the prosperous young property owners and he would have to struggle to earn a meager living. He had hope that some good soul would take pity and see fit to hire him. He dreaded the thought of revealing all of this to dear, gentle Giuseppina.

"God give me strength to carry on. I have ruined my life and Giuseppina's."

As he approached the farm he had left only a few months earlier, he was surprised by the compassionate glances he received from passing acquaintances. Although no one spoke, it was clear that an unexpected sympathy poured forth as he rode by on his donkey. Did these people perhaps understand his plight as a soldier? After all, it could have happened to anyone in a moment of fright. Suddenly, he was looking up at his farm and, in the distance, the house that he and Giuseppina fashioned from the hovel that it had once been. The farm had not been worked and there was no sign of life anywhere. There in front of the house stood Father Zinzi.

"Father, what is it? What's happened?"

"My son, your Giuseppina has gone to her reward. Shortly after you left for Reggio, she was taken with the fever and by the time we discovered her, she and her unborn baby were beyond help. Her last wish was that the two of you be reunited in heaven."

Now his agony was complete. Spared the torment of having to explain misfortune to his wife, he now suffered the ultimate pain of having lost the rest of his entire world. He placed his arms around Father Zinzi and wept hysterically.

"My son, no doubt it is of little solace to have me tell you this now, but you will have a home to go to whenever you are ready to rejoin society. And you will have work for as long as you wish." Astonished, Aldo looked up. "And who is my benefactor, Father?"

"Count Leone."

⊱──◆──○──◆──⊰

One would think that the news of becoming a father would appeal to Leone. His marriage to Beatrice of 30 years had not produced an heir, and his advanced years might easily have precluded that possibility forever. But Leone is displeased when Marianna tells him that he will be a father within the year.

"How did you allow this to happen? Did you not take precaution?" Leone shows an uncharacteristic anger.

"Of course I take precaution. Do you think this was deliberate? Do you think I am the first woman ever to become pregnant against her wishes?" But Marianna is not truthful. During one of Stella's visits, the two women secretly discussed the possibility of a pregnancy and how that would add the needed substance to the relationship with Leone to link Marianna to the Leone fortune.

"Leone, please don't be angry," Marianna pleads. "You will have your very own child soon and it will be yours to love for all time."

"How will I explain it?" Leone seems concerned, not merely for himself, but for Marianna as well. "You will be viewed as a tainted woman and I will be the fool among my friends. No, Marianna, there must be a solution to this problem."

"What can that possibly be?" Marianna's thoughts are confused, and she is disappointed that Leone is not somehow pleased with the prospect of having a child.

Finally, his thoughts yield to conversation. "Marianna, you must marry. Of course the marriage will be in name only, but the child must not be born a bastard. And you must not be unwed when the child is born."

"But who, Leone, who will marry me under these circumstances?"

"… A man who owes me much… Aldo Caristi. He is an older man, probably 50, a widower who will understand the situation and will be anxious to accommodate me. I will present this situation to him at once and offer him your hand. Do I have your consent?"

Marianna knows that her consent is mere formality and responds quietly, "Yes."

———◦———

Calabrian peasant women of the time were not free to act or to make decisions of importance. That role was left to *Il Marito*, the husband. To be sure, most women were strong of back and will, but they were almost always subservient to their men. Intelligence did not matter. Occasionally, alert women would stand silently aside while their husbands blundered through a negotiation or made senseless promises to others that were impossible to keep. They would say nothing and try not to show anger or irreverent laughter. Once in a great while, a woman of unwavering determination refused to accept the fiat to obey and asserted herself as the dominant force in her family. Such a woman was Stella Soluri.

Marianna seeks her parents' approval of her impending marriage to Aldo. Giuseppe rages, "Enough of this, Marianna. Isn't it bad enough that you are in the condition you are in? Why doesn't Leone do the right thing and marry you himself?"

"Father, please," Marianna is crying and holding her face, "Leone can't marry me. Our differences in age and status are too great. We will still be together, though. Aldo will be my husband in name only."

Giuseppe is about to shout his condemnation of the marriage when Stella holds up her hand. Giuseppe falls back against his chair and listens to Stella declare, "This is not what we intended, but Leone's will must not be challenged. All is not lost. Somehow, things will work out. Marianna, you have our permission to marry Aldo. Just remember that you are doing Leone a favor that he must one day repay."

Once again, Giuseppe yields his prerogative as the head of his family to his cherished Stella.

Weddings in Calabria are major celebrations, giving the extended families of the wedding couple a respite from the harsh, drab existence of peasant life. For the better part of two days, a wedding celebration is prepared. Streamers and lanterns are strung in the town square, where the reception is likely to be conducted. Musicians shine their brass instruments and freshen their uniforms for the procession of the newly married couple from the church to the reception. There is cooking of every sort. A pig is slaughtered and roasted. Cheeses are brought up from their storage bins and the traditional meats, pastas and pies are prepared. On the day of the wedding, the guests appear in their finery: the men in the suits they will likely be buried in and the women in the flightiest long-skirted dresses they can manage to assemble. In a sense, it is a denial of the reality that these impoverished people endure.

The marriage between Marianna and Aldo is far subtler. Leone arranges for the priest of The Church of the Holy Rosary in Gagliano to come to the villa. The bans having been waived, Father Zinzi quickly performs the ceremony before Giuseppe, Stella, Gesuzza, little Pietro and Giuseppe II, and the house staff. Of great importance is the paperwork that binds Marianna to Aldo for life. In this society, there is no parting of man and wife except by death. Nor is there any tolerance whatever of illicit pregnancies or births. Such maladies are dealt with in summary fashion: the pregnant girl is brought to a convent by her humiliated parents, where she is hidden from the world until she delivers her child and surrenders it to the nuns to arrange for adoption.

But this girl is different. She is the mistress of a man of great influence. She has had the *misfortune* of becoming pregnant, but she will not look upon the face of adversity. She will have her child to cherish as though it was born to an espoused couple. True enough, its name will be Caristi and not Capurro, but then one makes allowance for some transgressions in this life. And, as Stella has said, who knows what the future holds.

The wedding reception is uncharacteristically short and the local customs are dispensed with. There are no favors of candied almonds, no *abusta* bag to fill with cash gifts from the guests, no *Tarantella* to dance. There are sandwiches of the favorite meats and cheeses and the best wine of the region. A final champagne toast by Leone sends the couple off to occupy the gatehouse, where Aldo has lived these many years. But though they are under the same roof, every adult present knows that Aldo and Marianna will occupy separate bedrooms and there will be no marriage of the flesh. Marianna's marriage to Aldo is a mere formality of convenience. Her exclusive sexual relationship is still with Leone.

On September 10, 1892, Marianna delivers Leone's child, attended by a midwife in the gatehouse of the Capurro villa. It is a boy and Marianna is ecstatic. She dreams wildly about the unencumbered life that her infant son will lead and concludes that his name must be Allessandro, in anticipation of his importance. Unlike his cousins, Pietro and Giuseppe, who are already doomed to the life that the Calabrian system demands of the disenfranchised, Allessandro will be educated in fine schools and will grow up among the elite of society. Perhaps one day he will be a judge. Or, perhaps he will be mayor of

Catanzaro, the capital of Calabria. There, as the head of government, he will be in a position to mete out a justice of his own. He could favor his cousins, perhaps even deliver them from their confined existence. And what of Marianna herself? Surely, Allessandro will understand his mother's predicament and come to her aid. He might arrange an annulment of her marriage to Aldo so that she might be free to seek out her true love, Lorenzo.

Marianna suddenly realizes that she has thought of Lorenzo after all this time, and in terms that elevate her feelings for him to true love. She thinks that perhaps she should determine his whereabouts in America and communicate with him. Surely, he will forgive her for her affair with Leone when she delineates her feelings for *him* and her motivation in all that has occurred between her and Leone. If only Allessandro had resulted from her love for Lorenzo. How simple life would be.

Marianna is brought abruptly to reality as Aldo enters the room.

"Congratulations, Marianna, you've become a mother and borne a beautiful child. And a boy! What shall we call him?"

Marianna is repulsed by the thought that Aldo would share in this moment and in the decision regarding the newborn infant's name. She takes on the persona of her controlling mother and responds in a curt tone, "Thank you, Aldo, but I have already named the boy. He is Allessandro."

"And a good choice it is." Aldo shows the good side of his nature.

⊱──⊰

Five years later, Alessandro has grown into a young boy. His appearance seems to have captured the best of both parents. Already it is clear that he will one day have his father's height and even now Allessandro has Leone's mild olive complexion. His gangly walk also speaks clearly of Capurro parentage. But his jet-black hair and sparkling brown eyes are his mother's. And his firm jaw, set in defiance of all, is that of Stella. Allessandro and Marianna have been inseparable, and Aldo has seized every opportunity to be with his "son". Already, Allessandro shows signs of intellect and inquisitiveness and Marianna grows concerned.

He is undoubtedly ready for school, thinks Marianna, *I must talk to Leone.*

But Leone shows no interest in the child. To Marianna's disappointment and torment, Leone does everything to suppress any knowledge of Allessandro's lineage. He almost never is seen in the same place as Allessandro and any talk of the boy is quickly quelled by a wave of Leone's hand.

Leone's denial of Allessandro encourages Aldo, who now acts as the child's father and begins thinking of his future. "Allessandro will follow in my footsteps," he thinks aloud, "and become a laborer in Leone's employ, relieving me of the responsibility of driving Leone's carriage when I do not wish to drive it myself and digging and manuring what has become a much larger garden than I can now handle. Besides, Leone won't object to my having an assistant if the helper is Allessandro, and I am growing older and less capable."

Marianna explodes. "Like hell! My son will not be a footstool for anyone. He is of high rank and I will not accept anything less for him." She storms out and makes her way to the main house. There, she sits alone for a few moments to gather her composure and cool her temper. It would do great harm for Leone to observe an outburst of anger from Marianna, whatever the reason might be. She enters his room. He is sitting behind the large desk across the room in concentration. He neither sees nor hears her, so deep is his absorption in his work.

"Leone, I must have a word with you."

"Very well, then, come in. What is it, Marianna?"

"I must talk to you about Allessandro. He is growing up and we need to decide on his future. Unless we now choose a life for our son, Aldo will make the choice and turn him into a laborer, to dig and fetch and to surrender his birthright for all time. Leone, please, this is your only child. He is bright and loving and needs your help. Don't allow this to happen. You must act to save our Allessandro." Tears roll onto her cheeks and she sobs into her hands.

The reality Marianna describes in so emotional a tone strikes Leone like a light coming on. Finally, he realizes how foolish he has been in denying Allessandro and how close to misfortune he has allowed his only offspring to come. A laborer indeed. That fate will never be thrust upon his son. He resolves that he must act to provide a proper place in society for Allessandro. But what to do? How can he preserve dignity, while at the same time take his bastard son into his life? Only one man can help him to solve this dilemma: his closest friend, Renato Rizzo.

Chapter 8

Prigione dell Asinara

Sardinians call sea salt "the child of the sun and wind". Here, in the northern reaches of the island province, seawater is channelled into shallow fields and ponds. They are lined with clay deposited by the flow from freshwater streams and rivers in the mountains above the gulf of Asinara. The movement of water, wind and sun combine to promote evaporation, forming salt crystals on the clay beds. Crews of barefoot men rake the salt into wooden saltpans. The harvest is formed into pyramids to further dry and bleach out the salt. The flaky, delicate crystals that result are called *fiori di sala*, flowers of salt. It is backbreaking work that is left to the prisoners at Prigione dell' Asinara.

For several days, the view to the east had sporadically

revealed the cobalt-colored coast as the prison ship made its way slowly up the Mediterranean to the northern-most point of Sardinia. As the ship crawled toward the distant island, the men all sensed that they had at last reached the isolated province, a fortnight after leaving Calabria. Here, in the second century, the Romans sent their exiles to live out their lives in the rugged countryside, a penance for their misdeeds. In the eighth century, the Spaniards fortified the island against pirate invasion. For a time this was a stopping point for the Crusaders on their way to Malta, Rhodes and other points along the Eastern shores of the Mediterranean. And, as the skill for drawing salt from the sea developed, the great structure that had fortified the island for two centuries was converted to a prison for those who would work the salt bogs.

As the ship neared the island, the rock gray hills looked almost green, and an occasional whitewashed hut seemed to be reaching gratefully to the azure sky. The ship entered the tiny pastel-colored commercial port of Torres, bustling from trade with the Genovese merchants freshly arrived from mainland Italy. Shops lining the street that faced the sea were a collage of color offering all sorts of food and supplies. The sounds of the merchants calling out the plaintive cadence of their wares drifted over the bay and could be heard faintly aboard the prison ship. There was the loading and unloading of small sailing vessels and a steam-powered ship taking on a load of grain after depositing its cargo of citrus and olive oil. Streetwalkers propositioned seamen coming ashore to shake off the boredom of the sea.

At the very moment when it seemed that the prison ship would stop at the picturesque port, it veered to the north and made its way across the bay, leaving behind all connection to freedom and the false illusion that had been created. Twelve miles ahead lay the small island on which the prison was situated, looking gray and ominous. As they entered its grim, desolate harbor, the island revealed its principal source of activity, a huge salt marsh being worked by a swarm of prisoners under the watchful eyes of armed guards.

The thought of having arrived in this dreadful place that was to be our home for the years ahead depressed us all the more. Out in the marshes below the prison, we saw scores of prisoners working. They went on with their work as if they saw and heard nothing. There were those who chopped at the white earth with picks and those who raked the harvest into pans. There were many piles of white salt, which grew as the pans were emptied onto the piles. Some of the men looked strangely white in color, as though they had taken on the color of the salt. Others were in slime up to their waists, piling mud into a heap with a wooden shovel. We later learned that the mud pile was a temporary dam put in place by the prisoners to trap the seawater that was to surrender its salt. Once done, the dam was broken at low tide to allow the bland water to escape back into the sea in time for the next rush of fresh seawater.

The ship pulled up to the prison dock and was tightly secured so that the swells of the sea could not separate it from the centuries-old timbers. There was a restrained joy at the thought of getting away from the guards on the ship, especially Ernesto, but there was concern as to what lay ahead. The dock was lined with prison guards. They wore a pale green uniform consisting of a short-sleeved blouse and twill trouser. Their ankle-high shoes were a heavy military issue and their hats were campaign style, sporting a small yellow feather tucked in on the left side. They were not armed, but they wore service belts that held clubs and wrist chains.

The highlight of the landing came as we lined up on the dock to have our chains removed. In less than an hour, they were off and returned to the Carabinieri, to be used on the next group of unfortunates they would escort. Good riddance! The men stood rubbing their wrists and ankles and tending their wounds, by now at least partially infected. The Rossi twins were the worst off. They were both silent as they tore off bits of cloth to wrap around their ankle wounds. It would be a long time before they could forget the punishment they had experienced.

At last a prison official arrived, his aide giving the order for us to come to attention in our space on the dock.

"Men, my name is Roberto Caruso and I am captain of the guard. You are here because you have committed a serious crime. During your time at Prigione dell' Asinara we will work you hard so that, hereafter, you will give more thought to obeying the law. If you follow instruction, you will find that time will pass quickly. If you don't, you will face harsh punishment and you will regret resisting orders. It is not our wish to inflict pain, but we will not shrink from our duty to uphold the letter of the laws of this prison. Heed my warning! Now go to your cells and prepare to serve your sentence."

The prison was on a bluff overlooking the gulf of Asinara to the East and the Mediterranean Sea to the West. The sweeping view for as far as the eye could see made it evident as to why the Spaniards chose this spot to build their great fortress. Now it loomed as a prison, high above the sea marsh where the men labored.

"Atten…tion!" The aide marched us up the hill to the prison and into an area where we were stripped and doused with cold water one at a time by two guards who seemed to be enjoying their work. As we stood naked and shivering, we were nonetheless grateful to have the filth of the prison ship finally off of us. We were then issued prison clothes that were too large for many of the pris-

oners. *They were gray, short-sleeved shirts, and pants that tied at the waist with a drawstring. We were issued open sandals, as it was not expected that we would wear socks of any kind.*

The entire prison was constructed of stone with parapets around the top, giving it the look of a fortress more so than a prison. There were bars over every window, even those that were in stairways or on the interior of the building. The prison yard was completely encircled by the square of the buildings and was very large. On one end of the square there was a wooden platform about thirty square feet in size, a place from which the prisoners could be addressed as a body. Not far away, there were posts standing five feet up from the ground with a steel ring at midway and another at the top. They were obviously for securing prisoners while they received corporal punishment.

The prison wards were hellish. They, too, were constructed of stone, and their ceilings were very high. Each room could easily house ten men and there were that many mats strewn on the ground as a place for the inmates to sleep. Across the front of each cell were iron bars from top to bottom, creating the appearance of animal cages. There were two buckets in each cell. One contained drinking water and the other was to be used as a toilet. The newest of the inmates and those being punished were assigned the burden of picking up and replacing the buckets daily, keeping the water buckets carefully separated from the toilets. The men tried to avoid defecating into their toilet pails by regulating their bodily functions to coincide with latrine breaks during the day and using other toilets. There was a foul odor of urine throughout the cellblock area, which after a time dulled the senses and no longer smelled. The cellblock was sealed off from the other parts of the prison by a heavy, iron-reinforced wooden door. Each night, as the door was swung shut and the lock cranked into position, it was clear that we were here as a severe punishment. There was wailing from the weaker of the men, some weeping in despair for what they had done and others expressing the sheer frustration of being isolated from their loved ones. I thought endlessly of my beloved Gesuzza and my two sons. How would they live? Could Stella and Giuseppe, in their old age, provide assistance to my family through this nightmare? And what of the lost time with them, not seeing my boys grow up and giving them my advice and direction, not holding Gesuzza and providing for her, not protecting her from the horrors of the world? Oh, Lord what had I done to deserve this? Surely not that for which I had been falsely accused and convicted. Each day, I worked at my assigned task, and each night I repressed the misery of knowing that I could not be free and that I had committed no crime. I knew that I needed to drive these thoughts from my mind if I were going to survive nine years of imprisonment.

If the burning injustice of my imprisonment were not enough, the conditions that we all endured were even worse. We were allowed a freshwater bath weekly. If it became apparent that the seawater was eating away our skin, a quick rinse between baths was permitted. Seawater was plentiful and we used it to wash everything, including the prison cells and often our own clothing.

Food was another affront. In the morning, we were handed a cup of coffee with a piece of bread. This constituted the entire meal, which never changed. The main meal was taken in the middle of the day and required that we return from the bogs to the prison building. All two thousand prisoners ate at one time, crowding into four large rooms on the West Side of the prison. The rooms were hot and smelled of sweat and unwashed bodies. We were elbow to elbow at rough-hewn tables. Because of the tight control by the guards, there was rarely discord between the inmates, despite their hunger and desperation. Mostly, the food was tasteless and foul smelling, almost as though it was

*made from the leftovers of meals a week old. There were beans as
soft as jelly that had a musty smell and were flavorless. Cornmeal was served often and was somehow slimy and gritty at the
same time. We knew that the "coffee" was really chicory, since a
special detail would be dispatched to gather it along the roads
outside the prison.*

*Surely the crimes committed were different, but we all suf-
fered the same persecution. In the midst of all of this depressing
desperation, we developed a camaraderie founded on our common misery. We had been deprived of all comforts except for
each other's company.*

*"Hey, Angelo, is this what they eat in Calabria?" The North-
erner chided.*

*"Only when we're acting like Genovesi." The good-natured
mocking continued.*

*"How long does it take that barge to get Genoa's garbage
over here so we can salvage it as food?"*

"Just smell your food and you'll know."

*Hunger was constant in the prison. It resulted in a large
number of sick prisoners and an occasional death. Somehow it
didn't seem to matter that a prisoner died. They simply notified
nearest of kin and that was that. Mostly, the body was placed in
a coarse sack and buried at sea off the coast of Asinara. Very few
were ever sent home for a proper burial. The rich family of one
deceased prisoner requested his body a few days after he was
buried at sea. Since the prison officials could not produce the
body, another cadaver was substituted that had bloated beyond
recognition during the prisoner's failed attempt to swim to freedom. The family accepted the replacement with full confidence
that they had received the remains of their loved one.*

*Floggings were the usual punishment in Asinara. They were
sentenced and officiated over by Captain Caruso at the posts in
the yard. A multi-tailed whip was used and the sentences varied*

between ten and fifty lashes, administered by a large, dark-skinned guard, known only as Sputagna. The maximum sentence given to a frail prisoner was sometimes fatal. The punishments were carried out in the evening just before the final meal of the day, and the prisoner was left tied at the post, frequently unconscious, until after the meal was over. So disturbing were the whippings that despite the hunger among the men, many were unable to consume the cornmeal and bread that was their final nourishment of the day. Passing up a meal could result in serious illness, but such were the circumstances.

Armando Catera was from the hamlet of Teramo in the province of Abruzzi. In his early life, he was a fisherman in the Adriatic Sea, just a few miles away from his home. He had established himself as a master of his craft when a boom fell on him during a squall at sea, crushing his right hand. He was never able to use the hand again. Though his employer and the crew of his fishing vessel heaped sympathy upon him, they could no longer rely on his strength and skill. He was unable to practice the only craft he had ever known. After several failed attempts at other work, Armando turned bitterly to a life of crime. He first held up a grocer at gunpoint and stole his day's receipts. The act was so simple that he later increased the stakes by focussing on the private homes of the region, breaking in and stealing their valuables while they were away from home. Encouraged by his success, he again upped the stakes, moving to the city of Genoa where there were larger, richer homes to loot. After several close calls, he was finally captured and sent to prison for twenty years. He was 39 years old.

With fifteen years of his sentence left, Armando reasoned that he would be almost sixty when he would be freed. He became cavalier about carrying out his orders and brushed up against the authority of Captain Caruso.

"What do you mean he refused your command? Who is in charge of this place, anyhow? Bring that Catera in here to me." Caruso is enraged by yet another infraction of his authority by Armando.

"Sir, I mean no disrespect, but I am tired of being expected to do the same work as the other men. Can't you see that I have a deformed hand?"

"Catera, I can see your deformity, but I can't give you special treatment. I'll have the whole place offering excuses to get their work reduced. Now get back to work."

"Dammit! I won't go back to work. You try to make me."

Both men were incensed beyond their boiling point. The two guards in the room with them were shocked by the exchange and seemed riveted to their space. Just then, the captain brought his swagger stick around, intending to swat Armando across the face. He was met by Armando's good hand, which caught the stick and ripped it from Caruso's hand. He would have brought it down on the captain's head except that the guards sprung to life and saved the day for Caruso. Holding Armando in their grip, the guards rendered him helpless. Caruso stepped forward and slapped the helpless man across the face.

"You'll take twenty lashes for that!" Caruso had ruled. But that was not enough for Armando. It enraged him further.

"You son of a bitch. You'll never tame me. Turn me loose and fight me, why don't you? Because you're a coward, that's why."

At this point, Caruso became very still. His rage had been somehow mollified and he coolly responded to Armando.

"Very well, then, you have left me no choice. Your punishment will be the maximum that I can give. Fifty lashes, to be laid on at the post in the yard at the end of the workday. Take him away."

I can remember it as though it happened yesterday. We had worked an exhausting day, and as we lined up to walk back to the prison, we were informed that there would be a punishment that all prisoners were obliged to witness. It was Caruso's way of infusing fear into the men. After that experience, no one would dare to defy the orders meted out at the beginning of the workday.

As we entered the prison yard, three guards were dragging Armando to a post in front of the platform. There, he was tied securely to the top ring of the post. His shirt was ripped from his back and a leather guard was placed behind his neck to prevent an errant lash from piercing his face or neck. He seemed to be breathing heavily and his eyes were opened wide and appeared wild. There were sympathies expressed as the men filed in and took their position, standing in a huge semi-circle.

"Men, this morning I was attacked by this man in the presence of two of my guards. Were it not for them, he would have struck me with a stick that he tore from my hand. His uncontrollable anger resulted from my refusal to give him preferential duties because of his deformed hand. He then had the audacity to challenge me to fight him, calling me a coward. I have no choice but to punish this man for gross insubordination. His punishment will be fifty lashes. We will see who the coward is."

The men had groaned at the announcement of the punishment, and now, seeing the huge, bald Sputagna come out from the prison block, stripped to the waist, wearing leather breeches and carrying a dreadful whip in his hand made us all tense up. Sputagna unfurled the thick, leather whip and untangled its several tails, each bearing an end knot. He stood back five feet from his victim and waited, his superb shoulders and arms at the ready.

"You may begin the punishment. You, there, count out the lashes." Caruso had given the ugly task of counting to a nearby prisoner.

The first lash caused little reaction from Armando, whose muscles had hardened from the years of hard work. "One!" Spatagna seemed to gain rhythm with the second lash. A redness appeared on Armando's back. He tensed. "Two." The third lash produced a quick breath and a small trickle of blood. "Four."… "Five." It now occurred to Armando that fifty lashes was a lifetime of pain and he cried out. "Ugh!" There were several more lashes, each lessening Armando's resolve a little more. By now his back had been torn open and was bleeding copiously. At twenty-three, his spirit broke and he cried for mercy.

"Stop!"

"Twenty four."

"Oh, god. Help me."

"Twenty five."

"Stop! Please! I beg you!"

"Twenty six."

"Now, who is the coward!?" The captain's voice blurted out vengefully for the act that Armando had taken against him and the vocal abuse that he heaped on him.

"Twenty seven."

"Please! Stop! Forgive me!"

But the only man who could stop the punishment besides the captain, Warden Biale, was not there. The punishment continued. I don't remember the point at which Armando cried out, "Arrggh!," and fell unconscious. The punishment went on until the final number, "Fifty," was announced. A huge sigh of relief came from the men, who by now were swimming in their perspiration and simultaneously feeling emotions of rage, servility and sympathy. We were dismissed and filed into the mess *hall, where there was not a word uttered. As we returned to our cellblocks for the night, all eyes were on the spot where the whipping took place. Armando had been removed and taken somewhere, probably the infirmary. There was blood still on the spot where he had been beaten to a pulp.*

That night, I lay awake without a moment of sleep. My thoughts were on the purity of justice that men talk about in life and how rarely it is actually visited upon them here on earth. To be sure, the men in that prison were there for legitimate reasons and deserved the loss of years of freedom to be with their loved ones and move about as they wished. But the inhumanity that I witnessed there in Asinara and at the hands of the Carabinieri in Catanzaro and on the sea was unnecessary. I resolved that I would simply and carefully serve out my time and avoid contact with prison officials.

Chapter 9

Generoso

At age 49, Generoso Spadaro has served almost ten years in the penal colony at Prigione dell' Asinara. A convicted murderer, he will spend the rest of his life in prison. But, unlike the rest of the prisoners, Generoso answers to no one. In his prior life in Sicily he has been a Mafia chieftain, and though his friends in the government have not been able to quash his conviction, arrangements have been made to provide him with a comfortable life within the confines of the prison. While the others arise at dawn and begin their daily work at the salt marshes, Generoso sleeps until he is well rested, after which he eats a leisurely breakfast prepared specially for him by the prison cook. Eventually, he strolls over to the area where the prison infirmary stands and tends a garden filled with flowers and vegetables that he has planted. His meals are taken in the privacy of his large, comfortable cell and he is usually accompanied by one of his prison cronies. Occasionally, the warden dines with him. The guards know him well and cater to him.

Generoso grew up in the Sicilian village of Pozzo di Gotto, some 18 miles west of Messina. Life for the Spadaro family held out the same lack of promise as that of their fellow Calabrians on the nearby mainland. He and his four siblings were taught the work of the peasant farmer from the time they could reason and handle a hoe. When Generoso was nine, a local hoodlum reputed to be a soldier in the Messina arm of the Mafia, murdered his father, simply because he would not *bend to the needs of the Friends of the Friends*. His murder was an example to others that might dare to defy him. The same man also killed Generoso's older brother two weeks after his father's death, in order to preclude an attempt to avenge his father's murder. The other children were spared since three were girls and Generoso was believed to be too young and feeble to understand what had happened. Four years later, at age thirteen, Generoso tracked the man down and followed him until he was alone in a remote warehouse area of Pozzo di Gotto. There, he confronted him.

"Gabriello De Santis, you must answer for the deaths of my father, Vincenzo Spadaro and my brother Giacomo." The man turned to see a wiry boy armed with a knife. He strained his memory to place the name and the face, but couldn't.

"And who might Vincenzo and Giacomo Spadaro be?"

"My father was a poor family man that you killed because he would not agree to look away while you forced his employer to pay you protection money. My brother

Giacomo was his eldest child, whom you also murdered. It all happened four years ago."

"Aha! You are the son of that saintly fool who stood in my way of earning a living, and the brother of that young man who would surely have caused me trouble. I allowed you and your sisters to live. I did not think that you would ever be big enough to challenge me."

"I am here now and I am prepared to avenge my family."

"And just what do you think you can do with that stick pin in your hand?"

"It's a knife and I intend to kill you with it."

"Ha, ha! You're a joke." Gabriello seemed nervous, though he was confident that he could easily overtake the boy and disarm him. He was wrong. As he walked forward and reached out toward Generoso, the boy feigned back and then lunged forward and plunged the knife into the older man's forearm.

"Arrgh! You little son of a bitch. I'm going to teach you a lesson." The arm was out of commission and the wound caused a great deal of pain. Gabriello used his other hand to stop the bleeding and found himself at a disadvantage as the boy moved in on him. The older man made a desperate lunge at the boy and found himself slipping to the floor. In an instant the boy was on him shouting, "Die, you murderer of my father and brother. May you roast in Hell." Then, he plunged the knife into Gabriello's heart and ripped his chest in both directions. Gabriello's eyes looked out in disbelief as the last light of life passed through and he became very still.

The murders of his father and brother had been avenged. Now Generoso had to save his own life. After all, this dead person was a man of some influence in the

Sicilian Mafia and could not be attacked with impunity. The boy reasoned that he must go to the head of the crime family in Messina and give himself up to them. Because of his age and because of his act of surrender, the boy rationalized, his life would be spared. Perhaps he would have to give them something, a favor of some sort, but in the end they would see that his act was one of love of family and not at all vindictive. He dragged the body to an empty lot nearby and buried it under a huge pile of refuse. Then, he started out for Messina.

Making contact with the Mafia was as simple as Generoso had imagined. They were the unofficial government in Messina as they were in every other area of Sicily. Their operations were conducted openly and went virtually unchallenged. In Messina, they controlled the distribution of water, allowing them to hold the city hostage to an impending shortage or even discontinuance of service. In addition, they ran the city's brothels, a numbers lottery and collected *insurance* money from every business in the area to keep them free from crime of any sort. They were consulted on every venture that entered onto their turf and gave the needed approvals after receiving their customary arrangement, a share of the profits. The city officials stood smilingly by with "hat in hand," fearing retribution if they dared to interfere. To salve their pride, they were paid stipends to pledge their loyalty and to "look the other way."

Generoso easily spotted the *collector* making his rounds of the city's businesses and collecting the money to which the Friends were *entitled* for their protection services. He followed the man for the remainder of his route, staying sufficiently out of sight and being patient not to generate suspicion. Eventually, the collector reached the place that was apparently headquarters. It was a coffeehouse not far from the town square. Walking into the place, Generoso announced to the counterman that he had important information to be discussed only with the head of the organization. Fearful that he might be later criticized for turning away a source of valuable information, the man was able to convince a well-dressed gentleman in the corner of the room to meet with the boy.

"All right, young man, what can I do for you?" The man looked down at this seemingly harmless boy and smiled with condescension.

"I am here to confess to an act against the Friends, that I performed. I must meet with the Don to explain to him why it was necessary for me to do what I did."

"What is it that you did? It would have to be serious for me to bring it to Don Eduardo. He is, after all, a busy man and does not like to be disturbed by trivial matters."

"I have deliberately killed a member of the Friends." The man sat down in a chair and stared at the boy for a moment. "Who are you? And who is this man you speak of?"

"My name is Generoso Spadaro and I am from Pozzo di Gotto. The man I killed was Gabriello De Santis. Four years ago, he murdered my father and my brother for no reason at all. My family was left in deep mourning and with no one to support us."

"Can you describe this man De Santis?"

"He was about forty years old, average height and very overweight. He wore a large gold ring on his right hand with a shiny stone in the center."

"Did he have a tattoo?"

"Yes, of a skull, on his right arm. Did you know him?"

"Wait here. I'll be back shortly." The man then left and did not return for two hours. When he returned, there was another man with him. From the acknowledgments being extended to him as he entered the building, he was obviously a man of great respect. Generoso had been sleeping and was wiping his eyes as the two men walked in.

"Generoso, this is Don Eduardo. I have told him everything you have told me and he would like to speak to you directly." The Don took the boy's hand and shook it. Then he sat down beside the boy and addressed him in a kindly tone.

"My boy, you have committed a grave crime. Along with the penalties placed on you by the law, you could be severely punished by the man's friends and family. What could possibly have possessed you to perform this hideous act?"

Generoso knew that his life could depend on his answer. He mustered up every ounce of intelligence and eloquence that he could. Don Eduardo would be impressed with the poise and understanding of this mere boy.

"Don Eduardo, I have come here on foot from Pozzo di Gotto to see you, willingly and on my own, because I believe that I may have offended you and wish to have your pardon. Gabriello De Santis murdered my father because he would not agree to absent himself from his work so that he would not witness acts of persuasion planned for his employer. And, if the wasteful murder of my father were not enough, Gabriello then murdered my brother to prevent an act of vengeance against him. He allowed me to live because he did not think that I would ever try to avenge my family. But, Don Eduardo, what kind of man would I become if I let these murders go unpunished?" At this point, tears appeared on Generoso's cheeks and his voice quivered as he continued. "I loved my father and my brother deeply and I witnessed what it has done to my mother to have lost them both."

The Don could see that Generoso would like to have continued, but he held up his hand in a motion meant to end the boy's plea. "My boy, you have said enough to explain the situation. No amount of pleading or logic could ever win you a pardon for the killing of a Friend." Generoso looked up at the Don, looking disbelieving and stunned by his words. The Don continued, "In this case, what is left to say is that you did not offend the Friends because Gabriello De Santis was never part of our organization. He had given many people that impression, and that caused me great concern. Frankly, your act solved that problem for me. There is no need to ask my forgiveness. You need only answer to your government and to God."

Generoso was enormously relieved and could not help showing it. He smiled ear to ear, his warm and generous glow giving the Don a sense of closeness to him.

"How old are you?" The Don seemed interested in the boy.

"Thirteen." The Don marveled.

"And what will you do now that you are a man?" Generoso was not quite sure what to respond and thus remained still. The Don continued, "You have proven that you can do a man's work. I have an assignment for you that is equally as difficult as the extinction of that fraud, Gabriello De Santis. It is an opportunity to earn a very good living and make an excellent future for yourself."

Generoso flushed and looked up at his new mentor. "What is it that you want me to do?"

><+>−0−<+>−<

He was not often in our company, but when he was, there

was a different attitude taken on by the guards. It was as if they were in the presence of a man who could influence their lives sufficiently to merit their attention. I could not help but notice that the man we all knew as Don Generoso peered at me at times as though he had something to say to me. I knew somehow that he would one day approach me and reveal his interest in me. One day, in the exercise yard, he walked over to me, trailed by his usual band of followers.

"Are you Angelo Chiarella?" There. He spoke to me at last.

"Yes, Don Generoso, I am."

"Ah, you know me."

"Only of you."

"Very well, then. I would like to have a private conversation with you."

My suspicion had become reality. There was indeed a reason that this man of respect had glanced in my direction often enough for me to take notice.

"How is that possible with all of these guards and prisoners present?"

"Come to my cell tomorrow at daybreak. You will be relieved of your duties for the day. A guard will come for you and escort you to my cell."

The following morning a guard came for me as the cell door was being opened to allow the other prisoners in my cell to assemble for the work detail. The other men looked at me with questioning faces as they made their way from the cell. I did not try to answer their silent query.

"You will follow me." The guard spoke only after the men had gotten out of earshot. "Speak to no one of what you see or hear."

As I neared the place where I was being taken to my meeting with Don Generoso, I could see a decided difference in his cellblock from the others I had seen. It was clean and did not have the sharp odor that was ever-present elsewhere in the prison buildings. As we approached his cell, I could not believe my eyes. The cell was as large as the others, but it housed only three men, the Don and two other men. It was not difficult to discern that the men had been placed there to protect him and to keep the cell orderly. There were three beds in the cell, the equal of which I had never seen. Huge mattresses sat on top of metal frames that seemed to groan softly each time someone sat on or arose from the beds. Don Generoso's bed was immense and made up with fine linen and two large, fluffy pillows. There were several massive wooden armchairs in the room along with two upholstered sofas. A table sat in the center of the room on a big square rug. There were settings for two people to eat breakfast.

"Good morning, Angelo. I am about to eat breakfast. Will you join me?"

Would I join him? Was he serious? I had not had a true meal since I left Gagliano. Here on the table was coffee, sweetened breads, fruit and condiments of all kinds. The aromas of the food filled my nostrils. My mouth watered and I felt a little faint.

"Yes, of course, Don Generoso." I sat at the table and we began to eat. Suddenly, all of the memories that I had worked so hard to suppress returned. I thought of Gesuzza and all of the happiness I had shared with her and our sons. I imagined having the freedom to venture out to my herd of animals and lead them up to a grassy knoll overlooking Gagliano, feeling the lust for life, and cherishing the gifts that God had given me. My stomach was being filled, but my heart ached. We chatted throughout the meal in what seemed to be endless discussion of trivialities of his past and mine. I was intensely interested and curious about why he had singled me out and was anxious for him to begin the discussion. Don Generoso finally signaled his men to clear the table and leave.

"Angelo, I have summoned you here for a specific purpose.

In order for you to understand my motives, I must tell you a very confidential story. I will expect you to keep that knowledge secret."

"You have my word."

Generoso told of how he became associated with the Friends at a very early age and how he developed a friendship bordering on a father/son relationship with the head of the organization, Don Eduardo. Since Generoso's own father had been murdered, he welcomed the kinship of this powerful man. He was favored when opportunities arose in the organization and, over time, rose to the highest level below the Don himself. His meteoric rise was not without its price. One of the Friends was so enraged at being passed over several times that he convinced his *capo* to break away from Don Eduardo and form his own organization. War broke out between the two factions and many were killed on both sides. Then, the impossible happened. The original instigator of the war, Emmanuelle Cassa, caught Don Eduardo in an unsuspecting moment and killed him by emptying a nine shot army pistol into him at close range.

Generoso refused to release tears for fear he would be viewed as a weakling. But Don Eduardo's violent death at the hands of a hideous criminal mirrored his father's murder. He vowed on the heads of his dead father and brother that he would avenge Don Eduardo's murder, just as he had avenged theirs.

He assumed Don Eduardo's post, the highest in the organization. As *capo de capi*, Generoso ruled the city of Messina and the surrounding area. Eventually, he overtook the rebellious faction and peace returned to the area. Only the revenge against Emmanuelle Cassa remained an open sore. Generoso ordered that the man be captured and brought to him to receive his final punishment. Cassa had fled to the mountains and was difficult to find and so Generoso decided to take on the task himself. Wearing a disguise and pretending to be a cheese merchant, he skillfully worked his way into the confidence of Cassa's wife. Late one night, he followed her into the hills surrounding the city, where he knew her husband would be waiting. As he appeared from behind a huge tree to greet his wife, Generoso drew a pistol and held him at bay. Assunta Cassa was so frightened that she froze in her tracks as her husband's captor came within arm's distance of the two. Then, he asked Emmanuelle to beg for forgiveness for the cowardly act of murdering Don Eduardo. Without hesitation, Cassa fell to his knees and asked Generoso to forgive him, believing that his humiliation in front of his wife would win him reprieve. Instead, Generoso plunged a dagger through his throat and, as Emmanuelle gasped for air, his life was ended in the same manner as Don Eduardo's. Generoso fired nine times into the face and body of Emmanuelle Cassa. As the body fell forward to the ground, Generoso looked at the frightened face of Assunta. Expecting death, she cried to him, "Spare me and I will take an oath of silence." Having not intended to take her life, he nevertheless accepted her pledge never to reveal her husband's murderer.

Nine months later, Generoso was placed under arrest by a heavily armed troop of Carabinieri for the murder of Emmanuelle Cassa. He was taken out of Sicily to stand trial. In the Calabrian capital of Catanzaro, he was tried before a judge reputed to be the most honest and forthright in all of Italy. His name was Mario Martinez. Attempts were made to persuade judge Martinez that he should declare a mistrial or pronounce a dismissal for lack of evidence, but he could be neither bribed nor intimidated. At the appropriate moment, the widow Cassa was brought into the courtroom to testify against Generoso. So convincing was her testimony that the jury was instructed by Martinez that they must convict. And, convict they did. Over time, several motions were made for review of the case by a higher court, but each time judge Martinez used his influence to preclude an attempt at bribery or coercion of other judicial officials. His zeal earned him a formidable enemy. Generoso swore to even the score with the man who would send him to prison for life and then prevent the power of the Mafia from aiding him.

"Do you know the man named Don Mario Martinez who is the judge of the Criminal Court of Catanzaro?" Don Generoso began.

I looked at him with hate in my eyes. "Yes, I know him only too well. He is the judge who unjustly ruined my life and that of my family. He knew I was innocent and yet he sent me here to rot for nine years of my life."

"There was a reason that he convicted you, Angelo."

"What possible reason could there have been? And how is it that you know about it?"

The Don's face became very solemn, as though he were informing me of the death of a family member. He told me of the brief affair between Don Mario's daughter, Tina, and my brother Constantino. Despite Don Mario's rage at Constantino's romp with his daughter, he was not able to seek satisfaction because he himself had had an affair that would then be revealed by a friend of Constantino. My unjust conviction years later was his way of settling the score with Constantino. I was sickened by the thought of how my own brother could have allowed that to happen to me. Was he even aware of what had happened? Surely he knew I had been convicted, but was he aware of who the judge

was and did he know and believe that I was innocent? I raged,
"No! Stop, Don Generoso. I can't bear to hear any more."

"There is no more to hear, Angelo, only to know that we
have a common enemy and that we must work together to avenge
ourselves. Will you do that?"

"Yes, Don Generoso. Where do we begin?"

"We must begin a correspondence with your brother to learn
all that we can about Don Mario. Our scribe will be Ventorino
Cipriano, an unfortunate who, like me, will live the rest of his
life here." He turned to the prison inmate who had been out of
earshot and commanded, "Bring in Ventorino."

Chapter 10

Renato

It is not an easy decision for Baldassare Rizzo in the Italy of 1840. His son Renato's application to the School of Law at the University of Bologna has been accepted, but leaving Piedmont and the Kingdom of Sardinia for a Papal State could endanger his life. The Rizzo family has for years voiced support of their king, whose desire to unify Italy is condemned by the Church. Papal subjects are treated far better than Italians under the control of secular nations, but their will to be free is still harshly suppressed.

"Father, you must allow me to go. It is, after all, the finest school in this part of Europe and but a day's journey from home. Surely you won't let politics get in the way of this splendid opportunity."

"My son, there is no disputing the standing of the University of Bologna, but I am concerned that you will speak out against the government and be thrown into prison by those papal dogs. Then what will we do?"

"I give you my word that I will not partake in any political conversation or event as long as I am in school." Renato's young face looks pleadingly at his father.

"Very well, then, but remember your promise when you are enraged by these parasites in our country."

Renato proves himself right. Bologna's university provides him with the best law education in Italy. His years there form his mind for a formidable career ahead. And, true to his father's wishes, he avoids discussing the dream of a united Italy.

"Rizzo!" the mail courier calls out. Renato steps forward and collects a letter from his father. It reads:

"My dear Renato:

Greetings from your family. Your mother and I miss you terribly and look forward to your return to Piedmont....

I have been informed that there is a student in your midst whose lineage is of the court of Sardinia. His family has lived in Calabria for more than fifty years, having inherited a substantial property there, but have been the loyal subjects of the King of Piedmont and been uncompromising in their support of His Majesty. The student I refer to is Leone Capurro. His father is a count and Leone will one day succeed him. You are to offer him your friendship and invite him to join you on your next visit home...."

Renato is pleased with the prospect of having a friend with a connection to Piedmont and quickly seeks out Leone. Almost immediately, the conversation between the two turns to politics. Leone leads off, "The King of the Two Sicilies pretends to be an Italian, but fools no one. His orders come from Madrid and he is Bourbon. And his men treat Italians with contempt. Italians will have no justice or future until we drive the foreigners out."

"It is no better here in Romagna," Renato adds, "the Austrians do the Pope's dirty work for him. I saw them shoot two people in Bologna because they were accused of the theft of a cavalry horse. They later found the horse in a barn that he had walked into after breaking loose from his tie. They just laughed at the tragic mistake they had made."

The two men become hard and fast friends. They share the conviction of a free and united Italy and pledge their willingness to rise one-day against the foreigners. But they keep their feelings to themselves.

On November 15, 1848, the tide of sentiment erupts and Bologna finds itself in the midst of armed conflict. The freedom fighters declare today the time to unite with Piedmont in the drive for national unity. Renato and Leone emerge from the sanctity of academia. The excitement captures their attention and they are unable to contain themselves. The medieval city, with its narrow, winding streets and red brick enclosure is alive with gun and cannon fire. There is shouting and killing everywhere, and the smell of gunpowder fills the air, invading the lungs of everyone in the city. Both men choke as they make their way into the melee. Uniformed soldiers are randomly killing civilians. Bayonets are used on those who come in close, and muskets are used on those who dare to be seen on the streets of the city. Suddenly, three soldiers confront them. They are Austrians, shouting orders in a language that neither man understands.

Leone cries over the ear-splitting sounds of explosions coming from everywhere, "I think they are asking us to surrender."

One of the soldiers charges Leone, his fixed bayonet aimed at Leone's heart. Leone steps aside and in a quick motion takes his weapon and strikes the man down. As he looks up, he sees the two other soldiers taking aim at his head. He is certain that this is his last moment alive. Renato jumps headlong into the two men, thwarting their aim and knocking them down. Leone joins him in disposing of the troopers with quick thrusts of the bayonet. There is no returning to the University. They have taken their stand in defending themselves and must now join the freedom fighters.

They see what appear to be thousands of Austrian soldiers corralling the greatly outnumbered freedom force, indiscriminately firing into crowds of civilians that have gathered to support the cause of freedom. Blood and the corpses of the dead fill the streets, making it impossible to move quickly in any direction. The Italian freedom force fights to the death, hoping to divert the Austrians' fire away from the non-combatants. It does not work. After they are disposed of by point blank cannon-fire, the Austrians again turn on the crowd of dazed and incredulous civilians. As the crowd retreats from the bloody street, the Austrians charge after them, firing their weapons and plunging their bayonets into the backs of men, women and children alike.

"The battle is lost," says Leone, "but not the war. We will join the main force just outside the city."

But later they find that the war is indeed over. By sheer force of number, the Austrian army, brought in to defend the Pope's interests, has overwhelmed the freedom fighters and held the province for the pope. Leone and Renato make their way to Piedmont, where Leone is introduced to his ancestral land. The two men bond for all time, and pledge to meet again on the field of battle.

Renato will spend the next fifteen years of his life in the service of the king, eventually working directly with the Prime Minister, Count Camillo Cavour, and providing legal services to a private clientele of his peers.

—————

Leone is ecstatic as his friend Renato descends the carriage that has brought him from the train terminal in Lamezia Terme, some thirty-five miles away. He has been summoned to Villa Capurro to help his old friend cope with some yet unexplained calamity.

"Ciao, camerato," Leone calls to Renato.

"Hi, old comrade, it's great being back in Calabria after all these years."

That evening, after dinner, they recount past experiences.

"I shall always remember being in Calabria and fighting the Bourbons." Renato looks at Leone with obvious pride and continues. "No one ever believed that Italians would unite to expel the world's major powers from our Land. But here we are almost thirty years after we drove them out and formed our nation. Your Calabrian troop was the best that Garibaldi ever fought with. Their blatant heroism overcame the enormous odds on the beach below Reggio, and there began the momentum that ended at the palace doors in Naples."

It was Leone's turn to speak. "Yes, Renato, we Calabrians are tough. Do you recall the man who saved Garibaldi by leaping in front of him and taking a lance in his side? His name is Giuseppe Soluri, and he lives in the small village of Gagliano not far from here. He was amply rewarded for his selfless courage, but has since been something of a cripple. And, considering the enormous odds that day against a highly trained enemy, it is remarkable that only one Calabrian abandoned the field of battle. Actually, he was very young and under great family pressures."

The talk of war and camaraderie continues into the night. Finally, Renato sobers the meeting with a question.

"Caro amico, what is it that troubles you so greatly that you seek my help?"

Leone reveals the dilemma that has been torturing him for the past five years.

"As I believe you know, Renato, when I lost my beloved Beatrice, it was as though my world had ended. The first two years were sheer torment. I could barely eat and sleep. The advances of the eligible women my age repulsed me. My solace was found only in planning my place in the next life beside Beatrice. As time passed, I found myself directing my energies toward the business aspects of my life and feeling less pain from Beatrice's absence. Eventually, my manly impulses returned and I actually saw a woman who moved me to passion. She was a young peasant girl who was barely an adult, but her beauty and her graceful movements caught my attention. I did nothing to approach her, but one day her mother came to *me* with the thought that if the girl worked in my home, we could get to know one another and perhaps find one another attractive. That is precisely what happened and after a brief affair, the girl became pregnant."

Renato sat up in his chair. "Where is she now, Leone?"

"She is disguised as my gatekeeper's wife. At my request they were *married* more than five years ago and they have raised my son for that entire time. Alessandro has been acknowledged in law and by the Church as Aldo's son, and Aldo has thoughts of raising him as a gardener. I have fought off every impulse to acknowledge him, but now I realize that was wrong. Oh, Renato, what possible solution is there to this problem?"

"Do not worry, my friend. Every problem has a solution and so does this one. But first I must ask some very personal questions."

"Do not hesitate, Renato, you are my most trusted friend."

"Tell me, then, do you love this woman?"

"There is no woman alive who could ever replace my Beatrice. My heart, even now, is so full of her that there is no room for Marianna or anyone else."

"And what of your son, Leone, is there room in your heart for him?" Renato has chosen to blunt Leone's unnatural preference for his deceased wife's memory over his feelings for the living.

"Of course I love my son. That is why I am pleading with you to help me decide on what I must do."

"It is very late and I must give this some thought. Perhaps we can talk about this in the morning."

⊱⋅⊙⋅⊰

The following morning the two men meet at breakfast. It is clear from Leone's face that he has not slept well and that he is anxious to resume the conversation of the previous evening. Renato is sympathetic and allows the conversation to get to the point.

"I have a proposal that I believe will work for you, Leone."

"What is it, Renato, tell me."

"You must make arrangements with the child's parents to accept a generous gratuity in return for abandoning the child. In Aldo's case, he should be required to leave Calabria and never see the child again. As for Marianna, she must know that she will be permitted to see the child only sparingly and that, henceforth, the child will grow up away from home. The boy, himself, must be sent away to school, where you can visit him as frequently as possible and redirect his affection towards you."

"But how can I prevent Marianna and Aldo from asserting further claims on Alessandro later on?"

"I will prepare agreements which will be enforceable in the courts. Alessandro will be your son legally. And, I will prepare a codicil to your will to allow Alessandro, and only him, to inherit your wealth and position."

Renato works into the night, drafting the agreements between Leone and the boy's parents. First, he prepares the agreement with Aldo. Leone will adopt Alessandro and his surname will be changed to Capurro. Aldo is to sign over his parental rights to Leone and give up all ties to Alessandro. Further, he must leave Calabria for all time, never again to make contact with the boy. His departure will be described as a desertion of his family. In return, he will receive, free and clear, a one hundred acre estate in Sicily.

Marianna is given far more consideration concerning her future contact with her son. She will continue as the boy's mother and may visit with him, so long as she maintains her residence within the province of Catanzaro. Alessandro is to be sent away to a school of Leone's choice, and he will live at the Capurro villa when he is home. Marianna is to be described as Aldo's abandoned wife, left to live the remainder of her life alone. She may not remarry so long as either Leone or Aldo are known to be alive. She will have turned her son over to Leone in order to give him the life that he could never have had as Aldo's son. Her reward for agreeing to this arrangement is that she will be given a substantial home in Gagliano that Leone has reclaimed from the unfortunate former owners, who were unable to repay a debt. In addition, she will receive a sum of money each year that will not only preclude her need to work, but will allow her to spread her generosity to Stella and to other members of the Soluri family.

Having completed the agreements, Renato now turned his attention to Leone's will. While Italian law is not likely to allow Leone to disinherit his siblings, Renato follows Leone's instruction to direct most of his fortune to his only child upon his death. Alessandro is to be the next Count and will possess most of his father's power and wealth. Renato will be his guardian and will control the Capurro estate upon Leone's death, until Alessandro reaches the age of twenty-five.

⊷•◦•⊶

"Why do you hesitate to sign that paper, Marianna?" Stella has been presented with Marianna's doubts about the wisdom of signing Alessandro over to Leone.

"Because he is my flesh and blood and I love him. I don't know if I can live without seeing him for months at a time."

"Don't be silly!" Stella shouts, "The boy will have opportunity that few ever receive in this life. What's more, you will be able to help your sister and her poor little children. And what about me? Think about me, Marianna."

"This is not about you or me or anything other than my little boy. Leone and Renato are planning to send him away to school and he is only a small child. How will he get along on his own and who will be there to protect him when he needs help?"

Stella appeals again to Marianna. "My dear, you are imagining terrible things that cannot happen to the son of Leone Capurro. Wherever he goes he will be revered for his noble lineage and given all possible advantage. That includes the school that he will attend. You must be strong, Marianna. Don't you see? We have succeeded in securing a future for ourselves merely by agreeing to allow your child to take his place among the privileged. If you must balk in any way, it should be to ask for a greater amount of money. But, for heavens sake, don't fuss over the boy's future."

Stella's unshakable logic has reached Marianna. There are others to think about. Alessandro will be fine, the "silver spoon" in his mouth all the time that he is away from his mother. The real need is in the Soluri family. Stella and Giuseppe are advancing in years and Gesuzza is in her usual desperate fix. Marianna's thoughts turn again to Lorenzo. Perhaps this would be the time to rekindle his love. If only she could find him. Finally, she speaks, "You are right, as usual, mother. I will allow Leone to direct Alessandro's life as he proposes, but I will ask for more money."

⊱—•᠁•⊰

Marianna enters Leone's room, where she has been summoned. He is seated at his desk and Renato is with him. Leone is holding the signed agreement. The two men rise to greet her.

Leone speaks. "Thank you for agreeing to our arrangement, Marianna. You can be sure that our son will have an education befitting his station in life and that I will secure his safety all the while he is away from home."

Marianna notices Renato beaming with the pleasure of having returned happiness to his friend's life. "Renato," she says, "may I have a moment alone with Leone?"

"Of course." Renato makes his exit.

Marianna looks with meek tenderness into Leone's eyes. "You have been very generous with me, Leone. I now have enough money that I can lead an abundant life on my own. But, is that your wish …or…"

Leone gets her meaning and interrupts. "My dear, you are welcome here for as long as you wish. Should you decide to stay, you will no longer be a chambermaid. Your new occupation would depend on the type of work that appeals to you. However, I am a realistic man and I assume that you will leave, now that you are a woman of means, and I will understand if you so choose. Am I correct?"

"Yes, Leone, it is my preference to leave, but please know that my feelings for you are very deep and that you will always have a special place in my heart."

There is a note of regret in his voice as Leone asks, "What will you do, Marianna?"

"Tomorrow I leave for America."

Chapter 11

Ventorino

There was enormous misery and despair among the prisoners of Prigione dell Asinara. But one man, Ventorino Cipriano, seemed resigned to his fate of spending the rest of his life there. He was unusually literate for the time and place, having attended primary school, where he acquired the ability to read and write. In Asinara he was important among the illiterate and those who had known only crime and violence. Now they were treated to Ventorino's readings from Cicero and Virgil and his storytelling from his adventures at sea. And, for a price, they could engage him to read letters from home and even to scribe the responses. At times he seemed almost happy to be in Asinara, as though he had found his world of redemption.

A ship's bursar from the small Ligurian fishing village of Sestri Levante, Ventorino lived a happy home life on the infrequent days between voyages. He had married a beautiful woman from Calabria and she had born him two handsome sons. For almost ten years, Lisetta would be at dockside to welcome him home after his voyages. The couple would walk home arm in arm, obviously in love. There, Ventorino would play his mandolin and sing the popular Neapolitan songs of the day. Lisetta was a good cook, and filled her family's bellies with her celebrated pastas and desserts. Their sons seemed to take on the same good-natured virtues of the parents and the family lived in harmony and devotion to one another. The bliss was not to last.

Arriving after a long voyage at the port of Genoa, Ventorino was disappointed that Lisetta had not traveled the twenty-five miles from Sestri Levante to greet him in her usual fashion. Disappointment turned to fear as he now imagined that she was ill or perhaps injured. But, then why wouldn't someone there in Genoa let him know? Two hours later, as he descended from the wagon that had taken him home, Ventorino was horrified to find his home empty. A young girl of the neighborhood walked up to him.

"Signore, I think your children are with their grandmother."

"Why? What has happened? Where is my wife?"

"I don't know. I only saw the boys at their grandmother's home."

Ventorino rushed to his mother's house and found the boys there. "Mother, where is Lisetta? Has anything happened? She always greets me as I arrive."

"Why are you home, Ventorino? Lisetta told me that you were not due to return for another week."

"Didn't she get my message? We skipped Barcelona this time and came directly home from Tangier."

"I don't think she is expecting you or she would be home. She left the children with me this morning and went to help her friend who just had a difficult childbirth."

A strange feeling came over Ventorino. He knew nothing of her friend who was expecting. What's more, she had never left her children for an entire day. As he left his mother's house, he was summoned from across the street by Maria, the neighborhood gossip.

"Ventorino, I have valuable news for you. Do you have twenty cents?"

Ventorino quickly produced the currency. "What is your news, Maria?"

"Your Lisetta is not faithful to you. She has found another man."

"Damn you, Maria, you take that back this minute."

But, somehow Ventorino felt that Maria might not have made up the story. In spite of his happy life, he knew that there was something in Lisetta's past that she did not share with him. He had felt all along that one day he would learn something that would challenge their marriage. Perhaps that day had come. His mind was numb with spurious thoughts. He fought off the impulse to rage at Maria. He vowed to himself to kill Lisetta if she had been unfaithful to him. He worried about the children. He thought about the embarrassment to him of Lisetta leaving him for another man. Then, he dismissed the thought from his mind.

"Maria, where can I find Lisetta?" He produced another twenty cents.

"In La Spezia, at the edge of town, the Motto pensione. She is there with him."

Ventorino could no longer control himself. He quickly

rented a horse at the local stable in town and left for La Spezia at a full gallop. Two hours later he was in town, the horse breathing heavily and dripping foam from his mouth. It took Ventorino a few moments to force the room number from the frightened clerk. As he ascended the stairs, the police were summoned.

As he crashed in the door, Ventorino called out. "So! You dare to call me your husband. Prepare to die, the two of you." He was furious by what he saw.

There on the bed, completely naked, was Lisetta. She had been in the arms of Antonio Vanesso, the captain of a Carabiniere troop in Bologna, who was also naked on the bed. Ventorino dove for Antonio's holster, which was slung over the chair near the bed. He took the pistol in his hand. Next he looked at the frightened pair on the bed and cocked the hammer. The pleading eyes of Antonio and Lisetta would do no good.

"Vente, for the love of our children, don't do this."

"If you loved our children, you would not be here. Now you must meet your maker with this stain on your soul." He pulled the trigger over and over until he knew there was no life left in either of them.

⤐━⬦━०━⬦━१⤏

A few weeks after Don Generoso sent our letter to my brother, I was summoned to meet with him in his cell. In the meantime, I had noticed that the prison guards were less demanding of me than they had been. I was no longer given the bucket detail punishment for spilling water or for breaking their petty rules. I was even left alone in break areas so that I could now talk to my friends without interference. The other prisoners seemed to know that my new association with the Don had won me special privi-

lege. No one questioned me as to what the connection to Don Generoso was and I did not make any attempt to explain.

"Come in, Angelo, we have a response from Constantino. He has told us all that he knows, he says, but we may need to ask him a few questions to prompt his memory." I noticed that Ventorino was in the cell, ready to read me the letter.

In his letter, Constantino told of the way that he had met Tina and how they had become friends. He also told of the surrender of her virtue to him and how enraged Don Mario was when he became aware of it. He went on to describe his conversation with Maria, the House madam, and how she assured him that Don Mario would not act against him because of his involvement with a long-time resident of Maria's house of ill repute. He emphatically denied that he had any knowledge of my being linked to his indiscretion with Tina and offered to help in any way that he could by shedding light on the injustice imposed on me. He told of how Tina had later married and bore two children, a boy and a girl, to Don Mario's enormous delight and pleasure. Like Tina, they had become the focus of his life. The hidden relationship with the woman living in Maria's brothel flourished, uninterrupted, though Constantino claimed not to know her name or history.

I was pleased that my brother had not known of the circumstances of my conviction. I was comforted by his offer to assist in clearing me of the charges. It was not possible, however, because of my new association with Don Generoso and the enormous judicial scrutiny leveled at him because of his affiliation with the Friends.

"Angelo, I think we have the information we need and, with a few more details from Constantino, I can devise a plan of revenge never before seen anywhere in Calabria."

Chapter 12

Revenge

Cassandra Sercu was a gypsy, having been born in the Romanian province of Dolj on the outskirts of Craiova. Her parents raised her in typical Gypsy fashion, to be very independent and generally indifferent to the law. Most of her life was spent on the cusp of criminality, often on the wrong side of it. Her crimes ranged from petty theft and picking pockets to pandering for the whores of her tribe. Eventually she began offering her own sexual services and found that she could be very successful at it. Now in her late teens, her chiseled features and dark skin made her an interesting curiosity to Romanian men. When her parents ordered her to stop her illicit behavior, she packed up and left the tribe. Her father tracked her through Romania and Hungary. When he discovered that she had crossed over into Austria, he returned home to Craiova and gave her up as dead. She eventually found her way down the Italian Peninsula, to Maria's whorehouse in Gagliano. There, she found an environment that was warm and accepting, despite her alien appearance and broken speech. She had had enough of roughing it through the cities of Eastern Europe one step ahead of the police. She would settle down in this little Italian village where her trade was accepted by many and where she was protected and provided for by Maria.

In very short order, she was asked to cater to a powerful man of the community and to be extremely discreet about having ever met him. He was the magistrate of the Criminal Court of Catanzaro, was wealthy and had a respected family. His name was Mario Martinez. To say that they were magically paired would be an understatement. From the very start, Mario felt a passion beyond that of any of the women he had bedded in his lifetime. For Cassandra, there was exposure to a quality of individual she had never before met. She felt herself bonding to a man for the first time in her life. They decided that she would be his exclusive lover and that he would seek no other outside of his home. Arrangements were made with Maria so that Cassandra would be available only to Don Mario. At times Cassandra longed for the traditional, nomadic life of the gypsy, but her attachment to Mario and her fear of his wrath, were she to leave, kept her loyal to him. To all appearances, she was the happy mistress in love with her man.

Maria called to the second floor of the building from below, "Cassandra, would you please come down? There is a gentleman here who has a message for you from home."

Quickly, Cassandra descended the stairs to greet the

man with news from home. This had never happened before. How did they even know where she was or how to reach her? This was a strange moment indeed.

"My name is Giovanni Bianchi and I must talk to you privately."

"What is it? Has something happened to my parents?"

"Nothing has happened to your parents. But, it is important that I talk to you privately."

"Very well, come this way." Cassandra was careful not to lead him by the wrong room, lest he be startled by what he might see. She led him upstairs to her room. On the night table stood a picture of Don Mario in leisure clothing, probably taken during their trip to the Alpine city of Stresa. He was alone in the photo.

"Now then, tell me, what has happened? What is wrong?"

"There is nothing wrong. I am here to make you the offer of a lifetime."

Her eyes widened. "What do you mean?"

"I have been sent here by a man of great respect. He wishes a favor of you and is willing to pay handsomely for your help. He has reason to believe that you are bored with your current situation and are ready to move on, that only the fear of reproach by your lover prevents you from leaving him."

Cassandra's thoughts spun a web of possibility. Could this be Mario testing her? Had she slipped and said something to make him doubt her? Was she now talking in her sleep and perhaps giving her inner thoughts away? Was she really prepared to leave Mario? Could anyone really protect her from him should he become infuriated? She decided to chance that this offer was from a genuine source.

"Who is this man and what does he want?"

"It is not necessary for you to know who he is. If you decide to grant him this favor, you will have more money than you will need for the rest of your life."

Cassandra drew in a deep breath. "What is this wish of his? Must I kill someone?" She was trying to add levity to an otherwise somber conversation, but she was not entirely certain that murder was not the "favor" that the mysterious man wanted.

The man looked up at her placidly and did not take her comment as humor. "Murder is not a subject to joke about. No, that is not his wish. Do you know Tina and her two children, Serena and Adolfo?"

"Yes. They do not know me, but I am aware of them and see them occasionally when I am at the market. Serena is seven years old and Adolfo is five. Sometimes I think they are Mario's reason for living."

"My padrone wishes that you take the children and leave Italy forever. In a year or two, you are free to release them to anyone you wish, so long as they never return to their parents."

So that was it. Put a crimp in Mario's life for all time. Not to say what it would do to Tina and her husband. This man had a vendetta worse than she had imagined. She ventured forth with the conversation more out of curiosity than true interest. "And how much will he pay?"

"You will be paid outside of Italy in Pound Sterling, five thousand pounds."

"How much is that in lire?" Cassandra wasn't sure what Sterling was.

"Fifty thousand."

Whoa! She didn't know that much money existed. This was an offer she had to consider. She cared for Mario and for the comforts that their relationship provided, but the glamour of their association had faded. She had no reason to hurt Mario by taking away his grandchildren, but wasn't that what happened to others all over Europe? Didn't children get taken away all the time? And who knows what Mario had done to so anger this man that he was willing to pay a King's ransom for this act?

"How much time can you give me to think it over?"

"You have until I reach the door of the room. You may refuse, but understand that, if you do, you must never talk of this offer, under pain of death." He stood up and turned.

"Wait... I'll do it."

⊷⊶○⊷⊷

I was again summoned to Don Generoso's cell, this time to hear the reading of a letter to Don Generoso.

Don Generoso.

I trust this letter finds you in good health and of good cheer. There is news from Catanzaro that I believe you should know, since it involves none other than Don Mario Martinez. It is about his grandchildren, who are believed to have been kidnapped by a gypsy woman who was living in the brothel run by the madam Maria of Gagliano. They are believed to be across the border in France, where the woman has rejoined her family, a tribe of itinerants who work in the vineyards of the Languedoc region. All attempts to find them have failed and the family has resigned itself to the permanent loss of their two young children.

Needless to say, Don Mario is disconsolate to the point of being unable to speak or even hear those around him. He has confounded the physicians who think he may have experienced a stroke, despite a lack of symptom. His daughter, the mother of the children, has frantically blamed the tragedy on an act of re-venge by some unspecified party who may have been wronged by Don Mario. They fear for the well being of the children and are reluctant to cast blame on any particular person. It seems as though Don Mario's career as a Justice is over and perhaps the rest of his life as well.

That is the news of the moment, Don Generoso. Perhaps my next letter will have some cheerier information for you.

With all good thoughts for your well being, I remain your faithful servant.

Giovanni Bianchi

I am not sure why I took such pleasure in hearing Ventorino read the letter that Don Generoso received from a source in Messina reporting the kidnapping of Don Mario's grandchil-dren. It was sordid. But somehow I revelled in having taken part in settling the vendetta that existed between two powerful men and taking revenge for myself at the same time. Somehow this whole experience made my life in Asinara more tolerable. Now, my time in prison seemed to pass more quickly.

Chapter 13

Lorenzo

The Italian steamship, S.S.Giuseppe Verdi, arrives in New York harbor in August of 1897 with a full contingent of passengers after a 22-day voyage from Naples. Hundreds of steerage passengers from southern Italy, immigrants all, swarm out onto the lower deck for their first look at *La Merica*. Dressed in the garb of the Italian peasant and anxious about finally arriving in the new world, they are mostly silent as they absorb the sights. As the ship makes its way up the bay, they are awestruck by the colossal sculpture of a woman with arm uplifted, torch in hand, standing on a tiny island in New York harbor. The immigrants are yet uncertain of her welcome. They hear from a ship orderly of the famous French architect and sculptor, Frederic Bartholdi, by whose hand this structure was fashioned and of how the iron lady came to be placed in this spot, to which so many have traveled to seek their destiny.

High above, on the main deck, Marianna stands pensively. She is dressed appropriately in a summer dress and wide-brimmed, straw hat for her arrival as a visitor to the land adopted by the man she is here to find. Now that Leone is but a memory, she is free to search out Lorenzo Fusco to determine if there is anything left of their relationship. She thinks of the years that have passed and of how her looks may have changed. She worries that Lorenzo will find her less attractive. Then she dismisses the thought, knowing that her new position in life has given her stature. This will surely appeal to him. She has written to her friend, Rosa Vartone, who left Gagliano with her husband as a newlywed, to immigrate to the new world. Rosa's husband, Mario, believes that he can lead Marianna to the farm in Queens where Lorenzo lives with his American girl friend. The thought of Lorenzo with another woman hurts Marianna, but she knows that it was her liaison with Leone that caused Lorenzo's sudden departure for the new world. She must now find Rosa at the dock in New York, where her letter said she would wait for Marianna's arrival. The search for Lorenzo would depend on Mario, and Rosa would take Marianna home so that she could meet him.

Marianna addresses a ship steward, "Can you tell me how I can locate my friend waiting for me on the dock below?"

Certainly, signora, simply look over the side of the ship. If your friend is there, you will sight him."

"...Her!"

"Uh, yes, signora... her."

Suddenly, she hears her name being called by a woman in the small crowd of fashionably dressed ladies and men on the pier below, awaiting the arrival of the cabin class travelers. "Marianna! Marianna! Over here! Look!" After a few frantic moments, she sees Rosa's smiling face, arms waving frenetically in the air. She cannot help but notice that Rosa is looking very American, yet standing apart from the others, her dress worn and her shoes tattered. Looking down from the ship, Marianna thinks that she must help her friend by purchasing a garment or two for her, and perhaps even some new shoes. She disembarks and the two friends hug and greet one another.

"Marianna, I walked to the pier from home, a distance of about two miles. Can you walk in your high shoes that far?"

"Certainly not. And I have a steamer trunk coming off the ship. There it is among the passenger baggage. Will you call us a carriage while I arrange for a porter?"

As they make their way to the lower East Side of Manhattan, Marianna is startled by the unexpected. Steeped in the myth of America, she has formed erroneous notions of the promised land, that of a pristine and abundant civilization, open to all who agree to leave the familiar behind and venture to the unknown. Her first impression is one of amazed disappointment. First, there is the noise from crushing traffic and from the hordes of workers lining the streets, their chatter combining to create a constant assault on her ears. There is the dirt and ugliness of the tenement buildings, standing five and six stories high and sporting the soot of decades of smoke from the tens of thousands of fires needed to heat and light the homes and streets. The streets are filled with manure from the draught horses used for transport. The driest horse dung is lifted into the air by breezes coming in off the bay, making breathing very difficult. Marianna holds a handkerchief to her face. The smell of human feces rises from the pavement, where buckets are dumped at the curb. As they ride by, they dodge a pail of gray liquid slop thrown from a third story window.

"Rosa, how far away is this Mulberry district that you live in?"

"We are almost there, Marianna, just a few more blocks."

As they approach the building that Rosa and Mario live in, Marianna is horrified to see the squalor of the neighborhood. There is the smell of smoke combined with a profusion of cooking odors coming from hundreds of kitchens simultaneously. Children are dressed shabbily and play in the streets with makeshift toys made by fathers and uncles. Garbage lines the streets and dogs fight to claim food scraps in among the trash.

"You must tell me, Rosa, why are these people here? They are no better off than they were in Italy. And there, at least the sky is blue."

"That may be true, Marianna, but these people have hope that one day their fortunes will improve. What hope was there in Italy?"

<hr />

Matthew Feeney grew up in the Irish city of Limerick, where he prospered from a livery business handed down for three generations in his family. During his tenure as head of the company, the business grew from a few wagons to no less than sixty, each requiring a minimum of two draught horses. When he was not immersed in the business, Matthew was involved with a leading branch of the IRA, plotting the revolution that would free Ireland from the grip of England. Eventually, the group went from talk to action, tossing homemade bombs into British enclaves and fighting the Brown and Tan militia on the streets. Following several such clashes, an IRA operative was captured and tortured until he identified all of his superiors. Matthew thus became a marked man and promptly went into hiding. All of his assets were seized, including his company, and his family was placed under constant surveillance. He had little choice but to leave Ireland. Reluctantly, he emigrated to the U.S. with his wife, three sons and a daughter. He purchased a rooming house in New York's Greenwich Village with the funds he was able to take with him from Ireland and took a job running a local hauling company. His sons went to work for him, and his daughter, the youngest at age nineteen, helped her mother operate the rooming house. Most of the roomers were Irish immigrants who had fled Ireland for much the same reasons as their landlord. One man was an Italian, from the region of Calabria. His name was Lorenzo Fusco.

Lorenzo Fusco was indeed a fortunate man. He had escaped the misery of life in the Italian ghetto of the lower east side of New York City. And, he would have the capital to establish himself as a businessman in the New World. The price of this privilege was the loss of Marianna to the man who sponsored his good fortune, Count Leone. Following the shock that Marianna had become involved with Leone, Lorenzo Fusco sought out the Count, wishing to appeal for Marianna's *release*. Sensing this, Leone appointed Aldo to the task of dealing with the situation for him. Their meeting place was the courtyard outside the entrance to the main house.

"Young man, the Count is not here at the moment. However, I can handle this matter in his absence. What is it you wish?"

"I understand that Marianna Soluri is here. We are betrothed and I am here to take her to her home."

"That cannot be. Marianna has said nothing about a betrothal. And, besides, this is her home now. She need not go anywhere else."

Lorenzo tensed with frustration, clenching his fists and looking upward towards the top floor of the house, hoping for a glimpse of Marianna. His large size, somewhat intimidating, prompted Aldo to again question his purpose for coming to the Capurro villa.

"I am here to take Marianna with me. Please don't anger me."

"My boy, be practical. There are guards all over the property. There is little chance that you could get very far should you choose to fight us. Allow me to present a more sensible alternative to you. Leone is prepared to finance your immigration to the New World, if you will abandon the idea of ever seeing Marianna again."

"No, dammit! I want Marianna. I'll finance my own trip to America."

At this point, Aldo mustered all of the diplomacy of which he was capable, hoping to save Lorenzo the pain and humiliation of defeat from an altercation with Leone's guards.

"Lorenzo, you seem like an ambitious man. You will undoubtedly find yourself in America one day. Are you aware of the hardships that are endured by Italians who immigrate to America? The stories that are told of found wealth and cordiality are great exaggerations of the truth. Most immigrants are desperately poor and are abused beyond belief until they find their own way. You need not subject yourself to that misery. You can go to the New World as a gentleman. Take the money that Leone is offering you and forget Marianna. There are many women just like her in America looking for a good man like you."

It is clear from the pinched look on his face that Lorenzo had not changed his mind. He had not even asked about the amount of money that Leone was proposing to give him. Aldo turned and nodded in the direction of a guard standing just within the line of sight. In turn, the guard signaled to three men standing hidden in the garden. They knew what they had to do.

"Where is Marianna? Where is she?" Lorenzo was frantic.

Just then, the four guards flooded in on him from different directions. They carried small bats, which they swung at him as they approached. Lorenzo covered his head with one arm and fought with his other bare hand. Despite being larger than his opponents, a blow eventually struck his head and took him down. As he lost consciousness and fell to the ground, the men continued to pummel him mercilessly. Blood emerged from his face and mouth and he moaned.

"Enough." Aldo ended the violence with one word. "Now, take him away."

When Lorenzo awoke, he was on a bed in the infirmary of a steamship out at sea. His body pained all over and one eye was completely closed. The ship's medic was in the room with him.

"Where am I? What happened?"

"You were brought here by two men a week ago. They had you sedated by a nurse and asked me to look after you for a few days. They left this envelope for you. It contains a letter and some money."

"Please, read the letter to me." The man carefully opened the letter, fingering the cash that was enclosed.

"It says, *Dear Lorenzo, I was unable to make you see the mistake you were making in refusing Count Leone's offer. I took it upon myself to send you off to America in spite of your refusal. I have enclosed fifty dollars in cash for you to use until you can get to the J.P. Morgan bank in New York and identify yourself. They are holding five thousand dollars in an account that Count Leone has opened in your name. It is the equivalent of twenty five thousand lire, an amount that is sufficient to give you a handsome start in America.* It is signed Aldo."

"When do we arrive in New York?"

"In three weeks."

Upon arrival, Lorenzo found that his immigration had been expedited through the officials in Ellis Island and that an official of the J.P. Morgan bank had come to greet him. As he looked around him at the others who had arrived under less luxurious circumstances, he began thinking that perhaps Aldo was right after all. Scores of weary people waited for hours to be questioned about how they intended to support themselves now that they were in the U.S. They were tugged at and pushed and were subjected to physical examinations and immunizations. Often they were told that they had an illness that meant they would have to return to their native country. And frequently, they were separated from their loved ones when they were deported. The thought of having given up Marianna still pained Lorenzo, but the reality of his privileged status in the New World seemed to compensate. The young banker from the Morgan Bank introduced himself and explained how the banking arrangement that had been set up for Lorenzo would work. The discussion was in Italian, the only language that Lorenzo knew.

"You will want these check forms," the banker said in his broken Italian, "so that you can draw against your balance. I can instruct you on the signing of your name and how to complete the forms. By the way, do you have a place to live?"

"No. I know only one person in New York and I don't know how to contact him. He lives in a place called Mulberry."

"Oh no, signore, you don't want to go down there. I can arrange for you to have a nice room in the Feeney House in Greenwich Village. Kathleen can teach you to speak English and you can begin thinking about how you want to invest your money. If I can help in that regard, let me know."

"I am a farmer and I would like to own my own farm…and earn a good living."

"All right then, we'll see what we can do."

When Matthew Feeney was asked to take Lorenzo Fusco into his boarding house, he groaned. In only a few short years, he came to adopt the "American" attitude towards Italian immigrants. They were filth from the south of Europe, coming to the new world to escape poverty and to take advantage of a system of government that was not available to them in their own country. But he quickly agreed to take him in when he was told that Lorenzo was no ordinary immigrant. He was well provided for by an Italian nobleman in southern Italy. In fact, he had a handsome sum of money on deposit with the Morgan Bank and would likely use it to purchase land in New York somewhere. In the meantime, Matthew would have a boarder who could afford to pay a high rent for one of the lesser rooms of the house.

"I'll take the dago in, but he'll have to pay two dollars a week and eat the food we prepare without complainin'."

"All right, but it will have to include English lessons. He'll need to learn the language if he intends to succeed in New York." The Morgan Bank had done their duty as requested by Leone in assisting young Lorenzo in finding his way upon arrival in his new country.

Lorenzo's first glimpse of Kathleen occurred within moments of his arrival at the Feeney house. It was almost dinnertime and she was busily helping her mother with preparation of the evening meal. The aromas of food that emanated from the kitchen were unfamiliar, but so interested him that he peeked in through the swinging door from the kitchen to the dining room. The two women he saw resembled one another, their ruddy freckled faces surrounded by lots of straight auburn-colored hair tied neatly back and held in place by a small white bonnet. The older woman was large, obviously the mother, and moved at a deliberate pace, confidently placing cooked foods onto serving plates. The younger woman was tall and slim, radiating a sweetness that caught Lorenzo's attention. The plates by now contained slabs of meat cooked gray, boiled potatoes and cabbage. None of it looked familiar to Lorenzo, but it caused him to reflect on the fact that he was hungry. Unable to speak their language, he retreated to his room before he would be noticed.

"Gents, this here's our new roomer, Lorenzo Fusco. He doesn't speak any English yet, but Kathleen is goin' to learn him." The twelve boarders looked up drearily from their dinner to acknowledge Lorenzo, but didn't attempt to speak to him. They seemed confused about what one says to a man who doesn't speak their language. It was Lorenzo's first encounter outside of his own very limited circle of friends and acquaintances, all of whom spoke some form of his native language. Bewildered, he finished his dinner and returned to his room. "Mr. Fusco, may I come in?" It was Kathleen, coming to call on Lorenzo for the first time. Realizing that he was unable to understand her, she entered the room and began coaching him on some basic words.

"My name is Kathleen. Are you Lorenzo?"

"Si."

"No, not si, say yes."

"Yesa."

It would be several weeks before Lorenzo would learn enough English to carry on a conversation with Kathleen, the other boarders and certain of his new acquaintances at the wholesale produce market where he took employment while learning the ways of his new environment. But unlike other Italian immigrants, he was speaking English almost immediately. His sessions with Kathleen continued even after he was sufficiently grounded in English to make his way among Americans. During their sessions, Kathleen would look at Lorenzo's handsome, olive-complexioned face and become distracted from their effort. His light brown eyes, long eyelashes and full lips captivated her. It was not long before he took notice of her adoring stare and began to look back. He had much for which to be grateful to her. She had befriended him from the outset along with becoming his teacher. When the other roomers questioned him about the source of his money and his plans for spending it, he innocently told the sordid details of Leone's generosity, and of his intent to purchase farmland. Kathleen quickly warned him to keep to himself lest he provoke the hatching of a plot to separate him from his fortune.

By now his friendship with her had turned to affection. She was a lovely woman indeed, standing a slim five and a half feet tall, her full breasts filling the inside of her blouse. She had large, penetrating green eyes and gleaming white teeth. When she smiled, it lighted the room. There was no shortage of suitors who came to call on her, but somehow none seemed to interest her. It was an extraordinary act, therefore, when she took his hand in hers during one of their English lessons.

"Lorenzo, I think I am falling in love with you."

"You are a very lovely woman, cara. It would not be difficult for me to love you as well."

"But do you care for me?"

Lorenzo took her in his arms and pressed his body to hers. "Yes, Kathleen, I care for you intensely. I may be falling in love as well." Then, they kissed deeply and held one another for a long time.

The messenger came to the Feeney House with a letter for Lorenzo, which he found waiting for him on a small table in the front hallway. He had learned enough reading that he might have muddled through it. Instead, he waited for Kathleen to finish her kitchen duties so they could meet in the parlor away from the others. There she could read it to him quickly and accurately and perhaps even counsel him on its contents. The letter was from the same Morgan Bank official who had met with him at Ellis Island the previous winter.

"Please, read it for me."

"It reads, *Dear Lorenzo, I hope this letter finds you well and that you are enjoying your time at Feeney House. You may recall my interest in helping you find a suitable land investment for development as a farm. Well, it appears that an oppor-*

tunity has arisen that might suit you well. It is a twenty-five acre parcel of land in Queens with a lovely house on it, situated east of the city some fifteen miles. The previous owner owed the bank a debt which he was unable to repay, and we have thus taken over the property. It is easily worth the four thousand dollars that it would take to purchase it from the bank and we would pay for all of the costs to transfer it to you. It has been farmed for corn and winter wheat and there have been a small number of cattle raised for beef. At the moment it is bare land awaiting an owner. I will come by on Saturday morning at ten o'clock to pick you up and take you out to see the property. It is signed, Frank Mullin."

"Oh Lorenzo, this sounds like the perfect opportunity for you. And, it's being offered by someone you already know." Her eyes welled with tears. "I suppose this is the time we'll say goodbye."

"No, Kathleen, we'll stay together. You can come with me." Her look in response was filled with surprise and hope, but included a note of despondency.

"My father will never allow me to live anywhere but here, nor be with any man who is not Irish."

"But I can tell him we're to be married. You will marry me, won't you?"

"Yes, but only after we've had a proper amount of time to be sure that we want to spend the rest of our lives together. I will need to defy my father to marry you, and there will be no returning to him."

At ten o'clock on Saturday morning, Frank Mullin of the Morgan Bank arrived at the Feeney House in a carriage drawn by a sturdy bay gelding. A third generation American, he was the product of Irish, German and English parentage. Taller than average, his straight black hair and soft blue eyes projected genuineness that instantly won the confidence of his clients. The first of his family to earn a college degree, he was hired by the bank as a teller, upon graduation from Columbia College. He ascended to officer status in short order, having shown an interest in commercial lending and deftness with foreign languages. His first assignment was in the Foreign Department of the bank, which put him in contact with clients such as Count Leone. His Italian was a bit weak at first, but he was eventually able to converse in two dialects, enough to be understood by most Italians.

"Good morning, Lorenzo, are you ready to ride out to the country to see the property for sale?"

"Yes, and Kathleen will be coming with us."

Lorenzo thought that he spotted a look of disappointment on Frank's face and asked, "Is it all right for her to come along?"

"Yes, of course." Frank's expression seemed not to agree with his words, but Lorenzo chose not to pursue the point further. Though Frank had not revealed the fact to Lorenzo, he had previously approached Kathleen with the prospect of courting her, and despite revealing intense feelings for her, she declined his advance, reasoning that she was not yet ready to court. Now, only months later, she showed obvious feelings for Lorenzo, ending the possibility that she might be available.

It was a crisp morning and the three placed a comforter over their legs as they proceeded on in the mostly open carriage. It would take two hours to reach their destination, and the roads in Queens were narrow and unlighted. They would need to be back in the city by nightfall or risk traveling in the dark most of the way. Kathleen had anticipated their need for a midday meal and brought along a lunch for three. As they continued on from Greenwich Village to City Hall and across the decade-old Brooklyn Bridge, Frank began briefing Lorenzo on the possibilities that lay ahead for the property he would be considering purchasing.

"You might be interested to know that Queens will be incorporated into the city of New York as a borough, probably within a few years. That means that roads will be constructed and a surge in population will follow. The property you are about to purchase, as a site for homes, would be worth many times more than your purchase price."

As the carriage came to a stop on the edge of the property, Lorenzo drew in a breath. The rolling verdant hills, the dark soil and the cool breeze coming in from the north captured him immediately. It was apparent that much work would need to be done to restore the land to a farm, but the ingredients were there. Lorenzo recalled an observation he had made at the wholesale produce market where he had been working. There seemed to be an increase in demand for Italian vegetables from week to week as the thousands of new immigrants arrived. And, there were many of the favorites of the Italian countryside that were not available at all. Then, he looked up at the house that stood in the farthest corner of the property. It was an unfamiliar style of building to him, but it seemed inviting, with its dark pitched roof and exterior of contrasting white composition.

"Can we get into the house?"

"Yes, of course. I have a key."

The two-story cottage was finer than any home that Lorenzo had ever seen in Calabria, except for the Capurro villa. It stood in the open, away from the farm and livestock areas and had the remnants of flowerbeds that had been placed along the ground beneath the windows. The heavy wooden entrance door was split horizontally, so that it was possible to open only the top. Inside, the main room had heavy beamed ceilings eight feet high, and plaster walls with oil lamp fixtures. The floor was concrete and everywhere there were rugs covering the areas that would be used for family dinners, gatherings and as an office for operating the farm. The other room on the first floor was a kitchen that faced to the east, allowing the morning sun to stream in. There was a fireplace on the common wall of the room that provided heat for the first floor; and a wood-burning stove for cooking. The second floor had two bed-rooms, the larger being the sleeping quarters for the mas-ter of the house. The former owners had left behind much of the furniture, the property having been hastily vacated. Outside, a large barn sat half way between the house and a fenced area once used to contain cattle.

"Frank, this is beautiful! How do I get started?"

"The bank will charge your account for the purchase price of the property. We will also lend you up to twenty five hundred dollars to get the farm re-established. Your remaining capital should be adequate to see you through to your first harvest, after which you should be able to operate effectively on your own.

Lorenzo looked squarely at the young banker. "How can I ever thank you for all that you've done?"

"Don't thank me. Thank Count Leone. Now can we have some lunch? I'm starving."

It was almost evening when the carriage rolled to a stop at Feeney House. Lorenzo and Kathleen said their goodbyes to Frank Mullin and entered the house, laugh-ing and talking about the day's adventure in Queens. Matthew Feeney came to the front hall, glancing impa-tiently at Lorenzo and looking ominously at Kathleen. He waited for Lorenzo to catch his meaning and proceed on to his room and then lashed out at Kathleen.

"And where the hell have you been?"

"I went to Queens with Lorenzo and Frank Mullin to see the property that Lorenzo is buying."

"And of what matter is his property to you?"

"Dad, I wasn't expecting to tell you this here and in a moment of anger, but I'm going with Lorenzo to the farm in Queens. We'll be married as soon as possible and we're hoping to get yours and Ma's blessing."

"What! Are you crazy? You want my approval to marry a dago? Not on your life! You'll marry a good Irishman when the time comes. And in the meantime, you'll stay here with your mother and me. Do you understand?"

"I know what you're saying, Dad, but I'm not going to stay here as your housemaid while I wait for a man who doesn't exist. Lorenzo is the first man who ever made a difference to me, and he wants me as his wife. If you can't give your blessing to our union, then we'll go ahead without it."

"Then you'll have to leave now! I don't want you around any longer. And that goes for him, too. I should never have allowed him to live here. I should have known that he'd seduce you if you let him."

At that point, Colleen Feeney came to the front hallway and took both of them by the arm and pulled them into the kitchen. She had listened patiently to father and daughter arguing and now had her own anger to deal with.

"What in God's name do you think you're doing, arguing in public like that? And what's this about a marriage to a foreigner?"

"Mother, I'm going to marry Lorenzo Fusco. Dad has called him awful names and wrongly accused me of allowing him to seduce me. He refuses to give his approval to our marriage."

"No, and I'd rather croak than to see you marry that man."

"Now, Matthew, if that's who she's chosen, we have no right except to warn her of the problems of marrying outside of her own kind."

"Look, Mom and Dad, Lorenzo and I want to be together and nothing is going to stop us. To hell with any differences in culture. We're going to his farm in Queens to live as soon as the property is his and that's that."

"Then you might as well be dead."

Within a year, Lorenzo had the farm restored and yielding enough cash crops to live comfortably and even use the excess of cash to reduce the amount he owed the Morgan Bank. His contacts at the wholesale produce market in New York proved to be invaluable. The buyers gave him orders a year in advance for the vegetables they were familiar with and he, in turn, gave them ideas for new products that they had never heard of.

"You're trying to sell them foods they are unfamiliar with instead of finding the products they want. Eventually, someone will offer those products and you'll be out of business. Here, I have the sweet basil that Italians want, a Neapolitan strain that I managed to get from a friend. I am able now to grow it the year round and can keep you supplied all twelve months of the year." By now, Lorenzo had several employees and a greenhouse in which to germinate seed and grow produce throughout the cold winter.

Kathleen, meanwhile, had transformed the house into something special. Every window in the house had been treated to her handmade curtains and she had purchased the few pieces of furniture that were needed, arranging them to advantage. The kitchen table held a white pitcher filled with fresh flowers cut from the little patch she tended. Her training was such that she needed no coaching in housekeeping. For Lorenzo's sake she had become a skilled Italian cook, having learned from the wife of one of the men working for him. Though she and Lorenzo shared a bed, there was no furthur talk of marriage once they left the Feeney House. It was understood that they were man and wife and no municipality or priest was needed to sanction their relationship. Though they kept to themselves, they were the envy of their neighbors, who labored at their farms and could not seem to produce a comparable living. Most importantly, they had proven to Kathleen's parents that they were meant to be together and could succeed on their own.

Chapter 14

Home at Last

An oppressive and monotonous sun beats down on Calabria in July. It is unmerciful, at times stamping the countryside with a mid-summer blight that can be caused only by intense heat and humid air. There are large, black flies and mosquitoes everywhere. Farmers are unable to work in the fields for more than a few hours at a time and animals left unsheltered are likely to succumb to exposure and disease. The older, weaker inhabitants are confined to the indoors, where they will stay until they are released by a change in the forces of Nature. Such was the July of 1896.

It took me a month to get home to Calabria after I was freed. First, there was a three day wait at Asinara for the boat that sailed for Reggio. Then, the persistent Southern winds kept us at a crawl as the ship's crew tacked from side to side, gaining only a few yards each time. It seemed that the crew worked day and night weaving from side to side, seeking each little puff of wind to drive us forward toward Calabria. It was the time of year for the Sirocco wind to blow its white hot air from the Sahara, gather moisture as it crossed the Mediterranean, and heat Italy to a crisp. The voyage seemed endless. It was as though a year had been added to my sentence, and gave me the eerie notion that somehow Asinara was not satisfied with the nine years of my life that I had given up. The food was only slightly better than the sparse diet we were fed on the trip to Asinara nine years ago. There was some polenta and occasionally the cook prepared risotto for us. Some days, the sea would rage and produce great swells. Many of us would puke up from motion sickness. Needless to say, we were treated differently from the prison ship. Though still disciplined, the atmosphere aboard was one of great relief, an almost joyful undercurrent at finally being free after years of imprisonment.

I did not know any of the other former prisoners. Roberto Borrelli was the only one I knew at Asinara whose release date coincided with mine and his release was held up for lack of paperwork. I had a feeling that my release was processed on time because of my connection to Don Generoso. There were twelve of us ex-convicts in all and they kept us busy helping the crew to clean and sail the ship. There was a large consignment of salt on board and we joked as how it was likely that we had produced it and were therefore entitled to a part of the proceeds. There was word aboard the ship of a severe summer heat affecting much of Italy. Calabria in particular was steaming. My thoughts turned to Gesuzza and my boys. I wondered if they would know how to cope with this extreme weather. I could not wait to see them again after all these years. I wondered what they would look like and if I would recognize them. What did I look like after nine years and would they recognize me? The ship was moving so slowly that, in my frustration, I wanted to jump into the sea and swim home.

Gesuzza had been out for the brief period of the morning when there is light by which to see but when the new day's sun has not yet begun its torment of heat. She and Pietro, now fifteen years old, had carried and placed a gallon of water on each of the olive and citrus trees that they could irrigate in the span of an hour. Giuseppe, almost ten, was busy mucking the animal pen. She gave Pietro instruction to head for home to take refuge from the heat. The perspiration had begun to flow down from her forehead and to blur her vision as she turned to look up the hill descending from Gagliano's main road. She thought she saw Angelo walking down the hill towards her, a bag slung over his shoulder. She crossed herself in defense of false hope caused by some demon. Then, as he moved closer, she knew this was no false illusion. It was Angelo. His thin, drawn look gave her immediate reflection on herself. What did she look like to him after nine years of separation? She was older, less a woman and more a provider to her children. He would be grateful to her for her loyalty, but would he still love her? She straightened her back and pulled back the hair that fell in front of her face.

"Angelo?"

"Yes, Gesuzza, it's Angelo. How are you?"

"I think I'm all right. All three of us are all right…now that you're home." Tears flowed involuntarily down her cheeks.

Angelo stepped forward and put his arms around her. "Gesuzza… my poor, dear Gesuzza. I have lived only for this moment. I love you more than anything on earth, more than I have ever before." They embraced and kissed for a long moment. Then they stepped back and stared at one another.

"Are you hungry, Angelo?"

Back at the house my son, Pietro, greeted me enthusiastically. He flung his arms around me and hugged me. "Father, welcome home, we are so glad that you are back with us."

"Yes, Pietro, it's good to be home. You've done a good job while I was gone. I could see the farm as I walked down the hill. Now, it's time for us to work together and make a life for us all."

I could not help noticing that little Giuseppe was holding his hand behind him. I scooped him up into my arms and hugged and kissed him. "What's that you have in your hand?"

Gesuzza cut in on the conversation. "He has nothing in his hand. Two of his fingers are folded into the palm of his hand."

"Why is that?"

"Two years ago, when I worked in the afternoons and evenings, cooking and cleaning for the Minnelli family, the boys went to my parents home at the end of their work day. One day, Giuseppe picked up a hot skillet from the stove and burned his hand badly. Our neighbor, Signora Bova, treated it, stretching the two fingers out on a board so they would heal straight. Each day, I made sure that the fingers were fastened to the board and each night I found them curled and the board cast aside. I pleaded with my mother to be sure that Giuseppe keeps his fingers out on the board while he was in her care, but she just couldn't seem to keep after him, except to punish him each time his behavior slipped. I couldn't wait until I could again care for him myself, but by then, it was too late. His fingers, so piteously deformed, would remain so for the rest of his life."

"Damn that Stella! What will poor Giuseppe do without the use of two good hands? He'll have to become a priest. A hand like that is only good to give benedictions and nothing

else." I could not help lashing out at the clergy, who I felt should have helped bring the injustice of my imprisonment to the authorities and who should have given my family assistance during my absence.

"He will do just fine, Angelo, now that you are home to teach him. I just never want to place him in Stella's care again, so she can feed him and beat him."

"And neglect him."

I was amazed at how well my young family had done in my absence. The orchard that I had contracted for with Count Leone and the small vegetable patch behind the house were in excellent condition. The trees were thicker and taller than I remembered and the garden was full with tomatoes and squash. The sheep and goats numbered about the same as before, and there was no sign whatever of disease or malnutrition among the animals, despite the intense heat of the season.

To be sure, it was dreadfully hard on them. The lines on Gesuzza's face were evidence of the pitiless life she had lived these nine years. And, the boys seemed very serious and gloomy most of the time. But in short order, I was able to take charge and give them back a more normal life. Having lost nine years of life together, it could never have been the same. I had no remembrances of my children growing up those years, and my wife had gone through nine years in the prime of her life without a husband to care for her and to love her. And for what reason? The fact of my innocence gnawed at me and often kept me sleepless. I knew that I had to forget what had happened or I would lose the part of my mind I had not already left on that godforsaken rock called Asinara.

A week later the whole town turned out to celebrate my homecoming. It was more than an excuse to celebrate. They were genuinely happy for me. Many townspeople came up to me to tell me how badly they felt about my being sent to jail for a crime I *didn't commit. They knew how hard my family had to struggle to support themselves in my absence.*

"Angelo, that boy Pietro is about as good a worker as men twice his age. I can remember him coming home from a workday in the orchard, dead tired, and having to care for the animals before supper. He never let it bother him. He's quite a young man."

"That Gesuzza is a splendid mother. She and the boys worked endlessly to produce enough of a crop to earn their living. She never let up for a moment. She's a great example to those boys."

I knew for sure that all the celebrating and praise was genuine when two weeks later Roberto Borrelli showed up and was virtually ignored. Only his family celebrated his release from prison and not very enthusiastically at that.

Chapter 15

Adolfo

A dolfo Liotta was the captain of the Carabinieri in Gagliano. As such he was the highest-ranking military officer in town, with authority to direct police activities. Adolfo started life in the hamlet of Sacco, in the province of Campania. He was the third child of a moderately successful small-town attorney, Antonio Liotta. For a time, Antonio served as a military magistrate in the army of Francis II, the Bourbon King of the Two Sicilies. As an Italian patriot, however, he abandoned his Bourbon post when he heard that war to unite Italy was imminent. He escaped with his family to Catanzaro, where his identity was kept secret until after the war. There he met many of the influential people of the provincial government. He became a close friend of the newly appointed

Magistrate of the Criminal Court, Mario Martinez. When Antonio's oldest son, Giulio, announced his intention to marry Tina Martinez, Antonio was ecstatic. Eventually, the marriage summoned the arrival of the next generation of the two families into the world, a boy and a girl. As an act of gratification to the Liotta family, Don Mario used his influence with the military to bring Antonio's younger son, Adolfo, by now an officer in the army of the Kingdom of Italy, to Gagliano as head of the local Carabinieri.

All was well until Don Mario's mistress kidnapped the two little children and ran off to France, leaving the two families in acute distress. Don Mario was precluded from determining who it was who dared to arrange the abduction of his grandchildren in such a grotesque manner as to include public embarrassment of his family by his mistress. Such an inquiry could have meant harm or even death to the children. A valiant effort was made to secretly determine the whereabouts of the children, to no avail. Don Mario was so dispirited that he was left unable to speak for several weeks.

Adolfo took on the responsibility to find his nephew and niece, beginning yet another search into the matter. He was able to determine that a certain life-term prisoner at Prigione dell' Asinara, one Don Generoso Spadaro, could have been the perpetrator. His past record as a leading figure in the Sicilian underworld and his sentencing by Judge Martinez to life imprisonment were facts that could easily have caused a vendetta. He then discovered that a former prisoner by the name of Angelo Chiarella, from Gagliano, had a brother who was very close to Tina. What's more, Don Generoso had befriended Angelo in Asinara and had received letters from Angelo's brother referring to Tina. Adolfo thought that perhaps this was enough coincidence to get Don Mario's approval to bring Angelo in for questioning.

"No! No! Don't you understand? Those poor little children will be killed if I make any move against Don Generoso or any of his friends. Stop the investigation at once." Don Mario had finally spoken his first words since the kidnapping and they were strong words condemning any further action that Adolfo might have taken.

"Does this mean that Angelo Chiarella can do as he pleases?"

Don Mario strained to get his words out. "Certainly not! But he must never be questioned about the children or about his connection to Generoso Spadaro."

⊢┼◆○◂┼◅

I could not believe my ears when I heard that a goat was missing from Don Leone's herd. I immediately thought of Roberto Borrelli, that bungling fool who had gotten me into the mess that led to my imprisonment in Asinara. Could he have been so dumb as to again confuse his herd with Don Leone's just a few months after returning from a prison term for the very same confusion? I felt a renewed anger towards Roberto and found myself wishing that he were put away for good so that he could not implicate innocent people in his idiotic exploits. Just then, I heard a knock on my door.

"Angelo Chiarella, open up. We are here to examine your herd."

It was the Carabinieri. I sprang up and went to the door. "What is it? What do you think I've done?"

It was the captain himself, Adolfo Liotta, with two other officers, calling on me to verify my guilt or innocence. They blustered into my home as though they had already found the evidence to accuse me of the theft of the missing goat. In my younger days, I would have thrown them out. Now, I exercised great restraint and understanding. After all, they had their work to do and they would soon see that I was innocent.

"We are looking for Don Leone's missing goat. Do you know of its whereabouts?" The captain glared at me as though I was hiding something.

"No, but you are welcome to look at my animals to satisfy yourself that it is not here."

"That was our intention in coming here. Stand aside." The three went swiftly through the house and out to the animal pen. They carefully examined every beast. From the amount of scrutiny, it seemed that they wanted to find something to accuse me of. Having found nothing, they left without saying a word or acknowledging my innocence. It was late and Giuseppe had been asleep. Gesuzza placed her arms around him protectively as the conversation had awakened him. Pietro stood quietly by, looking toward me as if to seek an answer as to why this was happening.

The following day, Gesuzza made an inquiry of her sister, Marianna, who was a chambermaid in the home of Count Leone and could easily determine the outcome of the incident.

"Marianna, what has happened to the goat that has been found missing from Leone's herd?"

"I don't know, but I'll find out."

That evening, Marianna came to our house to let us know that there was no missing goat at all and to warn me that, for some reason, the captain was trying to connect me to a crime. I was stunned. What did I do to anger the authorities? And what could I do to avoid their wrath? Marianna was in a position to provide the answer. Over the past several years, she had been the mistress of Don Leone and had secretly borne him a son. To protect Leone's reputation, Marianna was married to his groundskeeper prior to the birth of Leone's son. The marriage *was merely a convenient cover for the ongoing relationship between Marianna and Leone. Now she could influence Leone to come to my assistance. Surely the Carabiniere captain would listen to him.*

───

The young captain stood and greeted the older man as he arrived at his appointed hour. The ruggedness of Leone's casual dress impressed the uniformed Adolfo.

"Welcome, Don Leone, your presence here honors me. To what do I owe the privilege of your company?"

"I will come to the point quickly, so as to avoid taking up too much of your valuable time. I have come here on behalf of Angelo Chiarella. He is married to the sister of my personal chambermaid. She is very disturbed at the prospect that Angelo is being unduly pursued by the law for a crime that is unspecified. The crime I refer to is the theft of a goat from me that was never reported as stolen in the first place. Moreover, it is believed by many that the sentence that he just completed at Asinara was for a crime he did not commit. Is there a reason that you or others seek to punish this man?"

"No, Don Leone, we do not seek to blame Angelo for something he did not do. Surely you understand that when a crime is reported to us we must act quickly. As a matter of routine, we seek out those who are likely to be perpetrators of criminal acts by virtue of their past history. Angelo Chiarella was put away as an accessory to the theft of a goat from your very herd. As such, he is a probable suspect. We merely performed our duty."

"Forgive me, captain Liotta, but I must tell you that I believe there is something you are leaving out. The fervor of your inspection of the Chiarella home troubles me. Normally you yourself would not make a preliminary investigation for the loss of a goat. And, your disappointment at finding everything in order was noted. What is it that you are not telling me?

"Nothing. I am merely doing my duty to investigate crimes and uphold the law."

"Then you must treat Angelo Chiarella fairly."

"Yes, Count, you can be sure that I will."

Naturally, I was elated to know that a man of such great position had come to my rescue. I thought of how my mother-in-law had encouraged Marianna to create a friendship with Leone and how she was criticized for it by her husband and even by my own wife. Now there was tangible benefit to Marianna's family arising from the friendship. The fact of the sinfulness of the relationship between Marianna and Leone did not bother me at all. Those matters I left for Gesuzza to think about. I went happily about my business.

But Gesuzza was not satisfied. Beyond her disapproval of the illicit bond between her sister and Leone, she feared that all was still not right between the law and me, and that even the great Leone had limited influence in matters such as these.

"Angelo, what will we do if Adolfo continues to harass you? I can't stand even thinking about what it was like here without you. I don't know what I would do if you ever left me again."

"Gesuzza, for Christ's sake! Will you stop worrying about something that will never happen? The Count has spoken. He will not allow his word to be trifled with."

I wish that I could say that I was right. Three weeks later Adolfo was at my door again. This time it was a pig that Michele Morretti had lost and believed stolen. I didn't even own a pig at that time, but still the Carabinieri repeated their search with Captain Liotta at the head. I was considerably less tolerant by now and let them know it.

"Do you troopers have nothing else to do other than to intrude on the privacy of innocent people? Can't you see that I *don't even own a pig? How can you possibly suspect me?"*

I thought of reporting the incident to Leone, but my pride prevented me from bothering him over what seemed trivial. To be sure, I was concerned, but I had always relied upon myself to settle my own affairs and I felt that I could handle this as well. What I had failed to consider was my temper, which was growing steadily worse with each incident. Two more incursions into my family's privacy occurred, each over alleged thefts and each making it increasingly difficult to restrain my anger.

▷─┼─◆▷─◯─◁┼─◁

At last the exhausting heat was over. It was fall and the harvest began. There were grapes and olives to pick and most of the fruits that were normally harvested later in the year were ready now, because of the hot summer. The days for all of us were very long. Gesuzza, Pietro, Giuseppe and I were up with the first light of day and went to sleep only after the sun had set. There was barely time set aside for noonday meals, most of which came from the fruit trees we were harvesting. I felt sorry for the young Giuseppe, who struggled to use his small, deformed hand to pick fruit. I estimated that it would take us another month to bring in the remainder of the crops and deliver the landlord's share to his warehouse. Despite the unseasonable heat of the growing season, we had an abundant crop and expected to have enough wine, olive oil and fruit to see us through to the next year. We could also sell enough of our crops to obtain the cash we would need to purchase the other necessities of life. Each evening, as the day drew to a close, the boys and I made our way home before the darkness closed in on us. Gesuzza would leave earlier so that she could prepare the evening meal.

Darkness had come by the time Angelo got home with his two boys. The boys cleaned up for dinner while Angelo looked after the animals. Then he, too, washed and joined the others. There was pasta made with olive oil and garlic. There was some broccoli, too, and some of Gesuzza's wine to wash it down. The four of them were dogged at the end of a long day and looked forward to laying their heads to rest in their beds. Angelo and Gesuzza talked about their work while the boys prepared for bed.

"The work is too great for just the four of us. We will need to ask the Paone's for help. Their relatives from Maidu are young and strong and can stay with us for the rest of harvest. I have used them before and they have been a Godsend." Though Gesuzza had made such arrangements during Angelo's absence, she now deferred to him in her tone, inferring that she was asking for his permission to make arrangements for help with the harvest. They would be relieved of the enormous burden of the following weeks, but they would also have to share their bounty.

"Yes, I agree that it is beyond the four of us to handle all the work without help. Make your usual deal with them and get them here as soon as possible."

Just then, there was a knock on their door. It was Adolfo Liotta and his two Carabinieri troopers. They had come on one of their forays, intruding on the calm that Angelo and Gesuzza had come to enjoy at the end of their exhausting days. As Gesuzza opened the door, Adolfo swung it open and entered the house gruffly.

"Bring a lantern to the back," he said to Angelo.

"What is it? What is it this time?"

"There is a pig missing, once again. I want to check your animals."

Angelo was very tired and it became evident that he was losing his patience. "Captain Liotta, why are you calling on me at this late hour? My children are asleep and my wife and I are about to put our heads down to rest. I have done nothing. You have been here several times in the past and found nothing. What must I do to prove to you that I am innocent?"

"What do you mean innocent? You are a convicted felon."

"Now, look here, Captain, what right have you to say that? I was the unfortunate victim of a gross injustice. I did not steal anything. Yet, I was taken away from my family for nine years. I paid a debt to society that I did not owe; yet, here I am being persecuted for heaven knows why." Angelo stood up and walked over to the Captain. He towered over him. His hands on his hips, he shouted, "Get out! You have no right to be here."

Gesuzza froze, her face ashen and showing fright. Tears welled up in her eyes. Adolfo looked surprised, his face turning beet red. The others gripped their weapons and awaited their leader's command. Just then, Giuseppe entered the room, rubbing his eyes and calling out, "What is it, ma? What's happening? Are we going to jail?" He began to cry and ran to his mother. Pietro appeared as well and peered at the three uniformed men, looking also to his father for direction.

Giuseppe's innocent intrusion completely altered the aura of confrontation and deflated the conflict. Adolfo stepped back and waved his arm in a downward sweep, signaling his men to put away their weapons. Despite the hatred that he had built for Angelo, he could not bring himself to commit a further act of recrimination in front of his family.

"Prepare yourself, Angelo, we will be back and next time we will not be so generous." Adolfo was goading him and Angelo knew it. Try as he might, Adolfo was unable to provoke Angelo any further. What had become a fierce, uncontrollable hatred of Adolfo now simmered as the three men made their exit.

I never felt more devastated than at that moment. My family had witnessed the law closing in on me for whatever reason they chose. The boys had been frightened out of a sound sleep and had seen me come to the brink of breaking the law. Would that change their opinion of me as a respectable person? What had I done to deserve this persecution? What could I do about it? If I didn't act now, I would run the risk of being blamed again for a crime I did not commit. I put my pride aside and asked Gesuzza to arrange a meeting for me with Leone. She was relieved that I had finally decided to act sensibly. But, the following day, we learned that Leone had been summoned to Turin. He was not expected back for two weeks.

Two days later, the Paone's showed up, three boys all under the age of fifteen. They greeted us in the field as we worked the harvest. It was a moment of celebration and joy. Gesuzza knew each of them by name. Pietro and Giuseppe smiled broadly during this brief respite and had their moment of reunion with the Paone boys.

"It's about time you loafers got here. Did you hope we would finish before you arrived?"

"Look here, Pietro, just because you're so tall, don't think for a moment that I'll take your crap. I can run circles around you in the vineyard."

"Oh, yeah, well how many bins of fruit can you pick in a day?"

"Boys, boys, what will I ever do with you? Will we have no peace now that you've arrived?" It was great, seeing Gesuzza laugh and put on her stern mother act for them. We laughed and the boys played for a few short moments before we resumed our work, now assisted by the Paone boys. By late afternoon, we

had made such progress that I decided to go up to the house to check on the animals. To my amazement and anger, I spotted a Carabiniere guard posted on the road outside our front door. He was younger than the others and bore no evidence of military tenure or campaign badges on his uniform.

"What the hell are you doing here? Who sent you?"

"Are you Angelo?"

"Yes, I am. Why are you here?"

"I merely take orders and carry them out as instructed. I have been told to keep an eye out for what may be going on here."

"What!?! You get out of here! Do you understand?"

"Who do you think you are? You can't order a Carabiniere around like that."

Suddenly, I felt myself pushing the trooper, as if to prove that I meant what I said. I must have caught him off guard, for he lost his balance and fell. As he rose, he seemed to be clutching at his side arm. I did not wait to find out. I removed his pistol from its holster and pulled the rifle off the man's shoulder. I removed the bolt and swung the rifle at him, bloodying his head and rendering one of his arms useless. I held on to the pistol as the soldier fled, looking back at me and shouting.

"Now we have you, you son-of-a-bitch. You've broken the law in front of all these people and proven that you are a criminal."

It was then that I first realized that a group of the townspeople had gathered and listened and watched as I humiliated the young trooper. There was no doubt that I had committed a crime this time and would soon have Captain Liotta at my door with his whole troop. Then, out of nowhere I heard Gesuzza's voice.

"Angelo! What have you done?" She was returning at the end of the day with our sons and the three Paone boys and saw the crowd in the street outside of our house. We quickly went into the house so we could speak privately.

"Gesuzza, I need to get away. This is the moment that Liotta has been waiting for. I have no doubt he'll be here the moment that trooper returns to the barracks."

She looked at me with tears streaming down her cheeks. Then, she said the only thing she could. "Oh, Angelo, please hurry. The Carabinieri will be here at any moment. But, where will you go to be out of their reach? And how will I know that you're all right?"

"Remember, my dear, I grew up in the mountains not far from here. They will never find me there. I have many friends in those mountains and they will let you know where I am and lead you to me. Don't be frightened, and don't let them discourage you."

One of my neighbors, who saw the scuffle and knew what I had been up against all along, took pity and gave me a horse. I mounted and galloped away. As I reached the top of the mountain overlooking Gagliano, I looked back. Everything looked tiny, but I thought I could make out the street that my house was on. There were lanterns burning up and down the street, probably attached to the saddles of the mounted Carabinieri who were sent to find me. I hated them terribly. Then, my thoughts were of my family and of how they would survive this new ordeal. I had brought them pain and misery enough for a lifetime before now. As I thought of my poor young sons and my wife, I dismounted and fell to the ground in a crouch. I sobbed as I never had before.

Chapter 16

Escape

Angelo's escape to the mountains was virtually effortless. In a sense, it was a return home to the landscape that weaned him to manhood. While the Carabinieri assembled a troop and rounded up a team of bloodhounds, Angelo sped through a field of wild fennel on his way to his first stop, San Gimigliano, where his brother Constantino lived in their ancestral home. The powerful aroma of the fennel would throw off his scent and render the dogs useless. His brother would provision him for the hideaway he would have to locate and make his home. Along the way, there were fruits and vegetables in full season and the farmers understood as Angelo helped himself. The sparse inhabitants of the rugged hills took pity and even brought him prepared foods and wine. They commiserated with him, somehow knowing that he was the man that had been so wronged by the law. A fortuitous light rain on the second day of his escape helped to blend his tracks with the soil and, after a short search, the Carabinieri gave up the hunt and returned to Gagliano. The escape was complete.

It was not long before Angelo became less cavalier about his fate as an outlaw. As fall faded into winter, the crops had been collected and there were no more fruit trees and vines to visit for sustenance. The local peasants seemed not to remember that Angelo roamed the hills outside their villages, in constant need of their help. In order to bring down the wild deer and rabbits, he would need a rifle and ammunition. These he obtained one night when he broke into the general store in Cropani and stole them. He was sighted by the town baker, up in the middle of the night kneading dough for his next day's bread. Word spread throughout the area and Angelo quickly became persona non grata. There were other break-ins, this time in the neighboring town of Sersale. Angelo was blamed for them all, though in only one incident was he actually involved. That was the theft of a heavy jacket to warm him from the intense cold of the Calabrian mountains in the middle of winter. He had asked Constantino to steer clear of him and not try to help him, lest he lead the Carabinieri to his hideout. The one thing he required of Constantino was to get word to Gesuzza as to how she could rendezvous with him.

It was only a month since I made my escape, but I had never before felt this lonely and so in need of my family. My flight from the law had been successful, but I still feared the return of the Carabinieri or perhaps even their spies, sent to spot me on a visit to Gimigliano, to Constantino's house. From there they could follow me back to my hideout and get word to Adolfo Liotta of my whereabouts. Though it was never confirmed, I had heard that the Carabinieri offered a reward for information that would lead them to me. Nevertheless, my need to see Gesuzza compelled me to pay a visit to Constantino and ask him to bring Gesuzza to me. I longed to see the boys as well, but the risk was too great that they would be spotted by the police. Besides, they would be needed at home to work the fields.

It was not long after Angelo escaped that Adolfo called on Gesuzza to threaten her with aiding an escaped criminal and thus intimidate her into revealing Angelo's whereabouts.

"I suppose you know that you can be charged with committing a crime for helping Angelo to escape." Adolfo sneered at Gesuzza with beady dark eyes that blared intensely. He was surprised, as a composed Gesuzza gave her fiery retort.

"Is this the brave Carabiniere captain carrying out his orders to put fear into the hearts of the women and children of Gagliano? Have you no better mission to accomplish? No, IL Capitano, you do not frighten me. I have no knowledge of my husband's whereabouts. Nor did I assist him in his escape. Apparently, he did not need help. From what I hear, he did quite well on his own."

Adolfo was humbled and knew that there was little he could do to harass Gesuzza further without bringing the wrath of the townspeople on him. Instead, he changed his approach and appealed to her fear of facing the future without Angelo.

"What will you do for support now that Angelo is gone? Eventually we'll capture him and he'll be back in prison for a long time. If you tell us where he is, you'll be given assistance by the government for any time that he is in prison."

Gesuzza held back her fury and responded coolly. "I

have already told you that I don't know where he is. Now, please leave. I need to get back to my work."

The wind blew wildly in the overcast Calabrian hills as the new season approached. I lifted the collar of my wool jacket and watched as the two figures in the distance approached. From my perch high above the ascending field, I could see that they were not being followed. It had been several weeks since I left Gesuzza with a crop to harvest, but by now it was done and at this moment she climbed the slope that separated us, with Constantino at her side. When they were but a half-mile away, the two waved at one another and my brother turned toward home. Gesuzza made the last of the trip alone, carrying food that she had prepared for me. My heart broke for this poor, frail woman who had been so tortured by my misfortunes. I had all that I could do to avoid showing my feelings. To do so might weaken Gesuzza's resolve to survive this mess I had unwittingly thrust on her.

"Gesuzza, *cara*, come to me. It's been so long and I've missed you."

"Oh, Angelo, are you all right? I've worried so about you."

The two held one another for a long time, and then Angelo brought her into the abandoned shack that he had been using for shelter. It contained an old stone fireplace, but there was no fire for fear of discovery. There was a bed made from fragments of wool cloth, dried leaves and assorted objects that Angelo had found scattered about. Despite the cold, the enclosure was sufficiently dry and sheltered and was lit by a single candle that had been burning all afternoon and evening.

"Will you live here now, Angelo?"

"No. I wish I could, but a search party would be sure to look here. I have found a stand of thick trees surrounding a rock area large enough for me to build myself a safe hideout. It is near here, but so rugged that no one is likely to ever find me."

"How long will you stay here?"

"As long as necessary. I am hoping that when Leone hears of how I am being persecuted, he will help me to clear myself."

Gesuzza looked up to him. Her face was pained, her lips drawn tight.

"What is it, Gesuzza? Tell me!"

"Oh, Angelo, I went to Leone when he returned from his trip. At first, he seemed infuriated at the thought that his word had been disregarded and that you continued to be blamed for every crime committed in Gagliano. Then, he heard that the young soldier that you struck was hospitalized and might never again use his arm. His anger cooled and he seemed to lose interest in you. Marianna has brought your situation up to him several times, but he no longer feels as he once did about your innocence."

Angelo shouted angrily, "Damn the rich! They pretend to care and then they go back to their comfortable lives and throw us to the dogs. Well, we don't need him, Gesuzza, you'll see. We'll solve this without his help."

But they both knew that Leone was their only chance at challenging the new establishment. They sat on the seats that Angelo had constructed from fragments of fallen limbs. Gesuzza served her homemade bread, cheese and salami. Afterward, they sat quietly and motionless in one another's arms. Together, they drank the new wine of the vintage. Finally, they went to bed and made love, knowing that their lives were hopelessly damaged.

For another year, Gesuzza and Angelo met in their rendezvous in the Apennines high above Gagliano. The Carabinieri occasionally combed the area in the hope of finding a clue left carelessly by one of Angelo's visitors, or even by Angelo himself. But Gesuzza had worked out a ruse to avoid being spotted. She would feign illness, remaining indoors for two days. In the middle of the second night, she would steal away for the four-hour journey by mount, to where Angelo now lived beneath the stars and among the wild animals. The moonlit roads and meadows were well enough defined that her journey would be swift and relatively safe. If she were spotted, it would be by hill peasants, who were unlikely to give her away. Back in Gagliano, the police would continue to stalk her house, thinking that she was still in bed, nursing her illness. After a two-day visit with Angelo, Gesuzza would reverse the process. She would make her way back to Gagliano, sight unseen, and emerge the following day, completely recovered from her "illness."

><+●>-○-<●+<

I was afraid that Gesuzza would never return after a bear came into my camp looking for food while she was here. I was able to fight him off, but Gesuzza was so terrified that I had to take her back to within a few miles of Gagliano that day. But now, as the first light of morning shone, I could see her form on the hillside, making her way towards me, sidesaddle on her horse. I thanked heaven that she was there and hoped that she had overcome her fear of being attacked by the wild animals in the forest around us.

"Gesuzza! You're here! Will you stay?"

"Yes, of course I'll stay. I have faced danger before and the bears are not going to keep me away."

Over the course of her visit, she seemed a bit cool and distracted. I did not think much of it, but as she was preparing to leave on the second night, I decided to question her. Something was wrong and I had to find out what it was.

"Is something wrong, Gesuzza? Are the boys all right?"

From the moment she looked up at me to respond, I knew there was something she had wanted to tell me, but feared my reaction. "What is it, Gesuzza?" I said sternly.

"I'm with child."

The words burned in my brain. With all of the troubles that had descended on us since my conviction, by what right did she now see fit to become pregnant? How could she have allowed this to happen? Who was going to support this new being? I knew that my thinking was wrong, but emotion took over and I could not control my anger.

"How did this happen? Did you not take precaution to avoid this?"

"Yes, of course I tried to prevent this from happening. But, since it has, Angelo, let's make the best of it. We can name the child after your father: Raffaele, if it's a boy and Raffaela if it's a girl."

"And how will we feed this new child?"

"Don't worry, we'll find a way."

I raged at her acceptance of this new disaster. "You became pregnant, now you solve the problem or you can mangia catzo." Appalled at my invoking language that was not befitting her, Gesuzza climbed onto her horse and began to ride away. My rage continued, and I shouted after her, "Gesuzza, you bring that baby to the wheel as soon as it's born. Let the nuns raise it." I stood there and watched as Gesuzza continued her trek down the mountain. She was hunched over and appeared to be crying. I felt the urge to go after her and ask her forgiveness, but my anger was slow to ebb and I was unable to move or speak.

As Gesuzza rode off into the night, she could not contain the stream of tears that rolled down her cheeks. Surely, she had not tried to become pregnant. She washed herself thoroughly each time after having sex. That was all she could do. It had worked until now. She thought of how unfair Angelo had been to her. Perhaps if she had had the convenience of her home in which to douche, the pregnancy would never have happened. What's more, didn't he partake in the act that impregnated her? And how could he love her and want no part of this pregnancy? Then, her thoughts turned to the dreaded wheel to which she would take the new infant. All of her life, she had seen others bring their unintended offspring to this refuge for the unwanted. Now she had to face the torment of handing over her own child. It was too unbearable to contemplate. There were still months ahead before the child would be born and she would think about it then. After all, she might not even be able to carry the child to term at her age. She would be 39 years old when the baby was born, an age that, in this time and place, was far too old to be having children.

Chapter 17

Convicted

It is an overcast morning in Catanzaro as the three Carabinieri ride up the cobbled street to the jail where holding cells contain enough prisoners to fill the calendar of the honorable justice Mario Martinez for a week. The three have ridden through the night with their prey tied across the saddle of a fourth mount. They are tired and bear the ugly bruises they have received from their prisoner in the process of his capture. Their mission accomplished, they dismount and, while the lieutenant handles the paperwork with the jailer, the others allow their prisoner to slip off his horse and stand erect. Though he towers over his captors, he is no threat to them. His arms and wrists are tied securely and he is still barely awake. An elderly woman in black garb is permitted to approach him with a flask of water, which she holds to his face so that he is able to drink. "The Lord be with you," she says, as she is lead away.

"Here we are, Angelo, you can stop babbling now and answer for your crimes to the Criminal Court." The lieutenant winces from the broken arm inflicted on him by Angelo in the scuffle to apprehend him.

"Good riddance, Angelo. I hope you get what you have coming." The trooper whose ear was severed in the fracas peers menacingly at Angelo.

It's funny, but I never thought I had anything 'coming to me' throughout this ordeal. I always believed in my innocence and have mistrusted the authorities. Why else would I have fought them? Should I have agreed with them when they sent me to prison for trying to help my neighbor? Should I have allowed them to push themselves into my home over and over until they could fabricate yet another charge against me? No, I do not accept that I have any punishment coming that I deserve.

"This way." The jailer pointed to the entrance gate of the jail and pushed me towards it. He is a squat man with a bald head and wears a leather apron and studded leather cuffs that reach half way to his elbows. Were I untied and on an equal footing, he might not be so brave. Inside, I am lead to a cell, where I am finally untied and left to wonder if they will provide food and drink. I am again in the prison atmosphere and overcome with desperation. I have thoughts of escape. What have I to lose? Then, my thoughts turn to suicide. If I kill myself, no one will ever believe that my death was self-inflicted and my family will not be disgraced. Only a few guards and my Carabinieri captors even know that I'm here. They will want to quietly dispose of my body so there is no investigation. Gesuzza will come to our mountain rendezvous and wonder if I simply left, intending to contact her from my new hideout. Or maybe

she would think that a bear killed me and that a hunter or a trapper would one day discover my remains. I came back to my senses and decided that suicide, unfortunately, was not possible for me.

"Angelo Chiarella, you will be tried before the magistrate of the court tomorrow morning at ten o'clock. Your trial is being expedited because you are considered dangerous and we want you out of our jail. You will remain inside your cell for the remainder of your time here." *The stocky jailer let me know that I should expect to be convicted in the morning. Thankfully, he sent me a pan of pasta faggiole to eat and some fresh water to drink, the first since the old woman took pity on me out on the street.*

"Angelo Antonio Chiarella, you are called before the bar of justice to answer for your crimes. You are accused of an attack upon several Carabinieri, one in Gagliano and three high in the hills where you have been hiding from the law. Moreover, you have attacked citizens of Cropani and Sersale and stolen from them as well. What have you to say for yourself?" The robed prosecutor holds a record book from which he reads, occasionally looking up to stare at Angelo. Looking down from his perch above the others in the courtroom is Justice Mario Martinez. He is menacingly quiet and grim.

This morning, they chained my arms and wrists before leading me to the defendant's box. Since I have neither time to arrange for a defense nor money to hire a lawyer to represent me, I must defend myself. There is, of course, no hope. In their view, it is quite clear and simple. What possible excuse can I have for fighting the Carabinieri? And what excuse can I give for hurting innocent people in the two communities nearest my hiding place? I respond as best I can and hope that the testimony of an innocent man is heard and understood.

"Please understand that I was sent to prison for nine years simply because I assisted a neighbor in need of help. I did not contribute to any crime, nor was there any deliberate crime committed. Yet, my neighbor and I were both convicted of stealing and sent to prison for nine years. When I returned home, I tried to resume my life as a law-abiding citizen. The law hounded me as though I was a criminal. They came to my home and intruded on my family, searching for evidence that was not there. When I objected, they ignored my plea, placing a guard outside my home with instructions to find an infraction of the law so that I could be prosecuted. I eventually lost patience and struck out at the people who were trying to place blame on me for crimes I did not commit. I also fought the men who were sent to capture me and bring me here to answer for crimes of which I am innocent. I did not attack any person in Cropani and Sersale. My one desperate act was to take a jacket from a merchant in Cropani so that I would not freeze through the winter in the outdoors. Your honor, I am an innocent man and ask that I be cleared of the charges against me."

After a brief silence, the prosecutor stands and declares, "Your honor, the defendant has just admitted to several of the crimes he is accused of. He has admitted to the beatings of the Carabinieri and to the theft of a jacket. The people ask for a conviction of this man and a sentence of appropriate duration."

The judge responds to the prosecutor's plea, "Angelo Antonio Chiarella, do you have anything further to say in your defense?"

"No, your honor."

"Then, by the power vested in me by the Kingdom of Italy and the Province of Catanzaro, I hereby pronounce you guilty as charged of the crimes of stealing and using force to prevent the lawful authorities from performing their duty. Your punishment shall be imprisonment at hard labor for a period of twenty years. However, in recognition of the hardships that you have experienced at the hands of the law, your sentence is hereby reduced to nine years, to be served beginning immediately at the prison in Asinara."

Angelo stands quietly staring at the judge. Tears stream down his face and stain the collar of his shirt. Though there is no surprise in the outcome of the trial, it is now a reality. He knows that the years ahead will be far worse than his previous sentence. This time he is actually guilty and the crimes involve the beating of four of the Carabinieri. He will be singled out and treated to every possible hardship that the law can mete out. For all practical purposes, his life is over.

As I stand here, the reality of what is happening begins to sink in. I think not of myself but of my poor, dear Gesuzza and of my boys. I will probably never see them again. They will have to face life without me. Gesuzza will deliver our baby and will send it off for adoption. Pietro will take command of the family and be responsible for his mother and brother. Whatever hope he had of ever being youthful is forever gone. And Giuseppe, that high–spirited youngster, will have to be molded by his brother and mother. I hope they can handle him and that he stays out of trouble. I think of how they will even learn of my conviction and of my return to Asinara.

"Your honor, will my family know what has happened to me?"

"Don't worry, Angelo, they'll be told."

Chapter 18

Reunion

Mario Vartone has lived in New York for all of the nine years he has been in America. Arriving with his bride a few short weeks after their wedding, he was able to find a place to live in the Mulberry District and locate a job at the wholesale produce market on the lower west side. Rosa bore two children within a span of three years and also worked as a clerk in a local grocery store catering mostly to immigrant Italians. The couple's drive to succeed caused them to scrimp and save to the point of depriving themselves of all but the bare essentials of life. Now they observe the arrival of Rosa's dear friend Marianna, a lady of means from their hometown in Italy, who has earned her fortune as mistress to a wealthy Italian nobleman.

"Marianna, I am very pleased to meet you. Rosa has told me of the many happy moments she shared with you in Italy."

"Thank you, Mario. Your wife is one of my dearest friends. It is a wonderful coincidence that you know my love, Lorenzo Fusco. I understand that the two of you worked together at a market of some sort."

"Yes, when Lorenzo first arrived in New York, we worked side by side at the wholesale produce market. There were a few Italians there and we all became good friends. Lorenzo was the successful one of us, though. He never lived in this damned Mulberry district. He speaks English really well and was able to talk with the American bosses. Later on, he purchased a farm and grows Italian vegetables, which he now sells to the wholesalers we all work for."

"Have you been to his farm?"

"Yes, I worked on a wagon that we used to pick up produce from his farm. I got to spend some time there while we loaded up for the return trip. He is doing very well. He lives in a beautiful house and has a crew of men who do the planting and harvesting."

"And?" Marianna looked at him obliquely, alluding to the woman who lives with Lorenzo.

"Yes, Marianna, it's true. He lives with an American woman who cooks and cleans for him. They say she taught him to speak and read English and that he consults her on every move he makes in his business."

Marianna is suddenly unable to contain herself. "That whore! Lorenzo is my man and I aim to take him back. I did what was required of me back in Italy, but I never loved anyone but him." Then, eyes blazing, she sits back in her chair, covers her face with her hands and mumbles regrets for her outburst and for the impression she has made on her friends.

"Forgive me, Rosa, I am more angry with myself than with him. These last five or six years have been hard on me. I'm trying to put my life back together and I'm hoping that Lorenzo becomes part of it."

"Marianna, don't be angry with them. Lorenzo had no reason to believe he would ever see you again, and his woman friend has probably never heard your name."

The following morning, Mario borrows a buggy from a friend and heads for Lorenzo's farm with Rosa and Marianna, having passed by the Victoria Hotel to pick up Marianna. It is a sunny morning and the Brooklyn and Queens countryside is alive with color from the green hills and the late summer crops that they pass along their way. As they proceed, the roads narrow and become treacherous with ruts made by wagon wheels. There are some holes deep enough to require Mario to disembark from the carriage and lead the horse around them. Marianna does not seem to notice the poor road surface. She gazes instead, at the knolls and the fields. She is awed by the fruit hanging from trees and other crops reaching skyward from the earth.

"This is the America that is spoken of by the returning immigrants in Italy. It is truly beautiful."

"Yes, Marianna, but land is not available to poor Italians who save their pennies for the day they can afford to purchase a plot of land. Only those who agree to change their religion to one of the Protestant faiths are permitted to purchase land."

"Well, then, why don't they do what is required of them?" Marianna shows the effect of her upbringing by the ever-practical Stella. She receives no response from either Rosa or Mario.

Two hours later, they arrive at Lorenzo's farm. It is Sunday and all is quiet. As they roll up to the front of the house, Kathleen appears at the door.

"May I help you?"

"We are here to see Lorenzo."

"And who may I say is calling?"

"It is Mario and Rosa Vartone and a friend."

"Does he know you?"

Marianna can no longer hold back. She speaks in Italian. "Will you please tell him that Marianna Soluri is here to see him?"

"I'm sorry madam, but I don't speak Italian." She looks at Mario. "Will you interpret for us?" But it is not necessary for Mario to speak. By now, Lorenzo is at the door, a look of shock and disbelief on his face.

"Marianna! Good Lord, you're here!"

"May we come in?"

"Yes. Please come this way."

For the Vartones, it is their first time in a home of this quality. They stare and admire the surroundings openly. The aroma of a fruit pie baking in the oven and the crisp, clean air permeating the house is a stark contrast to the atmosphere of New York and especially Mulberry Street. Marianna's thoughts are more of curiosity about how Lorenzo has ordered his life in the new country than the sight of trappings so familiar to her new station in life. Kathleen stands by questioningly as Lorenzo escorts his guests to an area of the room containing several sturdy chairs.

"Will you have a drink? Anisette? Coffee?"

Mario speaks. "We have traveled a good part of the morning. Perhaps the ladies would like to freshen up."

"Ah, yes, this way please." Lorenzo takes them to the outhouse facility a short distance from the house.

When all are settled in their chairs, the obvious discomfort with discussing the subject that Marianna is here to talk about becomes apparent. In deference to Marianna, the conversation is conducted in Italian, and after twenty minutes of catching up on the events of the last several years in Gagliano, Lorenzo addresses Marianna.

"Where are you staying?"

"At the Victoria Hotel in Manhattan."

"Can you stay here for a few days?"

"Yes, I'd like that." Lorenzo looks up at Kathleen, whose puzzled look has not changed. She seems to understand the offer that has just been accepted and gives an inconspicuous nod that signals her consent.

"Very well, then, we'll send for your things at the hotel. You can use the guest bedroom."

"I'll get your things for you, Marianna, if you can arrange to settle with the hotel."

Marianna gives Mario more than a sufficient amount of money to check her out of the hotel and the five continue their conversation for another hour, during which time Kathleen serves lunch. Following the meal, the Vartones leave Marianna behind and begin their return trip to Manhattan.

"We'll see you all in a few days when we return with Marianna's trunk."

As they get on their way, Rosa says, "How could Lorenzo do that? He must know that Marianna is here to take him away from Kathleen and who knows what he has told Kathleen about his relationship with Marianna. I don't understand him."

Mario has the last word on the subject. "Don't worry yourself over what other people do. They'll work it out."

Kathleen takes Marianna upstairs to the guest room and gives her clothing of her own that Marianna will need for the next few days while they await the Vartones return. Marianna is shorter than Kathleen, but they are otherwise the same size. The clothes will be a bit long, but they will fit. She looks around the room cynically, remembering the days in her younger life when she and Lorenzo enjoyed one another's body on a straw mattress. Here she will sleep in a comfortable bed in the house of her former lover, while he sleeps in the room across the hall with another woman.

Downstairs in the kitchen, Kathleen encounters Lorenzo. "Who is this woman to you, Lorenzo?"

"She is the woman I have told you about. She remained with Count Leone despite my efforts to free her from him. I was beaten senseless by Leone's thugs and put on a ship bound for the U.S. Thankfully, I received the money he had offered to give me for leaving Italy. It is how I got my start here."

"Why did you ask her to stay? Do you love her still?"

"My darling, I must be honest. I don't know how I feel. I just know that I want her to stay here so that I can find out."

"Lorenzo, I'm afraid."

"Don't be, my dear. We must all face the truth about who we are and how we will live our time on earth. Sometimes it requires us to be brave."

Just then, Marianna walks into the kitchen. Unable to converse directly with Kathleen, she directs her comments at Lorenzo. "May I assist with preparing dinner?"

"Certainly. I will remain here to see that the two of you are able to communicate." Lorenzo navigates between the two languages. "Kathleen, Marianna wants to help you to prepare dinner." Good-naturedly, Kathleen looks at Marianna and smiles. She has decided to be brave.

Within two weeks, Kathleen has learned some more Italian and Marianna learns some English. They occasionally address one another without the assistance of Lorenzo, but they are grateful when he is there to translate. Marianna's trunks arrive after a few days, and she sleeps her nights in the guest room while Lorenzo and Kathleen sleep across the hall. But, as each day passes, Kathleen sees on Marianna's face, more and more, the longing to be with Lorenzo. It is only a matter of time until Marianna can no longer contain herself. Kathleen searches Lorenzo's face for an indication of his feelings and imagines that she detects in him, a yearning for Marianna. But, she will not question him. He has promised to take Marianna to an annual Italian festa, in the hamlet of Hempstead the following week. When they return home from that event, she will know for herself if Lorenzo's love for her is stronger than his feelings for Marianna.

Lorenzo comes out the front door and notices Kathleen posting a letter with the mail carrier. "What is it? Are you sending a letter?"

"Yes, it's a letter to a friend I haven't heard from in a long time."

"Darling, I hope you don't mind my taking Marianna to the festival in Hempstead. It's been a while since she has been in Italy and this is an opportunity for her to be among Italians and enjoy the food and festivities."

"Lorenzo, I must tell you that I don't like your being alone with that woman, but I won't fuss or try to stop you. As you have said, '…we must all face the truth…' Hopefully, you'll do that soon."

By the end of the 19th century, the village of Hempstead is already two hundred and fifty years old, having been settled by Scottish and English settlers in the mid seventeenth century. Situated four miles north of the ocean beaches of Long Island, the soil is thick and rich and lends itself well to farming. The early settlers farmed the land surrounding the settlement for tobacco, corn, wheat and barley. Over time, the farms grew large, requiring the use of hired labor. The waves of Italian immigrants arriving in New York in the last two decades of the nineteenth century were ideally suited. They were experienced farm laborers and they would work for low wages. Hempstead farmers welcomed them, so long as they worked hard and kept to themselves. As more and more Italians populated the east end of the town, it became an enclave and a society unto itself, with all of the traditions and customs of the old country. Once a year, a three-day festival is held in honor of the Madonna of Mount Carmel. The music, dancing, eating and drinking lures Italians from all over the area.

"Are you ready to go, Marianna?" Lorenzo eagerly awaits her in his carriage at the front door. Cleanly shaven and dressed in fine trousers and fresh linen shirt, he is as handsome as ever. She appears, dressed in a plain white summer dress with short sleeves and narrow skirt. Her dress clings to her and shows the sultry silhouette of her body. Her hair is combed carefully to the sides of her face and back, causing her eyes to appear larger than he has ever seen. She wears a white cap, creating a look of affluence that he privately fears may be out of place for the occasion. He drinks in the sight of her and says nothing. Kathleen is at the door as they pull away in the carriage. She does not speak, nor does her bland facial expression betray her inner thoughts.

The height of the day is spent as Lorenzo and Marianna make their way to Hempstead. The sun will be setting as they arrive, and the festival will have begun. For a time, they are without conversation. Then, Marianna speaks. "Lorenzo, I have thought of you all these years that we have been apart."

"And why is that? Didn't Leone keep you happy?" The sharp jab reveals years of submerged anxiety and painful memories. It makes its point with Marianna.

"There was no love between me and Leone, merely a business arrangement that has worked out rather well for me. It was my mother's idea and it succeeded just as she predicted it would."

"Then you must be happy."

"No, Lorenzo, I will never be happy as long as you are with someone else."

"And, I suppose that you want me to dispose of Kathleen now that you've shown up on my doorstep."

"Don't be cruel, Lorenzo. You must forgive me for what I have done to you. It was never my intention to hurt you."

"But, of course you did. I understand that, in addition to being with him, you have had his son."

"Yes, and that is how I was able to achieve my status in life. I am now independent of anyone, including Leone. I don't ever have to see him again if I don't wish to."

"And do you wish to?"

"No, Lorenzo, I wish only to be with you and no one else."

The carriage arrives at the outskirts of town and it is

no longer appropriate to discuss the subject. Lorenzo finds a safe place to leave his rig and the two walk the last fifty yards to the edge of the festival grounds. Already, their nostrils are filled with the aroma of food being cooked all around them. They are aware of being hungry and thirsty for the first time since they left the farm. This is their kind of food, the bowls of pasta with red sauce, the pizza with cheese and anchovy, the sausage and peppers. And, space permitting, a delicious dessert is theirs for the asking. Marianna is amazed at the number of acknowledgements that Lorenzo receives from dozens of people on both sides of the counters as they make their way from one exhibit to another.

"Who are they, Lorenzo?"

"Mostly, they are people who work for me at some time of the year, especially at harvest time. Some have steady jobs, but work for me in their spare time so they can have that special thing they want, like money to buy a pig for roasting around the holidays. Some are saving to put their children in private school. Others want simply to be able to send a few dollars to their relatives in Italy."

"Lorenzo, do you recall how different our lives were in Calabria years ago?" Marianna has struck a sentimental note that touches Lorenzo. He looks admiringly at her and places his arm around her shoulder. It is their first genuine touch since Marianna has come to America. There they stand as a couple of considerable means in the midst of a people still struggling for achievement. As they look at those around them, they can identify with their past life, but they can also measure the success that they have achieved. Marianna continues. "We have paid our price, but we have risen above the limits that were set for us before we were even born.

The rest of the evening is magical. They hold one another as they walk through the crowded street and talk with vendors and patrons. They are amused by some of the stories they hear and saddened by others. The procession of the Lady of Mount Carmel is at last begun and the music and fireworks begin in earnest. As the statue passes them, her long dress flowing to within reach of the crowd, first Lorenzo and then Marianna each pin a ten dollar note to the hem of the Madonna's gown. The crowd acknowledges their generosity with screams of delight and gestures of praise. They are eventually exhausted from the hours of walking and standing, and decide to call it a night. They walk, hand in hand, to where they had left the carriage and, as they climb in, they experience a swarm of pleasure from being off their feet. As they swing onto the dark road lit only by a large, full moon, they overcome the cool night air by placing a blanket around them. In a flash, their bodies are touching. Lorenzo holds the reins steady as the carriage races through the night, but Marianna places her arms around his waist and puts her head on his chest. Finally, Lorenzo cannot resist any longer. He pulls the carriage off the road and brings it to a stop behind a large elm tree. His hands are now free and he throws them around Marianna as he brings their faces together in a deep kiss. "Marianna, Marianna. I love you. I must have you." His hands pull at her clothing. Marianna is in a confused state. What will Lorenzo think of her if she gives in to him so quickly and without some effort to resist? Is this the moment that she has waited for these many years they have been apart? Will she lose him if she does not respond to his lust? Finally, she assists by removing her clothing, being careful to remain under the blanket. By now, Lorenzo has removed his clothing as well and is on top of her. The evening has served as an aphrodisiac for both of them and they waste no time in coming together as man and woman. As he plunges forward into her, she feels the release of the years of longing for him. Her cry is almost a scream. "Lorenzo! I love you! I love you!" As he climaxes, he calls out, "Marianna! Marianna!"

An hour later, they enter the farmhouse and are at once aware of a looming change. There is no light to welcome them home in the dark and there is no greeting from Kathleen. The door needs to be unlocked. The bolt between its sections is tightly secured. As they enter and light some of the lamps inside, Lorenzo spots a note pinned to the wall alongside the stairs leading to the second floor. He tears it from its berth, holds it up to the light and reads it.

"My dearest Lorenzo:

For the past few weeks, I have noticed the love in your eyes as you look at Marianna. Though you have tried to mask it, it is clear that the long separation has not changed the love that you both feel for each other and that you want to be together. It hurts me deeply to think of you with anyone else, because I am so in love with you myself. Nevertheless, I feel that I must not stand in your way any longer.

As for me, I have asked Frank Mullin to come for me at the precise time that you and Marianna are at the festival. I think you know that Frank has professed his love for me on previous occasions. He is my best choice now that I am leaving you, and I know that I will be able to make him happy.

I have taken all of the things that belong to me and have locked the house behind me. You will not see me again, but know that I will always love you and wish for your happiness. "It is signed, Kathleen."

Without looking at Marianna, Lorenzo buries his face

in his hands and sobs.

⊱─◦─◦─◦─⊰

In the weeks that pass, the Fusco homestead is redone to Marianna's tastes. The frilly lace curtains give way to a more formal drape and the kitchen countertops fill with the ingredients for Marianna's style of cooking. The bouquet of wine, cheese and bread replaces the aroma of apple pie. Pasta is a more frequent dish and almost always served with a fresh tomato sauce. There is less meat and more vegetable. The guest bedroom is no longer used. The two occupants of the house live as man and wife.

"Marianna, I have never been so happy. This is the life that we dreamed of back in Calabria. And, hopefully, some day we'll have children to complete our joy."

"Lorenzo, that day is coming sooner than you think. I'm already pregnant."

"How wonderful! Now we can be married and give our name to the child."

"Darling, I thought you were aware that I was married to Aldo Caristi, in order to cover up my having a child with Leone. In the eyes of the Church and the Italian government I am still married to Aldo, even though he was later bribed and sent off to Sicily to live."

"Godammit! What must I do to have a normal life with you? Must I live forever like a cavone?"

"Please don't be upset, Lorenzo, no one need know that we are not married. Our child can be raised by the two of us and have all of the entitlements of any other child."

On July 16th, 1902, a daughter is born to Lorenzo and Marianna. She is named Stella, in honor of her maternal grandmother and is registered in the Queens County record hall as the daughter of Mr. & Mrs. Lorenzo Fusco. She is the image of her mother, her sparkling brown eyes peering out at her proud parents and her supple dark hair already commanding notice. The pleased parents take her home and are ecstatic with their new family member. It is a matter of only a few months before Marianna is thinking of her home in Calabria and the family she has left behind.

"Lorenzo, I must take little Stella home to Gagliano to see my mother. She is in failing health and I dread the thought that she will pass away having never seen her granddaughter."

"I don't want my daughter leaving me at such a young age, for what will turn out to be three months or more. Perhaps next year I will be more able to leave the farm and can come with you. But not now."

"Lorenzo, I have been meaning to talk to you about our future. Have you considered moving back to Italy to live?"

"Absolutely not! I left that place forever. An occasional visit is all right, but I will not ever live in Italy again."

"Not even for me?"

"Don't be ridiculous, Marianna, we could never be happy there. We lead a substantial life here. In Italy, we would be mere pawns again, and we would be gossiped about for living as a married couple. Even our child would be victimized and called la bastardella."

"You're wrong, Lorenzo, you forget how money talks in Italy. Aldo is gone. Leone is old and frightened of the anarchists. Who would have anything to say? With the money from the sale of this property and with what I now have, we'd be able to live lavishly in Italy and never have to work again."

"No, Marianna, there is no way that I will leave this life to return to Italy."

Marianna does not accept Lorenzo's answer, but does not irk him with continued urging. Instead, she chooses her moments, when she believes he is in an agreeable mood, to press him for a favorable response. He does not yield to her. It becomes clear to Marianna that Lorenzo will not return to Italy with her, and that she must either remain in Queens or lose him. Once again, her life is beset with calamity. Her need to return to the place of her birth, where her young son lives, where her family has lived its centuries-old existence, and where the customs are more comfortable to her, is essential. Yet, to return to Calabria, she would need to give up the two people who now mean more to her than anything in the world. She thinks to herself, *Lord, why am I in constant dilemma? Is my sin of taking up with Leone so severe that you have condemned me to a life of longing and unhappiness?* Then, she reasons that her son, Alessandro, is safe and happy, and close to his father. She must stay with her lover and their daughter and give up the idea of ever going back to Italy.

⊱⊱⊰⊰

From the moment the Western Union carrier wheels his bicycle up to the house, Marianna knows that something terrible has happened. In her life, she thinks, telegrams are sent only to keep her instantaneously informed of tragedies. She has received a telegram only once, a short time ago, informing her of her father's death. That time, she cried for a whole week and then on and off for another month. She could not possibly have traveled to Calabria in time for his funeral. Instead, she sent her mother a letter of sympathy and enclosed a draft for a thousand lire and a promise of life-long care and support. Her life now has an emptiness, that of the memory of Giuseppe, smoking his rope cigars and muttering pridefully to his cronies about *his Stella*.

"Lorenzo, please see what terrible news we are receiving from Western Union this time. I can't bear to go to the door."

Obediently, Lorenzo accepts the telegram, tips the carrier and turns to Marianna. "It's addressed to you."

"Oh, God. Read it to me, Lorenzo." Her hands are against the sides of her head, covering her ears, as though she has already heard some tragic news.

"It's from someone called Renato Rizzo. It reads,

Marianna:

Unfortunate duty to inform you Count Leone Capurro has died, victim of uprising by anarchists. Strain of attack upon villa caused heart failure. His death mourned by many.

Question of succession and inheritance uncertain. Your absence violates agreement to live in Calabria. Successful outcome greatly benefits you and Alessandro. Return at once.

Renato Rizzo

"So this is it, Marianna! You're going back to Gagliano, aren't you?" Lorenzo is enraged by the prospect that Marianna will leave him and their baby daughter to pursue the wealth and position to which she and her young son are seemingly entitled. Marianna rages back.

"What would you have me do? Should I permit Leone's fortune to be forfeited to his relatives? Should I deprive my son of a noble status in life? Don't be ridiculous, Lorenzo, of course I'm going back. If you have any sense you'll come with me. And take our daughter to meet our families in Calabria."

"Stella is not going with you. If you go, you leave her behind."

"I expected nothing less from you, Lorenzo, but I must do this and nothing you say or do will change my mind. I understand how you feel about the success you have had here in America and your fear of being trapped by the caste system that pervades Italy. But what choice do I have? My place is in Calabria with Alessandro and the rest of my family. I hope someday you come to your senses and move with our daughter to Italy, where we can all live as a family. Until then, you will both have to live without me."

Marianna takes her cherished little daughter from her crib and holds her tightly and lovingly. She thinks of how she will remember this moment with regret and how she will miss her child intensely. Despite his anger, Lorenzo approaches them and places his arms around them both. They stand silently together for several moments, but neither of them speaks. The separation is unavoidable, and somehow Marianna and Lorenzo sense that the parting will not be temporary.

Chapter 19

Raffaele

When she is not otherwise occupied, Carmela Vasapollo is a midwife. Most of the time she follows the same course as other *Gaglianesi*, that of farming for the earth's bounty and sharing it with a landlord. She tends a fifty acre olive grove owned by Count Leone. In a good year, the yield of twenty barrels of fine cooking oil, of which Leone's warehouse manager claims half, raises only enough cash to sustain Carmela's household until the next year. And since her husband Carlo is a sloth, refusing even the slightest of work, Carmela is obliged to supplement her farm earnings in order to ensure the welfare of her four children. Fortunately for her, she was drawn to midwifery as a young woman, as she watched the miracle of childbirth being assisted by an aunt.

So taken was she with the craft that she began assisting with deliveries even before becoming a mother herself. She became used to the blood and the pain that were all a necessary part of the birthing phenomenon. By the time she was twenty-five years old, she was a respected midwife, having delivered no less than fifty-six members of the next generation, two having complications. Though there are others who are older and more experienced, Carmela is in demand by the families who have experienced her skills first hand. She thus receives enough business to earn the money that Carlo refuses to pursue.

The harvest in January of 1898 of the black Moraioli olive is sparse, and Carmela worries that her share will not be sufficient to generate enough money to feed her family. She has delivered her olives to the mill, where they have been pressed into oil. The entire crop filled only twelve barrels and the oil is now aging in wood barrels in the shed behind the Vasapollo house. As for her midwife enterprise, she has performed only three deliveries in the early part of the year, and it does not seem that enough money will be earned to make up for the short crop. Moreover, she has been asked by her mother to assist a neighbor who is also a distant relative, in her delivery of an unwanted child. Since the woman's husband is in prison, she is unable to pay for the service. Carmela's work will be a gift from her family to the elderly mother of the woman who is expecting.

"Carlo, dammit, will you get off your ass for once and check the condition of our oil? I need to get over to help that Gesuzza woman to have her baby."

"Don't bother me, Carmela, can't you see that I'm trying to sleep? Besides, why are you doing this at all? That woman can't even pay us for our work."

"What do you mean us? They pay me, for my work. This woman is Stella Soluri's daughter and my mother owes Stella a favor for heaven knows what. Besides, if I don't do this, who will? Do you think I want a mishap on my conscience?"

"I hear that she's going to take the newborn to the Wheel. What difference does it make if the child lives or dies? It will only end up in a strange home to be raised by strangers and end up like its father."

"I've heard enough, you fool! I'm going over to examine Gesuzza and you had better check on our oil while I'm there."

"How long will you be gone?"

"As long as it takes. You look after the children, too."

It is almost mid-April and the stars are out, proclaiming the season of new life and growth. Buds have appeared on the trees and vines, and the cool spring weather promises abundance. Carmela makes her way to where Gesuzza labors. She hears the expectant mother call out as the sudden, sharp pain reminds her that she will soon bear the child that she has been commanded to abandon. Her two boys have been sent to *Nonna's* so they may be spared the experience of their mother's agony. They will not return, except to perform their chores, until the newborn arrives and is taken to the Wheel.

"Gesuzza, it's me, Carmela. I'm here to help you deliver your baby. How are you doing?"

"I think my hour is fast approaching. The pains are moments apart. Thank God you've arrived."

The two women talk through the night as they wait for the birth to begin. Gesuzza relates her sad tale of how Angelo has been captured and sent off to serve yet another nine years in prison, and Carmela tells Gesuzza of her frustrating life with Carlo, who refuses to take responsibility for his family's welfare. She tells Gesuzza about the extremely low yield from the olive grove and how it will mean a year of struggle. Finally at four AM, Gesuzza cries out as the frequency of pain is nearly constant and the unborn child decides to enter the world.

"Gesuzza, it's a boy!"

"Is he all right?" Just then, the baby registers his first complaint with a loud and hearty cry. It is followed by several more. Carmela is busy with separating the baby from its afterbirth, and Gesuzza needs no response to her question. It is evident that the delivery has gone well. Both women are relieved. Moments pass and Carmela asks, "Do you want to hold the baby?"

Tears roll down Gesuzza's face, her eyes pressed shut and her body quaking with sobs as she reaches up to receive her newborn. It is the saddest moment of her life, as her eyes open onto the tiny bluish eyes and the bit of dark hair that reaches down into the infant's face. "Lord have mercy on you," she murmurs as her consciousness slips away and her grip on the child is lost. Carmela intervenes, preventing the child from slipping to the floor.

Hours later, as Gesuzza regains awareness, she hears the plaintive infant calling for her breast. Stella is there, greeting her back to consciousness and assuring her that all is well with the newborn.

"You've done a good job of having this baby, Gesuzza. Now you must quickly turn him over to the nuns and not become attached to him. Don't be concerned, everything will work out for him."

"Isn't there any way that I can keep him, mother?"

"Are you crazy? Do you want Angelo to learn that you defied him? Isn't it enough that he is away in prison and can't support you and his other children? Gesuzza, be realistic. You must give up this child. Be thankful that he will be placed with another family that can take care of him properly."

"I don't know that. He might not be adopted at all and could end up spending his whole young life in an orphanage. Or, worse, he could end up with the wrong family and be treated miserably." With that, Gesuzza begins to cry.

"Stop it Gesuzza, you need to be strong."

"No, mother, I know this is all wrong. Angelo is wrong. I just know it."

The following day, Gesuzza's friend, Maria Fanucci, comes to visit her. "Gesuzza, your mother has asked me to take the baby to the Wheel for you."

"Oh, Jesus, I can't do this. I can't let him be taken away from me."

"You must, Gesuzza, there is no one to care for him in your absence. Don't worry, he'll be all right." The tilt of Maria's head and the look of compassion on her face, convince Gesuzza that there is no choice and that all will work out in the end.

"Very well, then, but be quick about it. I don't want to weaken before you leave with him. But come back and let me know what happened."

In a flash, Maria takes the infant boy and is gone.

The convent of Our Lady of Mount Carmel is more than one thousand years old, having survived a plague, several epidemics of cholera, conquest by three Powers and four major wars. It is built in the ancient technique of stone fitted to stone without benefit of mortar. Two great arched doors made of heavy oak form the entrance to the convent, and a smaller door, built within one of the entrance doors, is used daily by the nuns and their visitors. Despite its long existence, it has had but one body of occupants: the dutiful handmaidens of the Lord, the Sisters of Charity, whose mission is to aid the Christian souls that fill their world.

The inside of the convent is a residence and chapel for twenty nuns, a refuge for unwed mothers and a sanctuary for criminals seeking God's forgiveness and protection from the long and often brutal arm of the law. In one end of the convent lies a huge wooden wheel, La Rota, which reaches, horizontally, to the street behind the building, out of the view of all who pass on either side. There, unwanted infants are placed by their desperate mothers. Once a day the wheel is turned by the nuns, bringing the infant children into the refuge. Once abandoned, the infant is never returned. If a surname is attached to its garments, a record is made that could later be used to identify a congenital parent. They are never reunited. Many of the cast-offs are adopted by childless, affluent parents and lead normal lives. Occasionally, to the great disappointment of the nuns, they are taken on by families who use them as slaves until they are old enough to escape to a better life.

Maria approaches the convent unhesitatingly and places the infant boy on the wheel. He immediately cries out as though he understands what is happening. As Maria leaves, she hears his cries. She knows Gesuzza will ask if he was left crying. She thinks, *I will simply tell her that he was sleeping comfortably.*

As she returns to Gesuzza's house, she can hear her crying in a frenzied state. From the moment that Maria walks in, Gesuzza holds her arms out and begs her,'"Maria, you must return to the Wheel and bring back my baby. I can't go on if I allow this to happen. Please, Maria, you must go back and get my baby." After several tries to calm Gesuzza down and reason with her, Maria realizes that she must return to the Wheel to retrieve Gesuzza's infant son. "I'll hurry back, Gesuzza. By the grace of God, they haven't turned the Wheel yet."

"Hurry, Maria, hurry."

Maria runs the mile and a half to the nunnery, all the while praying that she will arrive in time. As she approaches the Wheel, she can see a blanket with what seems to be a baby, kicking at the air. It is Gesuzza's baby. She snatches him up, and without looking back, brings the baby back to Gesuzza. The reunion of mother and child brings tears to Maria's eyes and she knows that she has done the right thing.

"Oh Gesuzza, I'm so glad that I was able to bring him back to you. Now that you will get to keep him, what will you name him?"

"I told Angelo that if I could keep him, I would name him after Angelo's father: Raffaele. Maybe it will make Angelo feel a little better about my having kept the baby."

Chapter 20

Return to Asinara

Angelo Chiarella is no stranger to the ship that ferries convicts from Calabria to Prigione dell' Asinara. It is one of the worst memories of his life. Now he is at sea again, on his way to the life that he prayed God would end during his first imprisonment there. There is no mental anguish worse than this. Even the death of a child has to be better. No, he thinks, even this is not quite that bad. He vows to build strength enough to survive. He thinks of the Carabinieri on the dock at Reggio di Calabria the day before and of how they singled him out and ordered him to load the ship of its provisions. The other prisoners stood by as Angelo did the work of the crew by himself. It was the Carabinieri's way of letting him know of their hatred for him for having injured and embarrassed several of their comrades during his capture. He hopes that their abhorrence will abate as the ship makes its way up the Mediterranean. It doesn't. It is clear that he is a marked man.

"Hey, Angelo, I hear that you're a tough guy. Is it true that you took three of us on when we came to escort you to Catanzaro?" The captain of the Carabinieri sneers at Angelo, looking for a fight with his shackled opponent.

"I only did what any man in my position would do."

"So, you think that suspects should fight the Carabinieri?" Angelo does not respond. The captain is in deep thought. Finally, he says, "Chiarella, you will tend the latrine pails for the whole trip,..prisoners, crew, guards…everyone's crap is yours to deal with. And that's in addition to your regular duties. You will work on deck like everyone else and you can handle the shit on your own time."

Angelo looks menacingly at the captain and finally responds, "You mean there is free time on this voyage?"

"Don't be a smart ass with me, Angelo. I'll make you sorry that you were ever born. Remember that I answer to no one on this ship, and I can do more than make you work the whole time you're here."

Again, Angelo does not respond. He decides that he will do whatever is asked of him without remark or complaint. His trip is one of constant work. Each time a chore is done, another is heaped on. He is allowed to sleep only a few hours a night. The other prisoners take pity, but they too are at the mercy of the Carabinieri and are unable to help him.

By the time the ship reaches Asinara, Angelo is physically exhausted, but he is elated that he will no longer be under the control of the Carabinieri. The prisoners are brought into the prison yard and are stripped of their clothing. They are doused cruelly with cold water and handed the clothing they will wear during their prison term. They are given the warning by the Captain of the Guard, that Angelo remembers well, "Men, my name is Roberto Caruso and I am captain of the guard. You are here because you have committed a serious crime. During your time at Prigione dell' Asinara we will work you hard so that, hereafter, you will give more thought to obeying the law. If you follow instruction, you will find that time will pass quickly. If you don't, you will face harsh punishment and you will regret resisting orders. It is not our wish to inflict pain, but we will not shrink from our duty to uphold the letter of the laws of this prison. Heed my warning! Now go to your cells and prepare to serve your sentence."

As the prisoners are led out of the compound, two guards approach Angelo. One of them announces gruffly, "Prisoner Chiarella, you will come with us." Angelo follows obediently. He is lead to the office of Captain Caruso. It is a large room that is comfortably outfitted with couches and chairs. A large desk sits on an oversized rug and is covered with paper files piled neatly in stacks. There are quills, an ink well and a brass stamp bearing the Captain's emblem. The accoutrements imply the power of the office.

"So, one term with us was not enough. Did our hospitality appeal to you?" The Captain opens a cigarette box and lights one. He draws in deeply and blows the heavy smoke into the room. The guards show no reaction to the choking atmosphere. He continues, "Angelo, it has been reported to me that you have been very hard on the officers of the law who were sent to apprehend you. Is it true?"

"Perhaps so, signore, but my actions were provoked. I am innocent of any of the charges that have ever been leveled at me. The Carabinieri have hounded me to the point of complete frustration. I was provoked into committing the acts that put me here again."

"And so you bit the ear off a soldier of the King's army." Angelo is silent.

"And you shattered the arm of another young Italian soldier so that he will never use the arm again."

"No, no dammit! That's not all there is to the story. I was being forced to step out of line so that I could be convicted again and brought here. There is a vendetta against me in the courts. I am here to pay for a blood feud of which I know nothing."

"How dare you infer that there is malfeasance in the court that convicted you? Angelo, you need to learn your place in this world. We will begin here in Asinara to mend your ways. First, you will be confined to a cell in which you will be the sole occupant. You will not leave your cell except to work. In the mornings and evenings you will perform latrine duty for the northeast quadrant of the prison. During the day, you will be assigned to sea salt production with the others. I have spoken to the sergeant-at-arms about your assignment. He has assured me that you will be given appropriate work. Do you understand?"

Angelo is devastated. He knows what lies ahead for the next nine years. His head hangs low as he responds. "I will do as I am told, but I do not understand."

The following morning, Angelo is awakened at four in the morning by the guard of the mid-watch. "Angelo, get up. Hurry, your instructor is here to show you what you must do." He has spent his first night in solitary confinement and feels the walls of his small cell closing in on him. It is a far cry from the freedom of the Calabrian mountains. He is tired, hungry and thirsty; but he must first respond to the command that he take instruction. Instruction, indeed! He is taking over the latrine duty from the happy prisoner who is unexpectedly relieved of the prison's worst duty.

"This is prisoner Bucco. He will show you what is expected of you."

Salvatore Bucco is a slight man of thirty years. His relatively young face shows the scars of his profession, that of a runner for the Camorra, Naples' version of the Mafia. The well-paid runners are expected to collect betting money from players of the Neapolitan numbers racket and to deliver it to the game's treasury. They also must pay winners on those rare occasions when they actually win a prize. One of the hazards of running bets is that there is sometimes, confusion as to which number has actually won, giving rise to claims of non-existent prizes. Since the runner then becomes the bearer of bad news, he is often recriminated by the disappointed bettors, sometimes violently. In Salvatore Bucco's case, he was arrested and convicted of bludgeoning an irate customer with the butt of a pistol. Though the customer had attempted to assault Bucco because he thought he was being deprived of a prize he had won, Bucco was unable to present the fact of self-defense in a court of law that considered his activity illegal. He has been in Asinara for four years of a seven-year sentence.

"There is very little to show you, Angelo. Just follow me and you'll get the hang of it in no time at all."

The two men walk through the corridors of the prison pushing a large, wheeled barrel. They stop at each cell and empty the contents of buckets placed into the corridor through a section of the bars that has been fitted to allow the movement of small objects to and from the cells. The foul smell that rises from the buckets turns Angelo's stomach, but there is too little in it to heave up. He continues on. As the barrel fills and the odor becomes unbearable, Angelo uses a cloth to shield his face from the terrible stench. The other man shows no aversion to the smells, having become acclimated to the smell. They proceed to an opening at the end of the cellblock, where there is a perch extending beyond the edge of the building and over a small inlet from the sea. Here, they invert the barrel, sending its contents hurtling sixty feet down to the sea. Then, they return to where they left off and continue. When they are done, they return with the barrel filled with water and rinse each of the buckets. Then, they wash their hands and faces thoroughly from a bucket that contains clean, fresh water and soap. The next time, and for the next two years, he will perform this ritual on his own.

"OK, Angelo, let's go. The tide is out and we need to prepare a dam for when the flats fill." This is Angelo's first learning of what is in store for him. The sergeant-at-arms escorts Angelo down to where the men are preparing for their daily work. On their way, he is handed a heel of bread and a cup of coffee to consume in haste.

"What do you mean 'prepare a dam'?"

"Come now, Angelo, you're no stranger to what goes on here. Have you forgotten how we make our sea salt? You've been assigned to the mud detail. From what I hear, it's a permanent assignment." The sergeant remembers Angelo from his prior sentence and has obviously been told to assign him to the most difficult and dangerous task in the salt-making process.

Twice a day, the tide of the sea roars in to shore, bringing with it the treasured salt that is deposited on the flats below the prison. The prisoners must trap the seawater until it yields its crop: that which remains when the water drains. To do this, a crew of men is lowered into the sea just outside the harvest flats so that a mud dam can be prepared to prevent the rushing seawater from returning to the sea. The men labor in mud the entire day as they place the dam and plug the holes that constantly appear. The tides must be predicted accurately and the crew must work quickly and in unison. So turbulent is the movement of water, that the crew is in constant peril of being swept into the undertow and vanishing from sight for all time. When this happens, the other prisoners joke that the victim had found a way of feigning accidental death and in reality has escaped.

"Hold on to the rope as we lower you down. The others are already there awaiting the rush of the tide." A trustee operating a boom lowers Angelo into the water beyond the flats. It is the only device by which he can return to safety. The tide has already begun to show its menacing force and Angelo is instructed to hold on to the side of the mud wall so that he will not be swept away. His instructor is Guido Rossi, one of the twins who became violently entangled with another prisoner during Angelo's first sail to Asinara more than ten years ago.

"Are you one of the Rossi twins?" Angelo chanced that Guido would talk to him and let him know what was going to happen during this new experience. He was startled at Guido's reply.

"There are no Rossi twins. I am Guido Rossi."

"Am I mistaken? Don't you have a twin brother?"

"My brother is dead, killed by these bastards." He looks away, not wanting to be seen mourning for his brother. His eyes fill with tears.

"What happened? Are you able to talk about it?"

"Yes, enough time has gone by that I can talk of my

brother, Luigi. He came to my rescue at sea, on our way
here ten years ago. We severely beat a man who attacked
me heatedly for no reason. The man was taken away and
eventually disappeared from the ship. No one knows
where he ended up. Luigi and I were nearly killed by the
Carabinieri on the ship for defending ourselves. When we
arrived in Asinara, we were told that we were going to
receive harsh treatment for our actions, rather than having to account to a magistrate. We were relieved that we
were not being accused of a vicious crime and made up
our minds to accept whatever punishment was handed
us. We were put on this mud duty for an indefinite time.
The other prisoners were reassigned after only two weeks,
but we were made to continue week after week with no
let-up. We were sure that it was their intent to tire us out
so we would eventually slip and fall into the sea. One night,
Luigi stole out of sight and remained behind on the flats
when the rest of us returned to the prison. By the time we
were accounted for and he was discovered missing, he was
well on his way, swimming to Stintino, just across the
straits of Asinara.

It was dark and almost impossible to see a swimmer
out in the shadowy water, the moon being hidden in the
clouds. A group of guards, a marksman among them,
climbed into a small craft and went after Luigi. When he
reached the shore on the other side, Luigi became a target
as the moon moved out from behind a cloud and lit up
the beach. In the next moment, a shot rang out and we all
knew that Luigi had been shot. They dragged his dead
body into the compound the next morning as an example
of what happens to prisoners who attempt to escape."
Guido can no longer keep his composure and weeps
openly. Horrified by the story, Angelo tries to console him,

"I'm very sorry, Guido."

Just then, the tide rushes against the wall and the men cling for their lives. When the sea is content, the men hurriedly construct a wall of mud at the opening to the flats to hold in the captive water. Then, as the seawater is directed to clay beds, they guard the dam to prevent its' opening. Angelo has learned yet another of his assignments this day, along with the possibility that he, too, may be marked for accidental death.

Chapter 21

Carmela

Carmela has been away from her family for several days, aiding Gesuzza in her most critical time following the birth of her new son. She dutifully registers the newborn with the provincial government, after determining from Gesuzza the desired given name.

"I must leave you now Gesuzza. My lazy husband has been looking after my children, and I can imagine what my house looks like. Also, it is nearing the time for me to pay Don Leone his share of the olive oil that has been sitting in my shed for the past few weeks and I need to be there to make certain that it's done properly."

Gesuzza is on her feet and able to care for the baby for the first time since giving birth. She looks gratefully at Carmela and expresses her appreciation. "Carmela, how can I ever thank you enough or repay you for your work? I will always be grateful to you for helping me to bring my son into the world. May God's blessings be on you for all time."

Carmela enters her home for the first time in four days. It is morning and her children are busily preparing breakfast for themselves as their father sleeps into the day. There is considerable clutter everywhere. The morning porridge that has gone awry covers layers of drippings from prior meals and the slippery floor shows traces of their attempts to clean up. Unfortunately for Carmela, the older of her children are boys, aged 9 and 11, and the girls, 4 and 6, do not yet involve themselves in the housework. The boys believe that the house is in tidy condition. Vincenzo greets his mother, "Hi, ma, we thought you were never coming home. Are you going to stay home, now?"

"Of course I'm staying home. Did you ever doubt that? This house looks as though the Sirocco has struck. Where is that father of yours? We need to get this place straightened up."

"Carmela! Dear! You're home!" Carlo has awakened and enters the room. He rubs his eyes and then his stomach. He is a handsome, slim man of average height. Carmela admires his good looks and resolves to continue her life of drudgery to accommodate his slovenliness. She has stayed with him despite his aversion to work of any kind.

"Damn you, Carlo, look at this place. It's a pit. And Grazia looks as though she hasn't had a change of clothes since I went over to help Gesuzza. I think that poor woman is better off with her husband in prison than I am with you."

"Watch that mouth of yours, Carmela. I'm not going

to take your shit. I'm doing the best I can. You know how tired I get all the time. Can I help it if I'm not a healthy man?"

Carmela becomes silent. They have been through this dozens of times before. It is useless. Maybe some day she'll do something about it, but not today. She needs to begin the work of cleaning up, and then she needs to taste her store of olive oil to see if it's ready to be used She thinks of the six barrels she will have after her payment to Leone and worries. How will they live the coming year with only six barrels of oil to sell? She puts away the bag with her birthing equipment and the spare clothing she had taken with her and begins to straighten her house.

It is a morning of the third week of April. Carmela thinks about the olive oil that by now should be sufficiently aged and ready to distribute. She clears away the breakfast clutter and heads for the shed. Little nine-year-old Paolo follows her, having missed her during her absence. The thought of her year's work in the twelve barrels swells her with pride despite the scant yield. After all, was it her fault that it was not a bountiful crop? Who could possibly fault her for the fickleness of Mother Nature? No, she need not worry about how she got into this predicament. She must figure out how to survive it. That damn Carlo. When will he grow up and take charge of his family's welfare?

The shed is but twenty steps from the house, separated only by the small livestock yard and a fenced in vegetable garden. The pen's aroma tells of the need to muck several days of animal excrement. The unwanted green among the vegetables cries for weeding. As Carmela nears the barn, she notices human footprints and markings made by barrels being rolled across the yard. For a fleeting moment, she fears that her precious cargo has been stolen during her absence. No, that isn't possible. Carlo is always at home and even he would not stand idly by while a theft of his family's sustenance was taking place. She peers into the shed and her fears are discarded as she views the twelve barrels sitting obediently in the shed. The aroma of olives and olive oil is in the air and Carmela thinks that perhaps it is nutty-smelling enough that its quality will allow for a little better price to partially offset the low quantity. She removes the burlap cloth from the top of one barrel and places her spoon into the liquid. She brings the spoon to her mouth. Her large brown eyes open wide and a look of horror comes over her face. The horror turns to panic as she tears the covers from the other eleven barrels and samples them as well. Paolo looks up to his mother, "What is it Ma? What's wrong?" Carmela's eyes seem not to see. She only babbles.

"What wretch could have done this to me? How will my children eat? How will I pay my landlord? What will become of us? Carlo! Carlo! Come quickly!"

"What is it? What's wrong?" Carlo shows uncharacteristic energy as he senses panic in Carmela's voice and instantly responds. She is barely able to speak.

"Water, Carlo, water. The oil barrels are full of water." She props herself up on the top of one barrel. Paolo is crying and biting on the sleeve of his shirt. He does not understand what is happening. He knows only that his mother is severely wounded by whatever she sees in the oil barrels.

"Carmela, you must not let whatever has happened trouble you to this extent. Come back to the house with me. You must rest. We'll figure it out." Carlo shows concern for his wife and seems surprisingly unconcerned about their material loss.

"Carlo, you stupid son-of-a-bitch, have you no thought

or fear of the future? Don't you see what has happened to us? We're ruined!" She draws in a breath as though it is to be her last, loses consciousness and falls to the floor of the shed. Paolo lets out a scream and the other children begin crying back at the house, where they have been watching their parents deal with a danger they are unable to perceive. Carlo scoops Carmela into his arms and carries her back to the house. He lays her on the bed and brings water to her. She begins to revive and sips the water. She looks up to Carlo with a strange face that he has never before seen. He is unable to make sense of it.

"Who are you? Why are you here?" Carmela seems not to recognize Carlo. She rises and wobbles over to where her children have huddled in horror. She places her arms around them protectively and shrieks at Carlo, "Get out of here or I'll call the police."

"Carmela, darling, it's me. Carlo. Don't you know me?" But Carlo's bid to reach her fails. She is unable to recognize him. The children's wailing overcomes her and she begins to fling pots, pans and anything within her reach at Carlo. He leaves quickly and heads for the doctor's house. "Doctor! Doctor! Come quickly. My Carmela has lost her mind."

It is surprising that, in the unrefined Catanzaro of 1898, there existed an institution capable of understanding and caring for patients afflicted with mental disorder. The *Instituto Della Mentale Male* had been founded by agents of the new Kingdom shortly after the Reunification, and had handled many a nervous condition similar to that visited upon Carmela Vasapollo. At the request of Doctor Umberto Villano of Gagliano, she was promptly admitted and lay fitfully strapped to a bed, twisting and turning and trying in vain to free herself.

"Why am I here? What is happening? Turn me loose! I must go to my children. They need me. They have no support without me." Carmela's eyes are wild. She looks threateningly at the doctor as he approaches. He wipes her tethered arm with alcohol, plunges a hypodermic needle into the sterile spot and presses the contents of the syringe into her blood stream. Carmela relaxes and goes into a deep sleep, all the while murmuring about the safety and welfare of her children.

Outside, Carlo is tense and outwardly remorseful for the part he has seemingly played in his wife's condition. There is no one to hear him as he pledges aloud that he will take charge of the family's fortunes and somehow settle with Count Leone for the oil that has mysteriously disappeared from his shed.

But, Carlo knows that he himself is the thief. He has arranged for the oil to be shipped silently across the border to France and sold at a high price to a French purveyor who will bottle it and place his own label on the face of the containers. In this year of shortage of olive oil, he has received enough francs to escape from his miserable life with Carmela. No more will he listen to her flurry of insults. No longer will he be the fool among his friends. "Lazy, indeed. That woman should know how capable I am." Without further hesitation, he proceeds to his home, where his children are in the care of their grandmother. He packs his bags and leaves, looking back only momentarily at his children's faces and the bewildered expressions that he will always remember.

The following morning, a doctor from the Institute arrives at the Vasapollo house, and addresses Carmela's mother, "Is Mr. Vasapollo at home?"

"No. He's gone. I am Carmela's mother. What is it?"

"I'm afraid I have some bad news for you. Carmela died during the night. She had an adverse reaction to the sedative we gave her and she expired."

The old woman falls back on her chair, weeping quietly and hoping that the children will not overhear the tragic news. Their lives have been forever altered, and they will find out soon enough.

Chapter 22

Reprieve

There is a fury in the sea below Prigione dell' Asinara that has not been seen in months; but unlike other times, this day the men are not excused from their daily chores. Production has been slow and to dismiss the work detail for a day is, under the circumstances, unthinkable. The men are warned to be extra careful, that the sea listens only to Mother Nature and that the tide does not forgive. The men of the mud detail are given a lifeline to take with them into the water, to clutch when the swells become unmanageable. The two most experienced men, Guido Rossi and Angelo Chiarella, protest to the guards, but are rebuffed. The seven-man detail enters the water cautiously and reluctantly.

"They have got what they want," says Guido, "a tide

that is too difficult for us to handle. Now they can get rid of us without blame."

"Don't give up, Guido. We must be strong and we must survive." Angelo shows determination and hope.

For most of the morning, the waves come crashing in on the men. They are unable to hold the dam in place, but the guards urge them on and order them to prevent the onrushing sea from damaging the flats. The lifelines prove their worth as the men cling to them with each assault of the sea. The men on the flats are unable to work, but are made to stay at their posts regardless of the peril. There is a feeling of hopelessness among the men in the mud detail as they hold on for dear life while the sea rages.

"Angelo, I'm losing my strength. I don't know how much more I can take. I'm losing my grip on the line a little more with each wave that comes in."

"Hold on, Guido, you must not give in to these *puttani*."

But the sea is unrelenting and the continual pounding of the waves is at last more than Guido can endure. His grip on the line gives way and he calls out. "Angelo! I am gone! I can't hold on!"

"Give me your hand! Guido! Give me your hand!"

In the next moment, Guido slips under the water and is immediately drawn out to sea. Angelo cries out, "God have mercy on his soul." The guards at last react to the situation and call in the men. They have worked in the squall for most of the day.

The thin, bent form of a man emerges from the sea as his day's work is done. The others line up, tired and hungry, to climb the steps to the prison above the salt flats. They are wet to the bone with the seawater in which they toiled. Angelo Chiarella is salt-white from laboring every day for months, submerged in the dense seawater at the mouth of the channel that feeds the flats. He walks in slow, deliberate steps. Only one other, Guido Rossi, had endured the mud detail for a longer time, and now he is gone. As he nears the others, Angelo is suddenly and completely overtaken with rage. He screams at the guards, "Bastardi! You killed him! Murderers!" He charges at the guards, but he is easily overtaken in his weakened state. He is clubbed to the ground and left behind as the others proceed to the prison, heads bowed.

"So, Angelo, you are at it again, are you?" The captain's voice rings out as Angelo returns under guard to the prison, exhausted and lifeless. Captain Caruso has been informed of Angelo's attempt at fighting the guards and has come to pass sentence for the act of violence.

"Bring him to the prison yard. He is to be given ten lashes at the post. Hopefully, it will teach him to behave."

Some of the others overhear the sentence and begin to murmur among themselves. "How much can this man take?" "It's grossly unfair." "Why are we standing around? Why don't we do something?" "What can we do? They have guns and they can starve us if we step out of line. There is no one to protect us and no one cares what happens here."

"Stop that mumbling and get in formation to witness the punishment."

Within moments, Angelo is lashed to a post and the dreaded Sputagna walks out, carrying his many-tailed whip and appearing to be irritated, probably because this event interrupted his dinner. Angelo's eyes are wild, but he has given in to his state of fatigue and stands unmoving, his wrists lashed to the top rung of the whipping post. Sputagna grunts as he whirls his whip in the air to unfurl its tentacles. Then, he begins the whipping as one of the trustee prisoners calls the cadence. The whip comes down on Angelo's bleached-white back like a hot poker.

"One." Angelo tenses.

"Two." "Three." "Four."

"Five." A trickle of blood streams down Angelo's back and he reacts to the intense pain. "Ugh!"

"Six." Angelo's head falls forward and he slumps as though he has lost consciousness. He makes no further sound or move for the remaining time. When the final lash is counted and the bonds are removed, Angelo's beaten hulk slumps to the ground and is carried away by the guards. The prisoners are lead away in a silent rage of disgust over what they have been forced to witness, unable to resist their tormentors.

Back in his cell, Angelo is unable to move. The pain of his swollen back has immobilized him so that it has taken away all sense of the world. He lies on his cot thinking of home and how Gesuzza would rub his back when it was stiff from working in the fields. He thinks of his boys and how they must miss not having their father to help them through their early years. Foremost among his regrets in this life is that his sons have had no real father. From the time of their youth, he was taken away from them, and was replaced only by their grandfather, Giuseppe. His thoughts turn to his third child, whom he has never seen. Was it a boy or a girl? Where did the child end up? Did the nuns place it in competent hands? Did he do right by Gesuzza in demanding that she place their newborn on the Wheel? His guilt overcomes him and he sobs quietly into his hands.

The next morning two guards show up at his cell. Angelo has been unable to rise from his bed and he has been reported as delinquent. "Let's go, Chiarella, get out of that bed and get on the latrine detail. The buckets haven't been cleaned since yesterday morning. Did you think that little spanking would free you from your job?"

"I'm sorry, but I'm unable to stand without falling. You'll have to get someone to take over for me today." His words are mere mumblings, hardly audible by the guards.

"Oh no you don't. Get up and get going, Angelo. And don't think you're getting out of mud detail. The sea is calmer today and we need to get production going again."

The reality of their intent to put him immediately back to work strikes him and he struggles to his feet, only to fall to his knees. "Come on, Angelo, get going. Don't try to get out of work by pretending to be sick."

"Can't you see that I am unable to stand? Do you think I'm kidding? Believe me, I'm not." Angelo's condition is very convincing, but the guards are simply not willing to accept his pleas.

"We'll be back, Angelo, after we've had a chance to talk this over with the captain. He'll know what to do with you." Angelo fears the worst. He simply cannot stand and perform any of his assigned duties and no one can make him do so. Is this the day of reckoning? Is this the time for the authorities to somehow end his life in a manner subtle enough to escape scrutiny? And by whom? Who cares about him other than his family and they will have to accept whatever is told to them. Angelo thinks, *cruel world. Why did all of this have to happen to me?*

An hour passes. Angelo hears the footsteps of the guards returning to announce his final sentence. He looks up at the ceiling of the cell and prepares himself for the worst.

"Angelo, you will have a week off to recover. Thereafter you will be reassigned to duty as a gardener on the prison grounds. All other duties have been canceled. Your meals will be brought to you until you are able to walk to the mess hall."

He is unable to fathom what has just been told to him. "What about the buckets?"

"I've just told you. That will be assigned to someone else."

"And the mud detail?"

"That too has been assigned to someone else."

That evening, as one of the trustees brings the evening meal to Angelo, he asks, "Why has the attitude towards me changed so suddenly? What has happened?"

"I don't know for sure, but the word among the prisoners is that Don Generoso has learned of your plight and has interceded on your behalf."

"Thank God. The man has saved my life."

Chapter 23

Suppression

The situation in Gagliano is hopeless for Gesuzza and her three boys. She and the older two labor all of the time, working their tenant farm, herding their goats and sheep and producing cheese from the goats' milk and wool from the sheep's coats. Low prices and scant production force Gesuzza to take on yet another task, that of nursing the male twin of fraternal twins born to a woman of slight physique. Still, the money is short to buy the grains and vegetables needed for their table. The family is relegated to supplementing their diets with whatever foods they can find. During the months of harvest, they are in abundance with chicory and fennel, which they find growing wild along the roads, and with handouts from their friends of fruits and vegetables they are unable to market. But, in winter and during the many months of the growing season, there are no alternatives except to do without. Stella and Giuseppe are now old and are hardly able to care for themselves, and Marianna is away in America.

"Ma, is there any milk for us to drink? I haven't drunk any in such a long time."

"Your brother is using the milk to make cheese. There may be some left. Ask him to get you some." But there is no milk that has not been curdled for cheese making. Only a watery solution remains after the curds have been removed, and the boys must share it. Their little five-year-old brother, Raffaele, looks up gloomily as his brothers consume the liquid.

"Do you want some too, Raffaele?" Pietro offers the ladle to his brother. "Yes, Pietro, give me some."

Pietro looks squintingly at the horizon as though he sees something that others do not. He thinks to himself of his burning desire to leave this suffocating countryside for a place where he might own his own land, where he could farm for himself and his family's benefit. Instead, he is inexplicably tied to this dreadful life of work and deprivation. He thinks of Count Leone, the major benefactor of his work, and he is angry. His thoughts turn to his mother and her dependency upon him. Were it not for her, he would be in America now, helping to build the railroad and earning the money to buy a farm. Many of his friends have already gone to America to seek their fortune. Gesuzza says that she would go with him to the new world were she not otherwise committed. But she must wait for Angelo's release from prison. Then they can go. The three years left before Angelo returns is as much a prison term for Pietro as it is for Angelo.

"What are you thinking about?" says Giuseppe.

"About how I would like to be in America on my very own farm."

"Pietro, take me with you. We can hold down two jobs and share expenses. That way we could save twice as much and have a farm that much sooner." It is apparent that Pietro has shared his dream with his brother.

"I won't leave Italy without Ma."

"Why not? She'll be all right."

"Don't be silly. I could not rest easy, knowing that she is here and wondering how she is able to live. I am the oldest of her children and I will support her for as long as necessary."

⊷―◦―⊷

The new century has brought with it a new boldness and the men of Catanzaro province renew their dedication toward changing the system of land ownership and sharecropping. What had been murmurs of dissatisfaction become shouts of discontent. Words finally give way to actions when a band of dissenters is organized and the first shots are fired at the Capurro villa.

"Damn you, Leone, come out and fight." "We'll fight until you agree to give us a fair deal." "This time we won't give in to you." The men of Catanzaro are determined to end the unfair system once and for all. In the end, however, a Carabiniere unit supplements Leone's small army of private guards and the object of the assault becomes impregnable. As the dissidents disband, all is quiet except for the frequent expressions of discontent and disappointment.

"How can we ever win against that man and the other landholders when the Carabinieri jumps in on their side with their troops and their guns?"

"Just wait until the next opportunity comes up. We'll be there. We'll fight to the last man if we are given half a chance of succeeding."

The complete lack of rejoicing within the walls of Capurro villa is noticeable and the men camp in the woods outside to determine what is going on. Several hours pass before a groundskeeper comes to the entry gate and posts a notice. After he leaves, one of the insurgents approaches the gate and reads the sign:

TO THE PEOPLE OF CATANZARO, BE IT KNOWN THAT THE HONORABLE COUNT LEONE CAPURRO HAS GONE TO HIS FINAL REST IN HEAVEN, HAVING EXPIRED SUDDENLY THIS MORNING OF HEART FAILURE... BURIAL WILL TAKE PLACE AT....

"Aha! Take heart, men, the villain has gone to meet his maker and soon we will have his successor to contend with. Our day will soon be at hand."

When the word reaches Gesuzza, she immediately thinks of Marianna and Alessandro. Marianna is in America for heaven knows how long and Alessandro is away at military school. They must learn of this event and prepare themselves for whatever claims they may have on the Capurro estate. It has been said that Alessandro is in line for the Count's title and will inherit his wealth. And Marianna must ensure that her arrangement is still secure, though as the mother of the principal inheritor, she will undoubtedly be dealt with satisfactorily. Surely the shrewd Torcia blood coursing her veins will propel her to come home immediately. Gesuzza smiles inwardly and thinks of her beloved sister whom she has not seen for several years. She prays God that word gets to Marianna soon.

The arrival of spring is noticed in Gagliano by the farmers' constant vigil. There are smiles and expressions of joy as buds appear on fruit trees and as the sun makes a more deliberate appearance. Another season arrives and there is again, promise of abundance. In the Chiarella home, there is another, long-awaited arrival.

"Mother! Mother! She's here! *Zi' Marianna e arrivato!*" Pietro is wild with delight as he calls to his mother of the arrival in Gagliano of his aunt Marianna, Gesuzza's younger sister by five years. She has gone directly to the vacant home that has patiently awaited her return, to rest from her weeks-long trip before meeting with the Capurro family. A few days later, Marianna comes to see Gesuzza. "My darling sister, what's happened? I am told that Angelo has again been sent away to prison. Is this true? When did this all happen?"

"Oh, Marianna, it seemed as though the whole world changed just after you left Italy. The Carabinieri hounded Angelo until he couldn't take it any more. He finally lashed out at them and had to run to the mountains to keep his freedom, after he injured one of them seriously. They finally caught him after more than a year and a half. Leone used his influence as much as possible, but in the end Angelo's enemies were able to manipulate him and get him to turn against Angelo."

"I'm really sorry, Gesuzza. I wish I had been here to help. You must be overcome with the work of caring for the animals and with farming the contract property. Are you and the boys able to cope with it? The boys are so young and they look tired and anxious." Marianna looks over to where Pietro, Giuseppe and Raffaele are quietly observing her and listening in on her conversation with their mother.

The enormous frustration in her life seems to well up in Gesuzza as she reveals her story to Marianna, reaching the point where she is unable to contain her emotions. She drops her face into her hands and sobs. Pietro runs to her and embraces her while an embittered Giuseppe looks on. Tears stream down Raffaele's face.

Marianna is greatly moved. "Gesuzza, I am home now, and I am prepared to assist you and your children."

Chapter 24

Rodolfo

At the moment of dawning over the cemetery surrounding The Church of the Holy Rosary, the small white tombstones rise from the turf to break through the morning fog. In their cautious symmetry, they resemble a newly planted field of saplings, their alignment suggesting the farmer's careful placement. As daylight sweeps the ground and names appear across the stones, it is evident that this is the place of interment for generations of farmers, shepherds, carpenters, and all others who have lived their lives in Gagliano. To earn entry, one must die in reasonable harmony with the Catholic Church. This is, after all, consecrated ground, restricted to Catholics who have lived in accord with the tenets of Holy Mother, the Church. All others must find their final resting place elsewhere.

Several modest mausoleums stand at one end of the cemetery, the eternal habitat for the most affluent of the village. Each structure is equipped with an entry door, allowing the entombed to receive visitors from among their families and friends. Trees and grass proliferate, creating a pleasant refuge from the often-blazing sun. Inside, the cool interior encourages extended prayer. Among the dwellings is a recently erected crypt inscribed *Capurro*, and inside are the vaults containing the earthly remains of two people, Leone and his beloved Beatrice. Despite his excommunication as a supporter of the Risorgimento and his alienation from the Church for the remainder of his life, Leone was in the end able to take his place beside his wife with a proper Catholic entombment. His final goal had been achieved, largely because of his generosity towards The Church of the Holy Rosary and his arrangement with its pastor, Father Saverio Zinzi.

At age sixty, Letizia Falcone is considerably younger than her recently deceased brother, Count Leone Capurro. And, for almost forty years, she has been married to a man detested by Leone as an opportunist who married his sister with the intent of getting his hands on the Capurro fortune. Rodolfo Falcone was thus shunned by Leone and kept as far away as possible from any of Leone's business interests. Now, with Leone gone, Rodolfo imagines that he will have an unfettered path to the Capurro riches. But first, he will have to deal with Marianna Soluri and her bastard son.

Raised by an aunt in the poorest part of Naples, Rodolfo Falcone never knew his parents, both of whom were murdered in an attempt to fight off gypsy brigands who had infiltrated their neighborhood and were systematically pocketing everything of value. During the skirmish between the gypsies and his parents, Rodolfo lay in a crib in the corner of a room and, in the heat of the fracas, was overlooked by the gypsies. His mother's sister, a dour and disappointed spinster, grudgingly took on the task of raising her orphaned nephew. Her lack of enthusiasm for her charge so disaffected the boy that he pledged at an early age to remedy this setback by acquiring wealth in any way possible. His greatest asset was his good looks. Almost six feet tall, his lean frame allowed him to project an air of superiority over his contemporaries, most of whom were shorter and less slender. And, if a splendid physique was not enough, Rodolfo had also inherited superb facial features. His classic nose sat between large dark brown eyes. His teeth were long and white as chalk and his smile showed off a long, square chin. He was the envy of his friends.

To earn his keep in his miserly aunt's house, he worked at various jobs almost from the time he was able to talk and carry a broom. At age nineteen, he signed on as a stable boy at a riding academy on the far side of the city. The Spanish Riding Academy catered to an elite clientele, most of whom were from the wealthiest families in Italy. It was not long before Rodolfo was being pursued by several of the young women sent to the academy to add equestrian skills to their repertoire. All of them were rich. Realizing that he would have his choice among these lucrative prospects, he chose the richest and most appealing maiden of the lot: Letizia Capurro. She was the daughter of a noble of the court of King Victor Emmanuel, her physical appearance was quite pleasing and she was intelligent. At twenty years old, she was typical of her Capurro heritage.

Tall and slim, she was lightly olive complexioned with long brown hair and hazel eyes. The smooth lines of her facial features combined with her graceful mannerisms to project a regal quality. At first, she was reluctant to become involved with Rodolfo, concerned that her family would not approve of a *fortune-seeker from the lower class*. Eventually, Rodolfo's considerable charms overcame her fears, and she was able to get her father's approval to marry him. Leone was appalled by the marriage, certain that this *Neapolitan gigolo* would ruin his sister's life. He was wrong. Despite his constant reliance on her for material support, Rodolfo appeared to have a genuine love for Letizia and soon became the father of two daughters. Nevertheless, he was never accepted into the family by Leone.

"Letizia, my dear, we must put aside our grieving for Leone for the moment. Marianna Soluri has returned from America and we need to deal with her." Rodolfo is concerned that Marianna has returned to Italy to lay claim to the Capurro fortune while he and Letizia are engaged in mourning the death of Leone.

"What do you want to do? What can we do to thwart my brother's will? If he wanted his bastard son to inherit what our family has cherished for generations, so be it. We have enough from my father's bequest to live on. Let Marianna have the rest."

"Absolutely not! The Capurro fortune belongs to you, not some harlot from the back streets of Gagliano. No, my dear, we must decide on what we have to do and act now. The law will understand our dilemma and perhaps even see Marianna as we do, a street tramp that lured Leone into an illicit relationship resulting in the birth of his only offspring. The boy can be provided for by the estate, but Marianna must be disinherited."

"How do you know she is in the will at all?"

"I don't, but we need to assume that your brother's arrangement with her was somehow connected to a final settlement upon his death. And, you can be sure at the very least, that Alessandro is the principal inheritor." Rodolfo's otherwise handsome face twists forebodingly, taking on a sinister appearance. His mind has been at work long enough. "We must discredit Marianna by revealing what we know about her. She has had many men and has a child in America with the man she lived with there for two years, all the while violating her agreement with Leone not to leave Calabria. What sort of mother would do that to her then only child? And what of Alessandro? Who is to say that he is the genuine offspring of Leone? He might very well be the child of one of the other men with whom Marianna shared her bed."

"That's not true and you know it."

"I know nothing of the kind and neither do you. The only person that has Capurro blood for sure is you. And the courts will see to it that Leone's fortune does not pass to a bastard son whose lineage is in question."

"You are forgetting something, my dear. The official record shows that Alessandro was adopted by Leone after his real father, Aldo Caristi, abandoned him and Marianna. It is clear that Leone intended for the child to be his inheritor."

"Not at all. I intend to make it clear that Leone believed that the child was of his blood. But, I will cast doubt on whether he really was. And let me tell you, that if Marianna insists on pursuing her claim, she will regret it."

"What do you mean?"

"There are ways of dealing with fortune-seeking scum like that. The courts may not turn out to be the answer.

Perhaps Marianna needs to meet with an accident."

"Rodolfo, I'll have no part in that."

"Don't worry yourself, my dear, you won't have to."

The hired carriage arrives at the front of the home that Marianna has left unused for the past two years. It is evening, and there are signs of life. Chimney smoke and candlelight indicate that Alessandro might be here to greet her. At the very least, a member of her family has gone to the trouble of preparing for her arrival. She climbs quickly down from the carriage and runs up to the door. As she swings it open, she is greeted by the aroma of quince. The fruit have recently been placed in a bowl on a table to scent the clean, orderly main room. Surely Gesuzza has been here to prepare the house for the arrival of her sister.

"Who is here? Alessandro, is it you?"

A tall and handsome boy, nine years of age, steps out from behind the door. His sandy-colored hair and hazel eyes are reminders to Marianna that this is the son of the now deceased Leone. She swells with pride that he is also of her blood. He is in his olive brown uniform, the shirt collar open and the cuffs turned back. To his mother he looks much like a miniature version of a soldier she had once seen walking on the streets of New York. In an instant, her eyes fill with tears and she is speechless as she confronts her guilt for having abandoned him by going to America to seek out Lorenzo.

"Mother! It's been such a long time. Did you miss me?"

"Alessandro. Come here and let me hold you. Yes, I missed you enormously. I thought of you every day and prayed for your safekeeping. The attack on the Capurro villa by irresponsible ruffians had me frightened that you would be exposed to danger."

"I wish that I had been there. I'd have taught those dirty share-croppers a thing or two."

"Alessandro, you must not talk that way. It is not the sharecroppers who are to blame. They are easily led to revolt because they are poor beyond your understanding."

"Perhaps so, but they are also responsible for my father's death and I will not forgive them. Some day, I will have my revenge."

"Don't talk that way. I can see that military school has created some false notions in your head. Remember that your family background from the Soluri side is humble and that many of your very own relatives speak of leaving Calabria for the Americas in order to escape the system that holds them down. Your father was aware of this problem. He would have helped the tenant farmers if he could."

For the next two days, mother and son tell of the events of their years apart. Alessandro talks excitedly of how he is training to be an officer in the King's army and how Italy will soon become an important Colonial power like the other nations of Europe. Marianna is appalled that her young child is being fed notions of warfare and conquest, but says nothing. She vows that she will somehow prevent Alessandro's return to a school that teaches such things. She tells him of her two-year adventure in the New World, omitting the amorous purpose of the trip and her affair with Lorenzo. She tells him of his sister living with her father in America and watches his eyes grow large and inquisitive. He declares that he will one day visit his half-sister and have a look at this fabled land that attracts so many of his countrymen. He glances questioningly at his mother, this woman whom he knows mostly from what others have told him, some casting her as the victim of a flawed social order, some inferring that she is an insidious opportunist. Now his adolescent mind can reach its own conclusion. She is here beside him. He can see for himself, and he likes the warm, loving mother who seems devoted to his well being. Marianna glances, too. She looks at this young boy, the product of her loins, who is of another order but who is none-the-less, hers. His father gone, Alessandro belongs to her only and, whatever the future holds, she is pleased with being his mother. Then, her thoughts turn to the purpose of her sudden return to Calabria and she decides to prepare Alessandro for the battle with his aunt and uncle over the Capurro title and fortune.

"Do you know your aunt Letizia and uncle Rodolfo very well?"

"No, mother, they have never been to my school and they are never present when I am at home visiting. I had the impression from father that he was not very fond of them."

"My son, I must be utterly frank with you. You are about to inherit your father's place in society. On the one hand, it means great power and wealth, but it also means that you will have enemies who will try to prevent you from taking your rightful place in the world. Your aunt and uncle are two such people. They will cast doubt on who your father is and tell terrible lies about me. They may even send malicious men to harm us. We need to be strong and stand up to them."

"Don't worry, mother, you can count on me."

⊢∙◆∘◆∙⊣

Capurro Villa has not changed in the years since Marianna has been absent. The stately old main house, surrounded by guesthouses and meticulous grounds filled with flowers and fruit trees, has been designated as the meeting place for the reading of Leone's will. Marianna is last to arrive, and has brought her son, Alessandro, to the event. As she looks around the massive room that was once Leone's study, she acknowledges the presence of Letizia and Rodolfo Falcone, Father Saverio Zinzi and Concetta, the head house servant. From behind the desk, in a dark suit and tie and looking drawn, Renato Rizzo greets Marianna and calls the meeting to order.

"Thank you all for coming. You have been asked to this meeting to witness the reading of the last will and testament of our dear, departed Count Leone Capurro. May God have mercy on his soul. Having written this will myself, I am quite familiar with it and will read only those sections of the will that are particular to the inheritance of property and title. Anyone wishing to see the entire document can arrange for that later. Do you all understand?"

"I would like to suggest that the boy be excluded from the reading. He is too young to grasp its meaning." Rodolfo has struck the first blow.

"No, I will not remove him. He is Leone's son and has every right to be here." Marianna responds in a strong voice and looks to Renato to defend her and Alessandro.

"I see no problem with the boy being present. Let's continue." Renato has settled the issue. There is a hushed silence in the room as Renato leafs through the papers in front of him until he finds the words that describe the legacy chosen for each of the people present in the room.

"Ah, I have found it. It reads: 'It is my final wish that … etc., etc… each of my house servants receive a year's wages, except for Concetta Russo, to whom I hereby bequeath a sum equal to two years' wages.' "

Concetta looks up with tears in her eyes, and whispers in a barely audible tone, "May he forever rest in peace. He was a good and generous man."

Renato continues, " 'To The Church of the Holy Rosary in Gagliano, I leave all of the property on which the church stands and all of the cemetery grounds, free and clear of encumbrance. In addition, I leave the sum of one hundred thousand lire for the perpetual care of the Capurro crypt in the cemetery of the church, to be administered by Father Saverio Zinzi for the remainder of his life and then by his successors as pastors of The Church of the Holy Rosary.' "

Father Zinzi sits up in his chair, trying to restrain his joy, but unable to contain himself. In a clear voice he declares, "The people of Gagliano will forever be grateful to this enlightened man. May God give him a special place in heaven."

Again, Renato resumes his reading, now sounding a bit guarded. " 'To my loving sister, Letizia Falcone, I leave the sum of five hundred thousand lire.' "

"What?" Rodolfo stands and shouts at Renato. "This is an insult. The Capurro estate is worth many millions. It needs to stay in the Capurro family. I protest!"

"Be seated, signor. And hold your tongue. This is not an auction. If you have anything to say, I will hear you out privately when this meeting is over." But there is great anger in Rodolfo's stare as he takes his seat reluctantly, Letizia tugging at his coat. It is clear that he does not intend to accept Leone's will as it is written.

"Please allow me to continue without further interruption. 'To Marianna Soluri, the mother of my child, I leave the sum of one hundred thousand lire. The remainder of my estate, including the title of Count of the Court of the Kingdom of Sardinia, I leave to Alessandro Capurro, who I now proclaim as my natural-born son.' "

"I demand a private meeting with you, Renato." Rodolfo's face is red and his chest is heaving from the anger that has overtaken him. As he looks across the room at Marianna and Alessandro, he is incensed further by what appears to him as a look of triumph on Marianna's face. "Don't think for a moment that I will stand for this, Marianna. I will do what I must to see that the Capurro fortune is not lost to the likes of you."

As the others exit, Father Zinzi remains behind for a moment to admonish Rodolfo. "My son, you should not allow your lust for riches to anger you so. Remember that in the end, you must answer to God."

"You tend to your own business, Father. I'll tend to mine."

<hr />

The early Spring rain falls noisily onto the cobblestones along the narrow main street of Gagliano. It is nighttime and the clacking of the large raindrops muffles all sound. Not far from the town square, on the first floor of Marianna's home, there is a light reflecting shadows against the shades of the main room. There is a struggle taking place between two people, one a large, hooded man and the other a boy. An arm is raised holding something that could be a rod for stoking the fireplace.

"You little bastard, I'll kill you." The man brings the bar down onto the boy, and a moment of quiet ensues. Then, a blaze of light appears as if the fire were being stoked and fed another log. A large man covering his face with a paper mask appears at the front door and makes his escape into the night. He leaves behind a smoldering mass creating smoke and flashes of light. It is the motionless body of Alessandro lying helpless across the bed of the fireplace, burning. The smoke surrounding his face is no longer drawn into his nostrils. The last vestige of life has been seared from the young corpse. As the rain and wind mix with the smoke escaping from around the door and windows, neighbors eventually observe it. They enter the house and make their way to the blackened corpse. Their eyes burn and they choke from the smoke-filled room. It is useless. There is no hope of saving the boy's life.

Earlier in the evening, Marianna had been summoned to her mother's side, a mile away, for fear that Stella could slip into a final coma. Drawn and old, she is now barely able to speak beyond a whisper. She numbers the remaining days of her life. The two women face one another and recall the past. Stella musters her strength to speak audibly.

"…. I did not wish for you to be alone. I thought your wealth would bring Lorenzo back to you. I'm sorry, Marianna."

"Don't apologize, mother. It was your plan that worked for me. Now that I have all the money I'll ever need, I won't ever be alone."

The old woman swallows hard. There is a rattle in her throat, the sound of approaching death. She pulls Marianna close to her and whispers, "Take care of your sister and her boys. Promise me."

"I promise, Momma."

Marianna is sorrowing as she leaves her failing mother and negotiates the wet, slippery street that leads back to her home. The rain has saturated her shawl, and the lamp she carries flickers as it swings from her motion. It is well past midnight, and she hears distant voices like plaintive wailing. She can see a crowd of neighbors around her door. Smoke is clearing from the blackened entrance. The rain has stopped momentarily as if to mitigate the horror that awaits her. Two of her neighbors have wrapped Alessandro in a blanket and are carrying his lifeless body toward the steps of The Church of the Holy Rosary, as if to unite the small corpse with its heaven-bound soul.

"Ayiieee! No, dear God. It can't be! Not my little boy. Oh, mother of God, have mercy." Marianna peers helplessly at the cruel, ironic reality. Having returned to her home from a faraway land and intending to take her place as mother to her beloved son, she must now somehow absorb the fact that she will live the remainder of her life without him. A surge of anxiety and fear combines with her grief. Her legs give way, and she falls to the ground weeping uncontrollably.

⊷⊶○⊷⊶

A carriage arrives at the Falcone home in Catanzaro, a small villa set back from the road on an acre of ground. The sole occupant of the cab steps down. It is Aldo Caristi, Leone's former groundskeeper. Rodolfo, who is preparing his legal attack on Marianna, has summoned him to Catanzaro.

"Good morning, Aldo. How was your trip from Catania?"

"The trip was fine, but I hate to leave my farm in the hands of the help. They are an unconcerned and careless lot. It's a wonder we are able to produce anything."

Rodolfo remembers how this former gardener and messenger was spared the disgrace of a firing squad by Leone's interceding. He then obediently became the nominal husband to Marianna and stepfather to Alessandro. Eventually, he rose to the position of landowner as payment by Leone for abandoning his conspired wife and child. Now he speaks with disdain of those who are in the position he was in less than a decade ago. Rodolfo thinks to himself, 'What short memory these peasants have.'

"I will not keep you long. We can arrange for your testimony to be recorded tomorrow. But for now, come in and refresh yourself. We have much to talk about."

That night, Rodolfo prepares Aldo for the statement that he will attest to: that Marianna had a love interest with at least one man other than Leone. Moreover, there is reason to believe that the child resulted from a liaison with a young man from Gagliano, considering the number of times that Marianna visited him secretly. Truth seems not to matter in the discussion between the two men. Of importance is the fact that Marianna must be defeated in her quest to obtain Alessandro's inheritance, and that Aldo will be further enriched for his trouble in returning to Calabria to give testimony. The fact of Alessandro's recent death by *accident* is not discussed. It is merely an unfortunate occurrence that will inadvertently assist Rodolfo in overcoming Marianna's claim to inheritance and places in prominence the question of who will inherit Leone's title.

"Marianna, you must be realistic. A court decision may easily void your claim to the boy's inheritance and surely give the title to the Falcones." Renato Rizzo meets with Marianna to advise her on her chances of defending her claim to the Leone fortune now that Alessandro is no longer the inheritor.

"I will not let that scum win. He arranged for my darling Alessandro to be killed and I cannot betray my son's memory by giving in to his assassin." Emotion overtakes Marianna and she sobs into her handkerchief.

"Very well, Marianna. I will do as you wish. But, remember, your life is in danger with this man. You must secure yourself against the possibility of an attack on your person."

"What do I do?"

"Hire a bodyguard."

"I don't know anyone who can protect me. Do you?"

"Yes, Marianna, I do. He is a former Bersaglieri officer with a very distinguished service in the Abyssinian war. Since his return from the fighting, he has been earning his living by protecting people in circumstances like yours."

"How do I contact him?"

"I will get a message to him. He lives in the city of Maida. His name is Franco Gagliardi."

Chapter 25

Franco

As a young boy, Franco Gagliardo was struck by the uniform of a Bersaglieri troop of soldiers marching in a parade. Their dark green uniforms and black boots showed off their tall, northern Italian frames. And their plumed, pointed hats gave them an air of distinction and splendor that little Franco had never before seen. They were reputed to be the best marksmen in Europe and had recently won honors for their triumphant combat in the Crimean War. As they marched past the parade stand, the swift roll of three drummers and the inspirational marching melody played by several other marchers stirred a memorable emotion in the boy. He swore at that moment that he would one day become a Bersaglieri. He never wavered in his conviction from that day on. When his father realized the sincerity of his son's desire, he inquired about the process one follows to join the Bersaglieri, an elite rifle corps of the region of Piedmont. Applications to Turin for his admission to the training camp were all turned down, citing such reasons as height requirements and ability to communicate in the dialect of the Piedmontese.

Franco's father would not give up. Having heard about the origins of the Capurro family of Catanzaro, he made arrangements to meet with Count Leone.

"Don Leone, is it true that your ancestry is Piedmontese?"

"Yes, my father was born in Rivoli and was himself a Count of the Sardinian Court. He located the family in Calabria so that we would be where our land is situated. It was he from whom I inherited my title."

"Then it is true. Signor, you are in a position to do me a great favor. My son has grown up with the unswerving desire to become a Bersaglieri soldier. His applications to Turin have all been rejected, citing all manner of reason to refuse him. He has no other aim in life. Who knows what will become of him if he fails to have this opportunity. Is there any way that you can help him?"

"The Piedmontese have never allowed anyone from outside their province to join their cherished Bersaglieri. But times are changing. The King has been persuaded to extend his influence beyond Italy and to colonize parts of Africa that are in need of a European protector. The military forces are being expanded to begin the campaign."

"Does that mean that you will help us?"

"Yes, it does. I will base my plea on the exceptional record of the Calabrian forces that fought with me in the Risorgimento. Perhaps that argument, along with their requirements for increasing their numbers, will persuade them to admit your son for training."

The Count's plea to the Bersaglieri worked. In the span of a few months, Franco received orders to report to a training camp in Chivasso, a remote town in the foothills not far from Turin. By now he was nineteen years old and stood five feet eight inches tall, an above average height for a Calabrian. His dark-complexioned face and black hair contrasted with blue eyes that were deeply set and appeared to gaze out on the world with compassion. He had fallen in love with Agostina Sicilia, a dark-haired, brown-eyed young beauty from his village of Maida, and until he was called to Chivasso, it appeared that he might ask for her hand in marriage. Now he had other more important business. His life's dream was about to come true. He could think of nothing else.

"Franco, if you care for me as you say you do, how can you go off to this place that no one has ever heard of and leave me to wonder if I will ever see you again?" Agostina is hurt by Franco's sudden willingness to leave her to pursue this dream that she had heard him talk about.

"My dear, I must follow my destiny. Don't lose patience with me. I'll be back when I've completed training and can arrange for a furlough."

Franco was true to his word. After completing military training, he returned to Maida on leave, to be with Agostina and their families. Dressed in the uniform he admired throughout his youth, he looked older and more adult than his years. Lines appeared in his otherwise smooth, handsome face. His blue eyes seemed more serious than ever, and his gait had taken on swagger. Though he did not ask for Agostina's hand in marriage, it was assumed by both families that they would one day marry.

Heavily chaperoned most of the time, they were once able to steal away unnoticed to a remote stand of evergreens overlooking the Tyrenian Sea. There, they made love and promised one another their fidelity for the rest of their lives. Only Agostina bore the pain of separation. For Franco, leaving Maida meant that he would join the others in his troop and go off to some new and interesting billet, where they would strut in their ceremonial dress and talk of war and conquest for Italy.

In 1896, in its campaign to colonize Ethiopia, Italy found itself more and more dependent on elite troops such as the Bersaglieri. Their bravery and fighting abilities were expected to compensate for the young nation's hesitation to pour great numbers of fighting men into battle at considerable expense. As a result, those involved in the struggle for empire found themselves vastly outnumbered by an incensed native people. For a time, the superior training and discipline of the Bersaglieri kept the enemy at bay and under their control. Eventually, the mammoth proportion of the opposing force overran their positions, ending the Italian quest for territory. Beyond the hopeless odds, Italy's fighting men were subjected to the terrors of fighting a war against an ancient people with crude ways of dealing with adversaries. Mutilations and death marches were routine for prisoners of war.

Franco's family was made aware that his troop had been sent to the Italian colony of Eritrea, ostensibly to join the forces fighting the Ethiopians in the adjoining territory. A month later, they were told that Franco was among the defenders of Macalle, a strategically important city in the center of the Ethiopian region of Tigre. As the world watched, the twelve hundred defenders of an otherwise impregnable fortress had run out of food and water, but had vowed to fight their opposing force of ten thousand natives to the death. At the last moment, they were saved by an unexpected settlement in which Italy agreed to withdraw from the territory. Both sides preserved their reputations with the international community by showing compassion for the doomed troopers. Sadly, Franco's mother experienced a stroke a week after she learned that Franco would be reassigned to a Bersaglieri troop fighting in another province.

Following the Macalle rescue, the most heroic of the defenders were given field commissions as lieutenants and put in charge of whole companies of fighting men. Such was the case for Franco. During the savage fighting at Adowa, in which most of his company was wiped out, he was taken prisoner, and after what seemed an eternity of negotiation, he was released and returned home. In Turin, he was lauded for his heroism and decorated with a royal sash. But, for some undeterminable reason, he was honorably discharged and sent home to Maida. To everyone's surprise, he became reclusive, refusing to see anyone other than his immediate family, and never venturing out during the hours of daylight. Despite his pledge to Agostina that they would be married upon his return from the war, he refused to see her or to offer any explanations.

"How can he do this to me? I'm entitled to an explanation, if nothing else. Has he found another woman? If so, he should let me know." Agostina was appalled at Franco's strange behavior and demanded an explanation. But none was forthcoming. He refused to see her or to offer any account of his behavior. After a while, she gave up trying to see him and went on with her life. As the months rolled by, Franco eventually faced the reality that he needed to choose a vocation. But what? He later learned that a town elder, Massimo Agnello, had been accused of betraying a special oath of loyalty to a secret political organization and had been threatened with bodily harm. Franco strapped on his service revolver and paid a visit to the old man.

"Signor Agnello, can I be of assistance to you in your disagreement with your political friends… or should I say enemies?"

"What do you know of this matter?"

"Nothing, except that I have heard that you are in trouble with some of your former associates and need bodily protection from them. I can offer you my expert assistance, should anyone attempt to harm you."

Massimo hired Franco in the nick of time. On the second day of his assignment, Franco encountered a leathery-looking tough sent to punish the elderly man with a few strokes from a long, thin rock covered in thick hide. Franco easily disarmed the man and sent him on his way with a few bruises from his own club. A week later, in the middle of the night, a second thug tried to break into the Agnello home, only to encounter Franco as he stepped through a window he had forced open. Surprising the man, Franco was able to beat him brutally with his bare hands, so that he pleaded for his life. He was sent away bleeding from his nose and mouth and holding a wrist that appeared to be broken.

After two unsuccessful attempts, the perpetrators finally realized that this war hero by the name of Franco Gagliardo, a former Bersaglieri officer, was not going to allow his charge to be injured. The onus of betrayal was quickly removed from Massimo, sending news of his defense by Franco coursing throughout Calabria. Thereafter, persons needing such protection called upon him. Eventually, he could pick and choose his assignments and

even favor those with potential for rewarding him gener-
ously. Such was the case with Marianna. Not only was she
the mother of a student of the military who had been
murdered, but she was also in a position to compensate
her protector handsomely. He approached his assignment
with enthusiasm.

"Since the assailant is likely to strike at any time, I will
need to be with you at all times. I will accompany you
everywhere during the day and will sleep outside your
bedroom door at night. Do you have concerns about the
appearance of that?"

"No, Franco. Everyone knows that my life is in danger, and that you are a bodyguard. Besides, who would
ever give me credit for discretion?"

The constant companionship of Marianna and Franco
had begun. Older than Franco by twelve years, Marianna
is not beyond suspicion of taking up with him. But, as the
town gossips observe, *'her manner is more to pursue older men
of substantial wealth.'* Yet, though she has reached the age of
forty, she is still shapely and her facial features are still neatly
contained by firm skin. The men at the coffee house enjoy
their speculation as to what goes on in Marianna's house in
the middle of the night. Still, to her great surprise, Franco
makes no move to indicate that he might be interested in
an affair with her. Has she grown old? Does Franco not wish
to cloud their relationship with *amore*?

Marianna dresses herself in her most provocative dress.
It is cut low at the bosom, clinging to the well-formed body
that has turned many a head. Her hair is carefully coiffed
in a twist behind her head, giving her eyes their utmost
focus. Her lips are heavily coated a bright red while her
eyelids are shadowed in gray. She wears large jeweled
earrings and several gold bracelets on each wrist. They

are alone in the house, the maid having gone home. Clearly, she is inviting Franco into a sexual encounter with her. But Franco does not respond. Marianna is frantic.

"Franco, may I ask you a question? Do you have a woman in Maida who dominates your interest?"

"No, Marianna, I do not. I am merely not interested in women."

"How can that be? Are you homosexual?"

"No, I am not." Franco seeks to end the conversation.

"You must tell me. Why are you so aloof all of the time?"

Franco's eyes stare ahead of him. He seems to be overcome with a truth that he cannot bear. He turns and stares at Marianna, his eyes gaping at her.

"Why do you question me? What business is it of anyone's?"

"Surely, you know my background. I am the last to criticize anyone's indiscretions. God knows I have had enough of my own. I am merely curious about you, now that we have spent all this time together. And, who knows how long I may continue to require your services. There seems to be no end to the negotiations with Rodolfo."

"Marianna, I will tell you my story. But first, you must swear that you will share it with no one, that you will carry it to your death."

Marianna draws in a deep breath, her eyes opening wide. "I swear that I will tell no one."

They are each in an easy chair and Franco lights a pipe as he begins his story.

In November of 1895, I was assigned to duty in the colony of Eritrea. It was not long before we were sent to a fortress in Tigre outside the city of Macalle to aid in its defense. All told, including the native Ascari troops, we were 1200 strong. Food and water were in very short supply and the enemy, who num-

bered 20,000, had seized the water source outside the fort. It was only a matter of time until we were either relieved by a greater force from the Colony or forced to fight to the death in defense of Macalle. The Ascari, who numbered 800, were amazing. They were loyal to us to the point of extreme self-sacrifice. They earned less pay and were given fewer rations than the white officers and men. Yet, they fought and died willingly, eagerly protecting the officers from enemy fire. When they were captured alive, they were mutilated by having their right hand and left foot cut off. Many of them simply bled to death from their injuries. Others lived the remainder of their lives so severely handicapped that they wished they had died.

The Ethiopian fighting men were supplied with rifles and ammunition by French and Russian gunrunners. They were the best-armed natives in Africa. Thankfully, our carbines were superior to most of their weapons. They dressed for battle in their finest clothing: flowing robes of various pastel colors, and turban-like headdress. They chanted endlessly to remind us that we were greatly outnumbered and they beat drums that signaled the arrival of more and more of them each day. One of our senior officers who attempted to negotiate a peace with them later described their leader to us. 'He was dressed in a long dark robe of purple silk with gold embroidery. Only his own grizzled hair covered his head. His skin was a rich chocolate color and his eyes were a pair of gleaming, tawny orbs that looked out on a frightened audience.' Is there any wonder that they fought so valiantly for this man? One morning, they began their attack. They came at us in waves and kept coming despite our cannon fire that tore away their lives. The plain in front of the fort was so densely populated that it was evident we could never drive them all back. We could only hope to hold them off. Once our water was gone, however, we would have to make a run for it in their midst. We were certain to be killed at that point.

On the day before our water ran out, a white flag was unexpectedly hoisted by an enemy horseman carrying a message to us from his leader. It was notification that a cease-fire had been negotiated by the War Office in Rome that would allow us to leave Macalle unharmed. A roar of joy and relief rose from the fort as the word was passed. We could see the disappointed faces of the enemy as we looked at them through our field glasses. Their leaders had deprived them of the pleasure of killing us. We verified the treaty terms with headquarters in the Colony and then left Macalle and the territory of Tigre behind.

Upon arrival in Asmara, the capital city of Eritrea, four enlisted men, including myself, were notified that we had earned field commissions, the rank of lieutenant, and that each of us was assigned to lead a full company of native soldiers into battle 70 miles to the South, near the city of Adowa. Considering the ordeal that we had just been through, we were allowed five days rest before departing. As we left for the front, each man carried his allowance of 112 cartridges, a reserve of two days rations and a bottle of water. Within two days, we had reached Adowa. It was a familiar sight. The numbers of hostiles was incredible. A hundred and twenty thousand men would fight less than twenty thousand of us. We would later learn that a reserve of another hundred thousand of the enemy lay in wait behind the lines to be thrust upon us at the critical moment. The lean, fierce-looking Ethiopians in their cloaks of brilliant color, some infantry, some horsemen, waited for their great feudal chieftain to signal the attack. When it came, the gallant men of Italy were overwhelmed by the staggering odds. The quiet discipline of the European soldier, and his superior training, enabled our side to hold out for a time, perhaps the better part of a day. In the end, the hail of rifle shot fired at us took its toll and we were then reduced to fighting at close quarters with bayonet and sidearm. The hand-to-hand struggle was dogged, lasting only an hour as the enemy's lances and swords cut into the bodies of our men. I found myself among the very few who had survived the final charge. Surrounded by several attackers, I managed to fire several shots with my revolver, killing two of them. It became evident that they had decided to take me alive. One of them stepped forward as I tried frantically to reload my pistol. He struck me in the cheek with the butt of his sword and I was knocked unconscious. When I awoke, my arms were closely bound behind my back and I was being taken to the enemy camp behind the lines. There, I was placed in a tent along with twenty of my fellow officers, some of them wounded. In the distance, we could hear the constant crackle of weapons being fired and the occasional report of cannon-fire from our guns. As the cannon fire became less frequent, it meant that our side was being overrun, the men and munitions captured. The following day, we were led down a long line of our native Ascari that had been taken prisoner and mutilated by having their right hand and left foot hacked off. Some of the men of my own company called to me as I went by, waving the handless arm. It was horrifying. An enormous guilt overcame me as I looked at these poor Ascaris who would go through the remainder of their lives in this maimed condition. We arrived at an open area, where we were tied spread-eagle to posts that were set firmly in the ground. There, we were left in the intense sun without benefit of shade, nor were we given water to drink. After a few hours, we were delirious from the deprivation and loss of blood at the hands of our captors and the ordeal of the previous day.

On the following morning, a strange ritual war dance was performed in front of us, while we continued to be stretched out before them. A team of fierce-looking dancers wearing only loincloths and wielding straight, two-edged swords - uncommon for them- twirled to the beat of intense music, all the while holding their rapiers high above their heads. When the music stopped, *with hundreds of their comrades looking on, the dancers charged at us and tore away the clothing below our beltline. Then, as we tugged and tore at the bonds holding us, they slid the sword between our legs and cut away our testicles. The screams of agony were terrifying. For me, it was the most pain I have ever experienced in my life. Thankfully, I passed out. I woke up several hours later lying in the tent we had first occupied. A bloody cloth was jammed between my legs and the pain was so intense that I dared not move. A mutilated Ascari tended me with his one hand, giving me to drink and feeding me a flour and meal concoction that sustained us all through the torment. Despite his own pain, he handled me carefully so as not to cause me any further agony. Life in that tent was sheer misery. It was filthy and crawling with ants, roaches and rodents all darting about. The water was a muddy yellowish brown and had a taste of rotten eggs. There was little to eat besides the standard Ascari fare and no medicine at all. We were the few who survived the loss of blood, the infection and enormous shock to our bodies. So intense was the pain that most of the survivors prayed for death. Weeks later, I was placed on a crudely constructed stretcher and taken to a cart containing eight other officers who had survived. The cart, drawn by a team of mules, was our transportation back to the colony. The war had ended and Italy had been defeated. There was outrage among the civilized world because of the mutilations that had taken place at the hands of the Ethiopians, especially the emasculations. The enemy offered only that they had followed the example of King David of Israel, who was reported in the Bible to have emasculated his enemies among the Philistines.*

Marianna is horrified by the story unfolded by Franco. Now she understands the strange behavior of this man who has become her protector. Her face is wet with tears as the man who sits next to her reveals the story of the tragic battle of Adowa. She leans over to him, places her arms around him and kisses him tenderly.

━─◆─○─◆─━

A message arrives from Renato Rizzo. Marianna is to meet him at the Capurro villa in Catanzaro to discuss the settlement he has been able to negotiate for her. It has been three months since attempts at conciliation with Rodolfo have begun, and almost that long since her son has been found dead. Now Renato feels that it is time to conclude the negotiation.

"Marianna, I believe that I have worked out a settlement that you can accept."

"What is it?"

"Your inheritance from Leone has been doubled. You will receive two hundred thousand lire, a very handsome sum."

"What about my son's title? And the rest of the estate?"

"The title will go to Letizia until there is a male heir who is of Capurro blood. The remainder of the estate will go to Rodolfo and Letizia."

"What kind of settlement is that? Why must Leone's fortune go to Rodolfo?"

"Because he is married to Leone's only living sibling."

"Renato, you know how Leone hated Rodolfo. How could you allow this to happen?"

"There is little alternative, Marianna. Rodolfo has prepared a very convincing case to take to court. He has Aldo's testimony of how you had a lover in Gagliano who most likely fathered Alessandro. He can prove that you abandoned your son in direct violation of your arrangement with Leone, by living in America for two years. And, perhaps most damaging is the fact that you have had another child with the very man who is identified as your lover."

"Except for the birth of my daughter, those are lies. The truth is that he had my son killed to eliminate the only person with a higher claim than Letizia's to Leone's title and fortune. Aldo is scum who would testify to anything for money. And it was never my intention to stay in America. Italy is my home and I would have returned eventually in any case."

"Nevertheless, I must advise you to accept the terms of the settlement. You can easily live very comfortably on the proposed amount for the balance of your life. To allow Rodolfo to bring the allegations to court will be very risky. You could lose everything."

"Don't you understand, Renato? To accept his offer is to betray the memory of my son. I won't do it!"

"Suit yourself, but you had better talk to another lawyer before you make up your mind. You will see that I am right."

"I have already made up my mind. I am going to fight him."

⊱──◦──⊰

The night is as stifling as any in Marianna's memory. The August sun had earlier combined with moist air to create humidity that is just below point of rain. Together, the heat and moisture create a punishing intensity. The aroma of sheep and goats permeate the air. An occasional bray of a donkey is registered, as though its owner could be told to reduce the heat. It is late and outside Marianna's bedroom door, Franco curls up on a mattress of straw, and tries to sleep. His arm curls around the mattress to finger the hidden nine-millimeter handgun that awaits his command. He is unable to sleep and concentrates on the thick, still air. A curious rustle is heard outside in the otherwise motionless night. Franco is too experienced to allow a minor sound to get his attention. Another sound, this time a crackle sounding more like straw crumbling under a man's foot, reaches him. Franco sits up on his bed and listens. The third report removes all doubt. Someone is coming. Franco takes the gun in his hand. His feet are bare and make no sound as he descends the stairs to the first floor. A shadow passes the shaded window on one end of the main room. He wonders why the intruder chose not to enter the open portal. Then, a whisper. The prowler is not alone.

Franco stands motionless for several minutes that seem an eternity. He must determine how many of these scum have come to do Rodolfo's bidding. He hears three distinct voices, whispering in the darkness. He peers from behind a shade. There are four of them. He thinks to himself about the odds being so like Adowa, only there they were even higher. He turns and runs quickly up the stairs to Marianna's room. She is sleeping. He places his hand gently over her mouth and awakens her.

"Marianna, they are here to harm you. When I leave, bolt your door. If you hear a scuffle, throw your mattress out the window to the ground below, and jump into it. Hopefully, you will not injure yourself. You must then make your way quickly to the police barracks."

"And what of you, Franco?"

He smiles. "Don't worry. I can take care of myself."

"Very well, then, I am ready." Marianna reaches under her bed and brings up a nine-millimeter Berretta pistol. She has spare rounds as well. The determined look on her face tells him that she is prepared to do what she must.

Franco smiles at her and leaves her room. He hears the bolt on her door slide shut as he descends once more to the first floor, gun in hand. There has been no further movement by the men outside towards the house. He crouches and waits. He hears a whisper.

"Are you ready?"

"Yes."

"Be quiet. We don't want him to awaken."

One man comes to the front door and determines that it has been bolted. He backs away and moves toward a front window. It is open. He raises the window and climbs carefully into the front room. At that same moment, another of the men climbs through the window at the far end of the room. Franco thinks to himself that they are experienced. They make very little sound. One of the men quickly opens the front door and, suddenly, there are four of them in the house. It is very dark as they make their way over to the staircase leading to the second floor. Franco swings into motion.

"What are you doing here, you *bastardi*?" Franco startles the men as he leaps up and pushes one through the open entrance door and onto his back outside. The others close in on him. He cocks the hammer on his pistol and in one instant rams his elbow into one of the intruders and fires a round point blank into the shoulder of another of them. The fourth man attempts to bring him down with a thrust of his knife, but manages only to slice his forearm. Franco uses the muzzle of his gun in a backhand swipe across the man's face. He is elated as he looks down on all four of his invaders lying on the floor, his mind racing about how next to disarm them and send them on their way. Suddenly from behind, a fifth intruder who has forced his way through the back door brings a club down on him, missing his head but landing solidly on his shoulder. Franco falls to his knees only partially conscious, now bleeding profusely from his forearm where the knife had cut him. The others recover and begin pummeling him mercilessly, until he collapses to the floor, now bleeding from the nose, mouth and head. A bat of one assailant strikes him hard in the face and eye. Another attacker takes close aim at his knee and strikes the kneecap, producing a heavy cracking sound.

The battle is over. The shot fired from Franco's gun has aroused the neighborhood and a Carabiniere presence could be expected any moment. The men look to their leader.

"*Andiamo.* There's no point in getting involved with the law." They scramble quickly to a carriage waiting up the street and disappear.

"Franco! What have they done to you?" It is Marianna, who in the suddenness of the confrontation, has decided not to leave Franco to face a group of assailants alone. But, when the fighting begins, she is frozen in her tracks, unable to come to his aid. Now she stands, gun in hand, trembling over his limp body, hoping to revive him. He lies very still and shows no sign of breathing. In a moment, a Carabiniere officer is leaning over him, checking for life.

"He's breathing. Quickly, we must get him to a doctor."

<hr />

A somber and shaken Renato Rizzo opens the door to the Capurro villa to receive Marianna. Word of the break-in of the five intruders on Marianna's home has reached him. Surmising that she would run to him for protection, her arrival is not a surprise. He has himself gone to the front door for just that possibility.

"Are you all right?"

"You might say so, but I will not breathe comfortably until I know that Franco is all right. He looked dead when they took him away."

"There is no way that you can help Franco now. The surgeon attending him is doing everything possible. You must help yourself. Bring this insanity to a conclusion. Agree to Rodolfo's terms before he kills you."

"No, I will not. The Carabinieri are aware of Rodolfo's intentions after this last attack. They will not let any further harm come to me."

Renato is furious. "Marianna! You can't be serious. You will be killed the moment that you are left alone."

Marianna looks back at him. "Get me a greater amount of money and I'll settle."

Morning arrives at the Capurro villa. Marianna has stayed the night, occupying a bed she once shared with Leone. She has had a restless night, despite the sumptuous comfort of her bed. As light comes in through the center of the window where the drapes were not pulled tight, she thinks of the turmoil that has been created as much by her own lust for riches as the greed of her adversary, Rodolfo Falcone. Tears come to her eyes as she thinks of her dead son's body being carried off before her very eyes. She thinks of the little daughter she left in Queens with her father, and how the three had hugged for the last time before she left for Italy to claim her inheritance from Leone. And now, Franco's life could well have been snuffed out. She gets up quickly and dresses. She goes down to the breakfast room and finds Renato eating.

"Renato. *Basta*. I am ready to end the war with Rodolfo. Draft the documents and I will sign them."

"Signora, you have made the right decision. I will inform Rodolfo at once."

—•—°—•—

The home of Don Luigi Nerli, the only physician in Catanzaro with surgical skills, is large enough to house emergency patients in one room on the first floor. There on a bed, Franco is very still and looking pale.

"Did I see him breathe?" Marianna looks down with hope and pity.

"Yes, signora, it is very possible that he will live, but he will never see from his left eye again. And he will be a partial invalid. His right leg is paralyzed and may eventually have to be removed at the knee. He will be dependent on others for the remainder of his life."

She is devastated. "See that he receives the best of care while he recuperates."

Marianna is exhausted as she returns to her home, free of the specter of death and violence that has dominated her life since her return to Italy. She is aware that her house has been put back in order for her during her short absence. She sits in a chair and leans back. There is a soft knock on her door. It is her sister, Gesuzza, looking down at the ground as though some catastrophe has occurred.

"Gesuzza, what is it? What's wrong?"

"It's Momma. She died last night."

Chapter 26

Migration

Angelo Martino was born in the town of Chiaromonte, in the region of Basilicata just north of Calabria. Having spent most of his young life farming an olive grove for a share of the crop, he had accumulated some capital in the hope of acquiring his own property. He was able to locate a small farm for sale in the countryside just outside of Gagliano and, with his bride of a few months, moved to Gagliano and made the purchase. Within a few months, he had an offer of purchase from Leone's farm manager, who had inadvertently missed purchasing the property on Leone's behalf. At first, Angelo resisted the offer, but when the purchase price was raised to three times his purchase price of only four months prior, Angelo agreed to the sale. Knowing that the possibility of finding another farm for sale among the landholders of Southern Italy was very remote, he and Maria decided to emigrate to America. There, in their adopted country, they would find a suitable farm for purchase. While they awaited their passports and immigration documents, Angelo decided to help his needy friend, Pietro Chiarella, and his family, with their farm. His excitement over his imminent migration spilled out in every conversation with Pietro and eventually dominated every conversation between them.

"It is a great country and there is much opportunity. There is so much land that the land grabbers can't get it all. Even young people like us can find land to own and farm. They don't have olives or citrus, but there are lots of other crops grown there, even in the cold temperatures."

"But how does one get the capital required to purchase a farm?"

"I have heard that there are many jobs there for laborers, that they pay well enough to allow the frugal person to save some money each week from his pay. I, myself, will work on the construction of an underground railroad in New York City until I have enough information about how best to get into farming."

"How did you find that job? Do you think I could work at such a job?" Pietro's passion for immigrating to America was never so intense. "I'm Sure that the padrone in America could find you a job, either on the railroad or elsewhere. Come with us, Pietro. You'll never regret it."

"What about Giuseppe?"

"He's very young, but he can come, too."

Pietro is torn between his loyalty to his mother and the irresistible urge to immigrate to America. He would have to determine that Marianna would indeed take responsibility for Gesuzza and Raffaele, and be certain that Gesuzza could withstand the absence of two of her sons for an indefinite time. Only then would he feel free to pursue his obsession with America. He chooses to approach Marianna first.

"Zi' Marian', may I share something with you?"

"Yes, of course, Pietro, what is it?"

"For the last few years, I have dreamed of going to America. I have offered to take my mother and my brothers. My intent was to eventually bring my father to a home we would have in America, upon his release from prison. My mother is inclined to go, but has steadfastly refused to leave Italy until she is reunited with my father. That will not happen for three more years. I am now faced with the possibility of a good job in America, and Giuseppe would probably have an equal chance at steady work as well. He has indicated that he wishes to go with me, if I so choose. However, I will not go unless I know for sure that my mother will be provided for. Can you tell me what you meant when you said that you will assist her?"

"My dear nephew, as you know I have just returned from America and I have had a chance to observe the life among Italians there. It is not as pleasant as some would have you believe. Mostly, Italians are used for work that others cannot or will not do. If you are a stonemason or an artisan, you can demand a reasonable wage that will permit you to live on a level with the poorest of Americans. If you are unskilled, you will be given the dirtiest of work and paid the lowest wage possible. You will live poorly and wish you had never left Italy."

"My friend Angelo Martino has a padrone there who will get me a good job with the railroad in New York City. I'll save and buy a farm as quickly as I get the money together."

"Very well, then. I will see to it that Gesuzza and Raffaele are provided for, for as long as your father is away."

"God bless you, Zi'."

Armed with the belief that his mother and brother have a source of support, Pietro runs to Gesuzza to determine her feelings.

"Ma, I was talking with Angelo Martino today. He and Maria are leaving for America as soon as their passports arrive. He tells me that his padrone in New York can get me and Giuseppe good jobs on the railroad in New York City and wants me and Giuseppe to go with them. Zi' Marian' has said that she will look after you until Pa is back. Then, we can send for the two of you and be together in America. This is the opportunity I've been waiting for, but we'll only go if we have your blessing."

"My son, of course you have my blessing. I will miss the two of you terribly, but I will not stand in your way. Make your plans and tell Angelo that you are going."

Raffaele misses his older brothers, but his greatest pain is that of watching his mother plunge into further depression. Three of her family members are now gone from her sight, no longer require her care and can no longer console her. At times, she wonders if she will ever see them again. She speaks only when she must, and prays constantly for the safety of her family. She lives only for the day when they can all be together. Outside, in the streets of Gagliano, Raffaele listens to his friends talk of the New World and of the day when they, too, will leave their shabby world for the shiny existence on the other side of the Atlantic. Antonio Pace and Antonio Marrella speak naively of America; "There are jobs for all and all live in large homes." "There are farms available for the taking, to own without having to pay for them." "There are laws that make Sundays a holiday and no one works on holidays."

Raffaele looks up and says solemnly, "I choose to live here in Italy where I was born. My grandfather fought to free Italy, and I'm proud of him. I'd fight as well if my country were threatened."

The two Antonio's glance at one another in puzzlement and change the subject.

Chapter 27

Angelo's Demise

The fall evening is cool and as night falls, the cooing of swallows signals the whereabouts of their perch for the night. Shadows lengthen as the scarlet sun makes its descent into the horizon, outlining the buildings of Gagliano. A buzzing sound fills the evening air as the insects sense that freedom has once more arrived with nightfall. The single bray of a donkey breaks the tranquil outdoors as the townspeople retreat indoors and light their candles.

In the Chiarella household, Angelo sits staring as though he sees nothing. His second nine-year imprisonment has at last ended and he has returned home. But, while he is physically present, his mind wanders back to the faraway place off the coast of Sardinia that has stolen his life. What remains of his once blonde hair is now a faded gray. His features are bloated and wrinkled. His back bears the scars of a whipping received years earlier in prison. His once tall frame is bent over from the years of tending the garden at Prigione dell Asinara, a duty he was thankful to have been granted as a special favor from his friend, Don Generoso. Indeed, it was this singular act that ended his persecution as a man marked for his physical effrontery to the Carabinieri. Becoming the prison gardener had saved his life. But for what purpose? Now in his late fifties, his life seems empty and spent. His wife has lead a difficult life of deprivation and sorrow. She, too, appears old beyond her years. Wrinkled and skeletal, she does not complain or lament. Deprived of a husband, she has been the principal provider for their children. His two older sons have gone to America. His one remaining son has never seen him before now, and looks upon him as a stranger.

Limping from an accident at the prison that left his left foot permanently damaged, Angelo pulls at a straw mattress kept inside the back door, taking it to the highest spot on a hill behind the row of houses on his street. There, under the moon and stars, he prepares for his night's sleep, the open air confirming his new status as a free man. As he lays back cradling his head, he covers himself with a flimsy blanket and gazes at the darkened sky. He thinks, *Of what further use am I to my family or myself? Why does God allow me to live? I have brought nothing but shame and misery to my wife and children and caused them to live a brutally hard life. I have survived, but I am looked upon by everyone as a hardened criminal who has spent his life shut away in prison. Even my wife and son don't know me.*

He sobs quietly into his cupped hands.

Why me? Why did I have to be convicted of a crime of which

*I was innocent? And why did my poor children have to suffer
so? My sons have had no real father. I was taken away from
them from the time of their youth. Thankfully, their grandfather
was alive to give them a fatherly presence. But now they have
no desire to be with me. Even Raffaele will leave when he is able.
And who could blame them?*

He rolls over and falls into a deep sleep, murmuring
senseless words that seem like muffled responses to prison
guards.

"Angelo! Come have your breakfast." Morning has arrived and Gesuzza calls out to Angelo to come in from his
outdoor slumber and prepare for the day ahead. He sits
up and shakes his head as though the sleep could be ex-
pelled by force. Though he is partly infirm, he must contribute to the support of the family. He is no longer able to
do the heavy work, but he can tend animals. There are
sheep to care for and goats to milk. Two hogs need to be
fattened for sale at the market. But the principal source of
support is still the farm belonging to the Capurro estate.
And, now that Leone is gone and Marianna can no longer
assert her influence over the farm manager, the Chiarellas
are simply another of the many sharecropper families
whose toil is exploited for the benefit of the landlord.
Gesuzza and her ten-year-old son Raffaele grow and harvest the olives, oranges and lemons from a farm a half-
hour away from their home. Each morning, the two pack
their midday sustenance and walk to the farm to begin their
day's work. Only siesta allows for a respite from their toil.
If they are fortunate, they are able to complete their day's
work early and return home in the early evening. Then,
their evening hours can be spent together, eating their
evening meal and listening to the music of neighbors strum-

ming their mandolins and singing lyrics describing the beautiful Calabrian vistas or some long lost love.

Though Marianna lives in Gagliano, Gesuzza rarely sees her. Somehow, Marianna has forgotten the vow made in her mother's final days to provide for Gesuzza and her boys. Though her riches are greater than she will ever need to provide for herself, she seems oblivious to her sister's plight. And, now that Angelo has returned home, her conscience is relieved of any burden of caring for Gesuzza. Though the abandonment hurts her deeply, Gesuzza defends Marianna against the insinuations made by Angelo and Raffaele.

"Marianna is my dear sister, and I will always love and respect her. She has had a heavy burden in life, what with the death of Alessandro and the refusal of Lorenzo to come home with their daughter to live in Italy. Money and position aren't everything. Marianna has her cross to bear in this life."

But Gesuzza must live with the reality that Marianna is more generous with her servants than with her. She sees a housemaid wearing a dress that Marianna tires of, while Gesuzza wears the same drab peasant dress that she has owned for years. Marianna sends her cook for a vacation interval in Sicily at a cost of a hundred lire, enough money to buy Gesuzza and her family some much needed clothing. Gesuzza says nothing and demands that her family do likewise.

Marianna enjoys her young nephew's company and will occasionally hire a helper for Gesuzza so that Raffaele can spend a day with her rather than going to work on the farm. The two develop a frank relationship and are outspoken with one another.

"You know, of course, that my mother constantly defends you to me and my father. Sometimes that can be difficult, considering your ways."

"Whatever do you mean, Rafi? What does my sister have to defend me about?"

"You're always spending your money on clothes that you seldom wear and junk that you have no real use for, while we're constantly working to have enough food to eat. Our clothes are worn and old and we sleep on straw, while other folks have cotton mattresses and several changes of clothing. What good is it having a rich aunt if we can't count on your help once in a while?"

Within a week following Raffaele's complaint, Gesuzza is showered with gifts from her sister. Dried pasta and fruits, herb seasonings and bottled wine arrive on the doorstep. A bolt of patterned cloth, needles, thread and scissors are contained in a large box that is delivered from the general store. The dressmaker brings her a readymade dress. Gesuzza is wild-eyed with excitement as she receives her sister's gifts, but she is furious at Raffaele for having asserted himself with Marianna and asked for her help.

⊱─◦─◦─◦─⊰

Raffaele is ten years old and has spent most of his young life working in the fields alongside his mother and brothers. He stands barely five feet tall, but his energy is more like that of an older, larger boy. His dark eyes and olive-complexioned skin resemble the maternal side of his family, but his temper and wit is suggestive of his father. Unlike most of his contemporaries, he is a happy and cheerful boy, taking every opportunity to add some little pleasure to his life. In the rare moments between chores, he hunts birds with a borrowed shotgun. In the evenings, he plays a mandolin he has taught himself to play and even sings along with the music. The serious side of his nature appears in his devotion to his lonely mother. He tries to compensate for the absence of his two brothers.

Now Raffaele meets his father for the first time. He no longer depends on the hearsay and descriptions of others who are older and who remember Angelo before he was sent to prison. Angelo has spent the prime of his life, some twenty years, either in prison or in the hills dodging the law. He is a bitter, broken man whose patience wears thin quickly. He is particularly impatient with Raffaele, often admonishing him for the least avoidance of his daily chores.

"Raffaele, where have you been? I need help with milking the goats and someone has to call in the sheep for the night."

"I'm sorry, Pa, but I've worked all day in the groves and I took a few minutes to hunt birds. See? I have some here for dinner tonight."

"Who asked you to go hunting? I need you here. When you finish work, you report to me. Get it?"

"I don't need to report to anyone. I've been doing fine without you. Don't think you can order me around."

Angelo flies into a rage. The boy has struck a nerve and the wild look on Angelo's face confirms it. Raffaele starts to leave.

"Come back here, you little bastard. Don't you ever speak to me like that!"

As Raffaele increases his pace, Angelo is furious. He picks up an axe that is used for splitting firewood and flings it directly at Raffaele. The axe whizzes past Raffaele's head and finds its home in a nearby tree trunk. Gesuzza stumbles onto the scene and is horrified.

"Angelo, are you crazy? Do you want to kill your own son?"

Angelo opens his mouth, but no sound comes out. He seems frozen in his tracks. Then, almost as though he had been shot in the back, he falls forward onto the ground, gasping for air. He is in desperate need of help.

"Raffaele! Come quick! Your father is having a stroke!"

But Raffaele is beyond earshot and happily engaged in strumming his mandolin under a tree. Gesuzza must drag Angelo into the house and onto their bed. There, she nurses him back to consciousness and assesses his health. It is not a stroke after all. Angelo is able to move and speak. But his breathing is heavy and his chest is heaving. Perhaps he is experiencing heart failure. He speaks in hushed tones.

"Gesuzza, I fear that I don't have a long time to live. I must see my boys before I die. Please, Gesuzza, ask them to come home to us. I want to die in peace with my family around me."

"Oh, Angelo, don't be so dramatic. You're in no danger of dying. You're just exhausted. You'll be all right tomorrow."

But in her heart, Gesuzza knows that Angelo is right. She visits a scribe on the following day and sends notice to Pietro and Giuseppe that their father is gravely ill and wants them at his side. Months before, the boys had asked Gesuzza and Angelo to come to America to live; but Angelo refused, saying that his health was so poor that he would be rejected at Ellis Island and returned to Italy. Now they are being asked to give up their existence in the New World along with its opportunity to work and live far better than they ever could in Calabria. Though they are employed at the bottom of the economic scale, they are able to have a flat of their own, sharing facilities with only one other family. They eat well, mostly foods that they were not accustomed to back home. The cheese is a strange variety and is purchased in a long wooden box; and the pasta is dried for convenience and stored until it is time to boil it for dinner. The price of most basic foods is reasonable, even for the poorest laborers. And, they are able to save something each week from their pay. Still, Pietro decides immediately to return home. He is lonesome for the sight of his mother and places a great value on being with her. He thinks also of the father he has not seen in a decade. He turns to Giuseppe and announces his intention to leave for Italy.

"I must go back, Giuseppe. I miss Ma and Raffaele, and Pa is in a bad way. Much as I hardly know him, I feel a responsibility to be there while he is so sick."

"Well, don't expect me to go with you. I've got a good job at last and I'm staying here."

"That's your choice, Giuseppe, but I'm choosing to go back."

Giuseppe is cross. He knows at this point that he must either replace Pietro with someone else to share the rent of the flat or move to a boarding house. The prospect of the latter troubles him. After all, he had raised his status by moving to a rented apartment with his brother. Returning to a life of storing his worldly belongings in a trunk and sharing a room with a dozen other men is more than he can countenance.

"Godammit, Pietro, what kind of brother are you? You're going to abandon me so that you can return to a father we don't even know. And then what? You'll get drafted and sent to some miserable place in Africa to fight the locals in the name of Italian conquest."

Pietro is uncharacteristically heated in his response.

"Giuseppe, you could never understand my motives. Yes, I am going back to be with our father in his last days, but it is more to protect Ma from the misery she will experience. To hell with the military. They can't take me now that I'm an American."

"OK, Pietro, but when you come back, bring me a bride from Gagliano."

Gesuzza has been at the olive grove since daybreak. It is winter and the trees require pruning. As she cuts away at the dense branches, a jubilant mood overtakes her and she senses that something in her life will change for the better. She looks down from her ladder at Raffaele, who is pruning the lower branches of another tree. She feels blessed that she was given this child at an age when most women would not have been able to bear children. He is a good and obedient son and has been a comfort at a time when she is separated from her other sons. Her thoughts drift to Pietro and Giuseppe. Have they gotten her letter? Will they heed her wish that they return to Italy to be with the family at a time when their father is so ill? Still, the jubilance endures. Something good will happen today. She descends the ladder, careful not to trip on her long skirt. She removes the shawl from around her head and mops her sweaty brow. The day has reached mid point. She is tired and thankful that siesta time has arrived. She and Raffaele eat their lunch of cheese and bread and drink their water. Then, they each select a tree and lie back against the trunk. They are soon asleep.

"Mother…ma…wake up, it's Pietro."

Gesuzza's awareness returns slowly as she awakens

and looks up. There she sees her son Pietro, standing six feet tall and looking as handsome as ever. Raffaele is by his side, his arm around his brother's waist and wearing a proud, broad smile. Joy has returned to her life. She leaps up from her roost and throws her arms around Pietro.

"The Lord has answered my prayers. I have lived a hundred years these past two and they were years of misery."

"I'm glad to be home, ma."

"But where is Giuseppe?"

"He isn't coming. He wants to stay and work and save his money so that one day he can own his own home in America."

"I understand, but it would feel good to have our whole family together at this time. As you know, your father is very ill and wants to be with all of you. His years in prison have worn him out. He is no longer able to work the farm and live a normal life. We must try to understand and be patient with him. Come, let's go down to the house and find him."

The three walk home in the mild winter sunshine, Pietro excitedly telling of his life in America and of the progress that he and Giuseppe made in just a few years. He reopens the question of immigration of the whole family and is again told of his father's stubbornness in wanting to remain in Italy.

"Why would Pa want to remain in a place where he was treated so badly and had his life ruined?"

"He has heard from many of his friends of the hardships of getting established in a new country and of the discrimination they suffered at the hands of the Americans. He has heard of a group of Sicilians who had established themselves in a place called New Orleans and were lynched by a jealous, angry mob. There is no way that you can change his mind."

"What about South America?"

"That's even worse. He learned that I had refused an offer to leave him to go to Argentina with a man to whom I was betrothed before I met your father. But that's another story from another time. Your father would never go to South America."

The boys look at one another and shrug. Perhaps their mother is more worldly than they know.

⊱─◌─◌─◌─⊰

The morning fog rolls in through the open window, chilling the house. Pietro is first to arise and closes the window. He builds a fire with the wood that he and Raffaele stacked on the hearth the previous day. As he brews the morning chicory he thinks about the day's chores. He has relieved Gesuzza of the need to work the fields and the orchards. He and Raffaele have taken that over, allowing Gesuzza to care for the animals and for Angelo, who is virtually bedridden with what is believed to be consumption. Pietro thinks to himself, *I must not allow my wish to be back in America to be suspected by my family. Although I do not regret having returned to my family, I know now that this is not the place to seek a life and a future. I envy Giuseppe for having remained behind in America, though I do not understand his willingness to live away from our family permanently. If only Pa would have allowed us to all be united in America, we would be able to care for him so much better and we would be building a better life for us all. Now it is too late. Pa's health will prevent him from ever entering America as an immigrant and Raffaele has strangely become a patriot of Italy, talking about the achievements of the Risorgimento and the pos-*

sibility of war with Turkey over possession of Libya.

Suddenly, Gesuzza appears from out of the bedroom. Her face is white with fright. Her eyes are moist and her lip quivers. She looks up at Pietro.

"Your father is not responding. He just lies there, staring up at the ceiling and not making a sound. Go to him, Pietro."

Pietro enters the room and sees Angelo lying very still in the bed. He feels a chill of fear of what he will discover, but overcomes his dread and touches Angelo. There is no motion in response. He feels Angelo's wrist, searching for a pulse. There is none. He places his hand near Angelo's mouth hoping for an exhale indicating life. Still there is not a sign. Finally, he places his hand carefully over Angelo's eyes and brings down the lids in acknowledgement of what he must tell Gesuzza.

"He's gone, Ma." Pietro's voice cracks as he announces his father's demise to his mother. Though he does not know Angelo as a son knows his father, there is sorrow in his voice. His sentiment is more with his mother, who he worries, will be wounded yet again in her troubled life.

"Lord have mercy on his immortal soul." Gesuzza is surprisingly strong and shows little emotion at first hearing Pietro's confirmation of what she had suspected. "His life was wasted, and for what? He never did what he was accused of, but they ruined his life just the same. Twenty years of strife and deprivation for him and for us. I hope they are satisfied now that there is nothing left to take."

Angelo is finally at rest. He had overcome the harsh mountain life and familial discord of his youth only to be unjustly pulled away from the happiness he had found in his marriage to Gesuzza. But now he is out of harm's reach. No Carabinieri will come to his door in search of contraband. He will never again face a judge in fear of being convicted. The prison guards in Asinara can no longer have their sadistic fun with him, nor inflict their punishments. He will never return to them. Neither will he ever experience the satisfactions of life. He will not see his sons marry and become fathers. He will not experience the joy of having grandchildren come into his life. He will never have the contentment of an old age spent with a loving spouse.

Chapter 28

War in Libya

The rainy winter lays siege to Tripoli, the capitol of a land in turmoil as the world considers her fate. The year's rainfall will occur over a few weeks time, creating the illusion of streams and rivers and inviting plant growth to spring from the sparse soil. It is mere fantasy, however. The scorching sun will reappear before the first flower makes its debut, and will void the landscape of all vegetation. Only the faraway oases, with their enormous springs of water, are verdant and abundant.

It is 1911 and, in the Turkish-owned colony of Libya, Turk and Arab alike abuse the unwelcome Europeans. Muggings and public beatings are commonplace. Police are openly sympathetic to the local populace and ignore the travesty that is taking place. Businessmen and explor-

ers from the Western European nations are being sum-
marily convicted on contrived charges that often result in
lengthy imprisonment in primitive Libyan prisons. Pro-
tests by embassy personnel go unresolved. It is incum-
bent upon the Europeans to either alter their ambitions
for trade with Libya or expel the Turkish government. After
a year of debate, the European nations encourage Italy to
include Libya in her sphere of influence and create a
friendly atmosphere there for her allies. To do so, Italy must
replace Turkey by taking possession of Libya. The result
is a war that will last a year and cost both sides dearly.

For weeks now, Gesuzza has been sorrowfully praying for the repose of Angelo's soul and been aloof from
the rest of her family. Even Marianna's sudden attention
to Gesuzza's welfare with gifts of food and trinkets has
not been acknowledged. She seems to be strangely and
totally preoccupied with her new status as a grieving
widow, as though nothing else were present in her life.

"Ma, we need to leave Italy before the war gets going
and they want me to serve in the military."

"I just can't leave Italy now, Pietro. Your father is buried here and it would be wrong of me to leave and abandon him. Besides, you're an American. They can't take you
into service for Italy, can they?"

"I'm afraid they can, Ma. I am told that there is something called *the Sanguine Law* here in Italy, which means
that they consider me an Italian citizen because I am born
of Italian parents, regardless of what other nationality I
adopt."

"I'll think about it, Pietro. It would be wonderful to
have my family reunited, but it would mean that your father is buried here and we will all be in America. Besides,
I have a feeling that Raffaele would object to leaving Italy."

"That's no reason to balk, Ma. Raffaele is only thirteen years old and doesn't know what he wants. And, yes, we would have to leave Pa in his grave in Gagliano, but what does that matter? What is important is the welfare of those of us who are still alive."

"We'll see."

A few weeks later, a Carabiniere lieutenant appears at the door of the Chiarella house carrying a folded document. "Is there a Pietro Chiarella living here?"

"Yes. What can we do for you?" Pietro is wary.

"Are you he?"

"Yes."

"It is my duty to inform you that you are conscripted into the service of his majesty's army. You are to report to the barracks of the Carabinieri in the morning, at which time you will be taken up north for training." The officer hands Pietro a document verifying his status as a draftee. It is signed by Major Adolfo Liotta, the commander of the Carabinieri in Gagliano. He is the same man who infuriated Angelo many years ago by searching his home and goading him into breaking the law.

"I am an American and I am planning to return to America."

"Not until you perform your duty to the King of Italy may you return to America." The Carabiniere lieutenant has heard the lament before.

Gesuzza looks up from inside the house where she is seated, a look of fear and guilt on her face. Could it be that her delaying of Pietro's return to America has trapped him into a tour of duty in the army? There could not be a more dangerous time to be in military service. A unit of one hundred thousand men is currently being assembled to be sent to the war front in Libya, where Italy has challenged Turkey's ownership of the colony.

"Pietro, I'm truly sorry that I held back on leaving for America. I should have agreed and we would all be gone by now. Now you will have to serve in the army."

"Don't be silly, Ma, we'd have waited until after harvest anyhow. There is no way that we could have purchased passage for us all without the share of the crop we all worked so hard to earn."

━┿━◇━◇━┿━

The battleship Sicilia steams across the Mediterranean towards its destination of Tripoli. It is early October of 1911, and the war for possession of Libya has begun. Twelve hundred troops are on board in their fighting gear. They will be landed on the beach below the capital city and will become the first to storm the garrison there. The Sicilia and its sister ship, the Garibaldi, open fire on the enemy and silence their guns. The landing of the troops begins. Among the men in the landing force is a Calabrian, Pietro Chiarella. He thinks: *It is believed that the Turks have abandoned their positions in the fortresses along the coast. Our Navy is so powerful that it can destroy the enemy at will from their position in the Mediterranean Sea out of range of Turkish guns. The Turks have had to move inland and fight us from there. We are being cautious in approaching the fortifications around Tripoli, but we have thus far met with no resistance. The smaller weapons and ammunition have all been taken away and the larger guns have been rendered useless, but we have all of the armament we require. And the Garibaldi has just landed thousands of reinforcements from a Bersaglieri troop that includes some Ascari's from Eritrea. Our biggest problem with Libya is the filth and lack of clean water to drink and to use for washing.*

The signal is given and the swarm of Italian foot soldiers charges the last one hundred yards to the edge of the city. There is no resistance. Only the mayor and his entourage are there to welcome the troops and assure them that the people of Tripoli are on the side of the Italians. The devastation caused by the bombardment of the city is evident everywhere. Whole buildings have collapsed and hardly one stands that does not have a gaping hole where it was struck by a shell from the Italian ships just off the shore. The citizenry of Tripoli who remain behind are mostly the Arabs and blacks who have decided that possession of their land by the Italians is preferable to occupation by the Turks. At least Italy's motives are clear. It intends to trade freely with as many of the inhabitants as possible and develop the vastly underdeveloped country as a farmland to be settled by the huge overpopulation of Southern Italy and Lombardy. The Turks, on the other hand, seem to have no desire other than to rule and tax the inhabitants for the benefit of the Turkish homeland.

But colonization of Libya is not easily achieved. The Turks are able to appeal to Libyans by stressing the commonality in their beliefs in Islam and the uncertainty of how they would be treated by Catholic Italy. The result is that hordes of native fighting men leave the city and comprise a formidable opposing force surrounding the city on three sides. Only the side on the Mediterranean Sea is left to the Italians. It is used to maintain a supply line for troop replacements, armaments, food and much needed fresh water. Already the incidence of cholera and malaria among the Italians is noticeable. Each day, they suffer the loss of 25 to 30 men to cholera. An equal number become infected with malaria.

"Sergeant, I'm feeling feverish and faint." Pietro has

shown the first signs of malarial infection. "You'd better turn in to the infirmary." The sergeant points to a tent erected in the center of a wide street with a large red cross on its side. As Pietro walks toward the tent, he suddenly begins to shiver and realizes that he has become very cold.

"Doctor, I'm not sure what is going on. I was feverish a moment ago. Now I'm freezing. What's happening to me?"

"My boy, I'm afraid you have become infected with malaria."

"Is it serious?"

"Normally, you would be treated over the period of a few days and your illness would end for a time. Chances are that it would return again, but with a dose of quinine, it would be for only a few days each time the infection re-occurs."

"Then let's get on with it. Inject me or however you do it." Pietro is beginning to feel faint and is brought to a cot on one end of the tent. A blanket is thrown over him to quell his shivers. The doctor walks over to Pietro and looks down at him from a standing position.

"Trooper, I'm afraid I have bad news for you. There is no quinine. We've used it all and I can't seem to get the bureaucracy in Rome to understand how serious the problem is and to get me some medicine so I can do my job. I'll have twenty more of you in here before the end of the day and all I can do is tell you what the disease is that you have."

"What will happen to me?"

"If you can keep the fever in check, you'll pull through. The rest of it is just having to put up with a lot of discomfort."

"OK. But how do I keep the fever in check?"

"Drink as much water as you can and stay out of the sun. We'll give you aspirin four times a day until this thing is over."

Two weeks later, a weak and drawn Pietro leaves the hospital with the malaria gone. He has suffered untold periods of alternating fevers and shivers and, at one point, had become convulsive. The doctor gives Pietro a final word of advice as he exits from the infirmary tent. "Stay out of the sun and drink plenty of water…as much as you can get."

⊱───••○••───⊰

Skirmishes between the Turks and the Italians continue through winter, resulting in huge casualties on both sides. The Italian strength is in the coastal areas, where the ground forces can call on their navy to provide heavy battery against the enemy. Inland, the superior numbers of Turks and Arabs maintain control. Both sides fight for territory, at great sacrifice, only to surrender their spoils in a subsequent scuffle. Pietro's unit, a half-regiment of 1250 men, is sent to relieve a force in the inland camp of Ain Zara, where an outbreak of malaria renders the defending Italians helpless. The town is a mere five miles from the front lines and is under constant attack from the Turks. Rumor has it that the enemy is amassing a force of six thousand men to storm Ain Zara and take it back from the Italians.

The infantry unit is quickly entrenched in the defenses of the town, which has been in the middle of the fighting for several weeks and has been laid bare by shelling from both sides. The fortress is little more than a steeply sloping knoll with trenches and parapets at the top that allow combatants to stand and fire their weapons without exposing themselves to the enemy. The compressed sand makes a poor defense, but the troop digs in and sets up their machine guns and cannon. Their firepower is enormous for the size of the fortress, but the opposing force is well armed and huge in number. There is talk among the Italians of the poor odds of holding the enemy back.

"How do they expect us to hold the line without an adequate force? They know that the Turks have six thousand men, or even more, and that they have some heavy artillery. Can you imagine the impact their shells will make against this sand?"

"Quit the griping. We're here to do a job and we're going to do as we're told." The commander hears the talk and reins in his men. They are not here to plan the defense. They are here to defend. It is dusk and, as they look out across the sandy plain, they can see large numbers of horsemen riding toward them. The rumble of hoofs and shouts can be heard coming from the enemy.

"Here they come!" A sentry announces the imminent arrival of the enemy. Even from afar, it is evident from their garb that there are far more Arabs than Turks. The flowing robes and girded headgear are everywhere. There is no time for discussing the odds or for attending to fortification. The enemy must be stopped. A sudden explosion inside the fort reveals the fact that the enemy has wisely placed a cannon within range and is preceding the assault with bombardment. The gun must be silenced or the enemy will reduce the fort to rubble, along with the men. It is spotted, and within moments put out of commission by return fire from a heavy gun with precise gun sights. The Turkish cavalry continues its drive up the slope to the fort and is repulsed by fire from five machine guns and hundreds of rifles. The retreat gives rise to cheering by the defenders. But the commandant of the fort knows that this attack was merely designed to reveal the extent of Italian defenses. The Turks will be back in even greater number, and they will not again be so easily repulsed.

Pietro's face is painted with a blank stare after the emotional trauma of battle. He has killed his first human being, deliberately and with dispatch. He had watched the Arab cavalryman pressing his mount to reach the crest of the hill, and took careful aim at his head. The crack of his rifle and its recoil were simultaneous with the man's plunge to the ground. He saw the horse continue riderless for a time, before it too met with a round in its throat. Two of Pietro's comrades, close to his side in the fighting, had been struck by enemy fire, one of them killed. As he sits in his stupor, he feels a strange sensation of power for having survived the battle unscathed. But then, he is attacked within his own body.

"Oh, my God. I think the malaria is back." Pietro senses a surge in his body temperature that he knows is the advent of a malarial attack. Within moments, he is shivering. There is no further doubt. He must somehow get some drinking water and try to reach the dispensary to the rear of the fort. He thinks, *why now? My comrades need me more now than ever. The Turks will be back soon and we need every gun possible to defeat them.* But he is unable to stay at his post. He obtains permission and leaves, heading for the rear. There, he finds the tent in which casualties are being tended and the dead are being prepared for their interment deep in the Libyan sand. He staggers as he enters, and falls onto a cot. He is not noticed. The medics are preoccupied with the urgent need for their focus, created by the skirmish that has just taken place. He senses that this attack of malaria is more intense than he has felt before.

"Aiute!" He calls out for help as he passes out. When

he awakens, he is aware that he has been attended. There is water at his side and there is a blanket over him that shields him from the cold shivers in his body. A chaplain approaches him.

"My son, would you like to unburden your sins and receive Holy Communion?"

"Yes, father, but I have a favor to ask."

"Of course. What is it?"

"I wish to write a letter."

⊢⊶⊙⊷⊣

The new season has once again brought singular beauty to Gagliano. Green buds appear on trees and vines everywhere. A spring festival, thanking the Deity for His beneficence, is held. There is gaiety and prayer of thanksgiving. All but one in the town join in a procession to the Blessed Virgin. Alone in her home, Gesuzza kneels at her bedside, her hands clasped in prayer. She implores the Lord to protect her son from harm.

"Lord, there is but one thing I would ask of you. Protect my Pietro from harm. He is a kind and gentle soul and his life has been one of devotion. He is good in every respect and I could not live on without him."

She continues, reciting the rosary and several prayers, appealing to God for the safety of her son. It has been six months since the fighting in Libya has commenced and she has heard nothing from Pietro. She imagines that he is wounded and in need of help. Then she dismisses the thought and tries to envision him standing tall in his uniform with medals glistening on his chest. It does not help her mood. She is miserable and cannot bring herself to leave the house for any activity other than her work. She and Raffaele are now alone and all the work is theirs to perform. They have reduced the size of the herd and have no time left for making cheese to sell. They toil endlessly at the farm that is their principal source of sustenance. Raffaele is now fourteen years old and, though he is much younger and considerably shorter than Pietro, his high energy compensates and he is able to cope with the absence of his brother.

"Gesuzza!" It is Anita Cecchini, calling out in one of the few times that Gesuzza is seen outside of her door. "There is a list of casualties from Libya on the board in front of police headquarters. I didn't see Pietro's name on it, but you might want to look it over."

"I've seen those lists and Pietro's name isn't on any of them." Gesuzza has tried to work up the courage to look for Pietro's name, but has not done so. Anita knows, but says no more.

As the sun rises in the morning sky and the day begins to warm, Gesuzza sees the postman riding his unsteady bicycle and depositing mail in a few of the doorways along the way. He stops in front of her home and hands her a letter. Her emotions run wild.

"What is it? Is it a letter from Pietro?"

"Yes, it appears so. It's from Libya...an army address."

Gesuzza takes the letter immediately to the Church of the Holy Rosary. There, she finds Father Zinzi and implores him to read it to her.

"It's from Pietro. Let me put on my glasses and I'll read it. Let's see. It says,

My dear mother,

It has been several months since I have seen you and Raffaele, and I miss you both terribly. I think of how you must be labor-ing without my help and it pains me. Perhaps when this awful war is over, I can convince you to go back with me to America. I know you will be happy there.

I have bad news, Ma. Malaria has caught up with me and it has gotten very bad. As I compose this letter, I am burning with fever and I am passing blood in my urine. The attacks have not been this bad before and I fear for my life, as there is no quinine for any of us. I would not tell of this, except that I want you to know that I am truly sorry for having left you those two years that I was in America. I expected that Za' Marian' would take care of you as she promised she would. Since she didn't, I feel it was my fault that you lived so poorly during my absence, and I ask your forgiveness.

The war here is as terrible as I imagined it would be. We are greatly outnumbered and the enemy is determined to drive us out. We have been able to hold them back thus far, but the odds against us are great and the enemy seems relentless. I am now unable to take part in the fighting because of my illness.

Stay well, Ma, and take good care of Raffaele. Ask Za' Marian' for help. You are her closest relative and she has an obligation to keep you secure. Pray that my health takes a turn for the better and that we can someday be together again.

Your loving son,

It is signed, Pietro."

Gesuzza has tried to hold back her tears, but her face is wet and she is sobbing as Father Zinzi looks up. "I'm very sorry, Gesuzza. I will devote a novena to his recovery and safe return home."

The Calabrian summer of 1912 is not unlike the summers before it. The blazing sun rises each day and partners with a searing wind blowing in off the North African continent to create a hellish landscape. The ground is parched and hot. Little vegetation remains green without deliberate assistance. Farmers take precaution that their crops do not burn up in the heat. They irrigate and fend off the army of marauding insects.

A scroll mounted on the wall outside of the police barracks in Gagliano gives notification of those who have been wounded or killed in the war that has raged on in Libya for ten months. The wounded arrive home from the warfront, sporting their decorations and concealing their injuries as best they can. Others return in wooden boxes, the unceremonious army caskets, draped in the flag of the Kingdom. They are home for burial in the cemetery adjoining The Church of the Holy Rosary.

"I must go down to the police barracks. I haven't read the casualty listing in a month." Gesuzza nervously notifies Raffaele that he will be on his own for the rest of the day. "OK, Ma, don't worry about me. I'll be all right."

Gesuzza has had an intuitive feeling since early morning, a premonition about the danger Pietro is facing. She vows to not allow herself to become distressed. She will determine the facts shortly. As she nears the area where the listing is posted, there are two women examining the names. They are the mother and spouse of one of the men fighting in Libya. The women leave as Gesuzza arrives. Their faces show relief from not having found their man's name. There are nineteen names on the list, a cross inscribed alongside six of them believed to have been killed. Five of the names have been added since Gesuzza was here last. Though she can neither read nor write, she has a small piece of paper with Pietro's name written on it by Father Zinzi. She holds it alongside the new entries on the list. "Oh, Jesus! No! No!" She has found Pietro's name on the list. There is no cross following the name, so at least he is alive. Then, she thinks: *Perhaps he is on the list because of his malaria. Of course, that's it! He isn't wounded, he's sick.* But much as she clings to the hope that he is merely ill, the possibility that he is wounded looms. She walks home dejectedly, fingering her rosary beads and praying the whole way. The thought of Pietro wounded or in the hands of the enemy frightens her, and she feels unprotected by any earthly force.

⊶◦⊷

The first relief from the intense heat of the Libyan summer has at last arrived. Summer in Tripoli has been extremely hot and violent, with sandstorms occurring frequently, humidity at a constant 95 percent and the Celsius continually above 50 degrees. Now the month of October cools and portends of a wet and cold winter ahead. The war would be fought in a tumult of winter weather, with more young men going to their graves and even more being maimed.

Reports from Libya are unchanging: The war is going well for Italy and soon it will be finished. The many young Calabrians will then come home to be reunited with their waiting families. This was Gesuzza's dream. Pietro has been away for many months and she prays daily for his safe return. She misses him desperately, his voice, his comforting words, his warm embrace. She has Raffaele with her and Giuseppe in America, and she loves them very much. But Pietro is her first born and is the very essence of her life. Even as a young boy, throughout the grief and torment of her existence, he provided the comfort that lifted her from her misery. She marveled at his intuitiveness, sometimes sensing the origin of her pain even before she did. He had none of the vices of other young men. He neither smoked nor drank anything more alcoholic than ordinary wine. He never used foul language or wasted his time in idle pursuit of women of the night. Rather, he spoke honestly to all and always engaged in productive labor.

To Calabrians, the hot, moist air of the Sirocco is a terrible annoyance. But, to Gesuzza, it is the wind that comes from the African desert, from her beloved Pietro. While others complain, she tills the soil, tends the livestock, scrubs her clothes and cooks the evening meal without uttering objection. When the wind stops and others express joy, she becomes ill at ease, sensing an impending fate and a disengagement from Pietro. She loves all of her family greatly, but Pietro she adores.

⊱─━─◦──◦─━─⊰

Finally and unexpectedly, the Sultan of Turkey declares surrender after a year of fighting. The killing is over at last, and the Italians have won the war and the colony of Libya. A thankful Italy celebrates as their army of 150,000 troops is relieved by an occupation force, and returns home. Gesuzza has heard nothing from Pietro. In the final months of the war, she attempts to determine his whereabouts and condition. Her efforts are in vain. The army does not cooperate with peasants seeking information.

They would otherwise be mired in a maze of correspondence beyond their capacity to handle. Gesuzza waits and
prays. She sees the other men of Gagliano return, and
hopes that Pietro will be among the next arrivals.

"Antonio, welcome home. Did you by any chance see
Pietro on your trip home?" Gesuzza questions returning
troopers, hoping that one may have seen Pietro.

"No, signora, but be patient and he will eventually
show up."

▷┼◁▷─○─◁┼◁

Doctor Pasquale D'Adamo is from a prosperous family in Cosenza, and unlike the great majority of Calabrians,
he has attended school from the time he was six years old
until he graduated from medical school at the University
of Bologna at the age of 29. His entry into the field of medicine coincided with the start of the Italo-Turkish War and
he was quickly drafted and sent to Tripoli to care for the
wounded. His beginning as a doctor was a baptism of fire.
Like Pietro, he was among the relief unit for the malaria-
ridden troops in the garrison at Ain Zara. Each day, dozens of casualties were brought in to him to receive medical attention. Mostly, they were wounds in need of
disinfecting and patching. Then, the malaria that had defeated the preceding unit began to affect several men in
his brigade. Pietro was among them. Untreated because
of a lack of quinine to quell the illness, many of the stricken
died. But Pietro's body was able to cope with the illness,
despite increasingly severe attacks. Too ill to fight but well
enough to assist at the infirmary, he became Pasquale's
orderly. Then, at the end of the war, Pasquale was returned
to his home in Cosenza. First, he stopped in Gagliano to

talk to Gesuzza Chiarella.

"Good day, signora." From the moment the doctor arrives at her door in his army officer's uniform, Gesuzza seems to have become speechless, as she looks up at his tall frame and listens intently. "May I come in? I have lots to tell you." Gesuzza motions him in, but she is still mute. "I would like to tell you about Libya and your son's heroic contribution to his country."

It was a year ago when we were all sent to Tripoli for the start of the war with the Turks. We were attached to the 7th army corps. The navy transported us across the Mediterranean and then bombarded the coast while we prepared for the landing. Thankfully, when we went ashore, the enemy had fled the city. We were unopposed for the whole time that it took to take possession of the city. The enemy had taken all of the food and water, so it was necessary to bring supplies from Sicily to feed the locals. There were detachments of our unit sent out to the garrisons around the city and one of them, the one at Ain Zara, was under attack by a large force of Turks. There was an outbreak of malaria among the men defending the fort and eventually they were unable to continue fighting. A replacement force from units stationed in Tripoli was formed and sent to Ain Zara. Pietro was one of the replacements, as was I.

There was terrible fighting there from the moment we arrived. The enemy was mostly Arab militiamen recruited by the Turks. There were thousands of them, all armed with repeating rifles. To them it was a religious war, and they came at us with a frenzied ferocity. They were Muslims defending Allah against the Christians. They even had some cannons, although our guns silenced them right away. Occasionally, a number of them would break through and get into our camp. That took hand-to-hand combat with side arms, swords and bayonets. The carnage was difficult to watch, even for a physician like myself. There were usually more of them than us, but they did not have the discipline of a European-trained army and were easily disorganized. Because we were in a temporary camp with very few facilities, we were unable to take prisoners and they knew it. The result was that every scuffle became a fight to the death. When one of them was brought down, he was killed on the spot, usually run through with a bayonet.

Pasquale could see by now that the talk of violence was affecting Gesuzza. She is drawing in deep breaths and looking very uncomfortable. He decides to limit further talk of the fighting except where Pietro is directly involved.

Pietro first came to the infirmary after several weeks of fighting. He had a serious case of malaria and could barely stand. Since we had no quinine, we had no way of curing his illness. We gave him lots of water to drink and kept his fever under control as much as possible. He did not recover, but he was sufficiently improved that he could hold a rifle to his shoulder and fire it, so we decided that he would guard the infirmary along with the detachment of healthy troops assigned to us. The Turks were determined to retake Ain Zara and at one point made a full-scale attack on our defenses. Their numbers were so great that our lines were forced back into the city from the garrison. Still they came, until it became obvious that we could no longer prevent them from taking the city. As our troop fell back, we made preparation to move the wounded and sick from the infirmary to the safety of Tripoli. Pietro remained behind with the rear guard, fighting to give us time to evacuate. As we left Ain Zara and looked back, we could see that the fighting in the rear was very intense. There were so many of them that there was no way anyone could have survived.

At this point, Gesuzza rises from her chair. She has regained her voice. "What are you saying? Is my Pietro dead?"

"Oh my God, signora, didn't you know? I was told that you had been informed of Pietro's death and that I was merely to fill in the facts for you. I'm very sorry, Gesuzza."

"No! No! It's not true! You're lying! He's not dead."

"Signora, please. I beg you. You must believe me. His body was buried with the others who fought valiantly that day. I'm so sorry… sorry." Pasquale realizes there has been some sordid confusion and that he has been caught in its wake. Gesuzza now stares, the painful truth setting itself firmly into her brain. She is again unable to speak. She looks at Pasquale and seems not to see him or know where she is. He has seen the stare before. It is the gaze of the mentally distressed. As he leaves the house, he encounters a frightened Raffaele, peering in from the doorway, wondering what is happening to his mother.

"Look after her," he says. "She will need all of the help she can get."

As Pasquale disappears from Raffaele's sight, his words become evident. Gesuzza falls to her knees, an empty despair overtaking her. It is true. Pietro is dead. She does not cry or curse, but utters indistinguishable groans. She tears at her face and head, drawing blood and tearing out clumps of hair. A bewildered Raffaele runs to her side and tries to restrain her. Finally, he seats her in a chair and ties her arms back with strips of old garments. It is obvious to Raffaele that Gesuzza has lost all perception. She neither understands nor is able to communicate. Confronted with the reality of the unthinkable loss of Pietro, she chooses the only fitting option, the abandonment of her sanity. Gesuzza is completely mad. She neither weeps nor moans. She sits silent and motionless. When it is safe, Raffaele unties her and leads her to the bedroom where she falls onto the bed.

After a period of a few days, Raffaele summons the local physician, Dr. De Pasquale. He treats her for her anemia, a condition brought on by poor diet, and exacerbated by complete refusal of sustenance following her despair over Pietro's death. He prescribes an increase in iron in her diet, which is accomplished by drinking a reddened liquid produced by placing rusty nails in water. Raffaele coaxes Gesuzza to ingest the crimson beverage along with any solid food that he manages to force on her. As for her odd behavior, he suggests only that in time it will pass. It is weeks before a noticeable change occurs. She finally rises and forces herself to engage in chores she has long neglected. She speaks not a word, but occasionally makes an almost inaudible hissing sound, accompanied by tears. She is finally permitting herself to grieve. At length, grief yields to examination of the causes for her anguish and to the actions that could have avoided this most terrible event in her life. She and Angelo could have left Italy and joined their two sons in America. She should not have summoned her sons to return to Italy to be with their father in his last days. Or, she and Raffaele might have returned to America with Pietro immediately after Angelo's death. The tragedy could have been avoided... if only. And where was God when she needed him? She had entreated him daily in her prayers to keep Pietro safe from harm. Had she not been a loyal and devoted subject? Why, then? For what reason? To gain a colony for the damnable Italian state: this country that she loved, whose freedom her father had fought for, of which she was so proud? The anger she now feels and the confusion in her sentiments mitigates the pain for a brief moment. Then, in a tumult of emotion, all of her thoughts and feelings are released in a desperate flood of tears and mournful sobbing. She has retreated from the brink of madness to the middle ground of complete hope-lessness. It will hereafter be her singular purpose to join her son in Paradise. She accepts the pain in her life as God's will. She thus enters the final phase of her recovery in constant prayer, continually kneading the beads of her rosary. When her hands are otherwise occupied, the movement of her lips lends testimony to her continued supplication. Gesuzza has survived, but her life is forever changed.

Chapter 29

Caporetto

A new spring has arrived and the Calabrian farmer turns the soil and plants his season's crop. He has already pruned his trees, trained his vines, and replaced the few that haven't greened with the new cycle. Rain now paints the landscape green, igniting the contrast with lignite furrows and russet trees. Tiny buds appear in rows on tree limbs and vine tops. There is much for which to be thankful, but one woman seems unaware. From the moment that the word of her son's death tramples her consciousness, Gesuzza is aloof from the World. Even Raffaele doesn't break through her sullen barrier. She goes through her chores mechanically, her mind in other places. She speaks sparingly, mostly in response to others. It is up to Raffaele, barely sixteen years old, to assert himself as head of the family. Though hardly able to read and write, he has learned to farm the crops for which Gesuzza is responsible: 12 acres of lemons, oranges, winegrapes and olives. He no longer needs direction from Angelo, Pietro or any of the other farmers. His arms have become stronger and more able to cope with the demands of the farm, and he works ceaselessly, except when he allows himself the minor pleasure of hunting.

"Ma, look what I've brought you. Six birds with one round from my shotgun." Gesuzza looks at Raffaele and tries to smile her appreciation, but can barely move her features. Perhaps only the passage of time will curb the heartache.

The army officer who appears at Gesuzza's door bears the cross of a chaplain on his collar. He is an army major and it is evident from his secular manner that, in addition to being a Catholic priest, he is a career soldier. He carries a small, leather-covered case as he quietly asks permission to come into the house. "Signora, may I come in? I have something that I must give you."

"What is it?" He has aroused Gesuzza's curiosity. He enters and sits his large frame in a chair opposite her.

"As the mother of deceased army private Pietro Chiarella, you are entitled to receive a decoration bestowed on him posthumously two years ago. The medal is the Medallion of the Order of the Kingdom of Italy. It acknowledges your son's great contribution to our nation and, of course, his enormous sacrifice. He will be remembered by his countrymen for all time."

As he prepares to hand her the case, now open to show the medal, she is on her feet. "Get out!" She is almost screaming. " Take that medal with you. Do you think that piece of metal can ever replace my son? Haven't I had enough heartache? Get out and don't come back!"

The major is shocked. "Signora, this is no way to behave. We can't give you your son back. We are simply trying to show our honor and respect for the heroes who fought and died for our country. Your son was a brave man. I am here to honor him in your presence."

"My son was an American and should not have fought in that stupid war in the first place. It was only because I convinced him to come to visit me here that he got into your clutches and lost his life." She is unable to contain herself and begins crying.

"I am very sorry, signora Chiarella. The medal will be held for you at the Carabiniere barrack here in Gagliano for a month. If you do not claim it, it will be returned to Rome and placed on display in the soldier's memorial museum."

When the chaplain is gone, Raffaele approaches his mother. "Ma, why don't you claim the medal awarded to Pietro? He fought for Italy and earned it and now you are letting it go to where it won't ever be appreciated."

"...That thing reminds me...of how I caused his death."

Raffaele thinks, *there isn't any way that she can understand that men must die for the glory of the Kingdom. Sure, we lost Pietro, and it was very painful, but Italy gained a colony. There will be more wars and more deaths. We need to accept that fact.* But, despite his youthful attitude towards the death of his brother, Raffaele is protective of his mother in her everyday life. He ensures that she does not overwork herself in the field and that she eats well enough to maintain her health. It is now two years since the death of Pietro and more than three since Angelo died. The passage of time seems at last to be taking effect on the depth of Gesuzza's grief. She is able to talk more copiously and can occasionally smile. But she will never forgive herself for asking Pietro to return to Calabria.

◦—◦—◦—◦—◦

By 1915, the fledgling Kingdom of Italy has whetted its appetite for empire with its victory in the fight for the colony of Libya. Now, war is in the wind again as Europe disputes the boundaries of its nations and the origins of its peoples. After a long deliberation, Italy allies with Britain and France against Germany and the Austro-Hungarian Empire. It will not be long before war is declared.

"Raffaele, you must leave Italy. You will otherwise be drafted and sent to fight in Austria." Gesuzza shows her fear of the inevitable war and its danger to the life of her only son aside from Giuseppe, who has been living in America for over a decade.

"Don't worry, Ma. If I need to serve, the army will take care of you."

"I'm not worried about who will care for me. But, what will I ever do if anything happened to you and I were left alone in the world without anyone?"

"You have others in your life besides me. Giuseppe is safe from the war. And, Marianna is right here in Gagliano."

"Marianna. Ha!" It is the first time that Gesuzza openly admits her bitter disappointment with Marianna. "She has not been considerate of me before. Why should anything change that?"

Raffaele allows the conversation to end. He must find a way to let Gesuzza know that he is actually eager to be drafted and to have the chance to fight the Austrians. Were it not for the loss of Pietro, he would volunteer for the army. But, such a thought is preposterous, considering

Gesuzza's state of mind. He understands her fears and concerns and even has some of his own. He has seen the invalids that have returned from Libya and Adowa, some with limbs blown from their bodies; others with eyesight lost to gaseous fumes from fires and bomb bursts. *It is possible, even, that Pietro was lucky to have died and not been returned home as an invalid. Ma would have labored her remaining days caring for him. And, much as I love him and miss him, I feel fortunate that he did not return as a burden to Ma.*

The Carabiniere officer sees Raffaele walking past the front of the barrack and calls to him. "Raffaele! Come here, I need to talk to you." Warily, Raffaele walks over to him.

"I have some words of advice for you. You need to prepare your mother for what is coming. The war is raging and there is a big battle that will take place up north in a border town called Caporetto. I think it was a Yugoslavian town before we took it over."

"Why are you telling me about it? And why does it concern my mother?"

"Because you are now eighteen years old and you are certain to be drafted. The army is going to put a large force together and that means that every able-bodied man will be called to serve. You need to talk to Gesuzza about it before it you are called and it surprises her."

"I'll be happy to serve when the time comes, but you're right, I'll have to let my mother know what's coming."

The evening is still and Gesuzza has washed and put away the plates from dinner. She sits silently knitting a shawl. Raffaele opens the conversation. "The Carabiniere lieutenant seems to know a lot about the war. He tells me that a huge force will be required by the end of the year in order to fight the enemy up north. That means that the army will be recruiting and drafting men."

"Yes, it's what I've been fearing. Has he said whether you will be called?"

"No, but it's going to happen soon. You know that, Ma."

"I have been praying to saint Joseph to keep you out of the army."

"Do you really want me to avoid military service? What if everyone did the same thing? Where would Italy be? Who would keep the Austrians from taking over our country as they did once before?"

"Raffaele, I don't care about any of those things. I only want you to be safe and here with me."

"I wish that were the way it could be, but surely you remember what it was like to live under the Bourbons. Italians were property to be pushed around and used by the Spanish throne. Is that what you want?"

"And what do we have now? Where was Italian justice when your father was falsely accused and convicted? Why are the northerners fighting war after war? Why don't they spend all that money to help us poor southerners? We don't need colonies. We need bread."

"I understand why you feel that way, Ma, but every great country has gone through this. We're just a little late getting started because we had to get rid of the foreigners. It's up to my generation to keep them out and to build Italy by adding colonies. That's where the future is for Italy."

"Does this mean that you are going into the army?"

"I don't have any choice. I'll be called very soon whether I want to go or not."

⊢⊸⊸–0–⊸⊢

The Mediterranean Sea glitters at the metropolis that forms a fan-shaped bay. It is surrounded by majestic hills, stretching inland from the bay and sloping upward to shape an earthen tiara. Formerly the capitol of the Kingdom of the two Sicilies, Naples now takes its place among the great cities of Italy. It is fifty-four years since the Risorgimento sent the Bourbons fleeing back to Spain, and unified southern Italy with the north. But, for all its past grandeur, the city has begun its slide into mediocrity. Population has tripled in the past half century, mostly the result of peasants streaming in from the countryside to claim opportunity created by the burgeoning port. Stevedores, food packers, seamstresses and clerks are fashioned from peasants whose work had been limited to farming. For the first time, Naples lays claim to the principal evil of commercial progress, the crowded slum. It is also a training ground for tens of thousands of army inductees preparing for the defense of Italy against the Teutonic threat of invasion. One of the recruits is Raffaele Chiarella.

The Carabiniere officer who informed me that I had been called to serve in the army told me that my skill with animals would make it likely that I would be assigned to an artillery unit to handle draught horses that pull cannon. He was right. After my basic training was completed at an army camp near Nola, I was held over, and received special instruction in artillery. Since we were only 12 miles away from Naples, I was able to visit the city often during the weeks of waiting to be assigned to a unit. Each time I went on leave there, I was amazed at the size and beauty of the buildings. Being from Calabria, I didn't know anything so large even existed. Everywhere, the structures were four and five stories high. There were even buildings that were used exclusively for trading. Indoor markets showed endless displays of food and clothing for sale. I never saw so many people, all in one place. Often, I would go down to the sandy white beach and walk along the huge promenade. Although the water there is not as clear and pristine as the seacoast of Calabria, it is far more spectacular. The bay stretches for what seems like fifty miles out to Mount Vesuvius, the treacherous volcano that has caused so much devastation. On a tiny island between the shore and the volcano sits the massive Castel dell'Ovo, a twelfth century fortress from which the ruling Bourbons fought invading pirates. And, dominating the shore stands the unrivaled Castel Nuovo with its huge Renaissance sculpted arch.

Far and away, the most memorable event of my Naples experience is having met my ideal of a woman one day while I was swimming in the bay with another recruit from the army base. I remember looking up from the water and seeing this beautiful young, shapely woman with shoulder length blonde hair and azure blue eyes. She was holding the red umbrella of the tourist guide and leading a group of overweight foreigners- they could have been Swedes from their appearance - along the shore and pointing out to Mount Vesuvius. Each time she gestured, her breasts seemed to crowd her blouse and her hair flowed away from her head as she whirled around to face her audience. I heard her voice in a strange language telling the tourists something. A lifeguard walked by and bellowed a command to her. Her response to him was in Italian and not accented at all. Could she have been Italian? I had to find out. I brazenly approached her, dripping wet, and asked, "What's that language you're speaking?" "Danish," she answered.

"But you're not Danish, are you?"

"No, I'm Italian, but they're Danes," she said pointing to the impatient group of sightseers as they waited for us to finish our impromptu conversation in Italian. Then, I knew I had to act quickly if I wanted ever to see her again. I bravely blurted out, "Can I see you when you are through with this tour?" To my utter amazement, she responded, "Meet me at the entrance to Castel Nuovo in an hour." My passion looped into orbit. In my eighteen years of life, I had known a few women, but never one so spectacular. "What is your name?" I asked? "Gabriella."

She was very different from the country girls of Gagliano. She wore makeup and her clothes were tailored and very feminine. She had a confident walk. Her head tossed as she addressed her audience and she obviously knew how to speak fluently in more than one language. And, to think that she agreed to meet me after work. Now I had to see if she really meant it. I dried myself off, explained the situation to Stefano, my companion from the base, and got back into my uniform. "Remember to be back on time, Raffaele," he counseled, as he headed back to Nola.

I proceeded to the boulevard and the spot she had designated for our meeting. I was forty minutes early. I wasn't sure that she would actually meet me, but she appeared at just the appointed time. She looked the same except for the absence of her red umbrella.

"Hello!" I tried to be calm and unaffected by her presence, but her straight white teeth, her cherry lips and her sapphire eyes all gave dramatic contrast to her pearly skin. I melted in her presence.

"Hi. I knew you were a soldier." She was looking at my uniform.

"How did you know?"

"Because all the young men are in uniform these days. Haven't you noticed?"

"Is that why you agreed to see me?"

"Not entirely. You look like a happy person and that's rare these days. Everyone is so involved with talk of the war."

"Well, then, we won't talk about the war."

༺━┄━०━┄━༻

The spring of 1917 is the season of romance for Raffaele and Gabriella. They see one another frequently, eventually developing a relationship that transcends that of the usual wartime fantasy. Gabriella sees Raffaele as the unspoiled country boy with a zest for living and a sincerity that reaches inward to his being. Raffaele perceives Gabriella as a complex and refined woman whose every move is gentle and every word thoughtful. They spend days at the beach and evenings on the promenade. They watch the sun descend and then rise again, its rays intruding on their lovemaking. Raffaele tells her of his life of hardship, avoiding a tone of self-pity, and revealing the fact of being separated from his father from before his birth. He is animated as he describes the farm that his family has managed for Leone. He describes the removal of the prior season's limb growth from the olive and citrus trees and the careful pruning of the grapevines. Gabriella marvels to hear of the size of the fruits that are harvested and how they are sorted and packaged for their various destinations. He speaks tenderly of his mother and of how her life was ruined by the incident that sent Angelo to prison. He tells of Giuseppe in America, of the death of Pietro in the Libyan conquest and of how their mother was crazed by her guilt in asking him to return to Italy from America.

When it is Gabriella's turn to reveal her history, the account is quite different from Raffaele's. She describes an affluent family life, her father being a contracts lawyer. She herself has been educated through most of her teen years, though as a woman, she is not expected to go on to university. Her natural affinity for languages suits her for the role of tour guide, and her surname of Garibaldi, though not by relation to the Liberator, attracts her to people of influence and national pride. She is thus given the coveted position of tour guide for the Naples promenade. As her talent establishes her as a premier guide, she leaves home in her parents' large flat in the city for a small beach house just below the public walk at the lido. Her good looks afford her ample suitors, but she is repulsed by the manner in which most men approach her, gawking at her and suggesting lewd behavior. She felt completely different when Raffaele walked up to her and asked her which language she was speaking to her tour group.

They soon acknowledge that they are deeply attracted to one another, and even fret over the expectation that Raffaele will soon be called to arms in the conflict that is about to be waged in the north. As fall arrives and the turning leaves impart a feeling of impermanence, they discuss the subject more and more. Finally, the moment arrives. It is morning and Raffaele has received special permission to leave the army post to see Gabriella.

"Gabriella, I have some news. We have learned that the Austrians have been strengthened by the arrival of two more divisions of German troops at Caporetto. My unit has been called up along with every other available troop."

"Oh, Raffaele, what will we do if we can't see one another? I will miss you every moment of our separation."

"We must be strong. Italy needs to defend its territory or all the human sacrifice of the past will have been wasted."

"I know that, but I suppose I'm thinking of myself."

"We'll have a few days more before I have to leave. I'll return this evening and we'll spend the time together on the beach."

In the evening that ensues, the young couple walks out to the beach holding one another. Raffaele is carrying his mandolin and Gabriella brings their evening fare, a dinner of fresh cheeses, mortadella, warm crusty bread and a bottle of wine. Raffaele plays the Finicula, Vicin' o Mare and other songs of his repertoire, creating an aura of sentiment that is testimony to their feelings for one another. They eat, sing to the music and drink their wine. The wine and what is by now recognition of their love intoxicate them. For the moment, the world is at peace. In their rapture, they do not notice the two military police officers approaching, their boots sinking into the soft sand and stilting their walk.

"Let's see your pass, soldier."

"I don't have one." Raffaele and Gabriella look at one another sadly.

"You are unauthorized to be off the army base. You are under arrest. Come with us."

"Wait....You don't understand."

"We understand that you are here without leave. Are you coming?"

Raffaele and Gabriella are frantic. "I'll get this straightened out and return tomorrow," Raffaele says, "but I must go with them now." They embrace one last time and part, looking despondently at one another as they separate. They will not see one another again.

———○———

Stefano Contini has been Raffaele's closest army friend. Unlike the great majority of his peers, Stefano's family migrated to Gagliano in the early 1800's from Palestine, where their Jewish faith was under constant assault by the Islamic majority. After one particularly bloody exchange, a large community of Jews that included Stefano's family left nineteenth century Palestine and journeyed across the Mediterranean to Calabria. They brought with them their knowledge of silk production, utilizing the silk worm and the mulberry tree. At first, they received a guarded welcome in the Calabrian countryside, but eventually were so completely accepted that they almost wholly integrated into Calabrian society, embracing the Catholic faith of their adopted culture. The difference in religious belief of the immigrant Jews was of little concern to other Calabrians, and their transported silk industry benefited the entire region. The Continis (a changed surname from Avram) chose to remain Jewish, their family having produced several rabbis. They also maintained a temple in their home in Gagliano to allow for traditional services to be conducted for the few remaining of the faith.

Stefano and Raffaele were conscripted on the same day and traveled together from Gagliano to Naples for their military training. Both were assigned to artillery duty. Their time in special training at the camp in Nola cemented their friendship and most of their leave time was spent together until Raffaele met Gabriella. It was Stefano's admonition that Raffaele ignored when he left the army base without authorization. The result was that Raffaele was brought before the commander and sentenced to thirty days in the camp prison.

"How was the stockade, Raffaele?" Stefano opens the conversation as he and Raffaele busily groom the horses in their unit and sulphur them for fleas and ticks. Their unit has been called up to the war front, and preparations are being made to board a train for the north.

"It was pretty awful. They fed us leftovers from the general mess and forced us to weed and cut away brush on roads between Nola and Naples. Thank goodness that our assignment finally arrived and we are on our way out of here at last. I couldn't have spent another day in that place. And all because of one unauthorized leave. What did they expect I would do when they put us all on alert and canceled all leaves?"

"Were you able to let Gabriella know what happened?"

"Yes. She says she knows someone who can tell her where we're heading and that she'll come there to see me."

"Raffaele, do you love her?"

"Yes, I think so. What I know for sure is that I miss her terribly. When this war is won and we can all go home, I'm coming back to Naples. If I still feel as I do now, I'm going to ask her to marry me."

"Then tell her not to follow you. War is no picnic. She should not be exposed to its horrors." Once again, Stefano cautions his friend against imminent danger.

"There isn't any way that I can dissuade her. I can only hope that the army prevents her from getting too close to the front lines."

>—·—◇—·—<

In the final weeks of 1917, the battle of Caporetto stands as the symbol of defeat of the Italian dream for empire. The hammered army retreats towards the Pieve River, where they are determined to make their unwavering stand against an advancing enemy. Belled cows and mountain deer watch curiously as the stream of humankind descends the hilled pastures and wends its way through frozen field towards their meadow of redemption. Bloodied and trodden, they are unnerved by the crackling sounds of distant gunfire from their Austrian pursuers. Thunderous booms are heard from cannons, now too far away to harm them. There is urgency in their movement, for to save the Kingdom requires salvaging the army and their armaments. Cannon must be hauled across the mud-slopped meadow and on to the safety of the Pieve River's southern shore. Every fighting man must be martialled and refitted to withstand a new confrontation with an age-old enemy. The defeated Italy seeks to redeem itself in subsequent encounter.

Among the maze of humanity, Raffaele and Stefano struggle to keep several draught horses pulling against their straps to haul the caissons bearing cannon to the temporary bridge that crosses the Pieve. Already there are dozens of the largest guns pointed north at the enemy. They wait in unison for the Austrians to come within their range. Caporetto is lost, but the Veneto will be defended at all cost.

Raffaele seems not to be aware of the confusion around him as he tugs at a lead strap that encourages a team of horses to pull forward against the weight of a large gun. His mind is oddly distant from the disaster that has his comrades fleeing anxiously.

Whoever would have thought that this would happen to me? I can remember as though it were yesterday: Gabriella insisting that she come to the warfront to be near me, Stefano warning me of the danger, the unit moving up toward Caporetto. Tales of the heroes of other wars abounded as the troop train heading north smoked and swept fly ash across the open tops of the troop carriers. We had to shut our eyes to keep the dust out and half the time the smoke made its way into the cars and choked us. There was an awful clamor whenever the train went over the points where the rails met and each turn brought a frightening screech as the wheels strained against the track. Eventually, the train came to a stop in a meadow that would become our camp for two days. We could hear distant explosions coming from the cannons of both sides. As our unit moved up to within range of the enemy's guns, the fabled accounts of war ceased.

At first, our battle routine was simple. We kept the horses fed and healthy, and available to move in at a moment's notice to provide the muscle required for repositioning a gun. Strangely, our greatest fear was that of falling into the latrine from the two planks positioned precariously above the open pit that daily became deeper with human waste so acrid that it brought tears to our eyes. We carried rifles, but there was no likelihood that we would ever use them. The enemy was far away and our cannon sent them a steady flow of deadly missives. They were, of course, happy to respond in kind and their bombs exploded in our midst as often as we scored a hit on them. Both sides lost men daily, but there was no territorial gain for either side.

Then, the inevitable happened. One morning we were told to fix bayonets and keep our eyes open for signs of the enemy. We did actually see them fairly regularly, but always at a distance that was not alarming. We could see them, looking like tiny ants, through our field glasses. They wore gray coats to protect them from the mountain cold, spiked helmets and high boots that gave them a strange appearance, as though they were horsemen in search of their mounts. As they drew dangerously closer, we could see that most of them were young, barely out of their teens. An officer carrying a pistol fired it into the air and they immediately charged across the rocky terrain that separated us, their rifles bearing long, pointed bayonets. Our cannons fired point blank at them, greatly reducing their numbers, but still they came, seeking to overtake our position.

I threw the sheath off of my bayonet and charged forward

along with the others. An Austrian soldier fired a shot at me, but he missed. He shrank back in panic, frantically working the bolt of his rifle. As he rose to aim a second time, I quickly plunged my bayonet into his chest. He looked up pleadingly for the instant before he died, still pinned to the end of my rifle. I pulled back, dropping the young corpse to the ground. Then, I turned and puked. I had no time to think of the act of killing I had just executed for the first time. There were others who would have taken my life that day and I protected myself by killing first, before I would be killed. Later, as the Austrians withdrew and left us to collect our dead, I thought of the senseless nature of war and the terrible waste of human life.

As I returned to camp through the barbed wire that encircled our position, there were five men surrounding an Austrian soldier who found himself behind the lines as his comrades retreated. He was unwilling to surrender. He lunged wildly at his captors, knowing that he would be stopped and probably killed. His bayonet sliced the forearm of one of the Italians. The others closed in and battered him on his arms and chest until he fell into submission. Then, just as he was about to be taken prisoner, one of the five removed the Austrian's bayonet and in a swift motion, slit his throat, killing him with one stroke. As the Austrian lay bleeding profusely onto the ground beneath his body, the Italians cheered. It was as though the taking of his life was the symbol of their victory in holding their position that day. I could only think of the mother that would soon hear of the boy's death. Would she react as my mother did? Did Austrians cry and feel pain at the loss of a loved one? Just then, one of the Italians walked over to the corpse and kicked it as if to show disdain for the whole of Austria. A feeling of disgust and reprehension overtook me and I felt rage.

"Enough! What do you think you're doing? Isn't it bad enough that he was killed in the first place? You son of a whore, get away from him!"

I felt my anger swell out of control and as I lunged at the soldier, three others restrained me and took me away. I was screaming obscenities at the man as the company commander approached.

"Are you Private Chiarella?"

"Yes, sir. Please...let me explain my behavior."

"That will not be necessary. Come with me."

I thought surely I would be tried as a traitor or defector and either shot or sent away to some remote prison as was my father. As we entered the command post in a trench some sixty feet from the gun mounts, he picked up a letter from his desktop and held it for a moment.

"Raffaele, I have some bad news for you. As you know the Austrians have been using aircraft to bomb some of the public buildings in the Italian cities surrounding the war zone. One of those is Taipana, just west of here. They bombed a pensione there, which housed several journalists and a group of women who have loved ones at the front. Among the ruins of the building we found this letter. It was found on a dead woman and addressed to you."

Wild-eyed, I looked at the letter. It looked familiar, but I could not be certain. —"Please...read it to me."

"It says,"

"my darling Rafi,

The war rages on and you are there at the front. I know because my sources have allowed me to learn where you are. I am here, too, at the Pensione Vallerga in the city of Taipana. The army has asked the women to leave, that it is too dangerous for us to be so close to the enemy lines. But my love for you is so deep and I miss you so much that I am willing to risk my life to be near you.

I do not expect to see you any time soon, but I want you to

know that I am here and will wait for as long as it takes for you to be allowed to visit me. Please do not be angry with me. I know that you asked me not to come here…'"

"Stop! Don't read any more. My God, what more terrible thing can happen to me? My life is ended. The only woman I ever loved is gone, killed because she followed me to this horrid place." Raffaele shrouds his face in his hands and sobs intensely, his body shaking and his throat emitting pitiful moans. He has been confronted by one too many tragedies and his mind is stretched beyond its limits.

The commander places his hand on Raffaele's shoulder. '"My boy, we have received orders from headquarters to join the re-treat from Caporetto. The Austrians have overrun our lines and we must save the army from total destruction. When we arrive at our destination on the Pieve River, I will arrange for you to have a two months-long furlough. You have seen and experi-enced too much and need to go back to wherever you're from to recover your senses."

Chapter 30

Giorgio

At age twenty-five, Giorgio Scaglione is very much the handsome anomaly that his contemporaries perceive. His auburn hair and freckled, ruddy face are far more common in the north than in Giorgio's hometown of Corigliano in the province of Cosenza. And, if facial appearance weren't enough, his height of six feet furthers the contradiction to that of the typical Calabrian. Raised in the familiar tradition of the sharecropper, Giorgio could only hope to perpetuate the plight of his desperately impoverished family into the future. Initially resigned to that fate, he soon found himself curiously attracted to older women of means as he grew to his height potential and developed the look of worldliness that young men take on in puberty. Curiosity eventually led to his seduction of a mature lady of the higher society, almost twenty years his senior. To his surprise, the happy dowager spread the word of her newfound pleasure among her friends, some of whom initiated their own liaison with Giorgio. Finding that a price would be paid for his services, Giorgio was soon in business providing a stable of matrons with pleasures they did not find in their conjugal beds. The war interrupted his venture, just as he seemed destined to either become rich or fall prey to a cuckolded spouse.

Reluctantly, he answered the call of conscription into the Italian army. He was sent to Caporetto along with many of Italy's young men, and fought at the side of fellow Italians like Raffaele and Stefano. When the army retreated to the Pieve River, he was sent home to console his mother, who had just been widowed a second time by the man she married following the death of Giorgio's father. As he sat on the train to Calabria, he found himself seated next to Raffaele, listening to the outpouring of misery that had befallen the young soldier. Eventually, he decided that he would not exit the train in Cosenza to go home to Corigliano to be with his grieving mother. After all, his stepfather had never acknowledged him as his son. He was not all that kind, either. Why create a pretense of grief when he could use the time constructively, seeing new sights and meeting new people. Anyhow, he would probably be killed in the months ahead by a shot fired by some German fighting in the Veneto.

"I've heard that the beach below Catanzaro is so pristine that tourists from all over Europe marvel at it. No doubt you've seen it, Raffaele. Is it worth seeing?"

"Yes, I think so, but you would have to stay on the train to Mezza Terme. You would not be able to see your mother."

"That's OK. I'd rather see the Ionian Sea right now. I can stop in on my mother on my way back to Veneto."

The journey of almost seven hundred miles is painstakingly slow, with stops at virtually every hamlet along the way and delays in the loading of foodstuffs and livestock. To contain their patience, the two men share stories of their youth in rural Calabria. They are amazingly similar up to the point that Giorgio begins his pursuit of freewheeling relationships with women. Both men are mere toddlers when they first become involved in the work of tending farm animals. The parents of both are unable to shake the yoke of poverty and thus hand down a legacy of toil that is unrelenting. Both have permanent scars to show where they had been cut or bruised in the process of performing tasks without adequate training. They have also both experienced the difficult life without a father in this harsh and demanding environment. In the ten days that it takes to reach Catanzaro, they become close friends, vowing to fight side by side at the next encounter with the Austrians. Giorgio tells Raffaele of a practice among European governments, including Italy, to absolve the last male member of a family from fighting at the warfront, upon receipt of a sum of money equal to one year's pay of the soldier involved. Raffaele's eyes open widely and he immediately thinks of the possibility that Marianna might be willing to rescue him from the next battle. He wonders if the existence of his brother Giuseppe in America disqualifies him as the sole male survivor. Raffaele brings Giorgio home with him where they bunk together for two nights. He is introduced to all of Raffaele's friends and given advice and direction for a thorough exploration of the Catanzaro province. When he leaves, Raffaele is saddened at the prospect that he might not ever see Giorgio again. They wave at one another and each shout, "Ciao, camerato!" They are indeed comrades.

⊶─◦─⊷

"Rafi!" Marianna looks from her window and spots her nephew walking in the town square in his uniform, his ever-present young admirer, Antonio Pace, present. Raffaele completes his sentence and turns toward Marianna.

"Well, if it isn't my dear aunt Marianna. It's been a long time, Zi, how have you been? Do you know that your sister has been sick with pneumonia and was attended by a doctor?" There is sarcasm in Raffaele's voice.

"Yes, I do. Who do you think got the doctor for her?"

"Zi, we need to talk. There is something important I need to ask of you."

"Come to my house, Rafi. We can have some dinner and you can tell me what's on your mind."

Marianna seems pensive and curious about what she will hear from Raffaele. She has not seen him for many months and had heard that he has returned home after a very close encounter with the enemy at the warfront. But she had not seen him before this. He had not come to her house with his usual gusto, seeking to spend time with his closest relative outside of his mother. Even now his greeting is less cheery and convincing than in past times. What does he want of her? Did she not send for the doctor to be at her sister's side when she heard that Gesuzza was ill with a dangerous malady? And didn't she call on Gesuzza to make sure she had received her medicine and was taking it? What in God's name does she have to do to please these Chiarellas?

The house is in its usual orderly condition. The house-keeper has seen to that before leaving for the day. But, as Raffaele enters, there is telltale evidence to reveal the fact that there is someone in Marianna's life whom she is not revealing. That someone might be somewhere in the house at this very moment for all he knows. A pack of Turkish cigarettes sits on a table in the living room and the room smells of cigarette smoke. There are two water tumblers half full of dry vermouth that appear to have been left hurriedly behind. Raffaele shakes his head and thinks. *Doesn't she realize what she is doing to herself and to the rest of us by carrying on this way? She has trashed the Soluri name and brought disrespect to the rest of her family. She has been used and defrauded of more money than it would take to provide a better life for us all. And for what? What can I say or do to make her understand?*

"Za Marian', I have missed our talks and your doting. I hope that we will make up for lost time while I am home on leave." Marianna is pleased that Raffaele still places value on their friendship. She had feared that something had come between them, since he had not visited for two weeks following his arrival in Gagliano.

"I will arrange for a woman to do Gesuzza's work for the next two weeks so that we can all spend as much time together as possible. Now, come have dinner with me."

Dinner is far more elaborate than one might expect on a moment's notice. There is an appetizer of seasoned egg-plant, a main course of veal, salad and wheat pie.

"Were you expecting someone else tonight?"

"What do you mean?"

"This is not your usual meal, is it?"

"I eat whatever my housekeeper prepares. She is a wonderful cook and her meals allow me to eat well without all the drudgery of the kitchen."

Raffaele accepts her account for the moment. He is anxious to get on with the conversation he has come here for in the first place. After dinner, they sit out on the terrace behind the house, drink coffee and sip anisette. The night is cool and the mood is right for conversation.

"Zi, how much would you be willing to do for me?"

She laughs. "Rafi, you know I would do anything for you. What did you have in mind?"

"As you know, I've been at the warfront recently and, despite several close encounters with the Austrians, I was not harmed. I was sent home because of the fatigue that comes with killing other human beings and watching comrades die. In my case, in addition to the horror of the fighting, there was a woman who had come to Caporetto to be near me who was killed by a bomb dropped on her pensione by the Germans. Had she lived, I would have asked her to be my wife."

Tears well in Raffaele's eyes and his voice thickens with emotion. He clears his throat and continues.

"My soldier friend, Giorgio, told me of a way that I could avoid returning to the warfront. It involves a payment to the government of a substantial sum of money along with showing proof that I am the last male member of my generation of the family. I don't think they count Giuseppe because he is in America. I need you to sponsor me, Zi. It would cost you two thousand lire. Will you do it?"

"You poor, dear boy. Of course I will do it. Does anyone know of this woman and the circumstances of her death?"

"I was told about it by my company commander. I don't know if her parents have been notified, but I am planning to visit them in Naples once I am out of the service and free to travel."

"Leave everything to me. Tomorrow, I'll ask my lawyer to look into it and get things started."

"Thanks, Zi, I knew I could count on you."

For the next two weeks, Raffaele and Gesuzza are virtually inseparable. Despite the presence of the woman
hired by Marianna to work in Gesuzza's place, they walk
together to the farm and work alongside her. They leave
early and go home to prepare their meal. Raffaele tells
Gesuzza of his experience with army cooking. She is not
impressed by how soldiers are fed. Following their morning calisthenics, each man receives his breakfast consisting of a loaf of bread and a large tin of brewed chicory.
They are expected to save a portion of the bread for the
midday meal, when the tin is again filled, this time with a
soup containing a small amount of meat. The evening meal
is broth and a half-liter of wine. Gesuzza smiles as she
listens to Raffaele. Her joy at being with him is evident.
Even her pallor turns to pink, belying the fact that she is
still recovering from pneumonia.

Raffaele tells Gesuzza about his love for Gabriella, how
they met by chance and how he was taken with her blonde
beauty and her intelligence. He tells of how the military
police interrupted their last moments together, of how she
was able to find out where he was billeted and of how she
traveled up to Caporetto to be near him. As he describes
the horror of her death and how he learned about it, he is
unable to contain his emotions. Gesuzza takes him in her
arms and consoles him as he releases his innermost feelings in a torrent of tears. She thinks of how she relates to
his feelings of guilt for having innocently lured Gabriella
to her death. She herself has the same guilt-ridden senti-

ment about the ill-fated return to Italy of her son Pietro. She prays that Raffaele will not allow this tragedy to affect his life as the death of Pietro has devastated hers.

Surprisingly, Marianna is nowhere to be seen. Most probably, she is arranging with the government for Raffaele's exemption from any further warfront duty for the duration of the war. She is somehow not missed. Raffaele and Gesuzza have much time to make up. They dread the moment when Raffaele must leave to return to military duty, wherever it is. Their thoughts of Marianna are only to wonder how far she has gotten in her quest to free Raffaele from duty at the warfront.

"Unless I hear something different, I will have to return to my old unit's camp in Treviso. They say that there isn't any fighting there just now, but that armies are building up on both sides for the next major conflict."

"Please, Raffaele, don't talk of the war. I can't stand the thought of all those young men being killed and maimed."

"OK, Ma, I understand."

⊷⊶⊙⊷⊷

The weeks of rest have helped Raffaele to regain his composure. His presence in Gagliano has contributed to Gesuzza's recovery and he has paid his respects to his friends and their families in town. There are but two weeks left for him to make the journey back to camp in Treviso before his leave expires. Still, there is no word from Marianna. What can possibly be wrong? Has she failed at getting his reprieve from the army? Is she ashamed to face him? Surely, he would understand if that were the case. Or, has she fallen victim to bandits or worse, a rapist? He must find out. He decides to knock on Marianna's door. At the very least, he can say his goodbyes to her.

There is no response to his knock on the door. He peers inside through a front window, but there is no sign of her. A young man walks up to him, looking uncertain of himself.

"Are you Raffaele?"

"Yes, what do you want?"

"There is a message for you from Marianna Soluri. You must go to her lawyer's office and he will give it to you. It's just down the street…"

"Yes, yes, I know where it is."

Could this be it? Has my exemption come through and be resting in the hands of an attorney? Could she have been called away and expected that I would follow up with her lawyer? How stupid of me. Here, I have waited to the very last moment before calling on her.

For most of his life, Raffaele has walked past the office of Don Luigi Ruffolo, the lawyer to whom Marianna entrusts her affairs following the departure of Renato Rizzo. He has somehow felt thankful that he has never had reason enough to enter through the heavy wooden door bearing the inscription *avvocato*. The only attorney available locally in Gagliano, Don Luigi claims to be descended from a noble Calabrian family of Norman extraction that traces back to the eleventh century. The Ruffolo family conveniently forgot their claim of attachment to Norman lineage during the time when vigilantes formed a local *Ndrangheta* and sought to expel French rule by force. Following the departure of the Normans in 1442, the *Ndrangheta* went underground and became a de facto government much like the Mafia in Sicily. In these more moderate times, Luigi corresponds regularly with his French "cousins" with the surname of Rouff. Though the name suggests that he might have red hair and beard, Luigi is dark-haired and shaven. He is actually quite typical of the local genre, an olive complexioned, rotund man of fifty years, standing not more than five feet four inches in height.

"Come in, Raffaele, don't hesitate. I have heard of your bravery at the front, and I have wanted to meet you and give you my personal thanks."

Raffaele is uneasy with Don Luigi's patronizing manner. *Why is he pandering to me? I'm not his client and I don't ever intend to be. He probably thinks that I'll report this conversation to Marianna.*

The elder man continues to show uncommon hospitality. He pours anisette into two glasses and places one in front of Raffaele. He toasts to the victory that the allies will ultimately achieve in their fight with Germany and the Austro-Hungarian Empire. He encourages conversation with Raffaele about the war and what the victory will mean to Italy. Finally, Raffaele stops the conversation.

"Don Ruffolo, please excuse my direct manner. I am here to ask you about the progress you have made toward securing my exemption from the warfront as Gesuzza's last remaining son in Italy. As you know, my brother Pietro died in Libya and my other brother, Giuseppe, left Italy years ago and intends never to return. My aunt Marianna told me that she sought your assistance in gaining the exclusion."

Raffaele notices that Don Luigi's hand is trembling as he holds his drink to his lips and thinks about what his response will be.

"No, Raffaele, Marianna did not ask me to seek an exclusion for you."

Raffaele's eyes widen with surprise and then squint with anger. *What is this fat little bastard trying to tell me? Why doesn't he come right out with it? What has happened? It can't be that Marianna is unwilling to do this for me.* His words become sterner as he pursues an explanation.

"Tell me, Don Ruffolo, what has happened? Tell me!"

Raffaele's demand to know what has occurred frightens Don Luigi. He sits back on the chair behind his desk, staring down at the heap of documents that he has pushed aside so that he might focus his attention on Raffaele. His hands are openly trembling now as his inquisitor looks at him with growing antagonism.

"Raffaele, my boy, you must try to understand. These are trying times and people sometimes do strange things. You really must not judge her."

"Damn it, stop your muttering and be honest with me. What is the answer to my question?"

"I will be totally honest with you. After all, it was she who directed me. I did only as my client asked, nothing more. She came to me to seek my assistance in obtaining a military exclusion for a soldier who she said was her only son. She offered to pay whatever the Government required for actions of this sort. She was in a hurry, since the man would be going back to the front in a few weeks."

"That was me! I'm the soldier she was talking to you about. Did you get the exclusion order?"

"I was able to get the order, but it was not for you."

"What do you mean? That's absurd! Of course it was for me. Where is it?"

Raffaele searches the desktop frantically, going through every piece of paper. Don Luigi looks on, his face twisted in a frightened curl. There is no document, Raffaele concludes. To the elder's relief, Raffaele falls back in his chair and dolefully exclaims, "Jesus, will you please tell me what has happened?"

"As I was saying, I was able to get the exclusion order, but it was for another soldier. I had never seen him before, but he was surely not her son, though he was a good deal younger than she...and very good-looking. Under the terms of the exclusion, he was ordered to report to a military base in Sicily, near Siracusa. Marianna left with him. She admitted that he was her lover and said that they would be married as soon as they could find a magistrate to preside over their wedding."

"And who is the lucky man?"

"His name is Giorgio Scaglione."

Chapter 31

Vittorio Veneto

The late winter snowfall gives the medieval buildings of Treviso a look of serenity, as though there is no war to fight. At peace since 1870, when the people of Veneto won their independence from Austria and opted to join the Italian Kingdom, Treviso currently faces the prospect of returning to Austrian rule. The old town's narrow, winding streets remain encircled by walls that once offered protection from invaders. Now, German planes fly over those same walls and drop their incendiaries onto the headquarters of the Italian army. In the Piazza dei Signori, thirteenth century structures are charred from fires. The people huddle in their homes when they are not required to navigate the streets for some unavoidable purpose. Since the defeat at Caporetto, their city has become the focus of the war in northern Italy. Everywhere, there is armament. Stockpiles of trucks, wagons, cannon and rifle all evidence Italy's determination to oust a seemingly invincible enemy. Armando Diaz, the distinguished young Neapolitan-born General, has been given control of the army. He is in Treviso to personally supervise the preparations for the battle ahead. Across the Pieve River, a huge opposing force brandishing the flags and weapons of the Central Powers awaits their commander's order to resume their drive south.

Twelve miles to the north of Treviso, the men in Raffaele's unit remove a dusting of snow from their tent roofs. The prelude to battle belies the ugliness of war. Neat rows of white tents stretch across undulating hills. Melting snow reveals patches of green grass. Smoke rising from the tented mess halls reaches skyward to join the mass of puffed white clouds above the Veneto. To the North, the Alpine mountains are the majesty of this vast and stunning realm.

Surprisingly, Raffaele is in good spirits. The sting of Marianna's betrayal behind him, his return to the warfront has been nothing less than spirited. He has experienced defeat at the hands of the Austrians, but now he must help Italy to redeem itself and earn for himself, the thrill of victory. His fear is that any ill fate that befalls him will affect Gesuzza all too profoundly. *I am her last remaining link to family. She will never allow Marianna to come near her or speak to her again, and the lack of correspondence from Giuseppe has her puzzled and resigned to his complete absence from her life. Why does God permit these tragedies to befall one so sweet and innocent? Surely, she does not deserve this tragic life. But,*

Raffaele vows not to allow his love for Gesuzza to affect his effectiveness in battle. If I must die, then so be it. The greater good is that Italy emerges from the conflict a victor.

On October 24th, 1918, fourteen Italian divisions lying in readiness at the bank of the Pieve River cross over and begin the offensive to win back the Veneto. The Austrians meet them with ferocious resistance, but ultimately they falter and begin their long retreat north. First, they yield the meadowland of the Veneto, which they had taken the previous winter at an enormous cost of human life. Eventually, they flee to the mountains, entrenching themselves in elaborate fortifications, built over a period of one hundred years to be impregnable to attack. Still the Italians come.

"Raffaele, I can't believe we're already at the base of the Alps. We've really got them on the run." Stefano excitedly expresses the ecstasy of victory. But, Raffaele is less euphoric. It is his turn to caution Stefano.

"Don't be fooled, Stefano. They are not defeated yet. The hard work is ahead. They are so entrenched in their defenses that it will take a great deal of fighting to get them out."

The cannons point up at a fifty-degree angle and fire their shells into the cavities in the sides of the mountains leading to the Austrian defenses. The recoil of the big guns firing at so high a trajectory sometimes causes them to tip over. The horses work tirelessly to keep the guns righted. The caves are deep and are little affected by the cannon fire. The enemy returns the cannon-fire, aiming downhill at the Italians. It is a definite advantage to be holed up high on a mountain in a long, deep cave.

"You men!" The Italian commander shouts orders at

the twenty or so young men handling the horses. "We are going to attack them with rifles and bayonets. Get your weapons and come with me."

His heart fluttering, Raffaele scoops up his rifle and throws off the sheath of his bayonet. He affixes the long blade to the end of his rifle and follows the captain. It is not his first experience at this. As he increases his pace, fear turns to determination and ultimately to rage. The men reach a point where they meet up with a Bersaglieri unit brought in to break the stalemate. The young artillerymen are electrified at the prospect of fighting alongside elite troops. They are immensely inspired. The closest of the caves contains several Austrian interlopers who might have had the sense to withdraw with their retreating unit, but remained behind to pick off some of the Italians as they closed in on the cave. The Italian approach to the cave opening is met by machine-gun fire. A Bersaglieri trooper tosses an incendiary into the cave and the interior is suddenly an inferno. As the enemy troopers stream out of the cave, the Italians engage them in hand-to-hand fighting. Blinded by smoke and fire, the Austrians are easily taken. Those who surrender are taken prisoner. The others are either shot or bayoneted.

Raffaele and Stefano are exhausted. They breathe heavily as they stop to catch their breath and thank God they have both survived the skirmish. Around them lie the bodies of several of their artillerymen comrades and three of the Bersaglieri.

"OK, you men. This is only the first cave. There are several others to take. Let's get going." The young Bersaglieri lieutenant rallies his men for yet another encounter. As the troop moves quickly forward, Raffaele notices a small cavern that may simply be a bear's home.

He and Stefano decide to investigate, dropping behind their unit and cautiously approaching the cave entrance. They are alone as they arrive within fifty feet of the cave, the rest of their unit having gone on to a much larger cave higher up the mountain. A strangely garbed Austrian soldier jumps up suddenly from behind a bush and runs shouting into the cave to alert the others. He is much larger than either of his Italian pursuers and looks fearsome in his fur-trimmed cloak, horned helmet and sheepskin vest.

Within moments three Austrians, similarly attired, dart out of the cave and charge straight at Raffaele and Stefano. Their bayonets fixed and pointing at the Italians, they also carry trench clubs, which they use as a mace in close combat. The first man to reach them, thick-necked and wearing a mouton cap, swings a spiked club as he approaches his enemy. Raffaele takes quick aim and disposes of his attacker with a well-placed shot in the forehead. As he plunges to the ground, a pink spray spouts from the spot where the bullet pierced his skull. Raffaele, working the bolt on his rifle, receives a blow across his back from behind. It is the second Austrian, who somehow managed to get past him. Summoning all of his strength, Raffaele whirls around, his bayonet blade gleaming. In his motion, he bumps his opponent's weapon to the side and plunges his bayonet into the man's chest. The Austrian groans hideously and convulses, his body trying senselessly to work free. As blood pours freely from the torn chest, Raffaele pulls back and the lifeless hulk falls fast to the ground. He turns ferociously and sees Stefano on the ground, the third Austrian standing menacingly over him. A mace has landed on Stefano's hand and severed the fingers clutching his rifle. His upraised hand pours blood and shows bone where once there were fingers.

As Raffaele rushes the offender, bayonet forward, the Austrian brushes his weapon aside with a sword and swings his mace at the stock of Raffaele's rifle, intending to knock it from his hands. The mace reaches its target, embedding itself into the rifle butt, but Raffaele refuses to let go. He jerks back on the rifle, pulling the mace from his assailant's hands. In the next moment, he knocks the sword away from his foe and lunges forward, plunging his bayonet into the Austrian's solar plexus. The Austrian's body shakes for a moment and then lies deadly still. Raffaele assesses the cuts and bruises he has received and then remembers that Stefano was left alone on the ground a few feet away. He rushes to his comrade's aid, only to be greeted by a hideous sight. Stefano has received a vicious blow from a mace and lies there, mouth open with blood seeping from his throat; his right eye is pushed into its socket like a squashed egg, and a pattern of spikes is imprinted on his face. His fingerless hand still points upward as if to be holding his weapon. Raffaele looks around. He is alone. He falls to the ground in a seated position alongside his dead friend and sobs into his hands.

⊱─━❍━─⊰

For the second time in his life, Raffaele travels the tedious route from the north of Italy to his home in the south. The train is filled with soldiers and civilians returning to their homes, and the mood is high-spirited. The war is over and the allies have won. The final victory is becoming known as Vittorio Veneto. Raffaele wonders why he does not feel the elation that he had expected would accompany victory. *It was the most incredible three weeks of my life. Who would ever have believed that the great army of the*

Central Powers could have been vanquished in so short a time? Surely, their leaders had considered surrender in what had become a hopeless undertaking for them. But, their troops fought hard and both sides lost men every day. The valor and determination of the Italian troops was incredible. Had the war continued, we would have been in Munich within a week. As it turned out, we were halted in Austria by the Kaiser's surrender on November 4th. I am told that we took 500,000 prisoners, and that they even sent some of them to Prigione dell Asinara, where my father, Angelo, spent eighteen years of his life. The prison was practically cleared of inmates by the offer made by the army to grant a complete pardon in return for their volunteering for infantry duty. I wish Pa were alive to hear about that. His descriptions of Asinara were horrifying.

I don't know how to tell Stefano's family about how he died. I only hope they have been notified of his death and that I won't be announcing it to them. I remember my poor mother learning of my brother's death from a military doctor who had no idea that she hadn't been notified. It took her two years to get over the shock and the pain is still with her. Stefano thought the fighting was over when the Austrians retreated to the mountains between Italy and Austria. But, that was when the fighting just really began. Fighting at close quarters is brutal. It's never easy to die, but having a bayonet pushed into you or being clubbed to death is monstrous. Stefano's family will want to know the details, but I can't be completely descriptive. They won't be able to handle it. At least this time it isn't Gesuzza who is getting the bad news.

"Raffaele!" Gesuzza watches as her son walks towards her in his uniform, his duffle bag over his shoulder. The war is over and he has returned. There is a God in heaven, after all. She reaches out for him and throws her arms around him. He is embarrassed as they stand outside their door and Gesuzza sobs into his chest. The neighbors watching all seem to understand. Most of them have lost a loved one in some recent war and know how it feels to long for the sight and feel of a returning son or husband.

"Come in. There is much to talk about. Have you eaten? Can I get you something?"

Gesuzza cannot remember ever being so elated. For a time, they talk about how she managed to survive on her own. She reminds Raffaele of the culture they share, of how the people of the village rally to the assistance of a needy neighbor, widows and elders especially. She was never alone, she insists. They carefully and purposefully avoid the mention of Marianna.

Chapter 32

Alfredo

The early morning light streams in on Marianna as she awakens in her tiny flat in the pensione Medusa. She reaches across the bed, feeling for the presence of Giorgio. She thinks that perhaps he is in the same mood that she herself feels, ready for making love. There is neither sound nor presence. Giorgio is not there. *Dammit! He's off at the army base, playing soldier again. Don't those people know the war is over? Why don't they leave him alone?* Her flat is in the little hamlet of Floridia, not ten miles from the city of Siracusa where, at Marianna's behest, Giorgio has been stationed since he was excluded from service at the warfront. Almost a year has passed and still they live in the pensione with the expectation that they will soon be married. The war's end has rekindled the likelihood that they would formalize their union and return to Gagliano, where Marianna's properties are located. After a quick breakfast, Marianna dresses and is taken by donkey-drawn cart to the army base. She intends to locate Giorgio and take him away with her, and while she is at it, inquire as to the delay in his discharge from the service. She is quickly admitted to the base, her face being one of the most familiar to the gate guards. To her surprise, it is relatively easy to gain an audience with Colonel Mancuso, the base commander.

"Sir, may I enquire as to where my fiancée, Giorgio Scaglione, is and what is holding up his discharge from the army?"

"Of course you may enquire, Signora. Just have a seat while we search the file." It is obvious to him that this is a lady of means. Her clothes, her manner and her bearing combine to project importance. This is the woman that Stella has created. This is Donna Marianna.

The large file of inductees with the first letter of "S" is brought to the colonel and he leafs through to Giorgio's record. He is pensive as he carefully reads and rereads the file.

"Signora, it appears that Giorgio Scaglione was among the first to be released from active duty at the conclusion of the war. As you may know, he held a special status as the sole survivor in the current generation of his family. Those men were discharged first so they could return home as soon as possible."

Marianna is unbelieving. "When was he released?"

"At 0800 hours on the 21st of December, 1918."

"Does the record have a forwarding address?"

"Yes, it's an address in Corigliano. I believe that's somewhere in Calabria."

"Thank you. I won't trouble you any further."

Stunned but undaunted, Marianna later queries the men of Giorgio's company until she finds one who seems to know more than the others. Nicola Gracco tells her of how Giorgio had a very light duty assignment over the past year and of how he would go off for days at a time without even the need to check in with the unit commander. It was assumed that he was spending his time with Marianna, until one day a young woman met him just outside the entry gate to the base and they left together in a horse-drawn wagon in the direction of Avola, a resort town on the Mediterranean Sea. From the way they held one another, it was evident that they were lovers. Marianna is appalled to think that Giorgio continues to sleep with her and to express his love for her. All the while he is seeing this other woman she has just learned about. She wonders whether the other woman knows about her.

Shocked by what she has heard and dismayed by the prospect that she has somehow lost Giorgio to another woman, Marianna directs her transport towards Avola. There, she continues her inquiry until she is directed to a squalid rooming house near the center of town. As her wagon reaches the end of the street, she sees Giorgio in an undershirt and worn pants, his auburn hair tussled on his forehead, a cigarette in his hand, talking with another man his age. As Marianna descends from her wagon and approaches, he turns toward her and his face reddens noticeably. The other man leaves as Marianna begins her reproach of Giorgio.

"Well! We meet in a strange place, my love. How is it you neglected to tell me of your interest in Avola?"

"Marianna, please, may we go to our home to talk

this over?"

"No! We may not!"

"Please, lower your voice. You'll invite the entire neighborhood to listen in on what we have to say."

"And what is it that you have to say?"

Giorgio sees that he cannot dissuade Marianna from an immediate confrontation. He decides to face her with the truth.

"I'm really sorry, Marianna, but I have not been honest with you. I never thought that I could ever feel anything more for a woman than I have felt for you, but I now know a woman with whom I have fallen deeply in love. I must be with her or I will be incomplete. Will you ever forgive me?"

At that moment, a young woman at least twenty years Marianna's junior descends the steps of the building behind the arguing couple. She walks over to Giorgio and places her arm around his waist. He places his arm around her shoulder. Her bland stare in Marianna's direction reveals her beauty. She has silken black hair curling down her back and gray-blue piercing eyes contrasting perfectly with olive complexioned skin. She is only slightly more than five feet tall and slim as a reed. She wears a worn print dress and scuffed flat shoes that are quite old.

"So, you are the one!" Marianna chooses to be blunt and frank, her anger and hurt showing.

"I am the woman that Giorgio loves, if that's what you mean."

"We'll let Giorgio speak for himself. Giorgio! Is this the woman that can make you happy? Is this where you want to be?"

"Marianna, I don't ever expect you to understand this, but –yes- this is what I have always wanted, but have been too preoccupied with the trappings of life to realize it. Now, that part of my life is over. I love Gina and I always will. I will live according to my best means and go wherever I must go to be with her."

"You may feel that way today, my young friend, but eventually you will tire of her pretty face and regret you have given up what really matters in life. Come away with me and I'll forget this little incident. In fact, when we get back to Gagliano, I'll make you a gift of the ten acre lemon grove you like so much."

Head bowed, Giorgio gives his response. "No, Marianna, I am staying here with Gina. She is all I will ever want."

Marianna turns to Gina. "And you, my little seductress, are you as generous as he? Leave now and you will have five thousand lire in your pocket within the week."

"No, Signora, no amount of money can separate me from Giorgio. We love each other and need nothing from you or anyone else to live in happiness."

"Very well, then." She turns to Giorgio. "This is the last you will ever see of me or my *trappings*."

━┈◦┈━

Domenico Presta is pensive as he surveys the sixty acres of farmland that he supervises for Marianna Soluri. There is a large stand of olive trees in the direction of Catanzaro, a citrus grove on the westward slope of the valley and vineyards with many grape varieties reaching up into the northern hills above Gagliano. *It was worth all the scandal and scorn she has had to endure in order to end up with this treasure. Any man alive who could have all this would be rich and powerful. All he would have to do is to get Marianna to marry him. And she is still a very pretty woman as well. Despite her middle age, she has an allure that turns many heads, some of them very young heads indeed. Now she's back in Gagliano without that damned gigolo she's been clinging to, and she's brokenhearted. Christ! In the last two decades, she's pissed away a fortune on her phony friends and all those fortune hunters who have pursued her. In that same time, her property has developed well, but if she doesn't change her wild lifestyle, she will eventually lose everything.*

At age sixty, Presta has little material wealth to show for a life of hard work, managing farms owned by others. His wife, Constanza, has given him a son and three daughters, and each of his daughters has married and added grandchildren to his life. But now, as he peers into the face of his mortality, he feels the need to leave behind more than his memory. Suppose...just suppose... that his son, Alfredo, were to catch Marianna on the rebound from Giorgio. That would fulfill Domenico's need for possessions beyond his wildest dream. He would have not the least problem living his dream vicariously...not if it were through Alfredo. To make it all happen, he would have to overcome any stumbling blocks that might arise. *What would Constanza think of her son married to a woman old enough to be his mother? What would anyone else think for that matter? Would Alfredo be willing to enter such a union? Does Marianna already have a husband that she hasn't told anyone about? What about that guy in America that she lived with and who fathered a daughter with her? And what about Aldo Caristi? Is she free of the marriage performed right in the Capurro villa by Father Zinzi?* Then, he decides to disregard the cautions he has dredged up. He calls his son to a meeting of just the two of them. Alfredo will surely understand.

The younger Presta has far more of his mother's good

looks and physique than his father's rather ordinary appearance. Tall and slim, Alfredo's wavy black hair and large brown eyes make him the focus of many of Gagliano's young maidens. At twenty-four, he is at an age when young men in Gagliano are expected to marry and settle down. A mere worker in his father's crew of farm hands, it is expected that he will assume his father's place in the future as age takes its toll on Domenico.

"What? Are you serious? Do you think that I would give up my freedom to marry a woman for money?" Alfredo does not accept his father's scheme. He is repulsed by the notion of marrying a woman almost twice his age that he has never even seen.

"I can understand your first reaction, but will you at least agree to meet her? After all, you will one day succeed me as the manager of her properties." Alfredo does not respond.

"Very well, then, I am meeting with her this morning to review expenditures for the time she's been away. Come with me to the meeting."

By now, Marianna's house near the town center is the prettiest house in Gagliano. The stones from which it is constructed have been cleaned of their centuries of weathering and grime. The new shutters are in perfect condition and hung with exact symmetry to one another. They are chartreuse, contrasting with the sandy brown of the limestone. Planter boxes filled with red geraniums span the girth below each windowsill. The inside of the house, likewise, shows the good taste that Marianna has acquired along with her wealth. Furniture much like the Tuscan-styled pieces she first saw in the Capurro villa surrounds her now in her own home. Heavy oak tables and benches are crafted with elegant designs of fruit and landscapes common to the surrounding area. There are colorful woven rugs on the floor of every room and the easy chairs are upholstered behind thick, patterned chenille. Paintings of land and seascapes hang from every wall. The aroma of fresh-brewed coffee permeates the air as Domenico and Alfredo arrive. They are seated alongside a table of freshly baked biscotti and invited to partake by Marianna's housekeeper. They are drinking coffee and eating biscotti when Marianna enters the room. She is dressed for the morning in a white blouse with vertical green stripes. A darker green skirt reaches just to mid calf, and her shoes are flat with string ties that encircle her ankles. She wears a touch of lipstick and rouge. Her wavy hair is shoulder length and small white earrings add light to her face. Both men stand as she enters the room.

"Welcome back, Signora. It's been a very long time since we last saw you. I would like you to meet my son, Alfredo."

Alfredo extends his hand, but does not speak. He appears to be staring at Marianna as though he has never seen anything like her. They shake hands and the three are seated. Marianna looks back at Alfredo and seems to acknowledge his stare.

"Well, tell me, Domenico. How has my farm done in my absence?"

"Very well, Signora. I have paid all of the bills and have put more than fifty thousand lire away for you. Here is the account of all of the money I received for the crops we harvested and the money spent. I believe you will find everything in order."

Marianna reviews the bills and the receipts and asks many questions about the size of the various crops and the prices obtained. She has not been idle in Sicily and compares her knowledge of the harvest there with the results on her property. She is satisfied that all –or most- of the receipts have reached her treasury. Likewise, she is content that the expenditures were, for the most part, genuine. If there is any chance that Domenico helped himself to any of her money, it is very small indeed. For the two hours that it takes Marianna to perform her review, Alfredo sits quietly and observes. His glances at Marianna are noticed by her and by Domenico. At last the meeting ends and Marianna makes a parting request.

"Domenico, there is a lemon tree on my patio that is losing its leaves. Would you take a look at it for me?" All three seem to understand that this is a ploy to allow Marianna to be alone with Alfredo for a few moments. Alfredo stands his ground at Marianna's side while his father walks quickly to the rear of the house and slowly examines the tree in question.

"Alfredo, since we have but a few moments, I will be very frank with you. I have noticed your stares and I am very flattered by them. Come back this evening and have dinner with me. We can get to know one another better."

"Yes, Signora. I do find you attractive. I will be back this evening."

As they return home, Domenico eagerly queries his son. "What did she say to you while I was inspecting her lemon tree?"

"What makes you think she said anything?"

"Well, for one thing, her lemon tree is perfectly healthy."

"She invited me back for dinner."

"Are you going to do it?"

"Yes."

"Didn't I tell you how attractive she is?"

"That she is. And, that beautiful house…and all that money…"

The two men arrive at their home in time for lunch. Constanza is there to greet them. "How did it go?"

Both men look at each other and smile broadly. They utter the same response, as though it had been rehearsed. "Fine."

Chapter 33

Stefano

The Contini home is unlike most in Gagliano. There is a mezuzah on the door, since this is a Jewish home. Inside, there is a menorah on a sideboard, flanked by Sabbath candles and a Kiddush cup. There are no votives to the Blessed Mother, nor any crucifix or favored saints. Instead, the walls are hung with scenes of the holy land. It is the place where the rabbi lives and where the weekly service is held for those few Jews who have held fast to their religious beliefs in this land of Christendom. In their youth, there were times when Stefano, the Rabbi's son, and Raffaele played together in this very dwelling. Now, Raffaele reluctantly returns as an adult to this playground of his early life.

If elation over the victory at Veneto somehow escaped

Raffaele, the dread that now faces him does not. He loathes the task at hand more than anything he has ever had to do. Stefano Contini is dead, killed by Austrians in the final days of the war, and it is up to Raffaele to visit his parents and answer their questions. He has already ascertained that Stefano's parents are aware of his death. Gesuzza has told him of the agony that beset the immediate relatives and the depression affecting those in their extended family.

"It brought back the painful memory of your brother's death. Poor Davide and Amelia cried continuously for a week. I know because I could hear them each time I walked past their house. I don't know who conducted their religious services in those early weeks, but they were held just the same. When the Contini's finally came out of the house, their faces looked drawn and they walked as though they had been beaten and were now going to their execution. They haven't been the same since. I doubt they ever will recover." Gesuzza knows better than most how it feels to lose a son to war, and identifies with the pain that the Contini's are feeling. She also imagines the repulsion that Raffaele must feel in having to relive the horrifying moments of Stefano's death with his parents.

As he knocks on the front door of the Contini home, Raffaele hopes that there will be no response, that the old couple will have gone to their daughter's home in Catanzaro. No such luck. Davide comes to the door wearing a religious shawl and yarmulke, signifying the lateness in the day and his duty to mourn his son's death by evening prayer. To Raffaele's surprise, the rabbi recognizes him.

"Come in, come in. We have been hoping and praying that you would come to visit us. Have you eaten? We have just finished our dinner, but Amelia can fix you something."

"No thank you. I've eaten."

Amelia comes in and walks silently over to Raffaele. She wears a plain black mourning dress and a black scarf covers her head. She says nothing, but places her arms around him and hugs him. Then, she turns her back to him so that he will not see her crying. Davide continues to lead the conversation.

"It took courage for you to come here, Raffaele. Surely you know that we will ask you to tell us of how Stefano was killed. The letter we received telling us of his death said only that he was killed in battle. We need to know more than that. You were there, were you not Raffaele?"

"Yes, I was there, but I prefer not to talk about how he was killed. I can tell you it was in battle and that he was heroic, but that's all."

Suddenly, Amelia has found her voice. She looks piercingly at Raffaele, her dark eyes gleaming and her lined face drawn into a mask of inquiry.

"Please Raffaele, we must know! These weeks of mourning over Stefano's death have been hell on earth. There is nothing that you can tell us that will make our lives any more miserable than they are already are. Please, Raffaele, tell us!"

"I will tell you, Signora, but it will not be easy to listen."

Raffaele sits facing the somber couple and draws in a deep breath, as though he is about to reveal a truth that has never been told. The elders sit nervously engrossed.

"As you know, your son and I were artillery stablemen. Mostly, we took care of horses and mules that were used to pull caissons carrying cannons to where they were fired. We helped fire the larger of the guns. We were also trained in the use of rifles and side arms, but it was not expected that we would ever use them. The enemy was usually a long way away from us. At Vittorio Veneto, we had chased the retreating Austrians across the plains and into the mountains. There, they made their stand. Once we reached their encampments above the foothills, our guns were almost totally useless. Their fortifications were placed deep into the sides of the mountains and had been there long before the Great War even began. The only way to have beaten them was to force them to come out and fight us hand to hand. Units of the Bersaglieri and Alpini were brought in to fight them.

As it became obvious that our big guns would be useless against them, our unit was ordered to fight alongside a Bersaglieri troop. They used incendiary explosives to draw the Austrians out of their caves and into the open. The men we fought were strangely uniformed, mostly Hungarians. The fighting was brutal. Men on both sides were bayoneted and shot to death. They were outnumbered and outclassed by the Bersaglieri and we soon routed them and took many prisoners. I saw Stefano fighting for his life. His ammunition was gone at the end of one of the encounters, but he stood there with his bayonet pointing in the direction of the enemy, ready to continue fighting.

At one point, we became separated from the rest of the men. We had sighted a small cave and decided to investigate. We were spotted by an enemy soldier who alerted others that we were approaching. There turned out to be three of them. They charged us and we killed all of them."

At this point, Raffaele hesitated. He could not go on without risking an emotional calamity. Davide and Amelia are already at the edge of their reserve and could easily burst into a flood of emotion.

"Go on, go on! Don't stop now. This is what we want to know. What happened?" Davide's eyes were teary, but he was not satisfied. He had to know.

"I had killed the first of the three with a shot from my rifle. The second man was on me before I had a chance to fire again and I fought him with my bayonet. When I turned to see how Stefano was doing, I was horrified to see him on the ground with an Austrian standing over him. I charged at the soldier, hoping that I could divert his attention. We fought for a while and I ultimately killed him, but when I went back to Stefano, it was too late."

"Tell us, Raffaele, how was he killed?"

"He was struck on the head with a mace. It crushed one side of his head and must have ended his life instantly."

At this point, Amelia rises and runs to another room. She tries to muffle her sobbing and is barely heard. Davide stands, tears running down his face. He is hardly able to speak. It is a whisper when words finally emerge.

"Thank you, Raffaele. We will be forever grateful to you."

The rabbi is unable to say more. Raffaele makes his exit and returns home, head bowed, thinking of his poor, dead comrade. He is unable to contain his own emotion and sobs softly into the night air. Gesuzza greets him at home and the two end the day in sorrow.

Chapter 34

Final Days

For Calabria, post-war Italy is a repetition of the past. There is talk in Rome of the development of the poorer regions, but there are few appropriations being made by the Government. Peasant life continues much as it has since the Reunification. The disfavored poor are still hostage to a system that greatly favors the rich and blocks any possibility of change. Millions of Italians leave for the New World, the United States being the favored choice. There are prospects for improving one's life in a foreign country, but there is no hope in Calabria. Immigration is the subject of every household. Even Raffaele and Gesuzza consider it, however reluctantly. Gesuzza wishes to be near her husband's grave and still senses the presence of Pietro in the Sirocco blowing across the Mediterranean from northern Africa, where he is buried. For Raffaele, his attachment is rooted in his patriotism. Their indifference towards immigrating is suddenly shaken when, unexpectedly, a letter arrives from Giuseppe.

"I had Father Zinzi read me this letter from your brother Giuseppe in America. Thank God that he has made contact with us at last. I was beginning to believe that some misfortune occurred and that we would never hear from him again. He is well and asks for us to leave Italy and join him in America. He is ready to marry and requests that we bring a woman from Gagliano with us to be his bride. He wants our family to be together in America. It's so confusing as to why we should leave now that there is peace and hope right here in Italy."

"I'm not so sure any more, Ma. I've been thinking that maybe it would all be for the best if we went to live in America. We'd have Giuseppe back in our lives and a chance at a better life than we would ever have here."

"I'm surprised at you, Raffaele. You are such a patriot, yet you consider leaving along with the rest of the fortune-hunters to a land where you don't even speak the language or understand the culture." Gesuzza admonishes Raffaele for his sudden willingness to consider leaving Italy for the United States.

"You're right, Ma, I really should be one to stay in Italy. But I won't continue to be embarrassed by 'Za Marian's conduct. She behaves like a *puttana* and disgraces our family. Instead of helping us, she ignores our troubles and squanders her wealth on strangers. Now that I'm back from the war, I want to marry and raise a family. Do you think I want my children to be around her? Or, for that matter, do you think I want my children being enslaved to this way of life? I can understand your wanting to remain here in Gagliano, but it's time I made my own way in life. Whatever I do will include you, Ma, but I can no longer wait in hope that our difficulties will resolve themselves."

Gesuzza can see that Raffaele has withstood as much exploitation as he can and that he is prepared to put aside his national pride in favor of a chance at prosperity. *If only Marianna had followed through as she promised our mother she would. We would have all of the prosperity we need right here in Italy. What is wrong with that woman? Sure, she's had some terrible tragedies in her life, but so have we all. The wars of the last twenty-five years have touched virtually every family in Italy. The loss of her son was no more or less than we have all suffered.* In her moment of anxious inner thought, it occurs to Gesuzza that Marianna has returned from her senseless flight to Sicily with Giorgio. *What if she has finally come to her senses? How would we know? We have avoided her since she turned her back on Raffaele. She may be hoping and praying that we forgive her. She may be ready to place the welfare of her family first.*

"Raffaele, I need to see Marianna and offer forgiveness. She's back and Giorgio is gone. She may well be ready to assist us."

"I will have no part of that woman. Let's just concentrate on our own fate and let Marianna care for herself."

"No! Please! We must know. We can't ignore the possibility that she may have changed and wants us to invite her back into our lives."

"Very well, Ma, but I'll be the one to approach her. I don't want her to think that you're forgiving her."

The first floor of Marianna's house is dark as Raffaele approaches. He notices a soft light through a second floor window and decides to knock on the door.

"Za Marian,' are you there?"

A head pops out of the lighted window. It is Marianna. "Rafi! I'm so glad you've come. Wait and I'll be down in a minute to let you in."

Raffaele watches as the shifting light disappears from the second floor and reappears at the front door, a lamp in Marianna's hand. It is only nine O'clock, but already Marianna is in her nightshirt. Her hair is ruffled and she appears slightly disheveled, as though she has been asleep.

"Did I wake you, Zi?"

"No, I was sitting up in bed when I heard your voice. Please come in and let's drink a glass of wine to celebrate."

"Thank you, but I'm here to talk about the last year and why it was necessary for me to go back to the warfront in Veneto."

"Rafi, I'm so glad you're here. If anything had happened to you in the war, I'd never have forgiven myself. Can you ever forgive me for using my one possible exclusion to keep that awful Giorgio out of the war? He promised to marry me and I thought he really loved me. I should have known better, considering his background as a womanizer."

A flood of retort to Marianna races through Raffaele's mind. *You are to blame as much as anyone. Are you any better than he? It was your nephew that went back to the front lines, not his. And why did you run off and leave Gesuzza to the mercy of her friends when you could have taken care of her while I was away at war?* He holds his temper and speaks coolly.

"Zi, since I am your nephew and the younger of us, it would be bold of me to either criticize or complain, but I hope you will allow me to do both. You have been fortunate to have acquired significant wealth in your lifetime. It came at a great cost to you and your family. The few of us who are your relatives are constantly amazed at the generosity you show others. It will ruin you if you are not more careful. And your lack of discretion in choosing men to include in your life is upsetting. They are all around my age and have a history of bad intentions. We are wondering if you care about us as others care about their blood relatives. If you do, you must not cause us embarrassment, but rather, show sincere concern when we are in danger and help us to the same extent as we would help you."

"Rafi, please go no further. Of course I have concern about you and Gesuzza and I will do whatever is necessary to protect you from harm. I was confused in the past and did stupid things. But, that's over now."

"You're a little late, Zi. My mother and I will be leaving Gagliano."

Stunned by what she has just heard, Marianna pleads. "Rafi, no! Please don't leave. Where are you thinking of going?"

"We are set to leave for America. My brother has written and asked us to join him there."

"Oh, no, you can't do that. You're too much an Italian to leave. And your mother needs to be here where she is close to the graves of her husband and her son."

"There is very little hope for us here. The system for working the land is too defeating to offer possibilities. America is the place that people like me can make our fortune by hard work and common sense."

Just then, a loud sound is heard on the second floor just above them. It could have been a chair turning over or a drawer being pulled out and dropped to the floor. Marianna looks up, obviously disturbed by the sound.

"Dammit, I wasn't ready for this." She shows her annoyance.

Raffaele looks at Marianna wide-eyed and suspicious,

his look demanding to know what Marianna has kept from him. He says nothing.

Marianna calls aloud, "Alfredo! Come down and meet my nephew."

The young man descends the steps and makes his appearance. He walks over to Raffaele, his right hand extended and open, inviting a handshake. Raffaele does not accommodate him. Marianna senses the discontent felt by Raffaele.

"Raffaele! This is not what you think. I would like you to meet Alfredo. Shake his hand."

"Why, Zi? Isn't he just one more of your indiscretions? Why do I want to meet him?"

"… because he is not an indiscretion. He is my husband."

Raffaele is shocked. "How is it possible for you to marry? Aren't you already married to Aldo Caristi?"

"No, I am not. Last year, when my interest in marriage rekindled, I went to Sicily to see if I could somehow convince Aldo to agree to an annulment. Since our marriage had never been consummated, annulment was possible. What I found in Aldo's house was the woman he had been living with and their three children. She is considerably younger than Aldo and is now living with a man her own age. When she introduced him as her husband, I asked about Aldo's whereabouts. She hesitated to tell me, but she eventually realized that I had the right to know. She told me that Aldo had died about six months before. They both begged me not to claim the estate as Aldo's widow. I offered to abandon any claim to the estate if she would admit that Aldo disclosed to her that he had never consummated his marriage to me. She admitted it, of course, and I later abandoned any claim to his property. I didn't know Alfredo then, but I knew I would someday want to be married."

"Didn't you do that so you could marry that gigolo, Giorgio?" Raffaele is showing reckless disdain for Marianna and her lifestyle. Marianna feels the pangs of having the truth revealed to the man whom she just married. Her eyes look with hatred at Raffaele and then turn softly to Alfredo.

"It's true, my love. But, he was not a gigolo. He was an unfaithful lout."

Alfredo walks to the rear of the house and exits to the patio. Marianna whirls around to Raffaele, her dark eyes more piercing than ever before.

"Damn you! Are you satisfied now?"

"No, Zi. I am not satisfied. I am still disgusted with you and your ways. Would it surprise you to know that I have known your precious Alfredo since he was a boy? And that we played together in the street when we were both toddlers? We are the same age, Zi. He is young enough to be your son. Why do you think he married you?"

Raffaele's candid remarks have brought tears of anger and defensiveness to Marianna's eyes. She loses all composure and self-control.

"Get out, you ungrateful bastard! Go do whatever you want. And don't come pleading here when you need help."

Raffaele is mute. He stares at Marianna for several moments. Then, he walks to the door and turns for one last look at her. "We'll see who pleads in the end."

⊢•→•○•←•⊣

Maria and Luigi Donato have labored all of their lives in much the same way as the majority of Calabrians. Married at an early age, they secured a sharecropper arrangement with Don Leone and took on the burden of farming to earn their living. As luck would have it, the property was one of the least fertile in Gagliano, yielding meager crops, and sentencing the Donatos to a life of hardship. They were dealt additional difficulty in that all four of their children were girls. Not only did Luigi not have a son to share the burden of farming a difficult property, but he also lacked the means to provide a dowry for the eventual marriages of his daughters. The result was that his daughters could not attract husbands in Gagliano, all of whom would have required a dowry. Fortunately, his two eldest daughters, Caterina and Carmela, were invited to marry Vincenzo and Tomaso Pizzute, two expatriate brothers who had gone off to America to make their fortune. The brothers were willing to forego dowries, but the women had to relocate to Kent, Ohio and probably never see their parents again. They agreed after some practical, though tearful, advice from Luigi. The two younger sisters, Concetta and Giuseppina, were left behind, hoping for the unlikely prospect of marriage. As they reached the ages of thirty and thirty-one, it was evident that they would remain spinsters for all time. They continued to live with their parents, becoming marvelous cooks and housekeepers, and aiding Luigi with his harvest. They had accepted their lot in life.

To Gesuzza, the primary factor in selecting a wife for her son in America is the woman's ability to care for him. It is natural, therefore, for her to think of the Donato girls, who are not only available, but who can be counted on as stalwart servants to the men who would marry them. In addition, their ages are not out of line for the thirty-four year old Giuseppe. Since their departure for America is imminent, she hastens the approach to Luigi and Maria.

"I am reluctant to ask you to give up yet another of your daughters to *L'America*, but I can promise you that she will be treated properly. My son, Giuseppe, is lonely for the arms of a woman from Gagliano and will marry your daughter upon her arrival in America. He has been there for almost fifteen years and has a steady income and a place to live."

Maria is first to respond. "Gesuzza, you are one of the finest people in our village, and I like and trust you. But, as I recall, your son has difficulty in getting along with people. How do I know my daughter won't be mistreated?"

"I will guarantee that he will get along with her. He is now older and more mature. How else would he be able to stay employed and be self-sufficient? Don't worry, Maria, I will look after her as I would my own daughter."

Then, Luigi speaks. "You know, of course that there will be no dowry?"

"Yes, I know that. It is unimportant to me."

"Then you may have her if she agrees." He turns and calls into the bedroom, where the two prospective brides are waiting. "Concetta. Come in and talk with us."

Suddenly, Gesuzza stops him. "It is not Concetta whom I want for my son. It is Giuseppina." Concetta hears Gesuzza's words and returns to the bedroom, a look of rejection on her face.

"But, Concetta is the older of the two. She is next to marry."

"No. It is Giuseppina that I want." Gesuzza gives no explanation, but she has a reason for insisting on the younger of the two women. Her sources for obtaining the most hidden of Gagliano's secrets have informed her that Concetta is conducting a liaison with a married man, and that she may even be carrying his child at present. The affair is so secret that even her parents don't yet know of the matter.

"This is most unusual, Gesuzza. Can you tell me why you choose not to take Concetta?"

"Luigi, for the last time, I am asking for Giuseppina's hand in marriage to my son. There is to be no dowry or any other cost to you. I will handle everything and guarantee her safety and happiness in America."

Luigi looks angrily at Gesuzza and scowls. "All right, if that's the way you want it." He calls into the room a second time. "Giuseppina, come and talk with us."

Giuseppina enters the room, trying to look demure and feminine. But her age and plain features betray her. Her cobalt eyes have lost their youthful sparkle and her dark skin is marked with pocks that could once have been mistaken for freckles. She is above the weight that would be flattering, and the faded dress she wears does not show her to advantage. She looks knowingly at Gesuzza, having heard most of the conversation from the other room.

"I would like to take you with me and Raffaele to America. My son Giuseppe has said that he will marry you when we arrive. He is established there and can make a good home for you. I will see to it that you are treated properly and given everything possible."

Giuseppina is unable to speak. Her eyes fill with tears and she looks at her mother. She knows that this may be her last chance to marry and she remembers vaguely the man who would be her husband. Her mother is right. He is a difficult man, or at least he was in the days before he left for America. But, perhaps Gesuzza is right. He might have matured in the fifteen years since she saw him last.

"Is it all right, Mother?"

"Yes."

She turns to Gesuzza. "When do we leave?"

›—›—‹›—‹—‹

The S.S. Dante Alighieri is guided through the maze of ships in the Naples harbor by a tugboat, its engines now straining to cut loose and make their own unfettered way to the New World. As he looks back on the verdant coast, Raffaele feels the pull of his past as he first sees the elegant Castel Nuovo on the shore and later the Castel dell'Ovo sitting serenely on its tiny land mass out in the bay. He wonders whether he will ever see this sight again. He wells with emotion as events of his young life come into focus. He thinks first of Gabriella and tears fill his eyes. How he loved that woman, her simple ruddy face, looking more Germanic than Italian, her blonde hair reminding him of Pietro. His migrating to his brother's adopted land strikes him as irony. He vows always to keep the memory of Pietro alive. As the wintry swells rise to sway the ship, his thoughts are now of his father, who must have endured the voyage to Asinara in these very waters. He feels the tragedy that befell Angelo, but his sympathy is with Gesuzza, his mother, who was left to shepherd her brood through life, giving of herself the whole time. He thinks of how she was blighted by the loss of Pietro less than two years after Angelo's death. He will acknowledge her sacrifices and her suffering by giving her a better life in America. Sympathy turns to rage as he thinks of Marianna. *Puttana!* How could she have turned her back so completely on her family? Forget what she did to him; think of how she might have helped Gesuzza. It would have been so easy. Instead, she left them to suffer while she lived comfortably in her selfish world. Stella is surely turning over in her grave with rage and disappointment. And what a reputation she has made for the whole Soluri family. First a mistress, bearing Alessandro out of wedlock and then becoming a rich dowager, buying the love of the men in her life, most of them younger than she; opting to keep Giorgio safe from the warfront so she could bed him, while Raffaele returned to face the Germans at Veneto. And, finally, her marriage to Alfredo…. *Basta!* Enough of the embarrassment this woman has heaped on him and his family. For all he cares, she can burn in hell.

Now his thoughts turn to Calabria, to Gagliano, the earth that he knows best, from infancy, where he learned to walk and talk. His thoughts are tender even as he evokes an admonition of his birthplace. *Ah, Calabria, you are like a pretty woman with no soul. You promise us freedom and abundance, but deliver only more of the bondage that our land has known since the beginning of time. Yet, your parched hills and fruit-filled orchards are seductive. And, your people are kind and gentle still. Those who remain behind and submit to the regime that is forced upon them by a selfish aristocracy are tribute to your beauty. It will be hard to live without daily witnessing the morning haze blurring the sun and yielding finally to the dry heat of the valleys. No longer will I hold your bounty in my hands at harvest and marvel at the gift which nature has bestowed. Farewell, my Italy. I leave you now, but you will always be my love. The world may entrance me with its riches and pleasures, but my soul will be here with you.*

Epilogue

The migration to America of Raffaele, Gesuzza and Giuseppina in 1920 mirrored the action of millions of Italians who migrated to the Western Hemisphere in the decades following the Risorgimento. The United States was the choice destination, but Argentina and Brazil were locations for many who were either unable to qualify for entrance into the United States or who preferred the language and culture of the southern Americas. Whatever their choice of destination, they were unified by the frustration they all felt for the hopelessness of the social order they had left behind. To advance, one had to leave Italy and emigrate to another land. For many of the immigrants, the sacrifice in leaving their homeland was justified by the progress they as individuals made in the new land. For others, it was not until a generation had evolved before progress could really be claimed. Still others returned home to be with loved ones who refused to leave or simply because they did not like what they saw in the new country. Many Italian immigrants were perceived as criminal, simply because they were desperately poor, their clothing tattered and their possessions minimal. Most were thought to be associated with the Black Hand. False charges, arrests and imprisonments were frequent and particularly painful, since they were unable to speak English and explain their circumstances to a police force made up of monolingual Americans who distrusted these new arrivals as interlopers on their turf.

Most of those who arrived on American shores came to Ellis Island to be examined before admission to the United States. Raffaele's arrival coincided with an outbreak of smallpox on the island gateway, so his ship was rerouted to Philadelphia. There, he and his mother and future sister-in-law were admitted to the United States. They made their way to New York, where Giuseppe met them. The Chiarellas established themselves in the New World in the 20's, languished in the Depression of the 30's, wretched at the thought of their Italy at war with America in the early 40's and began their journey to prosperity thereafter. There was never a doubt that leaving Calabria had been the right choice.

Those who remained in Calabria experienced a surge in demand for their labor, brought on by the huge exodus of the work force. The void led to better conditions for the working class, and eventually, land became more available for purchase by those who worked it. The system that perpetuated the poverty of the worker began at last to break down, inspired partly by a desire to discourage Communism. By the mid twentieth century, there was a move to devote government resources to prime the pump in the mezzo giorno. Estates such as Leone's were forced by the government to sell off idle farm property, and inheritance taxes forced the sale of orchards and vineyards. The workingman received assistance in obtaining ownership of land that he would work for himself. World War II had the effect of introducing farming techniques that were previously unknown in Calabria. Irrigation of crops became common, as did crop rotation and scientific row spacing. The war also brought rampant inflation, drastically reducing the value of the lire. Marianna found herself in financial straits, having liquidated most of her land to support her extravagant lifestyle. As her wealth vanished, Alfredo and the rest of her capricious and callous friends eventually abandoned her. During the war, she experienced the same shortages of food and other necessities as her contemporaries in Gagliano, and called for help from Raffaele. Despite his loathing of her, he obliged, sending the money and clothing she requested.

The era of dominance over the people of Calabria ended as the new Republic of Italy emerged following the war. Its charter was to bring fairness to the legal system and to promote equality among Italians. Calabrians were offered the opportunity to become educated, rebuild their region and take control of their destiny. The result has been astonishing. Though they maintain a pride in their past, Calabrians have advanced into contemporary times, building their region into a worthy economic force and ending dominance by outsiders.

About The Author

Peter Chiarella started life in the Bedford-Stuyvesant section of Brooklyn in 1932. He was educated in the public school system and at St. John's University. Retired from the corporate world, Peter lives in Napa, California and enjoys the life of a gentleman farmer as a wine grape grower and vintner. He is married and has four children.

Despite the shame and disgrace brought upon his family by his great aunt's improprieties and his grandfather's two prison sentences, his grandmother's steadfast choices and enormous integrity placed a stamp of honor on the family that has been passed on to subsequent generations. It has allowed them to succeed as Americans and has endowed them with the courage to reveal the past.

The author's father grew up in Calabria, immigrating to the U.S. in 1920 at age 22. His mother grew up on the lower East Side of New York. Because his paternal grandmother lived with his immediate family, Peter needed to speak Italian to include Nonna in his conversations. Consequently, Peter grew up speaking and understanding Italian while internalizing what it means to be Italian. In his first years of life, he heard the stories about life in Calabria directly from his grandmother, a principal character in the book. After her death, the stories kept coming, both from his father, also a character in Calabrian Tales, and from his mother, who had listened in on her mother-in-law's recollections over a period of fifteen years.

For as long as they can remember, the author and his older brother felt the compulsion to reduce to writing, the stories they heard and reheard over the years. Encouraged by his brother and other members of the family, Peter took on the task of writing Calabrian Tales, reflecting on the struggle and compromises that past generations of his family endured in turn-of-the-century southern Italy. At times you will have to remind yourself that these are true stories with real people.